George A. Henty

A March on London

Being a story of Wat Tyler's insurrection

George A. Henty

A March on London
Being a story of Wat Tyler's insurrection

ISBN/EAN: 9783744748063

Printed in Europe, USA, Canada, Australia, Japan

Cover: Foto ©Andreas Hilbeck / pixelio.de

More available books at **www.hansebooks.com**

"EDGAR STRUCK HIM A BUFFET ON THE FACE WHICH SENT
HIM REELING BACKWARDS."

A MARCH ON LONDON

BEING A STORY OF

WAT TYLER'S INSURRECTION

BY

G. A. HENTY

Author of " Beric the Briton ", " When London Burned ", " With Clive in India ", &c.

WITH EIGHT ILLUSTRATIONS BY W. H. MARGETSON

LONDON

BLACKIE & SON, Limited, 50 OLD BAILEY, E.C.

GLASGOW AND DUBLIN

1898

PREFACE.

The events that took place during the latter half of the fourteenth century and the first half of the fifteenth are known to us far better than those preceding or following them, owing to the fact that three great chroniclers, Froissart, Monstrelet, and Holinshed, have recounted the events with a fulness of detail that leaves nothing to be desired. The uprising of the Commons, as they called themselves,—that is to say, chiefly the folk who were still kept in a state of serfdom in the reign of Richard II.,—was in itself justifiable. Although serfdom in England was never carried to the extent that prevailed on the Continent, the serfs suffered from grievous disabilities. A certain portion of their time had to be devoted to the work of their feudal lord. They themselves were forbidden to buy or sell at public markets or fairs. They were bound to the soil, and could not, except under special circumstances, leave it.

Above all, they felt that they were not free men, and were not even deemed worthy to fight in the wars of their country. Attempts have been made to represent the rising as the result of Wickliffe's attack upon the Church, but there seems to be very small foundation for the assertion. Undoubtedly many of the lower class of clergy, discontented with their position, did their best to inflame the minds of the peasants, but as the rising extended over a very large part of England, and the people were far too ignorant to understand, and far too much irritated by their own grievances to care for the condition of the Church, it may be taken that they murdered the Archbishop of Canterbury and many other priests simply because they regarded them as being wealthy, and so slew them as they slew other people of substance. Had it been otherwise, the Church would not have been wholly ignored in the demands that they set before the king, but some allusion would have been made for the need of reforms in that direction.

The troubles in Flanders are of interest to Englishmen, since there was for many years an alliance, more or less close, between our king and some of the great Flemish cities. Indeed, from the time when the first Von Artevelde was murdered because he proposed that the Black Prince should be accepted as ruler of Flanders, to the day upon which Napoleon's power was broken for ever at Waterloo, Flanders has been the theatre of almost incessant turmoil and strife, in which Germans and Dutchmen, Spaniards, Englishmen, and Frenchmen, have fought out their quarrels.

G. A. HENTY.

CONTENTS.

ILLUSTRATIONS.

A MARCH ON LONDON.

CHAPTER I.

TROUBLED TIMES.

AND what do you think of it all, good Father?"

"'Tis a difficult question, my son, and I am glad that it is one that wiser heads than mine will have to solve."

"But they don't seem to try to solve it; things get worse and worse. The king is but a lad, no older than myself, and he is in the hands of others. It seems to me a sin and a shame that things should go on as they are at present. My father also thinks so."

The speaker was a boy of some sixteen years old. He was walking with the prior in the garden of the little convent of St. Alwyth, four miles from the town of Dartford. Edgar Ormskirk was the son of a scholar. The latter, a man of independent means, who had always had a preference for study and investigation rather than for taking part in active pursuits, had, since the death of his young wife a year after the birth of his son, retired altogether from the world and devoted himself to study. He had given up his comfortable home, standing on the heights of Highgate,— that being in too close proximity to London to enable him to enjoy the seclusion that he desired,—and had retired to a small estate near Dartford.

Educated at Oxford, he had gone to Padua at his father's death, which happened just as he left the university, and had remained at that seat of learning for five years. There he had spent the whole of his income in the purchase of manuscripts. The next two years were passed at Bologna and Pisa, and he there collected a library such as few gentlemen of his time possessed. Then Mr. Ormskirk had returned to England and settled at Highgate, and two years later married the daughter of a neighbouring gentleman, choosing her rather because he felt that he needed some one to keep his house in order, than from any of the feeling that usually accompanies such unions. In time, however, he had come to love her, and her loss was a very heavy blow to him. It was the void that he felt in his home as much as his desire for solitude, that induced him to leave Highgate and settle in the country.

Here, at least, he had no fear of intrusive neighbours, or other interruptions to his studies. The news from London seldom reached his ears, and he was enabled to devote himself entirely to his experiments. Like many other learned men of his age, it was to chemistry that he chiefly turned his attention. His library comprised the works of almost every known writer on the subject, and he hoped that he might gain an immortal reputation by discovering one or both of the great secrets then sought for—the elixir of life, or the philosopher's stone that would convert all things into gold. It was not that he himself had any desire for a long life, still less did he yearn for more wealth than he possessed, but he fondly believed that these discoveries would ameliorate the condition of mankind.

He did not see that if gold was as plentiful as the commonest metal it would cease to be more valuable than others, or that the boon of a long life would not add to the happiness of mankind. For some years he gave little thought to his son, who was left to such care as the old housekeeper and the still older man-servant chose to bestow upon him, and who, in consequence, was left altogether to follow the dictates of his own fancy. The child therefore lived almost entirely in the open air, played, tussled, and fought with boys of his own age in the village, and grew up healthy, sturdy, and active. His father scarcely took any heed of his existence until the prior of the Convent of St. Alwyth one day called upon him.

"What are you going to do with your boy, Mr. Ormskirk?" he asked.

"My boy?" the student repeated in tones of surprise. "Oh, yes; Edgar, of course! What am I going to do with him? Well, I have never thought about it. Does he want anything? My housekeeper always sees to that. Do you think that he wants a nurse?"

"A nurse, Mr. Ormskirk!" the Prior said with a smile. "A nurse would have a hard time with him. Do you know what his age is?"

"Four or five years old, I suppose."

"Nearly double that. He is nine."

"Impossible!" Mr. Ormskirk said. "Why, it is only the other day that he was a baby."

"It is eight years since that time; he is now a sturdy · lad, and if there is any mischief in the village he is sure to be in it. Why, it was but three days ago that Friar Anselmo caught him, soon after daybreak, fishing in the Convent pool with two of the village lads. The friar gave them a sound trouncing, and would have given one to your son, too, had it not been for the respect that we all feel for you. It is high time, Mr. Ormskirk, that he was broken of his wild ways and received an education suited to his station."

"Quite so, quite so! I own that I have thought but little about him, for indeed 'tis rarely that I see him, and save that at times his racket in the house sorely disturbs my studies, I have well-nigh forgotten all about him. Yes, yes; it is, of course, high time that he began his education, so that if I should die before I have completed my discoveries he may take up my work."

The Prior smiled quietly at the thought of the sturdy, dirty-faced boy working among crucibles and retorts. However, he only said:

"Do you think of undertaking his education yourself?"

"By no means," Mr. Ormskirk said hastily. "It would be impossible for me to find time at present; but when he has completed his studies I should then take him in hand myself, make him my companion and assistant, and teach him all that is known of science."

"But in the meantime?"

"In the meantime? Yes, I suppose something must be done. I might get him a tutor, but that would be a great disturbance to me. I might send him up to the monastery at Westminster, where the sons of many gentlemen are taught."

"I doubt whether the training, or rather want of training, that he has had would fit him for Westminster," the Prior said quietly. "There is another plan that perhaps might be more suitable for him. One of our brethren is a scholar, and already three or four of the sons of the gentry in the neighbourhood come to him for three hours or so a day. Our convent is a poor one, and the fees he receives are a welcome addition to our means."

"Excellent!" Mr. Ormskirk said, delighted at the difficulty being taken off his shoulders. "It would be the very thing."

"Then perhaps you will speak to the boy, and lay your

orders upon him," the Prior said. "He was in the village as I passed by, and I brought him up here, very much against his will I admit. Then I gave him in charge on arrival to your servitor, knowing that otherwise the young varlet would slip off again as soon as my back was turned. Perhaps you will send for him."

Mr. Ormskirk rang a bell. The housekeeper entered.

"Where is Andrew?" he asked.

"He is looking after Master Edgar, sir. His reverence told him to do so, and he dare not leave him for a moment or he would be off again."

"Tell Andrew to bring him in here."

A minute later the old servant entered with the boy. Edgar was in a dishevelled condition, the result of several struggles with Andrew. His face was begrimed with dirt, his clothes were torn and untidy. His father looked at him in grave surprise. It was not that he had not seen him before, for occasionally he had noticed him going across the garden, but though his eyes had observed him, his mental vision had not in any way taken him in, his thoughts being intent upon the work that he had reluctantly left to take a hurried meal.

"Tut, tut, tut!" he murmured to himself, "and this is my son! Well, well, I suppose he is not to be blamed; it is my own fault for being so heedless of him. This is bad, Edgar," he said, "and yet it is my own fault rather than thine, and I am thankful that the good prior has brought your condition before me before it is too late. There must be no more of this. Your appearance is disgraceful both to yourself and me—to me because you are in rags, to yourself because you are dirty. I had never dreamt of this. Henceforth all must be changed. You must be clothed as befits the son of a gentleman, you must be taught as it is right for the son of a scholar to be, and you must bear in mind that some day you will become a gentleman yourself, and, I trust, a learned one. I have arranged with the good prior here that you shall go every day to the monastery to be instructed for three hours by one of his monks. In future you will take your meals with me, and I will see that your attire is in order, and that you go decent as befits your station. What hours is he to attend, Prior?"

"From nine till twelve."

"You hear—from nine to twelve. In the afternoon I will procure a teacher for you in arms. In these days every gentleman must learn the use of his weapons. I myself, although most peacefully inclined, have more than once been forced, when abroad, to use them. A man who cannot do so becomes the butt of fools, and loses his self-respect."

"I shall like that, sir," Edgar said eagerly. "I can play at quarter-staff now with any boy of my size in the village."

"Well, there must be no more of that," his father said. "Up to the present you have been but a child, but it is time now that you should cease to consort with village boys and prepare for another station in life. They may be good boys—I know naught about them—but they are not fit associates for you. I am not blaming you," he said more kindly as he saw the boy's face fall. "It was natural that you, having no associates of your own rank, should make friends where you could find them. I trust that it has done you no harm. Well, Prior, this day week the boy shall come to you. I must get befitting clothes for him, or the other pupils will think that he is the son of a hedge tinker."

An hour later Andrew was despatched to Dartford in a cart hired in the village, with orders to bring back with him a tailor, also to inquire as to who was considered the best teacher of arms in the town, and to engage him to come up for an hour every afternoon to instruct Edgar.

Seven years had passed since that time, and the rough

and unkempt boy had grown into a tall young fellow, who had done fair credit to his teacher at the convent, and had profited to the full by the teaching of the old soldier who had been his instructor in arms. His father had, unconsciously, been also a good teacher to him. He had, with a great effort, broken through the habits to which he had been so long wedded. A young waiting-maid now assisted the housekeeper. The meals were no longer hastily snatched and often eaten standing, but were decently served in order, and occupied a considerable time, the greater portion of which was spent in pleasant chat either upon the scenes which Mr. Ormskirk had witnessed abroad, or in talk on the subjects the boy was studying; sometimes also upon Mr. Ormskirk's researches and the hopes he entertained from them, and, as Edgar grew older, upon the ordinary topics of the day, the grievances caused by the heavy taxation, the troubles of the time and the course of events that had led to them; for, although very ignorant of contemporary matters, Mr. Ormskirk was well acquainted with the history of the country up to the time when he had first gone abroad.

The recluse was surprised at the interest he himself came to feel in these conversations. While endeavouring to open his son's mind he opened his own, and although when Edgar was not present he pursued his researches as assiduously as before, he was no longer lost in fits of abstraction, and would even occasionally walk down to the village when Edgar went to school in order to continue the conversation upon which they were engaged. Edgar on his part soon ceased to regard his father as a stranger, and his admiration for his store of information and learning served as a stimulant to his studies, for which his previous life had given him but little liking.

For the last two years, however, his father had seen with regret that there was but little hope of making a profound scholar of him, and that unless he himself could discover the solution of the problems that still eluded him, there was little chance of it being found by his successor.

Once roused, he had the good sense to see that it was not in such a life that Edgar was likely to find success, and he wisely abandoned the idea of pressing a task upon him that he saw was unfitted to the boy's nature. The energy with which Edgar worked with his instructors in arms,—who had been already twice changed, so as to give him a greater opportunity of attaining skill with his weapons,—and the interest with which the lad listened to tales of adventure, showed the direction in which his bent lay. For the last two years his father had frequently read to him the records of Sir Walter Manny and other chroniclers of war and warlike adventure, and impressed upon him the virtues necessary to render a man at once a great soldier and a great man.

"If, my boy," he said, "you should some day go to court and mingle in public affairs, above all things keep yourself clear of any party. Those who cling to a party may rise with its success, but such rises are ever followed by reverses; then comes great suffering to those upon the fallen side. The duty of an English gentleman is simple: he must work for his country, regardless altogether of personal interest. Such a man may never rise to high rank, but he will be respected. Personal honours are little to be desired; it is upon those who stand higher than their neighbours that the blow falls the heaviest; while the rank and file may escape unscathed, it is the nobles and the leaders whose heads fall upon the block. I think that there are troubles in store for England. The Duke of Gloucester overshadows the boy king, but as the latter grows older he will probably shake off his tutelage, though it may be at the cost of a civil war.

"Then, too, there are the exactions of the tax-gatherers. Some day the people will rise against them as they did in

France at the time of the Jacquerie, and as they have done again and again in Flanders. At present the condition of the common people, who are but villeins and serfs, is well-nigh unbearable. Altogether the future seems to me to be dark. I confess that, being a student, the storm when it bursts will affect me but slightly, but as it is clear to me that this is not the life that you will choose it may affect you greatly; for, however little you may wish it, if civil strife comes, you, like everyone else, may be involved in it. In such an event, Edgar, act as your conscience dictates. There is always much to be said for both sides of any question, and it cannot but be so in this. I wish to lay no stress on you in any way. You cannot make a good monk out of a man who longs to be a man-at-arms, nor a warrior of a weakling who longs for the shelter of a cloister.

"Let, however, each man strive to do his best in the line he has chosen for himself. A good monk is as worthy of admiration as a good man-at-arms. I would fain have seen you a great scholar, but as it is clear that this is out of the question, seeing that your nature does not incline to study, I would that you should become a brave knight. It was with that view when I sent you to be instructed at the convent I also gave you an instructor in arms, so that, whichever way your inclinations might finally point, you should be properly fitted for it."

At fifteen all lessons were given up, Edgar having by that time learnt as much as was considered necessary in those days. He continued his exercises with his weapons, but without any strong idea that beyond defence against personal attacks they would be of any use to him. The army was not in those days a career. When the king had need of a force to fight in France or to carry fire and sword into Scotland, the levies were called out, the nobles and barons supplied their contingent, and archers and men-at-arms were enrolled and paid by the king. The levies, however, were only liable to service for a restricted time, and beyond their personal retainers the barons in time followed the royal example of hiring men-at-arms and archers for the campaign; these being partly paid from the royal treasury, and partly from their own revenue.

At the end of the campaign, however, the army speedily dispersed, each man returning to his former vocation; save therefore for the retainers, who formed the garrisons of the castles of the nobles, there was no military career such as that which came into existence with the formation of standing armies. Nevertheless, there was honour and rank to be won in the foreign wars, and it was to these the young men of gentle blood looked to make their way. But since the death of the Black Prince matters had been quiet abroad, and unless for those who were attached to the households of powerful nobles there was, for the present, no avenue towards distinction.

Edgar had been talking these matters over with the Prior of St. Alwyth, who had taken a great fancy to him, and with whom he had, since he had given up his work at the convent, frequently had long conversations. They were engaged in one of these when this narrative begins:

"I quite agree with your father," the Prior continued. "Were there a just and strong government the mass of the people might bear their present position. It seems to us as natural that the serfs should be transferred with the land as if they were herds of cattle, for such is the rule throughout Europe as well as here, and one sees that there are great difficulties in the way of making any alteration in this state of things. See you, were men free to wander as they chose over the land instead of working at their vocations, the country would be full of vagrants who, for want of other means for a living, would soon become robbers.

M 371

EDGAR TALKS MATTERS OVER WITH THE PRIOR OF ST. ALWYTH.

Then, too, very many would flock to the towns, and so far from bettering their condition, would find themselves worse off than before, for there would be more people than work could be found for.

"So long as each was called upon only to pay his fifteenth to the king's treasury they were contented enough, but now they are called upon for a tenth as well as a fifteenth, and often this is greatly exceeded by the rapacity of the tax-collectors. Other burdens are put upon them, and altogether men are becoming desperate. Then, too, the cessation of the wars with France have brought back to the country numbers of disbanded soldiers who, having got out of the way of honest work and lost the habits of labour, are discontented and restless. All this adds to the danger. We who live in the country see these things, but the king and nobles either know nothing of them or treat them with contempt, well knowing that a few hundred men-at-arms can scatter a multitude of unarmed serfs."

"And would you give freedom to the serfs, good Father?"

"I say not that I would give them absolute freedom, but I would grant them a charter giving them far greater rights than at present. A fifteenth of their labour is as much as they should be called upon to pay, and when the king's necessities render it needful that further money should be raised, the burden should only be laid upon the backs of those who can afford to pay it. I hear that there is much wild talk, and that the doctrines of Wickliffe have done grievous harm. I say not, my son, that there are not abuses in the Church as well as elsewhere; but these pestilent doctrines lead men to disregard all authority, and to view their natural masters as oppressors. I hear that seditious talk is uttered openly in the villages throughout the country; that there are men who would fain persuade the ignorant that all above them are drones who live on the proceeds of their labour—as if indeed every man, however high in rank, had not his share of labour and care—I fear, then, that if there should be a rising of the peasantry we may have such scenes as those that took place during the Jacquerie in France, and that many who would, were things different, be in favour of giving more extended rights to the people, will be forced to take a side against them."

"I can hardly think that they would take up arms, Father. They must know that they could not withstand a charge of armour-clad knights and men-at-arms."

"Unhappily, my son, the masses do not think. They believe what it pleases them to believe, and what the men who go about stirring up sedition tell them. I foresee that in the end they will suffer horribly, but before the end comes they may commit every sort of outrage. They may sack monasteries and murder the monks, for we are also looked upon as drones. They may attack and destroy the houses of the better class, and even the castles of the smaller nobles. They may even capture London and lay it in ashes; but the thought that after they had done these things a terrible vengeance would be taken, and their lot would be harder than before, would never occur to them. Take your own house, for instance—what resistance could it offer to a fierce mob of peasants?"

"None," Edgar admitted. "But why should they attack it?"

The Prior was silent.

"I know what you mean, good Father," Edgar said after a pause. "They say that my father is a magician, because he stirs not abroad, but spends his time on his researches. I remember when I was a small boy, and the lads of the village wished to anger me, they would shout out, 'Here is the magician's son'; and I had many a fight in consequence."

"Just so, Edgar; the ignorant always hate that which

they cannot understand, so Friar Bacon was persecuted, and accused of dabbling in magic when he was making discoveries useful to mankind. I say not that they will do any great harm when they first rise, for it cannot be said that the serfs here are so hardly treated as they were in France, where their lords had power of life and death over them, and could slay them like cattle if they chose, none interfering. Hence the hatred was so deep that in the very first outbreak the peasants fell upon the nobles and massacred them and their families.

"Here there is no such feeling. It is against the government that taxes them so heavily that their anger is directed, and I fear that this new poll-tax that has been ordered will drive them to extremities. I have news that across the river in Essex the people of some places have not only refused to pay, but have forcibly driven away the tax-gatherers, and when these things once begin, there is no saying how they are going to end. However, if there is trouble, I think not that at first we shall be in any danger here, but if they have success at first their pretensions will grow. They will inflame themselves. The love of plunder will take the place of their reasonable objections to over-taxation, and seeing that they have but to stretch out their hands to take what they desire, plunder and rapine will become general."

As Edgar walked back home he felt that there was much truth in the Prior's remarks. He himself had heard many things said among the villagers which showed that their patience was well-nigh at an end. Although, since he began his studies, he had no time to keep up his former close connection with the village, he had always been on friendly terms with his old playmates, and they talked far more freely with him than they would do to anyone else of gentle blood. Once or twice he had, from a spirit of adventure, gone with them to meetings that were held after dark in a quiet spot near Dartford, and listened to the talk of strangers from Gravesend and other places. He knew himself how heavily the taxation pressed upon the people, and his sympathies were wholly with them. There had been nothing said even by the most violent of the speakers to offend him. The protests were against the exactions of the tax-gatherers, the extravagance of the court, and the hardship that men should be serfs on the land.

Once they had been addressed by a secular priest from the other side of the river, who had asserted that all men were born equal and had equal rights. This sentiment had been loudly applauded, but he himself had sense enough to see that it was contrary to fact, and that men were not born equal. One was the son of a noble, the other of a serf. One child was a cripple and a weakling from its birth, another strong and lusty. One was well-nigh a fool, and another clear-headed. It seemed to him that there were and must be differences.

Many of the secular clergy were among the foremost in stirring up the people. They themselves smarted under their disabilities. For the most part they were what were called hedge-priests, men of but little or no education, looked down upon by the regular clergy, and almost wholly dependant on the contributions of their hearers. They resented the difference between themselves and the richly-endowed clergy and religious houses, and denounced the priests and monks as drones who sucked the life-blood of the country.

This was the last gathering at which Edgar had been present. He had been both shocked and offended at the preaching. What was the name of the priest he knew not, nor did the villagers, but he went by the name of Jack Straw, and was, Edgar thought, a dangerous fellow. The lad had no objection to his abuse of the tax-gatherers, or to his complaints of the extravagance of the court, but this man's denunciation of the monks and clergy at once shocked and angered him. Edgar's intercourse with the villagers had removed some of the prejudices generally felt by his class, but in other respects he naturally felt as did others of his station, and he resolved to go to no more meetings.

After taking his meal with his father, Edgar mounted the horse that the latter had bought for him, and rode over to the house of one of his friends.

The number of those who had like himself been taught by the monk of St. Alwyth had increased somewhat, and there were, when he left, six other lads there. Three of these were intended for the Church. All were sons of neighbouring land-owners, and it was to visit Albert de Courcy, the son of Sir Ralph de Courcy, that Edgar was now riding. Albert and he had been special friends. They were about the same age, but of very different dispositions. The difference between their characters was perhaps the chief attraction that had drawn them to each other. Albert was gentle in disposition, his health was not good, and he had been a weakly child. His father, who was a stout knight, regarded him with slight favour, and had acceded willingly to his desire to enter the Church, feeling that he would never make a good fighter.

Edgar, on the contrary, was tall and strongly built, and had never known a day's illness. He was somewhat grave in manner, for the companionship of his father and the character of their conversations had made him older and more thoughtful than most lads of his age. He was eager for adventure, and burned for an opportunity to distinguish himself, while his enthusiasm for noble exploits and great commanders interested his quiet friend, who had the power of admiring things that he could not hope to imitate. In him alone of his school-fellows did Edgar find any sympathy with his own feelings as to the condition of the people. Henry Nevil laughed to scorn Edgar's advocacy of their cause. Richard Clairvaux more than once quarrelled with him seriously, and on one or two occasions they almost betook themselves to their swords. The other three, who were of less spirit, took no part in these arguments, saying that these things did not concern them, being matters for the king and his ministers, and of no interest whatever to them.

In other respects Edgar was popular with them all. His strength and his skill in arms gave him an authority that even Richard Clairvaux acknowledged in his cooler moments. Edgar visited at the houses of all their fathers, his father encouraging him to do so, as he thought that association with his equals would be a great advantage to him. As far as manners were concerned, however, the others, with the exception of Albert de Courcy, who did not need it, gained more than he did, for Mr. Ormskirk had, during his long residence at foreign universities and his close connection with professors, acquired a certain foreign courtliness of bearing that was in strong contrast to the rough bluffness of speech and manner that characterized the English of that period, and had some share in rendering them so unpopular upon the Continent, where, although their strength and fighting power made them respected, they were regarded as island bears, and their manners were a standing jest among the frivolous nobles of the court of France.

At the house of Sir Ralph de Courcy Edgar was a special favourite. Lady de Courcy was fond of him because her son was never tired of singing his praises, and because she saw that his friendship was really a benefit to the somewhat dreamy boy. Aline, a girl of fourteen, regarded him with admiration; she was deeply attached to her brother, and believed implicitly his assertion that Edgar would some day become a valiant knight; while Sir Ralph himself liked him both for the courtesy of his bearing and the firmness and steadiness of his character, which had, he saw, a very beneficial influence over that of Albert. Sir Ralph was now content that the latter should enter the Church, but he was unwilling that his son should become what he called a mere shaveling, and desired that he should attain power and position in his profession.

The lack of ambition and energy in his son were a grievance to him almost as great as his lack of physical powers, and he saw that although, so far, there was still an absence of ambition, yet the boy had gained firmness and decision from the influence of his friend, and that he was far more likely to attain eminence in the Church than he had been before. He was himself surprised that the son of a man whose pursuits he despised should have attained such proficiency with his weapons—a matter which he had learned, when one day he had tried his skill with Edgar in a bout with swords—and he recognized that with his gifts of manner, strength, and enthusiasm for deeds of arms, he was likely one day to make a name for himself.

Whenever, therefore, Edgar rode over to Sir Ralph's he was certain of a hearty welcome from all. As to the lad's opinions as to the condition of the peasantry,—opinions which he would have scouted as monstrous on the part of a gentleman,—Sir Ralph knew nothing, Albert having been wise enough to remain silent on the subject, the custom of the times being wholly opposed to anything like a free expression of opinion on any subject from a lad to his elders.

"It is quite a time since you were here last, Master Ormskirk," Lady De Courcy said when he entered. "Albert so often goes up for a talk with you when he has finished his studies at the monastery that you are forgetting us here."

"I crave your pardon, Mistress De Courcy," Edgar said; "but indeed, I have been working hard, for my father has obtained for me a good master for the sword—a Frenchman skilled in many devices of which my English teachers were wholly ignorant. He has been teaching some of the young nobles in London, and my father, hearing of his skill, has had him down here, at a heavy cost, for the last month, as he was for the moment without engagements in London. It was but yesterday that he returned. Naturally, I have desired to make the utmost of the opportunity, and most of my time has been spent in the fencing-room."

"And have you gained much by his instruction?" Sir Ralph asked.

"I hope so, Sir Ralph. I have tried my best, and he has been good enough to commend me warmly, and even told my father that I was the aptest pupil that he had."

"I will try a bout with you presently," the knight said. "It is nigh two years since we had one together, and my arm is growing stiff for want of practice, though every day I endeavour to keep myself in order for any opportunity or chance that may occur, by practising against an imaginary foe by hammering with a mace at a corn-sack swinging from a beam. Methinks I hit it as hard as of old, but in truth I know but little of the tricks of these Frenchmen. They availed nothing at Poictiers against our crushing downright blows. Still, I would gladly see what their tricks are like."

CHAPTER II.

A FENCING BOUT.

A FTER he had talked for a short time with Mistress De Courcy, Edgar went to the fencing-room with Sir Ralph, and they there put on helmets and quilted leather jerkins, with chains sewn on at the shoulders.

"Now, you are to do your best," Sir Ralph said as he handed a sword to Edgar, and took one himself.

So long as they played gently Edgar had all the advantage.

"You have learned your tricks well," Sir Ralph said good-temperedly, "and, in truth, your quick returns puzzle me greatly, and I admit that were we both unprotected I should have no chance with you; but let us see what you could do were we fighting in earnest;" and he took down a couple of suits of complete body armour from the wall.

Albert, who was looking on, fastened the buckles for both of them.

"Ah! you know how the straps go," Sir Ralph said in a tone of satisfaction. "Well, it is something to know that, even if you don't know what to do with it when you have got it on. Now, Master Edgar, have at you."

Edgar stood on the defence, but, strong as his arm was from constant exercise, he had some difficulty to save his head from the sweeping blows that Sir Ralph rained upon it.

"By my faith, young fellow," Sir Ralph said as, after three or four minutes, he drew back breathless from his exertions, "your muscles seem to be made of iron, and you are fit to hold your own in a serious *mêlée*. You were wrong not to strike, for I know that more than once there was an opening had you been quick."

Edgar was well aware of the fact, but he had not taken

advantage of it, for he felt that at his age it was best to abstain from trying to gain a success that could not be pleasant for the good knight.

"Well, well, we will fight no more," the latter said.

When Albert had unbuckled his father's armour and hung it up, Edgar said: "Now, Albert, let us have a bout."

The lad coloured hotly, and the knight burst into a hearty laugh.

"You might as soon challenge my daughter Aline. Well, put on the jerkin, Albert; it were well that you should feel what a poor creature a man is who has never had a sword in his hand."

Albert silently obeyed his father's orders and stood up facing Edgar. They were about the same height, though Albert looked slim and delicate by the side of his friend.

"By St. George," his father exclaimed, "you do not take up a bad posture, Albert! You have looked at Edgar often enough at his exercises to see how you ought to place yourself. I have never seen you look so manly since the day you were born. Now, strike in."

Sir Ralph's surprise at his son's attitude grew to amazement as the swords clashed together, and he saw that, although Edgar was not putting out his full strength and skill, his son, instead of being scarce able, as he had expected, to raise the heavy sword, not only showed considerable skill, but even managed to parry some of the tricks of the weapon to which he himself had fallen a victim.

"Stop, stop!" he said at last. "Am I dreaming, or has some one else taken the place of my son? Take off your helmet. It is indeed Albert!" he said as they uncovered. "What magic is this?"

"It is a little surprise that we have prepared for you, Sir Ralph," Edgar said, "and I trust that you will not be displeased. Two years ago I persuaded Albert that there was no reason why even a priest should not have a firm hand and a steady eye, and that this would help him to overcome his nervousness, and would make him strong in body as well as in arm. Since that time he has practised with me almost daily after he had finished his studies at St. Alwyth, and my masters have done their best for him. Though, of course, he has not my strength, as he lacks the practice I have had, he has gained wonderfully of late, and would in a few years match me in skill, for what he wants in strength he makes up in activity."

"Master Ormskirk," the knight said, "I am beholden to you more than I can express. His mother and I have observed during the last two years that he has gained greatly in health, and has widened out in the shoulders. I understand now how it has come about. We have never questioned him about it; indeed, I should as soon have thought of asking him whether he had made up his mind to become king, as whether he had begun to use a sword. Why, I see that you have taught him already some of the tricks that you have just learnt."

"I have not had time to instruct him in many of them, Sir Ralph, but I showed him one or two, and he acquired them so quickly that in another month I have no doubt he will know them as well as I do."

"By St. George, you have done wonders, Edgar! As for you, Albert, I am as pleased as if I had heard that the king had made me an earl. Truly, indeed, did Master Ormskirk tell you that it would do you good to learn to use a sword. 'Tis not a priest's weapon,—although many a priest and bishop have ridden to battle before now,—but it has improved your health and given you ten years more life than you would be likely to have had without it. It seemed to me strange that any son of my house should be ignorant as to how to use a sword, and now I consider that that which seemed to me almost a disgrace is removed. Knows your mother aught of this?"

"No, sir. When I began I feared that my resolution would soon fade; and indeed it would have done so had not Edgar constantly encouraged me and held me to it, though indeed at first it so fatigued me that I could scarce walk home."

"That I can well understand, my lad. Now you shall come and tell your mother. I have news for you, dame, that will in no small degree astonish you," he said, as, followed by the two lads, he returned to the room where she was sitting. "In the first place, young Master Ormskirk has proved himself a better man than I with the sword."

"Say not so, I pray you, Sir Ralph," Edgar said. "In skill with the French tricks I may have had the better of you, but with a mace you would have dashed my brains out, as I could not have guarded my head against the blows that you could have struck with it."

"Not just yet, perhaps," the knight said; "but when you get your full strength you could assuredly do so. He will be a famous knight some day, dame. But that is not the most surprising piece of news. What would you say were I to tell you that this weakling of ours, although far from approaching the skill and strength of his friend, is yet able to wield a heavy sword manfully and skilfully?"

"I should say that either you were dreaming, or that I was, Sir Ralph."

"Well, I do say so in wideawake earnest. Master Ormskirk has been his instructor, and for the last two years the lad has been learning of him and of his masters. That accounts for the change that we have noticed in his health and bearing. Faith, he used to go along with stooping neck, like a girl who has outgrown her strength. Now he carries himself well, and his health of late has left nought to be desired. It was for that that his friend invited him to exercise himself with the sword; and indeed his recipe has done wonders. His voice has gained strength, and though it still has a girlish ring about it, he speaks more firmly and assuredly than he used to do."

"That is indeed wonderful news, Sir Ralph, and I rejoice to hear it. Master Ormskirk, we are indeed beholden to you. For at one time I doubted whether Albert would ever live to grow into a man; and of late I have been gladdened at seeing so great a change in him, though I dreamed not of the cause."

Aline had stood open-mouthed while her father was speaking, and now stole up to Albert's side.

"I am pleased, brother," she said. "May I tell them now what happened the other day with the black bull you charged me to say nothing about?"

"What is this about the black bull, Aline?" her father said as he caught the words.

"It was naught, sir," Albert replied, colouring, "save that the black bull in the lower meadow ran at us, and I frightened him away."

"No, no, Father," the girl broke in, "it was not that at all. We were walking through the meadow together when the black bull ran at us. Albert said to me, 'Run, run, Aline!' and I did run as hard as I could; but I looked back for some time as I ran, being greatly terrified as to what would come to Albert. He stood still. The bull lowered his head and rushed at him. Then he sprang aside just as I expected to see him tossed into the air, caught hold of the bull's tail as it went past him and held on till the bull was close to the fence, and then he let go and scrambled over, while the bull went bellowing down the field."

"Well done, well done!" Sir Ralph said. "Why, Albert, it seems marvellous that you should be doing such things;

C

that black bull is a formidable beast, and the strongest man, if unarmed, might well feel discomposed if he saw him coming rushing at him. I will wager that if you had not had that practice with the sword, you would not have had the quickness of thought that enabled you to get out of the scrape. You might have stood between the bull and your sister, but if you had done so you would only have been tossed, and perhaps gored or trampled to death afterwards. I will have the beast killed, or otherwise he will be doing mischief. There are not many who pass through the field, still I don't want to have any of my tenants killed.

"Well, Master Ormskirk, both my wife and I feel grateful to you for what you have done for Albert. There are the makings of a man in him now, let him take up what trade he will. I don't say much, boy, it is not my way; but if you ever want a friend, whether it be at court or camp, you can rely upon me to do as much for you as I would for one of my own; maybe more, for I deem that a man cannot well ask for favours for those of his own blood, but he can speak a good word, and even urge his suit for one who is no kin to him. So far as I understand, you have not made up your mind in what path you will embark."

"No, Sir Ralph, for at present, although we can scarce be said to be at peace with the French, we are not fighting with them. Had it been so I would willingly have joined the train of some brave knight raising a force for service there. There is ever fighting in the North, but with the Scots it is but a war of skirmishes, and not as it was in Edward's reign. Moreover, by what my father says, there seems no reason for harrying Scotland far and near, and the fighting at present is scarce of a nature in which much credit is to be gained."

"You might enter the household of some powerful noble, lad."

"My father spoke to me of that, Sir Ralph, but told me that he would rather that I were with some simple knight than with a great noble, for that in the rivalries between these there might be troubles come upon the land, and maybe even civil strife; that one who might hold his head highest of all one day might on the morrow have it struck off with the executioner's axe, and that at any rate it were best at present to live quietly and see how matters went before taking any step that would bind me to the fortunes of one man more than another."

"Your father speaks wisely. 'Tis not often that men who live in books, and spend their time in poring over mouldy parchments and in well-nigh suffocating themselves with stinking fumes, have common sense in worldly matters. But when I have conversed with your father I have always found that, although he takes not much interest in public affairs at present, he is marvellously well versed in our history, and can give illustrations in support of what he says. Well, whenever the time comes that he thinks it good for you to leave his fireside and venture out into the world, you have but to come to me, and I will, so far as is in my power, further your designs."

"I thank you most heartily, Sir Ralph, and glad am I to have been of service to Albert, who has been almost as a brother to me since we first met at St. Alwyth."

"I would go over and see your father and have a talk with him about you, but I ride to London to-morrow, and may be forced to tarry there for some time. When I return I will wait upon him and have a talk as to his plans for you. Now, I doubt not, you would all rather be wandering about the garden than sitting here with us, so we will detain you no longer."

"Albert, I am very angry with you and Master Ormskirk that you did not take me into your counsel and tell me about your learning to use your sword," Aline said later on, as they watched Edgar ride away through the gateway of the castle. "I call it very unkind of you both."

"We had not thought of being unkind, Aline," Albert said quietly. "When we began I did not feel sure that either my strength or my resolution would suffice to carry me through, and indeed it was at first very painful work for me, having never before taken any strong exercise, and often I would have given it up from the pain and fatigue that it caused me, had not Edgar urged me to persevere, saying that in time I should feel neither pain nor weariness. Therefore at first I said nothing to you, knowing that it would disappoint you did I give it up, and then when my arm gained strength, and Edgar encouraged me by praising my progress, and I began to hope that I might yet come to be strong and gain skill with the weapon, I kept it back in order that I might, as I have done to-day, have the pleasure of surprising you, as well as my father, by showing that I was not so great a milksop as you had rightly deemed me."

"I never thought that you were a milksop, Albert," his sister said indignantly. "I knew that you were not strong, and was sorry for it, but it was much nicer for me that you should be content to walk and ride with me, and to take interest in things that I like, instead of being like Henry Nevil or Richard Clairvaux, who are always talking and thinking of nothing but how they would go to the wars, and what they would do there."

"There was no need that I should do that, Aline. Edgar is a much better swordsman than either of them, and knows much more, and is much more likely to be a famous knight some day than either Nevil or Clairvaux, but I am certain that you do not hear him talk about it."

"No, Edgar is nice too," the girl said frankly, "and

very strong. Do you not remember how he carried me home more than two miles when, a year ago, I fell down when I was out with you, and sprained my ankle. And now, Albert, perhaps some day you will get so strong that you may not think of going into the Church and shutting yourself up all your life in a cloister, but may come to be famous too."

"I have not thought of that, Aline," he said gravely. "If ever I did change my mind, it would be that I might always be with Edgar and be great friends with him, all through our lives, just as we are now."

Sir Ralph and his wife were at the time discussing the same topic. "It may yet be, Agatha, that, after all, the boy may give up this thought of being a churchman. I have never said a word against it hitherto, because it seemed to me that he was fit for nothing else; but now that one sees that he has spirit, and has, thanks to his friend, acquired a taste for arms, and has a strength I never dreamt he possessed, the matter is changed. I say not yet that he is like to become a famous knight, but it needs not that every one should be able to swing a heavy mace and hold his own in a mêlée. There are many posts at court where one who is discreet and long-headed may hold his own and gain honour, so that he be not a mere feeble weakling who can be roughly pushed to the wall by every blusterer."

"I would ask him no question concerning it, Sir Ralph," his wife said. "It may be as you say, but methinks that it will be more likely that he will turn to it if you ask him no questions, but leave him to think it out for himself. The lad Edgar has great influence over him, and will assuredly use it for good. As for myself, it would be no such great grief were Albert to enter the Church as it would be to you, though I, too, would prefer that he should not be lost to us, and would rather that he went to court and played his part there. I believe that he has talent. The Prior of St. Alwyth said that he and young Ormskirk were by far his most promising pupils; of course, the latter has now ceased to study with him, having learned as much as is necessary for a gentleman to know if he be not intended for the Church. Albert is well aware what your wishes are, and that if you have said naught against his taking up that profession, it was but because you deemed him fit for no other. Now, you will see that, having done so much, he may well do more, and it may be that in time he may himself speak to you and tell you that he has changed his mind on the matter."

"Perhaps it would be best so, dame, and I have good hope that it will be as you say. I care not much for the court, where Lancaster and Gloucester overshadow the king. Still, a man can play his part there; though I would not that he should attach himself to Lancaster's faction or to Gloucester's, for both are ambitious, and it will be a struggle between them for supremacy. If he goes he shall go as a king's man. Richard, as he grows up, will resent the tutelage in which he is held, but will not be able to shake it off, and he will need men he can rely upon—prudent and good advisers, the nearer to his own age the better, and it may well be that Albert would be like to gain rank and honour more quickly in this way than by doughty deeds in the field. It is good that each man should stick to his last. As for me, I would rather delve as a peasant than mix in the intrigues of a court. But there must be courtiers as well as fighters, and I say not aught against them.

"The boy with his quiet voice, and his habit of going about making little more noise than a cat, is far better suited for such a life than I with my rough speech and fiery temper. For his manner he has also much to thank young Ormskirk. Edgar caught it from his father, who, though a strange man according to my thinking, is yet a singularly courteous gentleman, and Albert has taken it from his friend. Well, wife, I shall put this down as one of my fortunate days, for never have I heard better news than that which Albert gave me this afternoon."

When Edgar returned home he told his father what had taken place.

"I thought that Sir Ralph would be mightily pleased some day when he heard that his son had been so zealously working here with you, and I too was glad to see it. I am altogether without influence to push your fortunes. Learning I can give you, but I scarce know a man at court, for while I lived at Highgate I seldom went abroad, and save for a visit now and then from some scholar anxious to consult me, scarce a being entered my house. Therefore, beyond relating to you such matters of history as it were well for you to know, and by telling you of the deeds of Cæsar and other great commanders, I could do nought for you."

"You have done a great deal for me, Father. You have taught me more of military matters, and of the history of this country, and of France and Italy, than can be known to most people, and will assuredly be of much advantage to me in the future."

"That may be so, Edgar; but the great thing is to make the first start, and here I could in no way aid you. I have often wondered how this matter could be brought about, and now you have obtained a powerful friend; for although Sir Ralph de Courcy is but a simple knight, with no great heritage, his wife is a daughter of Lord Talbot, and he himself is one of the most valiant of the nobles and knights who fought so stoutly in France and Spain, and as such is known to, and respected by, all those who bore a part in those wars. He therefore can do for you the service that of all others is the most necessary.

"The king himself is well aware that he was one of the knights in whom the Black Prince, his father, had the fullest confidence, and to whom he owed his life more than once in the thick of a mélée. Thus, then, when the time comes he will be able to secure for you a post in the following of some brave leader. I would rather that it were so than in the household of any great noble, who would assuredly take one side or other in the factions of the court. You are too young for this as yet, being too old to be a page, too young for an esquire, and must therefore wait until you are old enough to enter service either as an esquire or as one of the retinue of a military leader."

"I would rather be an esquire and ride to battle to win my spurs. I should not care to become a knight simply because I was the owner of so many acres of land, but should wish to be knighted for service in the field."

"So would I also, Edgar. My holding here is large enough to entitle me to the rank of knight did I choose to take it up, but indeed it would be with me as it is with many others, an empty title. Holding land enough for a knight's fee, I should of course be bound to send so many men into the field were I called upon to do so, and should send you as my substitute if the call should not come until you are two or three years older; but in this way you would be less likely to gain opportunities for winning honour than if you formed part of the following of some well-known knight. Were a call to come you could go with few better than Sir Ralph, who would be sure to be in the thick of it. But if it comes not ere long, he may think himself too old to take the field, and his contingent would doubtless be led by some knight as his substitute."

"I think not, Father, that Sir Ralph is likely to regard himself as lying on the shelf for some time to come; he is still a very strong man, and he would chafe like a caged eagle were there blows to be struck in France, and he unable to share in them."

Four days later a man who had been down to the town returned with a budget of news. Edgar happened to be at the door when he rode past.

"What is the news, Master Clement?" he said, for he saw that the man looked excited and alarmed.

"There be bad news, young master, mighty bad news. Thou knowest how in Essex men have refused to pay the poll-tax, but there has been nought of that on this side of the river as yet, though there is sore grumbling, seeing that the tax-collectors are not content with drawing the tax from those of proper age, but often demand payment for boys and girls, who, as they might see, are still under fourteen. It happened so to-day at Dartford. One of the tax-collectors went to the house of Wat the Tyler. His wife had the money for his tax and hers, but the man insolently demanded tax for the daughter, who is but a girl of twelve; and when her mother protested that the child was two years short of the age, he offered so gross an insult to the girl that she and her mother screamed out. A neighbour ran with the news to Wat, who was at his work on the roof of a house near, and he, being full of wrath thereat, ran hastily home, and entering smote the man so heavily on the head with a hammer he carried, that he killed him on the spot.

"The collectors' knaves would have seized Wat, but the neighbours ran in and drove them from the town with blows. The whole place is in a ferment. Many have arms in their hands, and are declaring that they will submit no more to the exactions, and will fight rather than pay, for that their lives are of little value to them if they are to be ground to the earth by these leeches. The Fleming traders in the town have hidden away, for in their present humour the mob might well fall upon them and kill them."

It was against the Flemings indeed that the feelings of the country people ran highest. This tax was not, as usual, collected by the royal officers, but by men hired by the Flemish traders settled in England. The proceeds of it had been bestowed upon several young nobles, intimates of the king. These had borrowed money from the Flemings on the security of the tax; the amount that it was likely to produce had been considerably overrated, and the result was that the Flemings, finding that they would be heavy losers by the transaction, ordered their collectors to gather in as much as possible. These obeyed the instructions, rendering, by their conduct, the exaction of the poll-tax even more unpopular than it would have been had it been collected by the royal officers, who would have been content with the sum that could be legally demanded.

"This is serious news," Edgar said gravely, "and I fear that much trouble may come of it. Doubtless the tax-collector misbehaved himself grossly, but his employers will take no heed of that, and will lay complaints before the king of the slaying of one of their servants and of the assault upon others by a mob of Dartford, so that ere long we shall be having a troop of men-at-arms sent hither to punish the town."

"Ay, young master, but not being of Dartford I should not care so much for that; but there are hot spirits elsewhere, and there are many who would be like to take up arms as well as the men at Dartford, and to resist all attacks; then the trouble would spread, and there is no saying how far it may grow."

"True enough, Clement; well, we may hope that when men's minds become calmer the people of Dartford will think it best to offer to pay a fine in order to escape bloodshed."

"It may be so," the man said, shaking his head, "though I

doubt it. There has been too much preaching of sedition. I say not that the people have not many and real grievances, but the way to right them is not by the taking up of arms, but by petition to the crown and parliament."

He rode on, and Edgar, going in to his father, told him what he had heard from Clement.

"'Tis what I feared," Mr. Ormskirk said. "The English are a patient race, and not given, as are those of foreign nations, to sudden bursts of rage. So long as the taxation was legal they would pay, however hardly it pressed them; but when it comes to demanding money for children under the age, and to insulting them, it is pushing matters too far, and I fear with you, Edgar, that the trouble will spread. I am sorry for these people, for however loudly they may talk, and however valiant they may be, they can assuredly offer but a weak resistance to a strong body of men-at-arms, and they will but make their case worse by taking up arms.

"History shows that mobs are seldom able to maintain a struggle against authority. Just at first success may attend them, but as soon as those who govern recover from their first surprise they are not long before they put down the movement. I am sorry, not only for the men themselves, but for others who, like myself, altogether disapprove of any rising. Just at first the mob may obey its leaders and act with moderation; but they are like wild beasts—the sight of blood maddens them—and if this rising should become a serious one, you will see that there will be burnings and ravagings. Heads will be smitten off, and after slaying those they consider the chief culprits, they will turn against all in a better condition than themselves.

"The last time Sir Ralph de Courcy was over here he told me that the priest they call Jack Straw and many others were, he heard, not only preaching sedition against the government, but the seizure of the goods of the wealthy, the confiscation of the estates of the monasteries, and the division of the wealth of the rich. A nice programme, and just the one that would be acceptable to men without a penny in their pockets. Sir Ralph said that he would give much if he, with half a dozen men-at-arms, could light upon a meeting of these people, when he would give them a lesson that would silence their saucy tongues for a long time to come. I told him I was glad that he had not the opportunity, for that methought it would do more harm than good. 'You won't think so,' he said, 'when there is a mob of these rascals thundering at your door, and resolved to make a bonfire of your precious manuscripts and to throw you into the midst of it.' 'I have no doubt,' I replied, 'that at such a time I should welcome the news of the arrival of you and the men-at-arms, but I have no store of goods that would attract their cupidity.' 'No,' the knight said, 'but you know that among the common people you are accounted a magician, because you are wiser than they are.'

"'I know that,' I replied; 'it is the same in all countries. The credulous mob think that a scholar, although he may spend his life in trying to make a discovery that will be of inestimable value to them, is a magician and in league with the devil. However, although not a fighting man, I may possess means of defence that are to the full as serviceable as swords and battle-axes. I have long foreseen that, should troubles arise, the villagers of St. Alwyth would be like enough to raise the cry of magician, and to take that opportunity of ridding themselves of one they vaguely fear, and many months ago I made some preparations to meet such a storm and to show them that a magician is not altogether defenceless, and that the compounds in his power are well-nigh as dangerous as they believe, only not in the same way.'

"'Well, I hope that you will find it so if there is any

trouble; but I recommend you, if you hear that there is any talk in the village of making an assault upon you, that you send a messenger to me straightway, and you may be sure that ere an hour has passed I will be here with half a dozen stout fellows who will drive this rabble before them like sheep.'

"'I thank you much for the offer, Sir Ralph, and will bear it in mind should there be an occasion, but I think that I may be able to manage without need for bloodshed. You are a vastly more formidable enemy than I am, but I imagine that they have a greater respect for my supposed magical powers than they have for the weight of your arm, heavy though it be.'

"'Perhaps it is so, my friend,' Sir Ralph said grimly, 'for they have not felt its full weight yet, though I own that I myself would rather meet the bravest knight in battle than raise my hand against a man whom I believed to be possessed of magical powers.'

"I laughed, and said that so far as I knew no such powers existed. 'Your magicians are but chemists,' I said. 'Their object of search is the Elixir of Life or the Philosopher's Stone; they may be powerful for good, but they are assuredly powerless for evil.'

"'But surely you believe in the power of sorcery?' he said. 'All men know that there are sorcerers who can command the powers of the air and bring terrible misfortunes down on those that oppose them.'

"'I do not believe that there are men who possess such powers,' I said. 'There are knaves who may pretend to have such powers, but it is only to gain money from the credulous. In all my reading I have never come upon a single instance of any man who has really exercised such powers, nor do I believe that such powers exist. Men have at all times believed in portents, and even a Roman army would turn back were it on the march against an enemy, if a hare ran across the road they were following; I say not that there may not be something in such portents, though even of this I have doubts. Still, like dreams, they may be sent to warn us, but assuredly man has naught to do with their occurrence, and I would, were I not a peaceful man, draw my sword as readily against the most famous enchanter as against any other man of the same strength and skill, with his weapon.'"

"I could see that the good knight was shocked at the light way in which I spoke of Magicians; and, indeed, the power of superstition over men, otherwise sensible, is wonderful. However, he took his leave without saying more than that he and the men-at-arms would be ready if I sent for them."

CHAPTER III.

WAT TYLER.

THAT evening Mr. Ormskirk continued the subject of his talk of the afternoon.

"You looked surprised, Edgar, when I said that I told Sir Ralph I had made some preparations for defence, and that some of the compounds in my laboratory are as dangerous as the common people regard them, although that danger has nought to do with any magical property. You must know that many substances, while wholly innocent in themselves, are capable of dealing wide destruction when they are mixed together; for example, saltpetre, charcoal, and sulphur which, as Friar Bacon discovered, make, when mixed together, a powder whose explosive power is well-nigh beyond belief, and which is now coming into use as a destructive agent in war. Many other compounds can be produced of explosive nature, some indeed of such powerful and sudden action that we dare not even make experiments with them.

"Many other strange things have been discovered, some of which may seem useless at present, but may, upon further experiments on their properties, turn out of value to man. Such a substance I discovered two years ago. I was experimenting upon bones, and endeavouring to ascertain whether a powder might not be procured which, when mixed with other substances, would produce unexpected results. After calcining the bones, I treated the white ash with various acids and alkaloids, and with fire and water, returning again and again to the trials when I had time. While conducting these experiments I found that there was certainly some substance present with whose nature I was altogether unacquainted.

"One evening, going into the laboratory after dark, I observed with astonishment what looked like a lambent flame upon the table. In my alarm I ran forward to put it out, but found that there was no heat in it; lighting my lamp, I could no longer see it, but on the table I found a few grains of the stuff I had been experimenting on. Turning out the lamp the light was again visible, and after much thought I concluded that it was similar to the light given by the little creatures called glowworms, and which in its turn somewhat resembles the light that can be seen at times in a pile of decaying fish. I tried many experiments, but as nothing came of them I gave them up, not seeing that any use could come of a fire that gave out no heat. I produced a powder, however, that when rubbed on any substance, became luminous in the dark, presenting an appearance strange and sufficiently alarming to the ignorant.

"Thinking the matter over some time ago, I took a little

of this powder from the phial in which I had stored it away, and, moistening it, rubbed it on the wall in the form of circles, triangles, and other signs. I did this just before it became dark. As the moisture dried, these figures gradually assumed a luminous appearance. I saw the use to which this could be put in awing a mob, and, setting to work, made a large supply of this powder."

"How long does it retain its light, father?"

"That is uncertain. For some hours in a darkened room, the light gradually growing fainter, but if a bright day follows, the figures stand out on the following night as brightly as before; while if the day is dull they show up but faintly at night. I see not that any use can come of such a thing, for the light is at all times too faint to be used for reading unless the page is held quite close to it. Come downstairs with me and I will show you the head of one of the old Roman statues that was dug up near Rochester, and which I bought for a few pence last year."

They went down into the laboratory. The light was burning. "There you see, Edgar, I have painted this head with the stuff, and now you can see nothing more unusual than if it had been daubed with whitewash. Now I will extinguish the lamp."

Prepared as he was, Edgar nevertheless stepped back with an exclamation of surprise and almost awe. The head stood out in the darkness with startling distinctness. It had the effect of being bathed in moonlight, although much more brilliant than even the light of the full moon. It seemed to him, indeed, almost as if a faint wavering light played around it, giving the stern face of the old Roman a sardonic and evil expression.

"You can touch it, Edgar, but you will see that there is not the slightest warmth."

"It is wonderful, father."

"Yes, it is a strange thing; but is, so far as I can see, of no use save as a wonder, and it is just one of those wonders that to most people would seem to be magical. I showed it a short time ago to the Prior, having explained to him beforehand how I had discovered it. He is above the superstitions of folks in general, and knowing that I could have no motive in deceiving him, was much interested; but he said to me, 'This is one of the things that were best concealed. I can quite understand that there are many things in nature of which we are ignorant. I know that what you say of decayed fish sometimes giving out light like this is perfectly true, and everyone knows that the glowworms, when the weather is damp, light up the banks and fields, although no heat can be felt. Doubtless in your researches on bones you have discovered some substance akin to that which causes the light in those cases, but you would never persuade the vulgar of this.

" 'Nay, there are even churchmen and prelates who would view it as magic. Therefore, my friend, seeing that, as you say, the powder is not likely to be of any use to man, I should say that it were best that you destroy it, for if whispers of it got abroad you might well be accused of dealing in magic. All knowledge of things beyond them is magic to the ignorant. Roger Bacon was treated as a magician, and I doubt not that this will ever be the case with all those who are more learned than their fellow-men. Therefore my advice to you is, burn the stuff and say nought about it.'

"I did not take his advice, Edgar, for it seemed to me that it might well be used to awe any unruly mob that might come hither at night to attack me. I have made an experiment that, though I believe not in the supernatural, would have frightened me had I seen it without knowing anything of its nature. You know that old skull that was

D

dug up out of the garden last month. I have hung the lower jaw on wires so that it can be moved, and have to-day painted it, and now I will blow out the light again, and then take it from the cupboard."

A moment later the room was in darkness, and then an exclamation of surprise and almost terror rose from Edgar. In front of him there was a gibbering skull, the lower jaw wagging up and down, as if engaging in noiseless laughter. It was much more brilliant than the stone head had been, and a lambent flame played round it.

"What think ye of that, Edgar?"

"It is ghastly, sir, horrible!"

"It is not a pleasant object," his father said quietly as he struck the tinder and again lighted the lamp. "I fancy, Edgar, that if a mob of people were to break down the door and find themselves confronted by that object they would fly in terror."

"Assuredly they would, father; they would not stop running this side of Dartford. Even though I expected it, the sight sent a shiver through me, and my teeth well-nigh chattered. But this would only avail in case of a night attack."

"It would avail something even in daylight, Edgar. These downstairs rooms have but little light, and that little I intend to block up by nailing boards inside, and by hanging sacks over them outside. Then if I place the skull in the passage, those who sought me in my laboratory would be brought to a standstill. But there are other means. I have buried jars filled with Friar Bacon's powder round the house, with trains by which they can be fired. At present the common people know little of guns, and methinks that the explosion of two or three of these jars would send them about their business. I have other devices which it is not necessary to enter upon, but which would be effective, therefore you need have little fear that any mob will gain entrance here, and you may be sure that after a repulse they would be very loath to touch the place again."

"Yes, father, but they might bring accusation against you of witchcraft."

"I admit that there is that danger, but the Prior here has long taken an interest in my investigations, and can testify for me that these are but scientific products, and have nought to do with magic. Besides, if there is a rising of the common people, the king and nobles will be in no mood to listen to complaints against those who have thwarted the attacks of the rioters."

"No doubt that would be so, father; still, for myself, I would rather charge them, sword in hand, with a band of stout fellows behind me."

"But we have not got the stout fellows, Edgar; and for myself, even if we had them, I would prefer to set these poor knaves running without doing harm to them rather than to slay and maim, for their attack would be made in their ignorance, and in their hatred of those above them. They have been goaded by oppression into taking up arms, and the fault rests upon others rather than upon the poor people."

The next morning, however, Edgar went round to the tenants, of whom there were fifteen. They had heard of the affair at Dartford, which was, of course, in everyone's mouth, and their sympathies were wholly with the rioters.

"I think as you do," Edgar said to one of them. "The exactions of the tax-gatherers are indeed beyond all bearing, and if the people do but rise to demand fair treatment and their just rights as men, I should wish them success; but I fear that evil counsels will carry them far beyond this, and that they may attack the houses and castles of the gentry, although these may be in no way the authors of their troubles. I am sure that my father has oppressed no one."

"That he has not, Master Edgar. He is as good a lord as one could desire. He exacts no dues beyond his rights; and indeed if there be trouble or sickness he presses no one beyond his means. We have not been called upon for service for many years, and if the Dartford men should come hither to attack him they will find that they have to reckon with us."

"That is what I have come for," Edgar said. "Should you hear of any intention to attack the well-to-do, I would have you hold yourselves in readiness to gather at the house, and to aid in its defence. My father has means of his own for discomfiting any that may come against him; but as these may fail, it would be well that there should be a body of men ready to repel an attack."

"You can rely upon us, Master, but I say not that you can do so on our men. These are serfs, and their sympathies will be all with the rioters. I do not think they would fight against us, but I fear they would not venture their lives against those of their own class."

"That is more than could be expected; but if you yourselves come, it will, I think, be sufficient. I have no fear that these men will in the first place interfere with the gentry. Their first impulse will be to obtain redress for their wrongs; but they have bad advisers, and many will join them for the sake of plunder. When this once begins others will take part with them in the matter, and there is no saying what may come of it."

"Well, you can depend upon us, at any rate, Master. You will have but to ring the bell and all within hearing will run, arms in hand, to defend the house, and we shall, I hope, have time enough to gather there before the mob arrives."

"I doubt not that you will. I shall engage a trusty man to go down to the town and watch what is going on, and we are sure to have notice of any such movement. But as I have said, I think not that there is any chance of their beginning in such a way; it will be only after they have encountered the troops and blood has been shed."

Having gone the round of the tenants, Edgar rode down to Dartford. On the way he passed many men going in the same direction. Almost all of them were armed with staves, pikes, axes, or bows, and he saw that the country people had only been waiting for some act that would serve as a signal for revolt, in order to gather as their fellows in Essex had already begun to do. He found the streets of the town crowded with people; some were excited and noisy, but the mass had a serious and determined air that showed they were resolved upon going through with the work that had been begun. In many places groups of men were assembled in open spaces, listening to the talk of others standing on tables or barrels that had been brought for the purpose.

Their speeches were all to the same point, and Edgar saw that they were the result of a previous agreement.

" Men of Kent!" one exclaimed, "the day has come when you have to prove that you are men, and not mere beasts of burden, to be trodden under foot. You all know how we are oppressed, how illegal exactions are demanded of us, and how, as soon as one is paid, some fresh tax is heaped on us. What are we? Men without a voice, men whom the government regard as merely beings from whom money is to be wrung. Nor is this all. 'Tis not enough that we must starve in order that our oppressors may roll in wealth, may scatter it lavishly as they choose, and indulge in every luxury and in every pleasure. No. The hounds sent among us to wring the last penny from us now take to insulting our wives and daughters, and at last our patience is at an end.

"We have news this morning from all the country round that the people are with us, and before long tens of thousands of the men of Kent will be in arms. Our course is resolved upon. We and the men of Essex will march on London, and woe be to those who try to bar our way. All shall be done orderly and with discretion. We war only against the government, and to obtain our rights. Already our demands have been drawn up, and unless these are granted we will not be content. These are what we ask: *first*, the total abolition of slavery for ourselves and our children for ever; *second*, the reduction of the rent of good land to 4*d.* the acre; *third*, the full liberty of buying and selling like other men in fairs and markets; *fourth*, a general pardon for all past offences."

The recital of these demands was received with a shout of approval.

"This and nothing less will we be content with," he went on. "There are some of the king's advisers who had best not fall into our hands, for if they do their lives will pay the penalty for their evil deeds. But upon one thing we are determined: there shall be no plundering. Our cause is a just one, and for that we are ready to fight. But should any join us with the intention of turning this movement to their private advantage, and of plunder and robbery, we warn them that such will not be permitted, and any man caught plundering will at once be hung. They may call us rioters; they may try and persuade the king that we are disloyal subjects, though this is not the case. One thing they shall not say of us, that we are a band of robbers and thieves. By to-night we shall be joined by all true men of the neighbourhood, and will then march to Gravesend, where our fellows have already risen and are in arms; thence we go to Rochester and deliver those of our brethren who have been thrown into prison because they could not pay the unjust taxes. That done, we will go straight to London and demand from the king himself a charter granting the four points we demand. Wat the Tyler has been chosen our leader. He has struck the first blow, and as a man of courage and energy there is no fear of his betraying us, seeing that he has already put his head into a noose. Now shout for the charter, for the king, and for the commons of England."

Such was the tenor of all the speeches, and they were everywhere received with loud cheers. As Edgar rode down the main street on his way home he heard shouting, and a brawny, powerful man came along, surrounded by a mob of cheering men. He looked at Edgar steadily, and stepped in front of his horse.

"You are the son of the man at St. Alwyth," he said. "I have seen you in the streets before. What think you of what we are doing? I have heard of you attending meetings there."

"I think that you have been cruelly wronged," Edgar answered quietly, "and that the four points that you demand are just and right. I wish you good fortune in obtaining them; and I trust that it will be done peacefully and without opposition."

"Whether peacefully or not, we are determined that they shall be obtained. If it be needful, we will burn down London and kill every man of rank who falls into our hands, and force our way into the king's presence. We will have justice!"

"If you do so you will be wrong," Edgar said calmly; "and moreover, instead of benefiting your cause you will damage it. Your demands are just, and it will be to the interest of no man to gainsay them. Even the nobles must see that the land will gain strength were all men free and ready to bear arms in its defence; and save for the article about the price of land, as to which I am in no way a judge, I see not that any man will be a penny the poorer; but if, on the other hand, such deeds as those you speak of were committed, you would set the nobles throughout the land against you, you would defeat your own good objects, and would in the end bring destruction upon yourselves; so that instead of bettering your position you would be worse than before."

"And do you doubt," the man exclaimed with a scowling brow, "that the commons of England could, if they wished, sweep away these accursed nobles and their followers?"

"Were the commons of England united, well-armed, and disciplined, they could doubtless do so," Edgar replied quietly. "I know not whether you are united, but certainly you are neither armed nor disciplined. We saw how little an undisciplined mass, even if well-armed, can do against trained troops, when a few thousands of English soldiers defeated nigh twenty times their number at Poictiers. And I say that against a force of steel-clad knights and men-at-arms any number of men, however brave, if armed as these are, could make no stand. It would not be a battle—it would be a slaughter; therefore, while wishing you well, and admitting the full justice of your demands, I would say that it were best for your own sakes, and for the sakes of those who love you, that you should conduct yourselves peaceably, so as to show all men that no harm can arise from granting you the charter you ask for, and in giving you all the rights and privileges of free men."

There was a murmur of approval from many of those standing round. The Tyler, who had made a step forward, looked back angrily and would have spoken, but the man next to him whispered something in his ear. Without saying more he walked on, while Edgar touched his horse with his heel and proceeded on his way.

Although his father no doubt heard him ride up to the house, he did not ascend from his laboratory until his usual time, for although, since the Prior had called his attention to his son's condition, he had, when not at work, done all in his power to make the boy happy, and had even given up two hours every evening to him, at all other times he was absorbed in his work to the exclusion of aught else.

"You have been down into the town?" he asked Edgar, as they seated themselves at the table.

"Yes, father; and whatever may happen afterwards, there is no fear of any trouble at present. The speeches of almost all the men were quiet and reasonable. They urged that serfdom should be abolished, free right of markets given, the price of good land to be not over four pennies an acre, that all past offences should be pardoned; beyond this they did not go. Indeed, they declared that everything must be done peacefully and in order, and that any man caught plundering should be hung forthwith. By the applause that followed, these are evidently the sentiments of the great mass of the peasants, but I fear there are some of them—Wat the Tyler at their head—who will go much farther. At present, however, they will disguise their real sentiments, but it seems to me the march on London that they threaten will be far from peaceable. In the first place they are going to Gravesend, and, joining those gathered there, will then march to Rochester, free all those who have been thrown in prison for non-payment of the tax, and then march on London."

"It must end in disaster, Edgar; for if they obtain what they desire from the king—which they may do, seeing that his uncles are all away, and it will be difficult to raise any force of a sudden that would suffice to defeat them—what will they gain by it? Doubtless, as soon as Gloucester and Lancaster arrive in London, the charter will be annulled, and possibly the leaders of the malcontents punished for their share in the matter. Still, I say not that even so the movement will not have done good. The nobles have enough on their hands with their own quarrels and jealousies, and seeing that the continuance of serfdom is likely to give rise to troubles that may be more serious than this hasty and ill-considered movement, they may be content to grant whatever is asked, in order to make an end to troubles of this kind. The English are not like the peasants of other countries—so far, at least, as I have seen them. The feeling of independence is very strong among them, and there is none of the obsequious deference that the serfs in Italy and France pay to their masters."

The next morning Albert de Courcy rode into St. Alwyth.

"Why, Albert," Edgar said, as he went out to the door on seeing him approach, "have you got a holiday to-day?"

"I have a holiday for some time, Edgar. I have received a message from my father, saying that he deems it well that I should at once escort my mother and Aline to London, for he has heard of this trouble at Dartford, and as the king has asked him to remain at court at present, he would fain have Mother, Aline, and me with him. Old Hubert is to take command of the castle, and to bid the tenantry be ready to come in for its defence should trouble threaten. But this is not all; he has spoken to the king of you, praising both your swordsmanship and the benefit that I have derived from your teaching, and Richard desired him to send for you and to present you to him."

"It is kind indeed of Sir Ralph," Edgar exclaimed warmly, "and I will assuredly take advantage of his goodness, although undeserved. This is indeed a splendid opportunity for me. When do you start?"

"We shall leave at ten. I heard as I came along that

the peasants marched at daybreak this morning to Gravesend, therefore there is no fear of our crossing their path."

"I must run down and speak to my father. It is no
small thing that he will allow to disturb him at his work,
but methinks that he will not mind upon such an occasion."

In five minutes Mr. Ormskirk came up into the hall
with Edgar.

"My son has told me, Master De Courcy, of the great
kindness that your father has done to him. I would indeed
say no word to hinder his going with you. 'Tis an opportunity the like of which may never occur to him again. It
is only on account of the troubles with the peasants that he
dislikes to go away at this moment, but I deem not that
any trouble will come of it here; and I can myself, as he
knows, cope with them should they attempt aught against
this house, therefore I bade him not to let that matter enter
his mind, but to prepare himself at once to ride with you
up to town, so that you can rely upon his being at the
castle at the hour appointed."

"Then, with your permission, I will ride off at once, Mr.
Ormskirk, for I also have preparations to make, having
started at once on the arrival of my father's messenger."

As soon as he had gone, Mr. Ormskirk went up to his
chamber and returned in a minute or two. "Here, Edgar,
is a purse with money for your needs. The first thing you
must do when you reach London is to procure suitable
garments for your presentation to the king. Your clothes
are well enough for a country gentleman, but are in no way
fit for court. I need not say to you, do not choose over gay
colours, for I know that your tastes do not lie in that
direction. I don't wish you to become a courtier, Edgar;
for, though it is an excellent thing to be introduced at
court and to be known to high personages there, that is an
altogether different thing from being a hanger-on of the

court. Those who do naught but bask in a king's favour
are seldom men of real merit. They have to play their
part and curry favour. They are looked down upon by the
really great; while, should they attain a marked place in
the king's favour they are regarded with jealousy and
enmity, and sooner or later are sure to fall.

"You cannot but remember the fate that befell the
queen's favourites when Edward threw off his tutelage
and took the reins of power into his own hands. Such is
ever the fate of favourites; neither nobles nor the commonalty love upstarts, and more than one will, I foresee,
ere long draw upon themselves the enmity of the king's
uncles and other nobles for the influence they have gained
over the mind of the young king. I should wish you then
to make as many acquaintances as you can, for none can say
who may be of use to you at one time or another; but keep
yourself aloof from all close intimacies. It may be that, in
after years, you may find it well-nigh impossible to keep aloof
from all parties in the state, but do so as long as you are able,
until you can discern clearly who are true patriots and who
are actuated only by their own selfish ambition, bearing in
mind always that you are a simple gentleman, desirous when
an English army enters the field against a foreign foe to
play your part manfully and with honour, and to gain your
reputation as a soldier and not as a frequenter of courts."

"I will bear your instructions in mind, father, and indeed they accord with what you before said to me, and
which I determined to make a guide to my conduct."

"Now you had better see to the packing of your valise.
It will not be necessary for you to take many things, as you
can equip yourself in London."

An hour later Edgar, after bidding farewell to his father,
mounted his horse. "I shall look to see you back again in
two or three weeks at the longest," Mr. Ormskirk said; "it

is better to come home even if you go again shortly, though it may be that you will have no occasion for another visit to town for some time to come. If Sir Ralph would keep you longer it were best to make some excuse to return. I know that there are many at court but little older than yourself, for the king, being as yet scarcely fifteen, naturally likes to surround himself with those who are not greatly older, and who have the same love for pleasure and gaiety; but such associates will do you no good, though I say not that a little of it might not be of advantage, seeing that you are somewhat more grave than is natural at your age, owing to the life that you have led here with me. Young De Courcy,—although I have greatly encouraged your companionship with him, for he is a very pleasant and agreeable young gentleman,—is too gentle, and lacking in high spirits, which has increased rather than diminished your tendency to silence, and a little companionship with more ardour would not be amiss. You must remember that a cheerful spirit that enables a man to support hardship and fatigue lightly, and to animate his soldiers by his example, is one of the most important characteristics of a leader of men."

Edgar arrived at the castle of the De Courcys a few minutes before ten. Some horses were already standing at the door. He did not go in, deeming that he might be in the way, but sent in word to Lady De Courcy that he was there and at her service. In a few minutes she came out, accompanied by her son and Aline.

"I am glad to have so good an escort, Master Ormskirk," she said smiling; "for after what Sir Ralph told me I feel that I can safely intrust myself to your care."

"I will assuredly do my best, lady," he said, "but I trust that there will be no occasion to draw a sword. I deem that most of those who make the roads unsafe will have gone off to join the Tyler and his band, thinking that opportunities for plunder are sure to present themselves; but, at any rate, as you take, I see, two men-at-arms with you, it is unlikely that any one will venture to molest us."

He assisted Lady De Courcy and her daughter to their saddles, and the party soon rode off, followed by the two men-at-arms.

"Do you purpose to make the journey in a single day?" Edgar asked.

"Assuredly. Aline and I are both accustomed to ride on horseback, and the journey is not too far to be done before the evening falls, especially as it will be for one day's journey only; the roads are good, the day fine, and there will be no occasion to ride at speed. Why, it is but some seventeen or eighteen miles, and you must think but poorly of our horsemanship if you think we cannot traverse such a distance."

So they travelled on, the horses sometimes going at an amble, sometimes dropping into a walk. As they proceeded they met several little parties of men hurrying along, armed with pikes, clubs, or farming implements. These passed without speaking, and seemed to be much more fearful that they might be interfered with than desirous of interfering with others.

"They are miserable-looking varlets," Dame De Courcy said disdainfully. "Our two men-at-arms would be a match for a score of them."

"I doubt not that they would," Albert agreed, "though methinks that a blow with one of those flails would make a head ring even under a steel casque."

"I doubt whether they would think of anything but running away, Albert," Edgar said. "I am sorry for the poor fellows; they have great grievances, but I fear they are not setting about the righting of them the best way. I hope that no great ill may befall them."

"But surely these people have not your sympathy, Master Ormskirk?" Lady De Courcy said in some surprise.

"I have seen enough of them to be sorry for them," Edgar said. "Their life is of the hardest. They live mostly on black bread, and are thankful enough when they can get enough of it. To heavily tax men such as these is to drive them to despair, and that without producing the gain expected, for it is in most cases simply impossible for them to pay the taxes demanded. It seems to me that a poll-tax is, of all others, the worst, since it takes into no account the differences of station and wealth—to the rich the impost is trifling, to the poor it is crushing. It seems to me too that it is not only wrong, but stupid, to maintain serfdom. The men and their families must be fed, and a small money payment would not add greatly to the cost of their services, and indeed would be gained in the additional value of their labour.

"When men are kept as serfs, they work as serfs—I mean to say they work unwillingly and slowly, while, had they the sense of being free, and of having the same rights as others, they would labour more cheerfully. Moreover, it would double the strength of the force that the king and his nobles could place in the field. I am not speaking upon my own judgment, but from what I have learned from my father."

They had no sudden attack to fear from lurking foes, for an act of Edward the First was still in force, by which every highway leading from one market-town to another was always to be kept clear, for two hundred feet on each side, of every ditch, tree, or bush in which a man might lurk to do harm; while, as any ill that happened to travellers was made payable by the township in which it occurred, there was a strong personal interest on the part of the inhabitants to suppress plundering bands in their neighbourhood. Both

Edgar and Albert rode in partial armour, with steel caps and breast-pieces, it being an ordinance that all of gentle blood when travelling should do so, and they carried swords by their sides, and light axes at their saddle-bows.

It was but a little past three o'clock when they crossed London Bridge and then made for the Tower, near which Sir Ralph was lodged.

CHAPTER IV.

IN LONDON.

I AM glad indeed to see you, my young swordsman," Sir Ralph, who was waiting at the door to receive them, said to Edgar after he had greeted his wife and children. "This affair at Dartford threatens to be more serious than I expected. I was on the point of starting for home when I heard of the trouble, and should have done so had not the king asked me to remain here, seeing that at present his uncles and many other nobles are absent, and that, as he was pleased to say, my advice and sword might be useful to him should the trouble grow serious. When, therefore, we received news that all that part of Kent was in a blaze, I sent out a messenger to you, Dame, to come hither to me. What is the latest news?"

"Master Ormskirk can best tell you, Sir Ralph, seeing that he was himself yesterday in Dartford and learned something of their intentions."

Edgar then recounted what he had seen and heard in the streets of Dartford.

"Your account tallies with the news that came here but an hour since, namely, that a crowd of men were marching towards Rochester; a panic prevails in that town, and the wise heads have sent off this messenger, as if, forsooth, an army could be got together and sent down to their aid before these rioters reach the place."

"I am glad to come up, husband," Lady De Courcy said. "'Tis some time since I was in town, and I would fain see what people are wearing, for the fashions change so rapidly that if one is away from town six months one finds that everyone stares, as if one had come from a barbarous country."

"I was afraid of that when I wrote to you," Sir Ralph laughed, "and felt that your coming up would cause me to open my purse widely; but, indeed, in this case you are not far wrong, for there has been a great change in the fashions both of men and women in the last year. The young king is fond of brave attire, and loves to see those around him brightly arrayed, and indeed it seems to me that money is spent over lavishly, and that it were cheaper for a man to build him a new castle than to buy him suits of new raiment for himself and his wife. The men at court all dress in such tightly-fitting garments, that, for my part, I wonder how they get into them."

"And the women, husband?"

"Oh, as to that I say nothing; you must use your own eyes in that matter. However, just at present men's thoughts are too much occupied by these troubles in Essex and Kent to think much of feasting and entertainments, and it will be well to wait to see what comes of it before deciding on making new purchases."

"Is there any chance of trouble in the city, father?" Albert asked.

"I know not, lad. The better class of citizens are assuredly opposed to those who make these troubles, although they have often shown that they can make troubles themselves when they think that their privileges are assailed; still, as they know that their booths are likely to be ransacked, were bands of rioters to obtain possession of the town, they will doubtless give us any aid in their power. But the matter does not depend upon them; there are ever in great towns a majority composed of the craftsmen, the butchers, and others, together with all the lower rabble, who are ready to join in tumults and seditions; and like enough, if the rioters come here, they will take part with them, while the burgesses will be only too glad to put up their shutters and do or say naught that would give the mob an excuse for breaking into their magazines.

"Would that Lancaster were here with a thousand or so of men-at-arms," he went on gloomily; "there is no one at the court who can take command. The king this morning asked me if I would undertake the defence of the palace; but I said to him: 'I am but a simple knight, your Majesty, and neither the young lords of the court nor the citizens would pay any heed to my orders; moreover, I am not one of those whose head is good to plan matters. I would die in your Majesty's service, and would warrant that many of your enemies would go down before I did. I could set a host in battle array, were there a host here; but as to what course to follow, or how it were best to behave at such a pinch, are matters beyond me. As to these, it were best that your Majesty took counsel with those whom the Duke of Lancaster has appointed, and to whom such business appertains.'

"'If you will give me orders I will carry them out, even if I am bade to defend London Bridge with but half-a-dozen men-at-arms, and at such work I might do as well as another; but as to counsel I have none to give, save that were I in your place I would issue a proclamation to these knaves saying that you would hold no parley with men having arms in their hands, but that if they would peacefully disperse you would order that a commission be appointed to examine into their complaints, and that any ills that proved to be justified should be righted, but that if forced you will give nothing, and that if they advance against London their blood must be on their own heads.

"'Should they still come on I would shut myself up in the Tower, which has a good garrison, and where you may well hold out against all the rascaldom of the country until your barons can raise their levies and come to your assistance. Still, it may well be, your Majesty, that these fellows will think better of it, and may, after all, disperse again to their homes. I pray you, take no heed of my words, but refer the matter to those accustomed to deal with affairs of state. The noble prince, your father, knew that he could lay his orders on me, and that I would carry them out to the utmost of my strength. If he said to me, 'Lead a party, Sir Ralph, to attack that bridge,' I gave no thought as to whether the defences were too strong to be carried or not; or if he intrusted the command of a post to me, and said, 'Defend it against all odds until I come to your assistance,' he knew that it would be done, but more than that I never pretended to; and I deem not that, as I have grown older, I know more of such matters than I did when I was in the prime of my strength.'"

"And what said his Majesty, Sir Ralph?"

"He laughed and said that I was the first he had known who was not ready to give him advice, and that he would that all were as chary of so doing as I was. When I told him this morning that I had sent for you and my son and daughter, as I misliked leaving you in the centre of these troubles, he offered apartments in the Tower, but I said that, with his permission, I would remain lodged here, for that, seeing his lady mother was away, I thought that you would prefer this lodging, as there is here a fair garden where you and Aline can walk undisturbed, to the Tower, which is full of armed men, young gallants, and others."

"It will indeed be more pleasant, Sir Ralph, for in the Tower Aline could never venture from my side, and there would be neither peace nor quietness."

The city had already stretched beyond the walls, and on the rising ground between it and the Tower, and on the rise behind the latter, extending to some distance east, many houses had been built. Some of these were the property of nobles and officials of the court, while others had been built by citizens who let them to persons of degree, who only came occasionally to Court on business or pleasure. The house in which Sir Ralph had taken up his lodging was the property of a trader who, when the house was not let to one needing it all, resided there himself as a protection to the property it contained against robbers or ill-doers, often letting one or more rooms to those who needed not the whole house. Thus Sir Ralph was enabled to obtain good accommodation for his family.

"The first thing to be done," he went on, "is to take the lads to a tailor's to obtain clothes more suitable than those they wear."

"I was going to ask you if you would be good enough to do so, Sir Ralph," Edgar said. "My father has furnished me with money for the purpose."

"That is well," the knight said, "though indeed it would have mattered not if he had not done so, for I had intended that you and Albert should have garments of similar fashion at my cost, seeing how much I owe to you."

"Indeed, Sir Ralph, such obligation as there is, is far more than discharged by your kindness in speaking of me to the king and offering to present me to him; indeed, I am ashamed that what was a pleasure to me, and was done from the love I bear your son, should be regarded as worthy of thanks, much less as an obligation."

"Cannot we come with you also?" Lady De Courcy said. "From what you say we must need garments to the full as much as the boys; besides, this is Aline's first visit to town. We saw but little as we rode through, and we would fain look at the shops and see the finery before I make my choice."

"So be it, wife; indeed, I had not intended that you should stay behind."

It was but a quarter of a mile's walk to Aldersgate, and as they reached East Chepe, the young people found infinite amusement in gazing at the goods in the traders' booths, and in watching the throng in the street. It was late in the afternoon now, and many of the citizens' wives and daughters were abroad. These were dressed for the most part in costly materials of sober hues, and Dame Matilda noted that a great change had taken place since she had last been in London, not only in the fashion, but in the costliness of the material; for with the death of the old king and the accession of a young one fond of gaiety and rich dresses, the spirit of extravagance had spread rapidly among all classes. With these were citizens, of whom the elder ones clung to the older fashions, while even the young men still displayed a sobriety in their costumes that contrasted strongly with the brilliancy of several groups of young courtiers. These sauntered along the streets, passing remarks upon all who passed, and casting looks of admiration at some of the pretty daughters of the citizens.

Among all these moved craftsmen and apprentices, the former taking to their employers work they had finished at home, the latter carrying messages, hurrying nimbly through the crowd, or exchanging saucy remarks with each other, for which they were sometimes sharply rebuked by their elders.

From East Chepe the party passed on through Chepe to St. Paul's, and then having chosen the shop at which they could make their purchases the ladies entered a trader's booth, while Sir Ralph went in with the two lads to another hard by.

"What can I serve you with, Sir Knight?"

"I require two suits for my son and this gentleman, his friend," Sir Ralph said. "I desire clothes befitting a presentation to the king, and wish them to be of the fashion, but not extravagantly so."

At the trader's orders his apprentices showed numerous samples, most of them light and bright in colour.

"I want something more sober in hue," the knight said. "These are well enough for men with long purses, and who can afford ample provision of garments, but they would show every spot and stain, and would soon be past wearing; besides, although doubtless such as are mostly used at court, they would be useful for that only, for in the country they would be far too conspicuous for wear."

Other goods were brought down, and Edgar's eye at once fixed upon a rich maroon. Sir Ralph took longer before he made his choice for Albert, but finally fixed upon a somewhat light blue, which well suited the lad's fair complexion and light golden hair. While they were choosing, the mercer had sent in to his neighbour, a tailor, who now measured them. The goods were of satin, and both suits were to be made in precisely similar fashion, namely, a close-fitting tunic reaching down only to the hips. They had loose hanging sleeves, lined with white silk, which was turned over and scolloped; the hose, which were of the same colour as the doublets, were tight fitting.

The caps were to match the dresses in colour. They were turned up at the brim, resembling in shape those still worn in Spain. As the matter was pressing, the tailor promised that both suits should be ready by the following evening.

It took the ladies longer to make their purchases, and it was some time before they issued out from the mantua-maker's, when the Dame informed her husband that she had chosen white satin for Aline's bodice, which was to be tight-fitting, in the fashion, and trimmed round the bottom and neck with white fur, while the skirt was of lilac and of the same material. For herself, she had chosen a purple robe reaching below the knees, with white skirt, both being of satin. The caps, which were closely fitting to the head, were of the same material, and of light-yellow for herself and lilac for Aline.

"We shall have to economize, my lady," Sir Ralph laughed. "'Tis well that I am too old for foppery."

"That is all very well, Sir Ralph, but you must remember that you had a new suit the last time you were in London, and have not worn it from then till now, and I will warrant me that it cost well-nigh as much as Aline's garments or mine."

While waiting for the ladies, two sword-belts had been bought for the lads, Edgar's being embroidered with gold thread, Albert's with silver.

"Now, boys, I think that you will do," Sir Ralph said. "You may not be able to compete with some of those young peacocks of the court, but you will make a sufficiently brave show, and need not feel envious of the best of them."

When the shopping was completed they returned to their lodgings. Here they partook of a meal, after which Sir Ralph went to the Tower, while his wife and daughter, fatigued by their day's journey, speedily betook themselves to their beds. The lads sat talking for some time over the events of the day.

"I fear, Edgar," Albert said presently, "that from my father choosing for me so light a coloured suit, instead of a

graver hue like that which you selected, he has hopes that
I shall not go into the Church after all."

"Well, why should you, Albert? You are gaining in
strength, and I doubt not that you will yet grow into a strong
man. Of course as long as you were weak and delicate, and,
as it seemed, would never be able to bear the weight of
armour, it was but natural that he should regard a life in the
Church as one that was best fitted for you, and that you
yourself would be perfectly willing to follow that profession,
but now it is wholly different; besides, even if at present
you may not wish, as I do, to be a soldier, you may well
become a wise councillor, and hold high position at court.
There are few young nobles, indeed, who have so much
education as you, and surely such a life would be better
than burying yourself in a cloister."

Albert was silent for some time. "Do you really think,
Edgar," he said at last, "that I shall be ever able to bear
arms with credit? To become a councillor, one must needs
be a courtier, and I am sure that a life at court would suit
me no better than it would suit you, therefore that thought
I must put aside. My tastes are all for a quiet life in the
country, and you know I could be very happy living at
home as I have done from my childhood. But if I am to
be in the world I must bear my part, and if needs be follow
the king to battle, and unless I could do my duty manfully
I would rather follow out the life I thought must be mine,
and enter the Church. I should like, most of all, to be able
to be always with you, Edgar, and to fight by your side.
We have long been like brothers. I know that you will
win rank and fame, and though I have no ambition for
myself I should glory in your success, and be well content
with your friendship as my share in it."

"That, you may be sure, you will always have, Albert;
and as to your plan. I see not why you should not carry it

out. In war time you and I could ride together, and in peace you could live at the castle, which is so close to St. Alwyth that we can ride over and visit each other daily when I am there, which mayhap would not be very often, for when England and France are at peace, and there is no trouble between us and Scotland, I may join some noble leader of free-lances in the service of an Italian or German prince. Such, when there is peace at home, is the best avenue for fame and distinction."

"I cannot say yet what I may feel as I gain strength and skill in arms, but it may be that even there I may be your companion should strength and health permit it."

"That indeed would be good,—so good that I can scarce yet believe that it can be so, although there is no reason to the contrary. It has for years been a grief to me to know that our paths lay so far apart, and that the time must soon be coming when we should be separated, and for ever. It was with some faint hope that exercise might bring more colour to your cheeks, and that with strength and skill in arms might come thoughts of another life than that of the cloister, that I first urged you to let me teach you the use of arms. That hope has grown gradually since I found how much you benefited by the exercise, and acquired a strength of arm that I had hardly hoped for.

"Moreover, Albert, you cannot but be proud of the name your father and those before him have won by their gallant deeds, but if you went into the Church it would no longer appear in the roll of the knights of England. It would be ill indeed that a line of knights, who have so well played their part on every battlefield since your ancestor came over with the Conqueror, should become extinct."

"I had never thought of that before, Edgar," Albert said after a long pause. "You see, for years I have looked forward to entering the Church as a matter settled for me by nature.

I had no enthusiasm for it, but it seemed there was no other place for me. Of late, since I have gained health and strength, I have seen that possibly it might be otherwise. At first I struggled against the idea and deemed it the suggestion of the Evil One, but it has grown in spite of me, although I never allowed myself fully to entertain it until I saw the joy with which my father perceived that I was not altogether the weakling that he had deemed me.

"Since then I have thought of it incessantly, but until now have been unable to come to any decision. On the one hand, I should please my father, and at the same time satisfy the desire that has of late sprung up for a more stirring life than that of the Church, and should be able to remain your comrade. On the other hand, I have always regarded the Church as my vocation, and did not like to go back from it; and moreover, although stronger than of old, I thought that I might never attain such health and strength as might render me a worthy knight, and feared that when tried I should be found wanting. Thus I have wavered, and knew not which way my inclinations drew me most strongly, but I never thought of what you have just said, that if I were to enter the Church our line would come to an end. However, there is no occasion definitely to settle for another year yet, but I will tell my father to-morrow that if at the end of that time he deems that I have so far continued to gain in strength that he may consider me not unworthy to represent our name in the field, I shall be ready to submit myself to his wishes, while upon the other hand, should he think me, as before, better fitted for the Church, I will enter it at once."

"I am glad, indeed, to hear you say so, Albert. I think that there is no reason to doubt that you will continue to gain strength, and will prove worthy of your name."

Accordingly, the next morning Albert asked his father

to accompany him into the garden, and there detailed to him the conversation that he had had with Edgar, and its result.

"Glad indeed am I, Albert, that this should have come about," the knight said, laying his hand on the lad's shoulder. "What your friend said to you has often been in my mind. It was a sore thought, my son. There have ever been De Courcys on the battle roll of England since our ancestor fought at Hastings; and I might well feel grieved at the thought that it might possibly appear there no more, and the pleasure that you have given me is more than I can express. I will not allow myself to fear that, now you have made so fair a start, you will fail to gather fresh strength and vigour, and I will wager that you will bear our banner as forward in the fight as those who have gone before you.

"I blame myself deeply that I have misjudged you so long. Had I encouraged, instead of slighting you, you might long since have begun to gain strength, and might early have commenced the exercises that are so essential to form a good knight. In future, I will do all I can to make up for lost time. As far as swordsmanship goes, you can have no better instructor than your friend. I myself will train you in knightly exercises on horseback—to vault into the saddle and to throw yourself off when a horse is going at full speed, to use your lance and carry off a ring; but I will take care not to press you beyond your strength, and not to weary you with over-long work. My effort will be to increase your store of strength and not to draw unduly upon it; and I will warrant me that if you improve as rapidly under my tuition as you have under that of Master Edgar, before a year is up I shall be able to place you in the train of some noble knight without a fear that you will prove yourself inferior to others of your own age."

Going into the house again when the morning meal was served, Sir Ralph said:

"There is bad news as to the rioters in Kent, lads. Last night I heard that a message had arrived, saying that they had entered Rochester, broken open the jail, and released not only those held there for non-payment of taxes, but malefactors; that they had been joined by the rabble of the town, had slain several notaries and lawyers, and torn up all parchments, deeds, and registers; had maltreated some of the clergy, broken open cellars and drunk the wine, and that from thence they intended to march to Maidstone and then to Canterbury, raising the country as they went."

"This should at least give us time for preparations, Sir Ralph."

"So I pointed out last night," the knight replied; "but who is to make the preparations? A proclamation was drawn up by the council, warning all to return to their homes on pain of punishment, and promising an inquiry into grievances. It is to be scattered broadcast through Kent and Essex, but it is likely to have no effect. The men know well enough that they have rendered themselves liable to punishment, and as they were ready to run that risk when they first took up arms, it is not likely that they will be frightened at the threat now when they find none to oppose them, and that their numbers grow from day to day. Seeing that time is likely to do little for us, I would rather they had marched straight on to London; they would then have arrived here in more sober mood; but now that they have begun to slay and to drink, they will get fiercer and more lawless every day, and as their numbers increase so will their demands."

Day by day more and more serious news came in. Canterbury was occupied by the rebels, and they declared their intention of slaying the archbishop, but he had left before they had arrived. There they committed many excesses, executed three rich citizens, opened the prisons, killed all lawyers, and burned all deeds and registers as they had done at Rochester, and kept the whole place in a state of terror while they remained, which they did while the stores of wine remained unexhausted.

"Why should they be so bitter against lawyers, and why should they destroy deeds and registers, father?" Albert asked.

"It can be but for one reason, Albert. The great part of them have small plots of land, an acre or two, or perhaps more, on terms of villeinage, paying so much in kind or money, and their desire is to destroy all deeds and documents in order that they may henceforth pay no rent, claiming the land for themselves, and defying those from whom they hold it to show their titles as lords of the soil. There must be some shrewd knaves among them. This Wat the Tyler and the men of the towns can care naught for such matters; but they suffer those who have an interest in the matter to do as they choose. They know that their deeds have so far committed them that they will not dare to draw back, and must follow Wat's leadership implicitly. You will see ere long that from murdering lawyers they will take to murdering lords."

"If the Council here is taking no steps to summon the knights of the shire and the feudal lords to hasten hither with their levies and retainers, how do they think to arrest the course of the ill-doers?" Edgar asked.

"Their opinion is that the king has but to ride out and meet the rebels, and that they will all, on seeing him, fall on their knees and crave pardon, whereupon he will promise to redress their grievances, and they will disperse to their homes. I have no such hope. Is it likely that they will quietly go home, having once worked themselves up to fight for what they call their rights, and with the thought of taking vengeance on those they consider their enemies, and of unlimited drinking and feasting, and, on the part of some, of rich plunder in London, when they see that there is no one to prevent their taking this satisfaction? Nothing but force will avail, and though something might be done that way, it is more difficult than it looks.

"The knights of the shire could hardly raise their levies, for most of those who would be called out are already with the mob, and of the others few would venture to answer to the summons. When they returned they might find their houses burned and their families slain. You see we know not how far this fire may spread. We hear that both in Suffolk and Hertfordshire men are assembling and parties marching away to join those of Essex. In truth, lads, the thing is far more formidable than I deemed it at first, for they say that two hundred thousand men will march on London."

"But in the French Jacquerie there were as many as that, Sir Ralph, and yet they were put down."

"They were so, but only after they had done vast damage. Besides, lad, your English villein differs from your French serf. An Englishman, of whatever rank, holds by what he considers his rights, and is ready to fight for them. Our archers have proved that the commonalty are as brave as the knights, and though badly armed, this rascaldom may fight sturdily. The French peasant has no rights, and is a chattel, that his lord may dispose of as he chooses. As long as they met with no opposition all who fell into their hands were destroyed, and the castles ravaged and plundered, the peasants behaving like a pack of mad wolves. Our fellows are of sterner stuff, and they will have a mind to fight, if it be but to show that they can fight as well as their betters. Plunder is certainly not their first object, and it is probable that whatever may be done that way will be the work of the scum of the towns, who will join them solely with that object.

"I doubt whether less than five thousand men-at-arms and archers would be able to show face to such an array as is said to be approaching, especially as there will be many archers among them who, although not to compare with those who fought at Poictiers, are yet capable of using their weapons with effect. I see no prospect of gathering such a force, and the matter is all the worse, as the rascaldom of London will be with them, and we shall have these to keep in order as well as cope with those in the field. Besides, one must remember that in a matter like this we cannot fully depend on any force that we may gather. The archers and men-at-arms would be drawn largely from the same class as the better portion of these rioters, and would be slack in fighting against them. Certainly those of the home counties could not be depended upon, and possibly even in the garrison of the Tower itself there may be many who cannot be trusted. The place, if well held, should stand out for months, but I am by no means sure that it will do so when the time comes. I shall certainly raise my voice against the king abiding here. He with his friends could ride away without difficulty, if he leaves before the place is beleaguered."

"I suppose you will take my mother and sister into the Tower, father, should the mob come hither?"

"That I know not, nor can I say until I see the temper of the garrison when these rioters approach."

On the day after the new clothes arrived, Sir Ralph took his son and Edgar to the castle and presented them to the king.

"This is my son, your Majesty, of whom I spoke to you. I am happy to say that I think he will some day be able to follow you to battle as I followed the noble prince your father; for he has now resolved, should his health remain good, to take up the profession of arms."

"I am glad to hear it," the young king said, "for indeed 'tis more suited to the son of a valiant knight like yourself, Sir Ralph, than that of the Church, excellent though that may be for those who have inclinations for it. He seems to me a fair young gentleman, and one whom it would please me to see often at court."

"This, your Majesty, is Master Edgar Ormskirk, a young gentleman of good family, but his father has not, although holding more than a knight's feu, taken up that rank, his tastes being wholly turned towards learning, he being a distinguished scholar, having passed through our own university at Oxford, and those of Padua and Pisa. He is one of my most esteemed friends. Master Edgar, as I told you, is greatly skilled for his years in the use of the sword, to which he has long devoted himself with great ardour. It is to him my son is indebted for having gained health and strength, together with more skill in the sword than I had ever looked for from him. I beg to recommend him highly to your Majesty's favour, and can answer for his worth, as well as for his strength and skill."

"You could have no better recommendation, Master Ormskirk," the young king said pleasantly, "and I trust that although your father cares not for knighthood, you will have an opportunity of gaining that honour for yourself."

"I should value it, if won fairly, your Majesty, as the greatest honour I could gain. It is not that my father holds the honour more lightly than I do, but I know that 'tis his opinion that if given merely for possession of land 'tis but an accident of birth, but that if the reward of bravery, 'tis an honour that is of the highest, and one that, were it not that his thoughts are wholly turned towards scholarship and to discovering the secrets of nature, he himself would gladly have attained."

"Methinks that he is right," the king said. "In the time when every land-owner held his feu on condition of knightly service rendered whenever called upon, it was well that he should be called a knight, such being the term of military command; but now that many are allowed to provide substitutes, methinks that it is an error to give the title to stay-at-homes. I shall be glad, young sir, to see you also at court, though, methinks," he added with a smile, "that you have inherited some of your father's sobriety of nature, and will hold our pleasures at small price."

"I thank your Majesty for your kindness," Edgar said, bowing; "but indeed I should not presume to judge amusements as frivolous because I myself might be unused to them; but in truth two years ago I studied at the convent of St. Alwyth, and my spare time then, and most of my time since, has been so occupied by my exercises in arms that I have had but small opportunity for learning the ways of courts, but I hope to do so, seeing that a good knight should bear himself as well at court as in the field."

"You will have small opportunity now," the king said rather dolefully. "Our royal mother is absent, and our talk is all of riots and troubles, and none seem even to think of pleasure."

After leaving the king Sir Ralph presented his son and Edgar to Sir Michael de la Pole, who held high office; Robert de Vere, one of the king's special favourites; and several other young nobles, who all received them kindly for the sake of Sir Ralph.

CHAPTER V.

A RESCUE.

PERHAPS, boys, you could hardly have been introduced at court better than by myself," the knight said as they returned to the lodgings. "There are men much more highly placed, many more influential than I am, but for that very reason I can be friends with all. The king's mother is always most courteous to me, because I was the friend of the Black Prince, her husband; and she has taught her son that, whatever might come, he could rely upon my fidelity to his person. On the other hand, no one has reason either to dislike or fear me. I am a simple knight longing most to be at home, and at the court as seldom as may be; besides, I hold myself aloof from both parties in the state, for you must know that the court is composed of two factions.

"The one is that of John of Gaunt, Duke of Lancaster, uncle of the king. He is greatly ambitious; some men even say that he would fain himself be king, but this I believe not; yet I am sure that he would like to rule in the name of the king. He has a powerful party, having with him the Duke of Gloucester, his brother, and other great nobles. On the other hand, he is ill-liked by the people, and they say at Canterbury the rioters made every man they met swear to obey the king and commons,—by which they meant themselves,—never to accept a king bearing the name of John, and to oppose Lancaster and Gloucester.

"The king's mother has surrounded him with a number of men who, being for the most part of obscure birth, have no sympathy with John of Gaunt's faction, and oppose it in every way.

"Doubtless the majority of these are well fitted for the

office that they hold, but unfortunately there are some amongst them, for the most part young and with pleasant manners and handsome faces, whom the king makes his favourites. This again is well-nigh as bad as that John of Gaunt should have all the power in his own hands, for the people love not king's favourites, and although the rabble at present talk much of all men being equal, and rail against the nobles, yet at bottom the English people are inclined towards those of good birth, and a king's favourite is all the more detested if he lacks this quality. England, however, would not fare badly were John of Gaunt its master; he is a great warrior, and well-nigh equal in bravery to the Black Prince. It is true that he is haughty and arrogant; but upon the other hand, he is prudent and sagacious, and although he might rule England harshly, he would rule it wisely.

"However, I hold myself aloof altogether from state matters, and I trust that you will strive to do so. I would fain see the king take all power into his own hands as soon as he gets somewhat older; but if he must be ruled, I would prefer that it was by a great Englishman of royal blood rather than by favourites, whose only merits are a fair face, a gallant manner, and a smooth tongue, and who are sure not only to become unpopular themselves but to render the king himself unpopular. It is for this reason that I journey so seldom to London, and desire that you should also hold yourself aloof from the court. I could not be here without taking one side or the other. It cannot be long, however, before the king becomes impatient of his tutelage by the dukes, and we shall then see how matters go.

"It will be time enough then for you to frequent the court, though it were better even then that you should do as I did, and leave such matters to those whom it concerns, and content yourself with doing service to England in the field. From my friendship for the Black Prince I of course know John of Gaunt well, and should there be, as seems likely, fierce fighting in France or in Spain—for, as you know, the duke has a claim to the crown of Castile—I will cross the water with you and present you to the duke, and place you in the train of some of his knights, comrades of mine, but who are still young enough to keep the field, while I shall only take up arms again in the event of the king leading another great army into France."

The two friends spent much of their time in wandering about the streets of London. To them all seemed peaceable and orderly; indeed, they kept in the main thoroughfares where the better class of citizens were to be seen, and knew little of those who lived in the lower haunts, issuing out seldom in the daylight, but making the streets a danger for peaceable folks after nightfall.

Upon one occasion, however, they took boat at Westminster and were rowed to Richmond. They had ill-chosen the occasion, knowing nothing of the hours of the tide, and so returned against it. It was therefore eight o'clock when they reached the Stairs, and already growing dark. They knew that orders had been given that the gates were to be closed to all at eight lest some of the great bodies of rioters should approach suddenly and enter the city.

The watermen, wearied by their long row, refused to carry them any further. There was nothing for it but to walk round the walls and so return to their lodging. The moon was shining brightly, and it seemed to them as they started that it would be a pleasant walk. They followed the Strand, where on the right stood many houses of the nobles, and the great palace of John of Gaunt at the Savoy, in which, after the battle of Poictiers, the captive king of France had been lodged.

Turning off to the left some short distance before they

M 371

"IN A MOMENT EDGAR'S SWORD FELL ON THE RUFFIAN'S WRIST."

reached the city wall, they held their way round the north side of the city. London had already overflowed its boundary, and although in some places fields still stretched up to the foot of the walls, in others, especially where the roads led from the gates, a large population had established themselves. These were principally of a poorer class, who not only saved rent from being outside the boundary of the city, but were free from the somewhat strict surveillance exercised by its authorities.

They were just crossing the road leading north from Aldersgate when they heard a scream and a clashing of swords a short distance away.

"Come, Albert, some evil deed is being done!" Edgar exclaimed, and, drawing his sword, ran at the top of his speed in the direction of the sound, accompanied by Albert. They soon arrived at the top of a street leading off the main road. A short distance down it a number of men were engaged in conflict; two of these, hearing the footsteps, turned round, and with a savage oath, seeing that the new-comers were but lads, fell upon them, thinking to cut them down without difficulty. Their over-confidence proved their ruin. Edgar caught the descending blow on his sword, close up to the hilt, and as his opponent raised his arm to repeat the stroke, ran him through the body.

"Do you want help, Albert?" Edgar cried as the man fell.

"No, I think that I can manage him," Albert said quietly, and a moment later slashed his opponent deeply across the cheek. The fellow turned and took to his heels, roaring lustily. One of the other men, who was stooping over a prostrate figure with his dagger raised, paused for a moment to look round on hearing the howl of his comrade, and as he did so Edgar's sword fell on his wrist with such force that hand and dagger both fell to the ground. The remaining ruffian, who was roughly endeavouring to stifle the shrieks of a young girl, seeing himself alone with two adversaries, also darted off and plunged into a narrow alley a few yards away.

Edgar paid no more attention to them, but exclaimed to the girl: "Cease your cries, I pray you, maiden, and help me to see what has happened to your companion. I trust that he is unharmed, and that we have arrived in time to prevent those villains from carrying out their intentions." He stooped over the fallen man. "Are you hurt badly, sir?" he asked. The answer was an effort on the part of the person he addressed to rise.

"I am hurt, but I think not sorely." He was unable for the moment to rise, for the man whom Edgar last struck lay across him. Edgar at once hauled the moaning wretch off him, and held out his hand to the other, who grasped it with more heartiness than he had expected, and rose without difficulty to his feet.

"Where is my daughter?" he exclaimed.

"She is here and unhurt, I trust," Albert replied. "The villain released her and ran off, and I saw her figure sway, and ran forward just in time to save her from falling. I think she has but swooned."

"Thanks be to the saints!" the stranger exclaimed. "Gentlemen, I cannot thank you at present for the service that you have rendered me, but of that I will speak later. Know you any place where you can take my child?"

"We are strangers, sir; but there should surely be some hostelry near where travellers could put up outside the walls."

The noise of the combat had aroused some of the neighbours, and on inquiry Edgar ascertained that there was an inn but a short distance away.

"Let me carry the maid, Albert. Her weight would be nought to me."

Albert gladly relinquished his charge, whose dead weight

hanging on his arms was already trying him. Edgar raised her across his shoulder.

"Albert," he said, "I know you have a piece of thin cord in your pocket. I pray you twist it round that man's arm as hard as you can pull it, and fasten it tightly. I have shorn off his hand, and he would very speedily bleed to death. If you staunch the wound he may last till his comrades come back, as they doubtless will after we have left; they will carry him away and maybe save his life. He is a villainous ruffian, no doubt, but 'tis enough for me that I have one death on my hands to-night."

"He is dead already," Albert said, as he leant over the man and placed his hand on his heart. "He must have been wounded by the traveller before we came up."

"Well, it cannot be helped," Edgar replied as he walked on with his burden.

"Did you see aught, kind sirs," their companion said, "of a servitor with three horses?"

"Nothing whatever," Albert answered, "though methought I heard horses' hoofs going down the road as we ran along; but I paid small attention to them, thinking only of arriving in time to save some one from being maltreated."

"I believe that he was in league with the robbers," the man said. "But," and his voice faltered, "give me your arm, I pray you. My wound is deeper than I thought, and my head swims."

Albert with difficulty assisted the man to the entrance of the hostelry, for at each step he leant more heavily upon him. The door was shut, but the light from the casement showed that those within had not yet retired to bed. Edgar struck on the door loudly with the handle of his dagger.

"Who is it that knocks?"

"Gentlemen, with a wounded man, who, with his

daughter, have been beset by knaves within a hundred yards of your door."

Some bolts were undrawn after some little delay, and a man appeared, having a sword in his hand, with two servitors behind him similarly armed.

"We are quiet people, my host," Edgar said. "Stand not on questioning. Suffice that there is a wounded man who is spent from loss of blood, and a young maid who has swooned from terror."

There was a tone of command in Edgar's voice, and the host, seeing that he had to do with persons of quality, murmured excuses on the ground that the neighbourhood was a rough one.

"You need hardly have told us that," Edgar said. "Our plight speaks for itself. Call your wife, I pray you, or female servants; they will know what to do to bring the young maid to herself. But tell her to let the girl know as soon as she opens her eyes that her father is alive, and is, I trust, not seriously wounded."

The landlord called, and a buxom woman came out from a room behind. Her husband hastily told her what was required.

"Carry her in here, sir, I pray you," the woman said. "I will speedily bring her round."

Edgar followed her into the room that she had left, which was a kitchen, and laid her down on a settle. Two maids who were standing there uttered exclamations of surprise and pity as the girl was carried in.

"Hold you tongues, wenches, and do not make a noise! Margaret, fetch me cold water, and do you, Elizabeth, help me to unlace the young lady's bodice," for the light in the kitchen enabled her to see at once that the girl was well dressed.

As soon as Edgar had laid her down, he hurried out of the kitchen, moving his arm uneasily as he did so, having discovered to his surprise that the weight of an insensible girl, though but some fourteen years old, was much more than he had dreamt of. In a parlour in front he found Albert and the landlord cutting off the doublet of the wounded man, so as to get at his shoulder, where a great patch of blood showed the location of the wound. He was some forty years old; his dress was quiet but of good quality, and Edgar judged him to be a London trader. His face was very white, but he was perfectly sensible. One of the servitors ran in with a cup of wine. The wounded man was able to lift it to his lips and to empty it at a draught.

"That is better!" he murmured; and then he did not speak again until the landlord, with considerable skill, bandaged up the shoulder.

"You have had a narrow escape," he said. "There is a sword-thrust just below your collar-bone. An inch or two lower and it would have gone hard with you; a little more to the left and it would have pierced your throat."

"It was a dagger wound," the man said. "I was knocked down by a blow from a sword which fell full on my head, but luckily I had iron hoops in my cap. One man knelt upon me, and endeavoured to strike me through the throat. I fought so hard that one of his comrades came to his assistance, and I thought that the end had come, when he sprung suddenly up. The other attempted more furiously than before to finish me, but striking almost blindly he twice missed me altogether, and the third time, by a sudden twist, I took a blow on my shoulder that would otherwise have pierced my throat. When he raised his dagger again something flashed. I saw his hand with the dagger he held in it drop off, and then the man himself fell on me, and I was like to be stifled with his weight, when my preserver hauled him off me."

"It were best not to talk further," the landlord said. "I have rooms fortunately vacant, and it were well that you retired at once."

"I will do that as soon as you have given me something
to eat, landlord. Anything will do, but I am grievously
hungry."

"I have a cold capon in the house," the landlord said.

"You will have to cater for three, for doubtless these
gentlemen need supper as much as I do."

"I thank you, sir, but we are very late already, and our
friends will have become alarmed, therefore, with your leave,
we will, as soon as we hear that your daughter has recovered,
go on our way."

"That I can tell you at once," the landlady said, entering.
"Your daughter has recovered, sir, and would come to
you, but I begged her to wait until my husband had done
dressing your wound."

"Then we will say good-night, sir. We will call to-
morrow morning to see how you are getting on;" and
without waiting for further words, they at once went out
and continued their way at a brisk pace.

"Let me congratulate you, Albert," Edgar said warmly.
"In good faith no old soldier could have been cooler than
you were. You spoke as quietly as if it were a lesson that
you had to finish before starting for home, instead of a
villainous cut-throat to put an end to. What did you to
him?"

"I but laid his cheek open, Edgar, and that at once let
out his blood and his courage, and he ran off bellowing like
a bull. He knew nought of swordsmanship, as I felt directly our blades crossed. I knew that I had but to guard a
sweeping blow or two, and that I should then find an opening; but you of course did much better, for you killed two
of the villains."

"I did it hastily and with scarce a thought," Edgar said.
"My eye caught the flash of the dagger, and I knew that
if the man was to be saved at all there was not a moment

to lose, I therefore parried the first blow he dealt me, and ran him through with my return. Then I had just time to chop the other villain's hand off as he was about to repeat his stroke. The ruffian you wounded caused the other to look round and pause for a moment. Had it been otherwise the traveller would have been a dead man before I had time to strike. I wonder who the wounded man is! He looked like a London trader. I wonder how he got into so sore a plight! but doubtless we shall hear in the morning."

The episode had taken only a few minutes, but it was nigh half-past nine before they reached home.

"What freak is this?" Sir Ralph said angrily when they entered. "Your mother has been anxious about you for the last two hours, and I myself was beginning to think that some ill must have befallen you. Why, what has happened to you, Albert, there is blood on your doublet?"

"'Tis not my own, sir," the lad said quietly. "I regret that we are so late, but it was scarcely our fault. You told us that we could take boat at Westminster and row to Richmond. This we did, but the tide was against us coming back, and though the men rowed hard, the Abbey bell was striking eight as we landed at Westminster, therefore, knowing that the city gates would be shut, we had to make a tour round the walls."

"Then, as you say, Albert, you were not to blame in the matter. But what about the blood with which, as I see, Edgar is even more deeply stained than you are? Have you been in a brawl?"

"We have, sir; but here, I am sure, you will not blame us when you know the circumstances. As we crossed the road running from Aldersgate Street to the north we heard screams and the clashing of swords; deeming, and as it turned out rightly, that some traveller like ourselves was being attacked by cut-throats, we ran on, and presently came

up to the spot where four ruffians were attacking a single
man who had with him a young girl, whose screams had
first called our attention. Edgar ran one through the body,
smote off the hand of another who was endeavouring to stab
the fallen traveller, and the other ran away."

"And what was your share of it?" his father asked sternly.

"His share was an excellent one, Sir Ralph," Edgar said.
"Two of the ruffians ran at us as we came up. One who
attacked me was but a poor swordsman, and I ran him
through at the first thrust. I then paused a moment to
ask Albert if he required aid, and he answered as quietly
as he is now speaking, 'No, I think that I can manage
him.' I had no time to say more, for I saw that a moment's
delay would endanger the life of the traveller. Just as I
reached him I heard a yell of pain, and knew that Albert
had done his work. That howl saved the traveller's life.
The man who was kneeling on him looked round for a
moment before delivering his blow, which gave me time to
smite him across the wrist. The blood you see was caused
by dragging him off the traveller."

"By our lady," Sir Ralph exclaimed, "but you have
begun well, lads! That you would do so, Edgar, was a
matter beyond doubt, but that Albert should stand up so
well and so coolly in his first fight surprises me indeed. I
had no doubt of your courage, lad. 'Tis rare indeed for one
of good blood to lack courage, but had you been nervous
and flurried the first time you were called upon to play the
part of a man, it would have seemed to me but natural, now
it gladdens me indeed to know that even in your first essay
you should have thus shown that you possess nerve and
coolness as well as courage. Anyone can rush into a fight
and deal blows right and left, but it is far more rare to
find one who, in his very first trial at arms, can keep his
head clear, and be able to reply to a question, as Edgar says

you did, in a calm and even voice. Now, tell me who was this man to whose aid you arrived just at the nick of time?"

"He looked like a London trader, father, and was some forty years old; but it was hard to tell, for by the time we got him to the hostelry he was well-nigh spent and scarce able to crawl along even with my help."

"He was wounded then?"

"Stabbed with a dagger, father, just under the collar-bone. He must have made a stout resistance, for we heard the clashing of swords for some time as we ran, and when he was struck down he struggled so hard that in spite of the efforts of two of his assailants they failed to slay him. As soon as his wounds were bandaged we left him to the care of the landlord, and hurried off without thinking to ask his name, or of giving him ours, but we promised to return to see him to-morrow morning."

"And what became of the daughter?"

"She swooned, sir, when all was over, and Edgar carried her to the hostelry."

"'Tis good. You have both entered well upon the profession of arms, and have achieved an adventure worthy of knights. Now to bed. Your mother retired long ago, but I know that she will not sleep until she has heard of your safe return and of this adventure that you have gone through."

Highly gratified at the knight's commendation, the lads went up to their room.

"Putting aside the saving of life," Albert said, "I am right glad that we have gone through this adventure. 'Tis true that I had decided upon yielding to my father's wishes and taking up the career of arms, but I had grievous doubts as to whether I should not shame myself and him in my first encounter. I thought of that as I ran forward with you, but as soon as the ruffian advanced against me, I felt

with joy that my hand was as steady as when I stood
opposite you. It was a good cause in which I was to fight,
and as soon as our swords crossed I felt how different it
was to standing up against you, and that the ruffian knew
little of sword-play. Twice I saw an opening for a straight
thrust, but I had no desire to kill him, and waited until I
could slash him across the face, and it needed but a few
passes before I saw the opportunity."

When Dame Agatha came down in the morning she
tenderly kissed Albert.

"My boy," she said, "I never said aught at the time, when
it seemed that you were never like to grow strong enough
to lay lance in rest or wield battle-axe, to show you that
I regretted that you were not able to follow the profession
of arms, as those of your race have ever done. I felt that it
was hard enough for you, and therefore tried my best to
reconcile you to the thought of becoming a priest; but now
that all that has changed, and you have shown that you will
be a brave and gallant knight, I can tell you that it gives
me as great a joy as it does your father. The Church is a
high and holy profession, but at present, as the preaching
of Wickliffe has made manifest to all,—although I do not
hold with all he says, and deem that he carries it too far,—
I feel that until many of these abuses are rectified 'tis not a
profession that I should, had I the choice, wish my son to
enter. I am glad, Albert, too, that your sword should have
been drawn for the first time on behalf of persons attacked
by cut-throats, and in saving life. God bless you, my boy,
and give you strength ever so to draw it in defence of the
oppressed, and for the honour of your country!"

Aline was exuberant in her pleasure. She was fondly
attached to her brother, and that he would be lost to her
as a priest had been a source of sorrow ever since she had
been old enough to understand that it would be so.

As soon as the morning meal was over, the two lads started for the scene of the previous evening's fight. The road from Aldersgate, with cars rolling in with loads of flour and other provisions, and with many travellers and foot passengers of all sorts passing along, presented a very different appearance to that which it had worn on the evening before. People were going in and out of the hostelries for their morning draught of ale, and all looked bright and cheerful. The day was fine and the air brisk. On entering, the landlord at once came up to them.

"Your friend is in the room where we dressed his wounds, sirs. He is doing well, and methinks will make a good cure. His daughter is with him. They have but lately risen, and are breaking their fast. He will be glad to see you, and was mightily vexed last night that we let you leave without asking your names."

"He was not in a condition for talking last night, what with the loss of blood and the smart of his wound and the suddenness of the affray. 'Tis not strange that he should not have thought of it; and indeed we ourselves did not ask his name, for we were pressed for time, and had to hurry away."

It was evident, indeed, as they entered, that things were going well with the wounded man, who was talking merrily to his daughter.

"Ah, sirs!" he said rising at once to his feet, "glad indeed am I that you have come, and that I can now thank you for the great service you rendered last night to myself and my daughter. First let me know to whom I am indebted for our lives?"

"This gentleman," Edgar said, "is Albert, son of Sir Ralph de Courcy. My name is Edgar Ormskirk. I pray you, speak not of gratitude. We are glad, indeed, to have been able to render service to you and to your daughter.

We hope some day to become knights, and it is a real
pleasure to us to have been able to draw a sword in earnest
for the first time, in so good a cause. But indeed there is
little occasion for glorification, seeing that the fellows were
but rough cut-throats, more accustomed, I fancy, to the use
of the dagger than of the sword."

"Do not belittle the action, Master Ormskirk," the other
said courteously. "It was a brave deed, for if I may say so,
you are but little more than boys, to pit yourselves against
four rascals of this kind. There are few in your place would
have ventured upon it. The landlord tells me that two dead
bodies were found this morning, and they are those of well-
known cut-throats and law-breakers, who would have long
since been brought to justice, had it not been that there
was no means of proving they were responsible for the many
murders that have been committed during the last few
months, on peaceful travellers and others. A search has
already been made of their haunts, and as it is found that
two others who generally consorted with them are missing,
and as much blood was found in the hovel they occupied,
no doubt one of them was severely wounded."

"His cheek was laid open by my friend," Edgar said.
"He could have slain him had he so chosen, but being as
yet unused to strife, and gentler hearted that I am, he contented himself by slashing his face."

"And did the other two fall to your sword, Mr. Ormskirk?"

"Yes; I saw that you were in sore peril, and so ran
one through at the first thrust; and then, seeing that my
friend was well able to hold his own, came on to your aid.
Before I reached you, Albert had struck his blow, and the
howl that the villain gave did more towards the saving
of your life than my sword, for your assailant paused in
the very act of striking, to see what had befallen his com-

rade, and therefore gave me time to deliver a blow on his wrist."

"As yet, gentlemen, you do not know my name. I am Robert Gaiton, and belong to the Guild of Mercers. I carry on trade with Venice and Genoa in silk and Eastern goods. This is my daughter Ursula."

The friends bowed, and the girl made a deep reverence. "Ah, sirs!" she said, "I cannot tell you how grateful I am for your succour. When you came running up it appeared to me that Heaven had sent two angels to help us, when it seemed that naught could save our lives."

"It was your scream, even more than the clashing of swords, that brought us to your aid, Madame Ursula."

"Ursula without the Madame," her father said. "She is the daughter of a plain citizen, and all unused to titles, save from my apprentice boys."

"I cannot think why the ruffian who held her," Edgar said, "did not stop her screams with a dagger-thrust. He must have been of a much milder sort than his comrades."

"It may have been that," the trader said, "but it seems to me more likely that they intended to carry her off and hold her to ransom. I dare say that you are surprised at my being abroad with my daughter so late, but I believe now that it was a preconcerted plot. It was but ten days before I left London, three weeks since, that I hired a new man. He had papers which showed that he came from Chelmsford, was an honest fellow, and accustomed to the care of horses. I doubt not his credentials were stolen. However, I engaged him, seeing that he appeared just the man I wanted. We journeyed down to Norwich without adventure. There I settled my business with some traders whom I supply with goods, and then journeyed back, stopping always at towns and always before nightfall, as I had a considerable amount of money in my saddle-bags.

"All went well until we started for town yesterday morning. I was detained somewhat late on business, and then, instead of finding the horses ready as I had ordered, it was nigh half an hour before they were brought round. We had not ridden very far when my horse fell dead lame, and I had to mount my servant's horse and let him lead the other, and it took us two hours to go five miles into St. Albans. As we went, I thought that, putting the first delay with the horse falling lame, this might be a plot to keep me from reaching London before the gates were shut, and while the horse's shoe was being taken off I slipped the bags of gold into my pouch, and going into the hostelry to get refreshments for Ursula and myself, I handed them to the host, and begged him to hold them for me until I sent for them. I further asked him to give me other bags of the same size, for I doubted not that my servant was in alliance with these thieves. He had doubtless observed me take the bags out, and I was the more confirmed in my suspicions as I noticed how he watched me when I mounted again.

"'What ailed the horse?' I asked the farrier.

"'Either the horse has picked up a nail on the road, master, or belike some knave has driven one in.'

"Then we rode on. I still hoped to pass the gates before they were closed, but the horse went lamely, and we were three miles away when I heard the city bells strike the hour. Still I hoped that they might open the gate for me when I gave my name, which is indifferently well known in the city, but the men at the gate were ignorant of it, and said that without an order from the Lord Mayor or one of the sheriffs they could open the gate to no man, for that since the country troubles had began, the orders were most strict. It happened that I had not been out through Aldersgate for two years past, but I had heard that an hostelry had been built for the accommodation of travellers who had arrived too late to pass the gates, or others who preferred to sojourn outside the walls. I knew not its position, and asking my knave where it was, he said that he knew not.

"We then rode back. Presently I saw two men standing at the corner of that street where we were attacked. I said to them, 'Where is the King's Head hostelry?' ''Tis but a house or two down here,' one of them said. 'The stables are a short way along this road. My comrade will show your man the way.' 'We may as well alight here, Ursula,' I said. It had been a long ride for her, and she was tired with sitting so long on the pillion behind me. ''Tis but three houses down; we may as well walk that distance. Reuben, do you bring round the valises when you have seen the horses stabled and attended to.' I jumped down and lifted Ursula off the horse, and went down the street. I had gone but a short distance when I saw that the locality was scarcely one where a man of sense would build a hostelry.

"'Which is the house?' I asked sharply. 'The very next door,' the man said. I had stupidly forgotten the suspicions that had been roused at the commencement of the day, and I stepped on. 'This is no hostelry,' I said when I got to the house. In reply he gave a short whistle, and three fellows, who had been hiding in the shadow of a doorway opposite, ran out, sword in hand. Seeing that I had been trapped, I pushed Ursula into the doorway and stood on my guard. For a short time I kept them at bay, Ursula screaming wildly the while. Then two of them rushed together at me. One struck down my guard, and then smote me on the head, and with such force, that although the steel lining to my bonnet saved me from being killed, it brought me to the ground. Then, as I told you, one of the fellows threw himself upon me and tried to stab me, but, although confused with the blow, I had still my senses, and struggled with him fiercely, grasping his wrist.

"Then the second one came to his aid, and with a blow from the pommel of his sword numbed my hand, and forced me to quit my hold. Then the other made three stabs at me, a third wounded me slightly, and together they would have finished me had you not come up. My horses were found on the road this morning, with the valises cut open. It must have been a rare disappointment to the rascals, for, save a suit of mine and some garments of my daughter's, there was nought in them. I should like to have seen the villain's face when he opened the money bags and found the trick that I had played him. He had best never show his face in London, for if I catch him he will dance at the end of a rope. And now, sirs, with your permission I will repair to my home, for my wound smarts sorely, and I must have it dressed by a leech, who will pour in some unguents to allay the pain. My wife, too, will be growing anxious, for I had written to her that we should return last night, and it is not often that I do not keep tryst. I pray you, gentlemen, do me the honour of calling at my house to-morrow at noon and partaking of a meal with us. I shall, of course, as soon as the leech gives me permission, wait upon Sir Ralph de Courcy to thank him for the service you have rendered me. I pray you to give me his address."

The invitation was cordially accepted, and, having given him directions by which their lodgings could be found, the two friends took their leave and returned home.

CHAPTER VI.

A CITY MERCHANT.

"ASSUREDLY it is well that you should go," Sir Ralph said, when his son had repeated the conversation they had had with the trader. "I know not the name, for indeed I know scarce one among the citizens; but if he trades with Venice and Genoa direct he must be a man of repute and standing. It is always well to make friends; and some of these city traders could buy up a score of us poor knights. They are not men who make a display of wealth, and by their attire you cannot tell one from another, but upon grand occasions, such as the accession or marriage of a monarch, they can make a brave show, and can spend sums upon masques and feastings that would well-nigh pay a king's ransom. After a great victory they will set the public conduits running with wine, and every varlet in the city can sit down at banquets prepared for them and eat and drink his fill. It is useful to have friends among such men. They are as proud in their way as are the greatest of our nobles, and they have more than once boldly withstood the will of our kings, and have ever got the best of the dispute."

"What shall we put on, sir," Albert asked his father the next morning, "for this visit to Master Gaiton?"

"You had better put on your best suits," the knight said; "it will show that you have respect for him as a citizen, and indeed the dresses are far less showy than many of those I see worn by some of the young nobles in the streets."

"And what is the young lady like?" Aline asked her brother.

"Methinks she is something like you, Aline, and is about

the same age and height; her tresses are somewhat darker
than yours; methinks she is somewhat graver and more
staid than you are, as I suppose befits a maiden of the
city."

"I don't think that you could judge much about that,
Albert," his mother said, "seeing that, naturally, the poor
girl was grievously shaken by the events of the evening
before, and would, moreover, say but little when her father
was conversing with two strangers.   What thought you
of her, Edgar?"

"I scarce noticed her, my lady, for I was talking with
her father, and so far as I remember she did not open her lips
after being introduced to us.   I did not notice the resem-
blance to your daughter that Albert speaks of, but she
seemed to me a fair young maid, who looked not, I own, so
heavy as she felt when I carried her."

"That is very uncourteous, Master Edgar," Dame Agatha
laughed; "a good knight should hold the weight of a lady
to be as light as that of a down pillow."

"Then I fear that I shall never be a true knight," Edgar
said with a smile.   "I have heard tales of knights carrying
damsels across their shoulder and outstripping the pursuit
of caitiffs, from whom she had escaped.   I indeed had
believed them, but assuredly either those tales are false or
I have but a small share of the strength of which I believed
myself to be possessed; for, in truth, my arm and shoulder
ached by the time I reached the hostelry more than it has
ever done after an hour's practice with the mace."

"Well, stand not talking," Sir Ralph said; "it is time
for you to change your suits, for these London citizens are,
I have heard, precise as to their time, and the merchant
would deem it a slight did you not arrive a few minutes
before the stroke of the hour."

As soon as they came into Chepe they asked a citizen

if he could direct them to the house of Master Robert Gaiton.

"That can I," he said, "and so methinks could every boy and man in the city. Turn to the right; his house stands in a courtyard facing the Guildhall, and is indeed next door to the hall in the left-hand corner."

The house was a large one, each storey as usual project-ing over the one below it. Some apprentices were just putting up the shutters to the shop, for at noon most of the booths were closed, as at that hour there were no customers, and the assistants and apprentices all took their meal to-gether. There was a private entrance to the house, and Edgar knocked at the door with the hilt of his dagger. A minute later a serving-man opened it.

"Is Master Robert Gaiton within?" Albert asked. "He is, we believe, expecting us."

"I have his orders to conduct you upstairs, sirs."

The staircase was broad and handsome, and to the lads' surprise was covered with an Eastern carpet. At the top of the stairs the merchant himself was awaiting them.

"Welcome to my house, gentlemen," he said, "the house that would have been the abode of mourning and woe to-day, had it not been for your bravery!"

The merchant was dressed in very different attire to that in which he had travelled. He wore a doublet of brown satin, and hose of the same material and colour; on his shoulders was a robe of Genoa velvet with a collar, and trim-ming down the front of brown fur, such as the boys had never before seen. Over his neck was a heavy gold chain, which they judged to be a sign of office. The landing was large and square, with richly-carved oak panelling, and, like the stairs, it was carpeted with a thick Eastern rug. Taking their hands, he led them through an open door into a large withdrawing-room. Its walls were panelled in a similar manner to those of the landing, but the carpet was deeper and richer. Several splendid armoires or cabinets similarly carved stood against the walls, and in these were gold and silver cups exquisitely chased, salt-cellars, and other silver ware.

The chairs were all in harmony with the room, the seats being of green embossed velvet, and curtains of the same material and hue, with an edging of gold embroidery, hung at the windows. But the lads' eyes could not take in all these matters at once, being fixed upon the lady who rose from her chair to meet them. She was some thirty-five years old, and of singular sweetness of face. There was but little about her of the stiffness that they had expected to find in the wife of a London citizen. She was dressed in a loose robe of purple silk, with costly lace at the neck and sleeves. By her side stood Ursula, who was dressed, as became her age, in lighter colours, which, in cut and material, resembled those of Aline's new attire.

"Dear sirs," she said, as her husband presented the visitors to her, "with what words can I thank you for the service that you have rendered me? But for you I should have been widowed and childless to-day."

"It was but a chance, Mistress Gaiton," Edgar said. "We saw a stranger in danger of his life from cut-throats, and, as honest men should do, we went to his succour. We are glad indeed to have been able to render your husband such service, but it was only such an action as a soldier performs when he strikes in to rescue a comrade surrounded by the enemy, or carries off a wounded man who may be altogether a stranger to him."

"That may be true from your point of view," the merchant said, "but just as the man-at-arms rescued from a circle of foes, or the wounded man carried off the field would assuredly feel gratitude to him who has saved him, so do we feel grati-

tude to you, and naught that you can say will lessen our
feeling towards you both. And now let us to the table."

He opened a door leading into another apartment. Edgar
glanced at Albert, and as he saw the latter was looking at
Ursula, he offered his hand to Dame Gaiton. Albert, with
a little start, did the same to the girl. The merchant held
aside the hangings of the door and then followed them into
the room where the table was laid. It was similar to the
room they had left, save that the floor was polished instead
of being carpeted. The table was laid with a damask cloth
of snowy whiteness and of a fineness of quality such as
neither of the lads had ever seen before. The napkins were
of similar make. A great silver ornament in the shape of
a Venetian galley stood in the centre of the table, flanked
by two vases of the same metal filled with flowers. The
plates were of oriental porcelain, a contrast indeed to the
rough earthenware in general use; the spoons were of gold.

The meats were carved at a side-table, and cut into such
pieces that there was little occasion for the use of the dagger-
shaped knives placed for the use of each. Forks were unknown in Europe until nearly three centuries later, the food
being carried to the mouth by the aid of a piece of bread,
just as it is still eaten in the East, the spoon being only
used for soups and sweetmeats. Two servitors, attired in
doublets of red and green cloth, waited. The wine was
poured into goblets of Venetian glass; and after several
meats had been served round, the lads were surprised at
fresh plates being handed to them for the sweetmeats.
Before these were put upon the table, a gold bowl with per-
fumed water was handed round, and all dipped their fingers
in this, wiping them on their napkins.

"Truly, Mistress Gaiton," Albert said courteously, "it
seems to me that instead of coming to court we country
folk should come to the city to learn how to live. All this

is as strange to me as if I had gone to some far land, by the
side of whose people we were as barbarians."

"My husband has been frequently in Italy," she replied,
"and he is much enamoured of their mode of life, which
he says is strangely in advance of ours. Most of what you
see here he has either brought with him thence, or had it
sent over to him, or it has been made here from drawings
prepared for him for the purpose. The carving of the woodwork is a copy of that in a palace at Genoa; the furniture
came by sea from Venice; the gold and silver work is English, for although my husband says that the Italians are great
masters in such work and in advance of our own, he holds
that English gold and silversmiths can turn out work equal
to all but the very best, and he therefore thinks it but right
to give employment to London craftsmen. The drapery is
far in advance of anything that can be made here; as to
the hangings and carpets, although brought from Genoa or
Florence, they are all from Eastern looms."

"'Tis strange," the merchant added, "how far we are in
most things behind the Continent—in all matters save fighting, and, I may say, the condition of the common people.
Look at our garments. Save in the matter of coarse fabrics,
nigh everything comes from abroad. The finest cloths come
from Flanders; the silks, satins, and velvets from Italy.
Our gold work is made from Italian models; our finest
arms come from Milan and Spain; our best brass work from
Italy. Maybe some day we shall make all these things for
ourselves. Then, too, our people—not only those of the
lowest class—are more rude and boorish in their manners;
they drink more heavily, and eat more coarsely. An English
banquet is plentiful, I own, but it lacks the elegance and
luxury of one abroad, and, save in the matter of joints,
there is no comparison between the cooking. Except in the
weaving of the roughest linen, we are incomparably behind

Flanders, France, or Italy, and although I have striven somewhat to bring my surroundings up to the level of the civilization abroad, the house is but as a hovel compared with the palaces of the Venetian and Genoese merchants, or the rich traders of Flanders and Paris."

"Truly these must be magnificent indeed," Edgar said, "if they so far surpass yours. I have never even thought of anything so comfortable and handsome as your rooms. I say nought of those in my father's house, for he is a scholar, and so that he can work in peace among his books and in his laboratory he cares naught for aught else; but it is the same in other houses that I have visited; they seem bare and cheerless by the side of yours. I have always heard that the houses of the merchants of London were far more comfortable than the castles of great nobles, but I hardly conceived how great the difference was."

"They are built for different purposes," the merchant said. "The castles are designed wholly with an eye to defence. All is of stone, since that will not burn; the windows are mere slits, designed to shoot from, rather than to give light. We traders, upon the other hand, have not to spend our money on bands of armed retainers. We have our city walls, and each man is a soldier if needs be. Then our intercourse with foreign merchants and our visits to the Continent show us what others are doing, and how vastly their houses are ahead of ours in point of luxury and equipment. We have no show to keep up; and at any rate when we go abroad it is neither our custom nor that of the Flemish merchants to vie with the nobility in splendour of apparel or the multitude of retainers and followers. Thus, you see, we can afford to have our homes comfortable."

"May I ask, Master Gaiton, if your robe and chain are badges of office?" Albert asked.

"Yes; I have the honour of being an alderman."

Albert looked surprised. "I thought, sir, that the alder-men were aged men."

"Not always," the merchant said with a smile, "though generally that is the case. The aldermen are chosen by the votes of the Common Council of each ward, and that choice generally falls upon one whom they deem will worthily repre-sent them, or upon one who shows the most devotion to the interests of the ward and city. My father was a prominent citizen before me, and I early learned from him to take an interest in the affairs of the city. It chanced that, when on the accession of the young king the Duke of Lancaster would have infringed some of our rights and privileges, I was one of the speakers at a meeting of the citizens, and being younger and perhaps more outspoken than others, I came to be looked upon as one of the champions of the city, and thus, without any merit of my own, was elected to repre-sent my ward when a vacancy occurred shortly afterwards."

"My husband scarce does himself justice, Master De Courcy," the trader's wife said, "for it was not only be-cause of his championship of the city's rights, but as one of the richest and most enterprising of our merchants, and because he spends his wealth worthily, giving large gifts to many charities, and being always foremost in every work for the benefit of the citizens. Maybe, too, the fact that he was one of the eight citizens who jousted at the tour-nament given at the king's accession, against the nobles of the court, and who overthrew his adversary, had also something to do with his election."

"Nay, nay, wife; these are private affairs that are of little interest to our guests, and you speak with partiality."

"At any rate, sir," Edgar said courteously, "the fact that you so bore yourself in the tournament suffices to explain how it was that you were able to keep those cut-throats at bay until just before we arrived at the spot."

"We are peaceful men in the city," the merchant said,
"but we know that if we are to maintain our rights, and to
give such aid as behoves us to our king in his foreign
wars, we need knowledge as much as others how to bear
arms. Every apprentice as well as every free man throughout the city has to practise at the butts, and to learn
to use sword and dagger. I myself was naturally well
instructed; and as my father was wealthy there were
always two or three good horses in his stables, and I learned
to couch a lance and sit firm in the saddle. As at Hastings
and Poictiers, the contingent of the city has ever been held
to bear itself as well as the best; and although we do not,
like most men, always go about the street with swords in
our belts, we can all use them if needs be. Strangely
enough, it is your trading communities that are most given
to fighting. Look at Venice and Genoa, Milan and Pisa,
Antwerp, Ghent, and Bruges, and to go further back,
Carthage and Tyre. And even among us, look at the men
of Sandwich and Fowey in Cornwall; they are traders, but
still more they are fighters; they are ever harassing the
ships of France, and making raids on the French coast."

"I see that it is as you say," Edgar said, "though I have
never thought of it before. Somehow one comes to think
of the citizens of great towns as being above all things
peaceful."

"The difference between them and your knights is, that the
latter are always ready to fight for honour and glory, and
often from the pure love of fighting. We do not want to fight,
but are ready to do so for our rights and perhaps for our
interests, but at bottom I believe that there is little difference between the classes. Perhaps if we understood each
other better we should join more closely together. We are
necessary to each other; we have the honour of England
equally at heart. The knights and nobles do most of our

fighting for us, while we, on our part, import or produce everything they need beyond the common necessities of life; both of us are interested in checking the undue exercise of kingly authority; and if they supply the greater part of the force with which we carry on the war with France, assuredly it is we who find the greater part of the money for the expenses, while we get no share of the spoils of battle."

"Have you any sisters, Master De Courcy?" the merchant's wife asked presently.

"I have but one; she is just about the same age as your daughter, and methinks there is a strong likeness between them. She and my mother are both here, having been sent for by my father on the news of the troubles in our neighbourhood."

"In that case, wife," the merchant said, "it were seemly that you and Ursula accompany me to-morrow when I go to pay my respects to Sir Ralph de Courcy."

After dinner was over the merchant took his guests into a small room adjoining that in which they had dined.

"Friends," he said, "we London merchants are accustomed to express our gratitude not only by words but by deeds. At present, methinks, seeing that, as you have told me, you have not yet launched out into the world, there is naught that you need; but this may not be so always, for none can tell what fortune may befall him. I only say that any service I can possibly render you at any time, you have but to ask me. I am a rich man, and, having no son, my daughter is my only heir. Had your estate been different and your taste turned towards trade, I could have put you in the way of becoming, like myself, foreign merchants; but even in your own profession of arms I may be of assistance.

"Should you go to the war later on and wish to take a

strong following with you, you have but to come to me and
say how much it will cost to arm and equip them and I
will forthwith defray it, and my pleasure in doing so will
be greater than yours in being able to follow the king with
a goodly array of fighting men. One thing at least you
must permit me to do when the time comes that you are
to make your first essay in arms: it will be my pleasure
and pride to furnish you with horse, arms, and armour.
This, however, is a small matter. What I really wish you
to believe is that under all circumstances—and one cannot
say what will happen during the present troubles—you can
rely upon me absolutely."

"We thank you most heartily, sir," Edgar said, "and
should the time come when, as you say, circumstances may
occur, in which we can take advantage of your most generous
offers, we will do so."

"That is well and loyally said," the merchant replied,
"and I shall hold you to it. You will remember that, by
so doing, it will be you who confer the favour and not I, for
my wife and I will always be uneasy in our minds until we
can do something at least towards proving our gratitude
for the service that you have rendered."

A few minutes later, after taking leave of the merchant's
wife and daughter, the two friends left the house.

"Truly we have been royally entertained, Edgar. What
luxury and comfort, and yet everything quiet and in good
taste! The apartments of the king himself are cold and
bare in comparison. I felt half inclined to embrace his
offer and to declare that I would fain become a trader like
himself."

Edgar laughed. "Who ever heard of such a thing as the
son of a valiant knight going into trade? Why, the bare
thought of such a thing would make Sir Ralph's hair stand
on end. You would even shock your gentle mother."

"But why should it, Edgar? In Italy the nobles are traders, and no one thinks it a dishonour. Why should not a peaceful trade be held in as high esteem as fighting?"

"That I cannot say, Albert," Edgar replied more seriously, "but whatever may be the case in Venice, it assuredly is not so here. It may be that some day, when we reach as high a civilization as Genoa and Venice possess, trade may here be viewed as it is there,—as honourable for even those of the highest birth. Surely commerce requires far more brains and wisdom than the dealing of blows, and the merchants of Venice can fight as earnestly as they can trade. Still, no one man can stand against public opinion, and until trade comes to be generally viewed as being as honourable a calling as that of war, men of gentle blood will not enter upon it; and you must remember, Albert, that it is but the exceptions who can gain such wealth as that of our host to-day, and that had you gone into the house of one of the many who can only earn a subsistence from it, you would not have been so entertained. But, of course, you are not serious, Albert."

"Not serious in thinking of being a trader, Edgar, though methinks the life would suit me well; but quite serious in not seeing why knights and nobles should look down upon traders."

"There I quite agree with you; but as my father said to me, 'You must not think, Edgar, that you can set yourself up and judge others according to your own ideas.' We were especially speaking then of the freeing of the serfs and the bettering of their condition. 'These things', he said, 'will come assuredly when the general opinion is ripe for them, but those who first advocate changes are ever looked upon as dreamers, if not as seditious and dangerous persons, and to force on a thing before the world is fit for it is to do harm rather than good. Theoretically, there is as much to be said for the views of the priest Jack Straw and other agitators as for those of Wickcliffe; but their opinions will at first bring persecution and maybe death to those who hold them. These peasants will rise in arms, and will, when the affair is over,—should they escape with their lives,—find their condition even worse than before; while the followers of Wickcliffe will have the whole power of the Church against them, and may suffer persecution and even death, besides being often viewed with grave disfavour even by their families for taking up with strange doctrines."

"No doubt that is so, Edgar, but I wish I lived in days when it were not deemed necessary that one of gentle blood should be either a fighting man or a priest."

In the time of Richard II. it was not considered in any way misdemeaning to receive a present for services rendered —a chain of gold, arms and armour, and even purses of money were so received with as little hesitation as were ransoms for prisoners taken in battle. Therefore Sir Ralph expressed himself as much pleased when he heard of the merchant's promise to present their military outfit to the two lads, and of his proffer of other services.

"By St. George," he said, "such good fortune never befell me, although I have been fighting since my youth! I have, it is true, earned many a heavy ransom from prisoners taken in battle, but that was a matter of business. The gold chain I wear was a present from the Black Prince, and I do not say that I have not received some presents in my time from merchants whose property I have rescued from marauders, or to whom I have rendered other service. Still, I know not of any one piece of good fortune that equals yours, and truly I myself have no small satisfaction in it, for I have wondered sometimes where the sums would have come from to furnish Albert with suitable armour and horse, which he must have if he is to ride in the train of a noble. In truth, I shall be glad to see this merchant of yours, and maybe his daughter will be a nice companion for Aline, who, not having her own pursuits here, finds it, methinks, dull. Just at present the court has other things to think of besides pleasure."

On the following day the visit was paid, and afforded pleasure to all parties. The knight was pleased with the manners of the merchant, who, owing to his visit to Italy, had little of the formal gravity of his craft, while there was a heartiness and straightforwardness in his speech that well suited the bluff knight. The ladies were no less pleased with each other, and Dame Agatha found herself, to her surprise, chatting with her visitors on terms of equality, and discoursing on dress and fashion, the doings of the court and life in the city, as if she had known her for years. At her mother's suggestion Aline went with Ursula into the garden, and from time to time their merry laughter could be heard through the open window.

" I hope that you will allow your daughter to come and see mine sometimes," the Dame said as her guest rose to leave. " When at home the girl has her horse and dogs, her garden, and her household duties to occupy her. Here she has naught to do save to sit and embroider, and to have a girl friend would be a great pleasure to her."

" Ursula will be very glad to do so, and I trust that you will allow your daughter sometimes to come to us. I will always send her back under good escort."

Every day rendered the political situation more serious. The Kentish rising daily assumed larger proportions, and was swollen by a great number of the Essex men, who crossed the river and joined them; and one morning the news came that a hundred thousand men were gathered on Blackheath, the Kentish men having been joined not only by those of Essex, but by many from Sussex, Herts,

Cambridge, Suffolk, and Norfolk. These were not under one chief leader, but the men from each locality had their own captain. These were Wat the Tyler, William Raw, Jack Sheppard, Tom Milner, and Hob Carter.

"Things are coming to a pass indeed," Sir Ralph said angrily as he returned from the Tower late one afternoon. "What think you, this rabble has had the insolence to stop the king's mother, as with her retinue she was journeying hither! Methought that there was not an Englishman who did not hold the widow of the Black Prince in honour, and yet the scurvy knaves stopped her. It is true that they shouted a greeting to her, but they would not let her pass until she had consented to kiss some of their unwashed faces. And, in faith, seeing that her life would have been in danger did she refuse, she was forced to consent to this humiliation.

"By St. George, it makes my blood boil to think of it! and here, while such things are going on, we are doing naught. Even the city does not call out its bands, nor is there any preparation made to meet the storm. All profess to believe that these fellows mean no harm, and will be put off with a few soft words, forgetful of what happened in France when the peasants rose, and that these rascals have already put to death some score of judges, lawyers, and wealthy people. However, when the princess arrived with the news, even the king's councillors concluded that something must be done, and I am to ride, with five other knights, at six to-morrow morning, to Blackheath, to ask these rascals, in the name of the king, what it is that they would have, and to promise them that their requests shall be carefully considered."

At nine the next morning the knight returned.

"What news, Sir Ralph?" Dame Agatha asked as he entered. "How have you sped with your mission?"

"In truth we have not sped at all. The pestilent knaves
refused to have aught to say to us, but bade us return and
tell the king that it was with him that they would have
speech, and that it was altogether useless his sending out
others to talk for him, he himself must come. 'Tis past
all bearing. Never did I see such a gathering of ragged rascals; not one of them, I verily believe, has as much as washed
his face since they started from home. I scarce thought
that all England could have turned out such a gathering.
Let me have some bread and wine, and such meat as you
have ready. There is to be a Council in half an hour, and I
must be there. There is no saying what advice some of
these poor-spirited courtiers may give."

"What will be your counsel, Sir Ralph?"

"My counsel will be that the king should mount with
what knights he may have, and a couple of score of men-at-
arms, and should ride to Oxford, send out summonses to
his nobles to gather there with their vassals, and then come
and talk with these rebels, and in such fashion as they
could best understand. They may have grievances, but
this is not the way to urge them, by gathering in arms,
murdering numbers of honourable men, insulting the king's
mother, burning deeds and records, and now demanding
that the king himself should wait on their scurvy majesties.
Yet I know that there will be some of these time-servers
round the king who will advise him to intrust himself to
these rascals who have insulted his mother.

"By my faith, were there but a couple of score of my old
companions here, we would don our armour, mount our
war-horses, and ride at them. It may be that we should
be slain, but before that came about we would make such
slaughter of them that they would think twice before they
took another step towards London."

"It was as I expected," the knight said when he returned

from the council. "The majority were in favour of the king yielding to these knaves and placing himself in their power, but the Archbishop of Canterbury, and Hales the treasurer, and I, withstood them so hotly that the king yielded to us, but not until I had charged them with treachery, and with wishing to imperil the king's life for the safety of their own skins. De Vere and I might have come to blows had it not been for the king's presence."

"Then what was the final decision of the Council, Sir Ralph?" his wife asked.

"It was a sort of compromise," the knight said. "One which pleased me not, but which at any rate will save the king from insult. He will send a messenger to-day to them saying that he will proceed to-morrow in his barge to Rotherhithe, and will there hold converse with them. He intends not to disembark, but to parley with them from the boat, and he will, at least in that way, be safe from assault. I hear that another great body of the Essex, Herts, Norfolk, and Suffolk rebels have arrived on the bank opposite Greenwich, and that it is their purpose, while those of Blackheath enter the city from Southwark, to march straight hitherwards, so that we shall be altogether encompassed by them."

"But the citizens will surely never let them cross the bridge?"

"I know not," the knight said gloomily. "The Lord Mayor had audience with the king this morning, and confessed to him that, although he and all the better class of citizens would gladly oppose the rioters to the last, and suffer none to enter the walls, that great numbers of the lower class were in favour of these fellows, and that it might be that they would altogether get the better of them, and make common cause with the rabble. Many of these people have been out to Blackheath; some have stayed there with the mob, while others have brought back news of their doings. Among the rabble on Blackheath are many hedge-priests, notably, I hear, one John Ball, a pestilent knave, who preaches treason to them, and tells them that as all men are equal, so all the goods of those of the better class should be divided among those having nothing, a doctrine which pleases the rascals mightily."

The next day accordingly the king went down with some of his councillors to Rotherhithe. A vast crowd lined both banks of the river, and saluted him with such yells and shouts that those with him, fearing the people might put off in boats and attack him, bade the rowers turn the boat's head and make up the river again; and fortunately, the tide being just on the turn, they were thus able to keep their course in the middle of the river, and so escape any arrows that might otherwise have been shot at them.

CHAPTER VII.

DEATH TO THE FLEMINGS!

THAT morning Aline had gone early to the city at the invitation of Mistress Gaiton to spend the day with Ursula, under the escort of her brother and Edgar. They were to have fetched her before dusk, but early in the afternoon Richard Gaiton himself brought her back.

"I am sorry to bring your daughter back so early," he said to Dame Agatha, "but I had news that after the king turned back this morning, the leaders of the rebels have been haranguing them, telling them that it was clearly useless to put any trust in promises, or to hope that redress could be obtained from the king, who was surrounded by evil councillors, and that, since they would not allow him to trust himself among the people, the people must take the matter into their own hands. They had remained quiet long enough; now was the time that they should show their strength. The rabble shouted loudly, 'Let us to London! Death to the Council! Death to the rich!' and having gathered under their leaders, they started to march for Southwark. As there is no saying what may come of the matter, methought that it were best to bring the young lady back again."

"I thank you," Dame Agatha said; "'tis indeed better that we should be together. This morning my lord was saying that if these knaves marched upon London, he had decided that we should move into the Tower."

"It were indeed best, madam. There is no saying what may happen when these fellows become inflamed with wine and begin to taste the sweets of plunder. We ourselves feel ashamed that we are not in a position to march out with the city force, and to maintain the law against this rabble; but it is clear to us that the majority are on the other side. They have taken into their heads that if these fellows gain rights and privileges for themselves, the city may also gain fresh rights. Many of the serving-men, the craftsmen, and even the apprentices have friends and relations among these people, for most of them belong to the counties round London.

"There are others better placed who not only sympathize, as I myself do, with the natural desire of the country people to be free from serfdom, but who favour the cause because they think that were all the people free to carry arms it would check the power both of the king and nobles. So it comes that the city is divided in itself; and in this strait, when all should show a front against rebellion, we are powerless to do aught. Even among those who talk the loudest against the rabble, there are many, I fear, who send them secret encouragement, and this not because they care aught for their grievances, but because the people are set against the Flemings, who are ill-liked by many of the merchants as being rivals in trade, and who have in their hands the greater portion of the dealings, both with Flanders and the Low Country; and indeed, though I see that in the long run we shall benefit greatly by this foreign trade, I quite perceive that the privileges that our king has given to the Flemings in order to win their good-will and assistance against France, do for the present cause disadvantage and harm to many of the traders of London."

"'Tis a troubled time," Dame Agatha said, "and 'tis hard to see what is for the best. However, in the Tower assuredly we shall be safe."

"I hope so," the merchant said gravely.

"Surely you cannot doubt it, Master Gaiton?" Dame Agatha said in surprise.

"I hear that the rabble are openly saying that the men-at-arms and archers will not act against them. It may be but empty boasting, but there may be something in it. The men are almost all enlisted from Kent, Sussex, Essex, and Hertford, and I have heard report that there is sore discontent among them because their pay is greatly in arrear, owing to the extravagance of the court. It were well, perhaps, that you should mention this to Sir Ralph, and, above all, I pray you to remember, madam, that so long as my house stands, so long will it be a refuge to which you and yours may betake yourselves in case of danger here. I say not that it is safer than elsewhere, for there is no saying against whom the rage of the rabble may be directed."

Sir Ralph came home late in the afternoon. He was gloomy and depressed.

"Things are going but badly, wife," he said. "Verily, were it not for the duty I owe to the king, we would take horse and ride to Kingston, and there cross the river and journey round so as to avoid these fellows, and get to our home and wait there and see what comes of this, and should they attack us, fight to the end. It seems to me that all have lost their heads—one gives one counsel, and one gives another. Never did I see such faint hearts. The Lord Mayor has been with the king. He speaks bravely as far as he himself and the better class of citizens are concerned, but they are overborne by the commonalty, who favour the rabble partly because they hope to gain by the disorder, and partly because the leaders of the rabble declare that they will slay all the Council, and, above all, the Duke of Lancaster, against whom many in the city, as well as in the country, have a deep grudge."

"What counsel did you give, husband?"

"I asked the king to give me the command of half the men-at-arms and archers, and that I would march them through the city across London Bridge, close the gates there, and defend them alike against the rabble on the farther side and that of the city until help could be gathered. The king himself was willing that this should be so, but the Council said that were I to do this, the gatherings from Essex, Hertford, Suffolk, and Cambridge would march hither and be joined by the rabble of the city, and so attack the Tower, being all the more furious at what they would deem a breach of their privileges by my taking possession of the gates; and so nothing was done. Have you looked out of the windows across the river? If not, do so."

Lady Agatha crossed the room and gazed out. From several points in Southwark columns of smoke mingled with flames were ascending.

"What is it, Ralph?"

"It is the rabble, who are plundering Southwark, and, as I hear, have broke open the prisons of the Marshalsea and

King's Bench. The malefactors there have joined them; and this has been done without a stroke being smitten in defence. Where are the boys?"

"They went into the city with Aline this morning, and have not returned. Ah! here they are coming through the gate."

"Well, Albert, what news have you?" Sir Ralph asked his son as they entered.

"The city is in an uproar, Father; most of the shops have closed. There are gatherings in the streets, and though the Lord Mayor and Robert Gaiton and many of the better class have been haranguing them they refuse to disperse to their homes. Robert Gaiton took us into the Guildhall, where many of the most worshipful citizens were assembled discussing the matter and what is to be done, but they have no force at their command. The Flemings are in great fear. Some have betaken themselves to the churches, where they hope that their lives may be respected, but without, as it seems to me, any good warrant; for as the rabble at Canterbury did not respect even the cathedral, it is not likely that they will hold churches here as sanctuary. Robert Gaiton advised us that if we entered the city to-morrow we should not show ourselves in our present apparel, for he says that if the rabble enter, they may fall foul of any whose dresses would show them to belong to the court, and he has given us two sober citizen suits, in which he said we should be able to move about without fear of molestation."

"Things have come to a nice pass, indeed," Sir Ralph grumbled, "when the son of a knight cannot walk with safety in the streets of London. Still, Gaiton is doubtless right."

"You will not let the boys enter the city surely, Sir Ralph?" Dame Agatha said anxiously.

"I do not say so, Dame. The lads are going to be soldiers, and it were well that they became used to scenes of tumult. Moreover, they may bring us news of what is doing there that may help us. I have obtained the use of a chamber in the Tower for you and Aline. My place, of course, will be by the king's side; and maybe the reports that the boys will bring us of the doings in the city may be useful. Is it your wish, lads, to go into the city?"

"With your permission, sir, we would gladly do so. There will be much to see, and it may be to learn."

"That is so. Above all take to heart the lesson that it is dangerous to grant aught to force; and that if the rabble be suffered to become, even for an hour, the masters, they will soon become as wild beasts. It was so in France, and it will be so wherever, by the weakness of the authorities, the mob is allowed to raise its head and to deem itself master of everything. All this evil has been brought about by the cowardice of the garrison of Rochester Castle. Had they done their duty they could have defended the place for weeks against those knaves, even if not strong enough to have sallied out and defeated them in the open, but the fellows seem to have inspired everyone with terror; and in faith, whatever befalls, it will be mainly the fault of those who should at the first outbreak have gathered themselves together to make a stand against this unarmed rabble, for it might at that time have been crushed by a single charge.

"I take blame to myself now, that instead of summoning you hither, I did not hasten home as soon as I heard of the doings at Dartford, gather a score of my neighbours with their retainers, and give battle to the mob. There were comparatively few at that time, and they had not gained confidence in themselves. And even if we had deemed them too strong to attack in the field, we might have thrown ourselves into Rochester and aided the garrison to hold the castle. I have seen troubles in Flanders, and have learnt how formidable the mob may become when it has once tasted blood; and it is well that you should both learn that, even when the commonalty have just grounds for complaint, they must not be allowed to threaten the security of the realm by armed rebellion.

"Would that the Black Prince were here instead of the Boy King, we should then have very different measures taken! Even if the king's mother had spirit and courage the counsels of those men who surround the king would be overborne; but she was so alarmed, as she well might be, at her meeting with the rabble on Blackheath, that the spirit she once had seems to have quite departed, and she is all in favour of granting them what they will."

Later on Sir Ralph again went to the Tower, and shortly returned. "Put on your cloaks and hoods at once," he said to his wife. "The Essex and Hertford men have arrived on the north side of the city and may be here in the morning, and it will be then too late to retire to the Tower. I will give you a quarter of an hour to pack up your belongings. The men will carry them for you. As to you, boys, you can safely remain here until daybreak, then put on your citizen dresses and make your way quietly into the city, as soon as the gates are open. Put them over your own clothes. I charge you to take no part in any street fray; but if the better class of citizens make a stand, throw off your citizen clothes and join them and strike for the king and country, for assuredly England would be ruined were the rabble to have their way."

In a quarter of an hour the ladies were ready; and their court suits and those of Albert and Edgar had been packed. The men-at-arms took up the valises, and, followed by them, Sir Ralph, his wife, and daughter made for the Tower.

In the morning as soon as they knew that the gates would

be open the two boys attired themselves in the citizen suits, and, buckling on their swords, left the house. As soon as they entered the city they found that the streets were already filled with people. It was Corpus Christi, at that time kept as a general holiday, and regardless of the troubles many were flocking out to enjoy a holiday in the country. The boys had debated whether they should first go to the merchant's, but they agreed not to do so, as he would probably be in consultation with the authorities, and would be fully occupied without having them to attend to.

As they advanced farther it was easy to see that there was another element besides that of the holiday-makers abroad. Bands of men carrying heavy staves, and many of them with swords at their belts, were hurrying in the direction of the bridge, and Edgar and Albert took the same direction. The bridge itself was crowded, partly with holiday-makers and partly with armed men, while the windows of the houses were occupied by spectators, who were looking down with evident apprehension at what was about to take place. Gradually making their way forward the two friends reached the other end. Here there was a group of citizens on horseback. Among them was the Lord Mayor, William Walworth, and many of the aldermen, Robert Gaiton among them. The mob were shouting, "Open the gates!" The uproar was great, but on the Mayor holding up his hand there was silence.

"Fellow-citizens," he said, "know ye not what has been done by these men at Southwark? Not content with plundering and ill-treating the inhabitants, breaking open the cellars and besotting themselves with liquor, they have opened the doors of the prisons, and have been joined by the malefactors held there. Assuredly if they enter the city they will behave in like manner here; therefore the gates cannot be opened."

A man stepped forward from the mob and replied:

"It has always been the custom for the gates to be opened, and for the citizens to go out to the fields to enjoy themselves on a holiday, and we will have it so now whether it likes you or not."

Then the uproar was renewed, swords and staves were raised menacingly, and cries raised of "Death to the Lord Mayor!" "Death to all who would interfere with our liberties!" The Mayor took counsel with those around him. It was manifestly impossible that some twenty or thirty men could successfully oppose an infuriated mob, and it was certain that they would all lose their lives were they to do so, and that without avail. Accordingly the Mayor again held up his hand for silence, and said:

"We cannot oppose your will, seeing that you are many and that we are few; therefore, if you wish it, we must open the gates, but many of you will regret ere many days have passed the part that you have taken in this matter."

So saying, he and those with him drew aside. With a shout of triumph the mob rushed to the gates, removed the bars and opened them, and then poured out, shouting and cheering, into Southwark.

While the dispute had been going on the two friends had quietly made their way almost to the front line.

"What had we best do, Edgar?"

"We had best keep quiet," the latter said; "this is but a street broil, against which your father charged us to take no part. It would not be a fight, but a massacre. Had these gentlemen been in armour, they might have sold their lives dearly, and perchance have fought their way through, but seeing that they have but on their civic gowns they can make no effectual resistance."

As soon as the gates were open they stood back in a doorway until the first rush of the crowd had ceased; then they followed the horsemen across the bridge again, and took their stand at the end of Gracechurch Street to see what would follow. In a short time they saw the holiday-makers come pouring back over the bridge in evident terror, and close on their heels were a great mob. At their head, on horseback, rode Wat Tyler and three or four other leaders. Behind them followed a disorderly crowd bran-dishing their weapons. Many of these were drunk, their clothes being stained deeply by the wine from the casks they had broached. Among them were many of the men who had been released from prison.

As they poured over the bridge, some broke off from the column and began to harangue the citizens, saying that these had as much to complain of as they had, seeing how they were taxed for the extravagancies of the court and the expense of foreign wars, and that now was the time for all honest men to rise against their oppressors. Many of the lower class joined their ranks. None ventured to enter into dispute with them. Some of the mob were dressed in ecclesiastical robes which they had taken from the churches. These as they went shouted blasphemous parodies on the mass. The leaders evidently had a fixed purpose in their minds, for upon reaching Cheapside they turned west.

"It is sad to think that these fellows should disgrace the cause for which they took up arms," Edgar said to his com-panion. "They had grounds for complaint when they first rose. I then felt some sympathy for them, but now they are intoxicated with their success. Look at Wat the Tyler. I believed he was an honest workman, and, as all said, a clever one. I do not blame him that in his wrath he slew the man who had insulted his daughter; but look at him now—he rides as if he were a king. He is puffed up with his own importance, and looks round upon the citizens as if he were their lord and master. He has stolen some armour on his way, and deems that he cuts a knightly figure. Let us go by the quiet streets and see what is their object."

The whole of the rioters moved down Cheapside by St. Paul's, and then to the Temple. So far they offered no wrong to anyone. They sallied out through the gates and continued on their way until they reached the Savoy, the splendid palace of the Duke of Lancaster, which was said to be the fairest and most richly furnished of any in the kingdom. With shouts of triumph they broke into it and scattered through the rooms, smashing the furniture and destroying everything they could lay hands upon. Some made for the cellars, where they speedily intoxicated themselves. Loud shouts were raised that nothing was to be taken. The silver vessels and jewels were smashed, and then carried down to the Thames and thrown into it.

In a short time flames burst out in several parts of the palace. One man was noticed by another as he thrust a silver cup into his dress. He was at once denounced and seized, and was without further ado hurled into the flames.

The fire spread rapidly. The crowd surrounded the palace, shouting, yelling, and dancing in their triumph over the destruction that they had wrought. Upwards of thirty of the drunkards were unable to escape, and were imprisoned in the cellars. Their shouts for help were heard for seven days, but none came to their assistance, for the ruins of the house had fallen over them, and they all perished. Thence the crowd went to the Temple, where they burnt all the houses occupied by lawyers, with all their books and documents, and then proceeded to the house of the Knights of St. John, a splendid building but lately erected. This also they fired, and so great was its extent that it burned for seven days.

The next morning twenty thousand of them marched to Highbury, the great manor-house of which belonged to the

Order of St. John, and this and the buildings around it were all destroyed by fire.

After seeing the destruction of the Temple, Edgar and Albert went back to Cheapside. The streets were almost deserted. The better class of citizens had all shut themselves up in their houses and every door was closed. On knocking at the door of the mercer the two friends were admitted. The alderman had just returned from a gathering of the city authorities. They told him what they had witnessed.

"It passes all bounds," he said, "and yet there is nought that we can do to put a stop to it. For myself I have counselled that proclamation shall be made that all honest citizens shall gather with arms in their hands at the Guildhall, and that we should beg the king to give us some assistance in men-at-arms and archers, and that we should then give battle to the rabble. But I found few of my opinion. All were thinking of the safety of their families and goods, and said that were we defeated, as we well might be, seeing how great are their numbers, they would pillage and slay as they chose. Whereas if we give them no pretence for molesting us, it might be that they would do no harm to private persons, but would content themselves with carrying out their original designs of obtaining a charter from the king.

"In faith it is cowardly counsel, and yet, as with the forces from the north and south there must be fully two hundred thousand rebels, I own that there is some reason in such advice. If the king with his knights and nobles and his garrison at the Tower would but sally out and set us an example, be sure that he would be joined by the law-abiding citizens, but as he doeth naught in this strait, I see not that peaceful citizens are called upon to take the whole brunt of it upon their own shoulders. However, I have little hope that the rioters will content them-

(M 371)   I

selves with destroying palaces and attacking lawyers. What you tell me of the execution of one of their number who stole a silver cup, shows that the bulk of them are at present really desirous only of redress of grievances, but they will soon pass beyond this. The jail-birds will set an example of plunder and murder, and unless help comes before long, all London will be sacked. My men and apprentices are already engaged in carrying down to the cellars all my richest wares. The approach is by a trap-door with a great stone over it in the yard, and it will, I hope, escape their search.

"Of one thing you may be sure, that as soon as the king shows himself and it is seen that he is in danger, there will be no hanging back, but we shall join him with what force we can. I think not that he can have aid from without, for we hear that the country people have everywhere risen, and that from Winchester in the south to Scarborough in the north they have taken up arms, and that the nobles are everywhere shut up in their castles, so they, being cut off from each other, are in no position to gather a force that could bring aid to the king. You can tell your good father what I say, and that all depends upon the attitude of the king. If he comes to us with his knights and men we will join him; if he comes not, and we learn that he is in danger, we will do what we can, but that must depend much upon how the rebels comport themselves."

The two lads went to the Tower, but the gates were closed and the drawbridge pulled up, and they therefore returned to their lodging, where they passed the night. On the following day they returned into the city; there the rioters had already begun their work. Thirty Flemings, who had taken refuge in the churches, were dragged from the altar and were beheaded, thirty-two others were seized in the vintry and also slain. Then parties broke into all the houses where the Flemings lived, and such as had not fled in disguise were killed and their houses pillaged. All through the day the streets were in an uproar. Every man the rebels met was seized and questioned.

"Who are you for?" Such as answered "The king and commons" were allowed to go unmolested, others were killed. The two friends had several narrow escapes. Fortunately Edgar had learned the watchword at Dartford and readily replied, and they were allowed to pass on. They were traversing Bread Street when they heard a scream behind them, and a girl came flying along pursued by a large number of the rioters, headed by a man in the dress of a clerk. She reached the door of a handsome house close to them, but before she could open it the leader of the party ran up and roughly seized her. Edgar struck him a buffet on the face which sent him reeling backwards.

With shouts of fury the crowd rushed up just as the door opened. Edgar and Albert stepped back into the doorway, while the girl ran upstairs.

"How now, my masters," Edgar said as he drew his sword, "is this the way to secure your rights and liberties by attacking women in the streets? Shame on you! Do you call yourselves Englishmen?"

"They are Flemings!" the man whom Edgar had struck shouted out.

"Well, sir, I should say that you were a Fleming yourself by your speech," Edgar said.

"I am but a clerk," the man said. "He who lives here is one of the Flemings who bought the taxes, and has been grinding down the people, of whom I am one."

"The people must be badly off, indeed," Edgar said contemptuously, "if they need to have such a cur as you on their side."

But his words were drowned by the furious shouts of

the crowd, "Death to the Flemings!" and a rush was made
at the door, headed by the clerk, who struck savagely at
Edgar.   The latter parried the stroke, and thrust the man
through the throat.   With a yell of rage the crowd now
strove furiously to enter, but the position of the two lads
standing back a couple of feet from the entrance rendered
it impossible for more than two or three to attack them at
once, and the clubs and rough weapons were no match for
the swords.   Nevertheless, although five or six of their
opponents fell, the weight of numbers pressed the friends
back to the staircase, where they again made a stand.

For five minutes the conflict raged.   The boys had both
received several blows, for the weight of the heavy weapons
sometimes beat down their guard; but they still fought on,
retiring a step or two up the stair when hardly pressed, and
occasionally making dashes down upon their assailants,
slaying the foremost, and hurling the others backwards.
Presently the girl ran down again to them.

"All are in safety," she said.   "Run upstairs when you
can.   Where you see me standing at a door run in and lock
it on the inside."

"One more rush, Albert, and then upstairs."

With a shout Edgar threw himself upon a man who had
raised a heavy pole-axe, and cut the fellow down.   Then, as
the man fell, Edgar flung himself on him, and hurled him
against those behind, while Albert at the same moment ran
an opponent through the body.   Then turning, they sprang
up the stairs.   On the landing above the girl was standing
at an open door.   They ran in and closed it, and then piled
articles of furniture against it.

"There is no occasion for that," she said; "this way."

The room was heavily panelled, and one of the panels
was standing open.   They followed her into this.

"Push it back," she said, "it is too heavy for me."   The

panel was indeed of great weight, the wood being backed with brick, the whole ran on rollers, but Edgar had no difficulty in closing it.

"Thank God, and you, gentlemen, that we are in safety! The keenest eye could not see that the panel opens, and, being backed with brick, it gives no hollow sound when struck. They will search in vain for it."

Taking a lamp from the ground, she led the way down a narrow flight of stairs. By the depth to which they descended Edgar judged when they reached the bottom that they must be below the level of the cellars. She opened a door, and entered an apartment some twenty feet square. It was lighted by four candles standing on a table. In one corner a woman lay on a pallet, two women-servants sobbing with terror and excitement stood beside her, while a tall, elderly man rose to meet them.

"Gentlemen," he said, "I don't know how to thank you. You must think it cowardly that I did not descend to share your peril; but it was necessary that I should go to the storey above that you reached to bring down my wife, who, as you see, is grievously sick. Her two maids were very nearly distraught with terror, and, if left to themselves, would never have carried their mistress below. Having had some experience of popular tumults in Bruges, my native town, I had this hiding-place constructed when I first came here twenty years ago. Now, to whom am I indebted for our safety?"

Edgar introduced his companion and himself.

"Then you are not, as would seem by your attire, merchants like myself?"

"No, sir. We but put on this attire over our own in order to be able to traverse the streets without interruption. May I ask how it is that your daughter was alone and unattended in the streets?"

"She was not unattended. She had with her my servant,

a Flemish lad, who has but recently come over. He speaks no English, and not knowing the tongue, could not be sent out alone. My wife was taken worse this morning, and the leech not having sent the medicine he promised, my daughter, thinking that there could be no danger to a young girl, went to get it, and as the servant was dressed in English fashion, and would not be called upon to speak, I thought that she could pass unnoticed did they fall in with any party of the rioters."

"So we should have done, father," the girl said, "had we not met a band headed by Nicholas Bierstadt."

"The villain!" the merchant exclaimed. "So it was he who led the party here. When these troubles are over I will see that he obtains his deserts."

"He has obtained them already, sir," Edgar said, "for I slew the knave at the first thrust."

"He was my clerk, the son of a man of some influence at Bruges. He was well recommended to me, and came over here to learn the business and the language, with the intention of going into trade for himself. It was not long before I came to dislike his ways, and when, a fortnight since, he asked me for the hand of my daughter, I repulsed him, telling him that, in the first place, she was too young to think of marriage; and that, in the second, I liked him not, and would never give my consent to her having him; and lastly, that she liked him as little as I did. He answered insolently, and I then expelled him from the house, when he threatened me that I should ere long regret my conduct. I gave the fellow no further thought, and did not know where he bestowed himself. Doubtless he was waiting to see whether this rabble would reach London and what would come of it, and when they entered doubtless he endeavoured to gratify his hatred by leading some of them hither. And now, Joanna, tell me what befell you?"

"We went safely to the leech's, father, and I got the medicine from him. He made many apologies, but said that he had heard so much of the doings of the rioters that he thought it best to stay indoors, and of course he had not heard that mother was taken worse. We had come half-way back when we fell in with a party of the rioters. Me-thinks they would have said naught, but Bierstadt, whom I had not noticed, suddenly grasped me by the arm, saying, 'This is the daughter of the Fleming to whose house I am taking you, one of the chief oppressors of the poor.' Johann struck him in the face, and as he loosened his hold of me I darted away. Looking back, I saw Johann on the ground, and the mob round him were hacking at him with their weapons. This gave me a start, and I ran, but just as I reached the door Bierstadt overtook and seized me; then this gentleman, who was passing, struck him a stout buffet in the face, and without waiting to see more I hastened to give you the alarm."

"Providence surely sent you to the spot, gentlemen," the Fleming said; "here we are absolutely safe. During the last two days I have brought down a provision of food, wine, and water sufficient to last us for a month, and long before that methinks this rascaldom will have been sup-pressed."

"There is no doubt of that, sir; my only fear is that when they cannot discover where you are concealed, they will fire the house."

"Against that I have provided," the Fleming said. He opened the door. "See you that stone slab, above a foot in thickness? it looks solid, but it is not. It is worked by a counterpoise, and when it is lowered," and, touching a spring, it began to descend, thus closing the stairway, "not only would it baffle them did they find the entrance above, but it would prevent any fire reaching here. The staircase is of stone, and above us is a strongly-arched cellar, which would resist were the whole house to fall upon it."

CHAPTER VIII.

A COMBAT IN THE TOWER.

I SEE that you are safe against fire, sir," Edgar said, when the stone slab had descended and they had closed the door behind it; "but were the walls of the house to fall in you might be buried here, as I hear many drunken wretches were yesterday in the cellars of the Savoy."

"I have means of escape," the merchant said, going to the other side of the apartment, where there was a massive iron door, which they had not before noticed. "Here," he said, "is a passage leading under the street; at the end it ascends, and is closed at the top by a massive panel in the hall of the house opposite. When I took this house a com-patriot lived there, and it was with his consent that I made the passage, which might be useful in case of need, to him as well as to me. He returned to Flanders three years since, and the house has been occupied by an English trader, who knows naught of the passage, so that, at will, I can sally out by that way."

"And how is your dame, sir?" Albert asked. "I trust that she is none the worse for her transport here."

"I trust not, young sir; she swooned as I brought her down, but I at once poured some cordial between her lips, and when she opened her eyes, just before you came down, I assured her that we were all safe, and that there was no cause for the least fear; thereupon she closed her eyes again, and is, methinks, asleep. When she wakes I shall give her the medicine that my daughter brought. I trust that she will ere long recover. Her attack was doubtless brought on by the news that we received yesterday of the murder of so many of our countrymen. We had already talked of taking refuge here, but deemed not that there was any pressing need of haste, for the front door is a very strong one, and could have resisted any attacks long enough to give us ample time to retire here."

"How do you manage to breathe here, sir, now that the stone slab is down and the door closed? I see not how you obtain air."

"For that I made provision at the time it was built. Here are two shafts, six inches square; this one runs up into the chimney of the kitchen and draws up the air from here; the other goes up to a grating in the outer wall of the house in the yard behind. It looks as if made for giving ventilation under the floors or to the cellar, and through this the air comes down to take the place of that drawn upwards by the heat of the chimney."

"And now, Mynheer Van Voorden," for such they had learned was the Fleming's name, "as there is a way of escape we shall be glad to use it."

"I pray you do not think of doing so at present," the Fleming said. "We know not yet whether the evil-doers have cleared off, and methinks it is not likely that they will have gone yet. First they will search high and low for us; then they will demolish the furniture, and take all they deem worth carrying; then doubtless they will quench their thirst in the cellar above; and lastly they will fire the house, thinking that although they cannot find us, they will burn us with it. They will wait some time outside to see if we appear at one of the windows, and not until the roof has fallen in will they be sure that we have perished. Moreover, you cannot well appear in the streets for the present in that attire, for you might well be recognized and denounced. First of all, let me persuade you to take such poor refreshments as I can offer you."

"Thanks, sir; of that we shall be glad, for 'tis now past noon, and we have had but a loaf we bought at a baker's as we entered the city."

The Fleming gave orders to the servant, and they speedily had a snow-white cloth of the finest damask on the table, and placed on it a service of silver dishes.

"'Tis well that I had my plate brought down here yesterday," the merchant said smiling, "though it hardly consorts well with the fare that I have to offer you. To-morrow, should you pay us a visit, you will find us better prepared, for, as you see, we have a fireplace at the bottom of the flue opening into the kitchen chimney. This was done, not only that we might have warmth, and be able if need be to cook here, but to increase the draught upwards, and so bring down more air from the other flue."

The lads, however, found that there was no need for apology, for there were upon the dishes two chickens, a raised pasty large enough for a dozen people, and a variety of sweets and conserves. The wine, too, was superb. They made a hearty meal. When they had finished, the Fleming said: "Now we will go upstairs; there is a peephole in the carving of the panel, and we can see how matters stand."

Opening the door they pushed up the massive stone. As they ascended the stairs they smelt smoke, which grew thicker at each step.

"We need go no further, sirs; the house is clearly on fire, and smoke has made its way through the peephole that I spoke of."

They waited for another half-hour, and then they heard a heavy crash on the other side of the stone barrier.

"The roof has doubtless fallen in, or one of the walls,"

Van Voorden said. "There is, be sure, a mob gathered to watch the flames, but in another half-hour it will have gone elsewhere; still, I should advise you to wait until nightfall."

They saw that this would be prudent, for their attire would certainly render them obnoxious to the rioters. They were, however, impatient to be off and see what was being done. The Fleming's wife was still sleeping soundly, and her husband said that he was convinced that the crisis was past, and that she would now recover. The Fleming asked them many questions about themselves, and where they could be found. They told him where they were at present lodging, but said they thought that as soon as the present troubles were over they should return to their home in the country.

"I myself shall be returning to Flanders, sirs. I have talked of it many times these last five years, and after this outburst it will be long before any of my people will be able to feel that they are safe in London. Had it not been that the populace are as much masters in Bruges as they are here, I should have gone long ago.

"There is, indeed, no change for the better there, but I shall settle in Brussels or Louvain, where I can live in peace and quiet."

At the end of half an hour Edgar said: "I think that they must have cleared off by this time. When we sally out, do you, Albert, go one way, and I will go another. There is naught in our dress to distinguish us from other citizens, and methinks that most of those who would have known us again are lying under the ruins above."

They had, on first arriving below, washed the blood from their faces, and bathed their wounds, which were by no means of a serious character. The Fleming agreed with them that, if they separated, there would be no great danger of their being recognized. After taking farewell of the girl, who had all this time been sitting silently by her mother's bedside, they passed through the iron door, preceded by the Fleming carrying a lamp. After passing through the passage they went up a long flight of narrow steps until their course was arrested by a wooden panel. The Fleming applied first his eye and then his ear to a tiny peephole.

"Everything is quiet," he said; then touched a spring, pushed the panel open a short distance, and looked out.

"All is clear; you have but to open the door and go out."

He pushed the panel farther back, pressed the lads' hands as they went out, and then closed the entrance behind them. There was but a single bolt to undraw; then they opened the door and stepped into the street, Edgar waiting for half a minute to let Albert get well away before he went out.

The front wall of the opposite house, having fallen inward, quickly smothered the fire, and although a light smoke, mingled with tongues of flame, rose from the ruin, the place had ceased to have any attraction for the mob, who had wandered away to look for more exciting amusement elsewhere.

Scenes of this kind were being enacted throughout the city. Already the restriction against plundering was disregarded, and although the men from the counties still abstained from robbery, the released prisoners from the jail and the denizens of the slums of the city had no such scruples, and the houses of the Flemings were everywhere sacked and plundered. The two friends met again at Aldgate. When they reached Tower Hill, it was, they found, occupied by a dense throng of people, who beleaguered the Tower and refused to allow any provisions to be taken in, or any person to issue out.

"What had best be done, Edgar? So menacing is the appearance of the rabble that methinks this attire would be as much out of place among them as would our own."

"I agree with you there, Albert, and yet I know not what we are to do. What we need is either a craftsman's dress or that of a countryman, but I see not how the one or the other is to be obtained. Assuredly nothing is to be bought, save perhaps bread, for the rioters have ordered that all bakers' shops are to stand open."

He stood for a minute thinking. "I tell you what we might do," he went on. "Let us go back into Aldgate, and then down on to the wharf. There are many country boats there, and we might buy what we need from the sailors."

"That is a good idea indeed, Edgar."

In a quarter of an hour they were on the wharf. Many of the craft there had no one on board, the men having gone either to join the rioters or to look on at what had been done. The skipper of a large fishing-boat was sitting on the wharf looking moodily down into his vessel.

"Are you the captain of that craft?" Edgar asked him.

"I used to think so," he said; "but just at present no one obeys orders, as every Jack thinks that he is as good as his master. I ought to have gone out with the morning's tide, but my men would not have it so, and just at present they are the masters, not I. A murrain on such doings, say I! I was with them when it was but a talk of rights and privileges; but when it comes to burning houses and slaying peaceable men I, for one, will have naught to do with it."

"Captain," Edgar said, "I see that you are an honest man, and maybe you will aid us. We find that there is peril in going about attired as we are, for we aided a short time since in saving a Flemish family from massacre by these fellows, and we need disguises. We want two countrymen's suits—it matters not whether they be new or old. We are ready to pay for them, but every shop is closed, and we have come down to the wharves to find some one who will sell."

"There is no difficulty about that," the skipper said, rising from his seat. "My own clothes would scarce fit you, but two of my crew are somewhat of your size. Step on board, and I will overhaul their lockers, and doubt not that I shall find something to serve your purpose. They will not mind if they find that there is money sufficient to buy them new ones. Indeed, there is no need for that, for if you leave behind you the clothes you wear they will sell at Colchester for enough to buy them two or three suits such as those you take."

There was in those days no distinctive dress worn by sailors. The captain went down into the little cabin forward and opened two lockers.

"There," he said, "suit yourselves out of these. They are their best, for they thought that aught would do for mixing up with the mob in the city."

So saying he went on deck again. The citizens' clothes were soon stripped off, and the lads dressed in those they took from the lockers, and in a few minutes they rejoined the skipper, looking like two young countrymen.

"That will do well," he said with a laugh. "Hob and Bill would scarce know their clothes again if they saw them on you. No, no," he added as Albert put his hand into his pouch, "there is no need for money, lads; they will be mightily content with the clothes you have left. Well, yes; I don't care if I do take a stoup of liquor. There is a tavern over there where they keep as good ale as you can find anywhere about here."

After drinking a pint of beer with the honest skipper, they again went off to the Tower, and mingled in the crowd. It was easy to see that it was composed of two different sections: the one quiet and orderly, the men looking grave and somewhat anxious, as if feeling that it was a perilous enterprise upon which they were embarked, although still bent upon carrying it out; the other noisy and savage—the men from the jails, the scum of Canterbury and Rochester, and the mob of the city. Between these classes there was no sympathy: the one was bent only upon achieving their deliverance from serfdom, the other was solely influenced by a desire for plunder, and a thirst for the blood of those obnoxious to them. Presently there was a loud shout from the crowd as the drawbridge was lowered.

"Perhaps they are going to make a sally, Albert. If so, we had best make off to our lodgings, throw off these garments, and appear in our own."

"'Tis the king!" Albert exclaimed; "and see, there is De Vere, the Earl of Kent, and other nobles riding behind him."

"Yes; and there is your father. The king and those with him are without armour or arms; if they had seen as much as we have seen the last two days, they would scarce trust themselves in such a garb."

A great shout arose as the boy king rode across the draw-bridge. The lads noticed that the shout proceeded from the men who had hitherto been silent, and that the noisy portion of the crowd now held their peace. The king held up his hand for silence.

"My friends," he said in a loud, clear voice, "there is no room here for conference. Follow me to Mile End Fields, and I will then hear what you wish to say to me, and will do what I can to give you satisfaction."

A great shout arose, and as the king rode off, most of the country people followed him. A great mob, however, still remained. These consisted principally of Wat the Tyler's following, who had ever been in the front in the doings that had taken place, together with the released malefactors and the town rabble. A few minutes after the king and his followers had left there was a movement forward, and a moment later, with loud shouts, they began to pour across the drawbridge.

"What madness is this?" Edgar exclaimed. "There are twelve hundred men there, and yet no bow is bent. It must be treachery!"

"It may be that, Edgar; but more like, orders have been issued that none should shoot at the rioters or do them any harm, for were there any killed here it might cost the king his life."

"That may be it," Edgar muttered; "but come on, there is no saying what may happen."

They were now near the drawbridge, for when a part of the gathering had left to follow the king, they had taken advantage of it to press forward towards the gates, and in a few minutes were inside the Tower. All was in confusion. The men-at-arms and archers remained immovable on the walls, while a crowd of well-nigh twenty thousand men poured into the Tower with shouts of "Death to the archbishop! Death to the treasurer!" Knowing their way better than others, Edgar and Albert ran at full speed towards the royal apartments. Finding themselves in a deserted passage they threw off their upper garments.

"Throw them in here," Edgar said, opening a door, "they may be useful to us yet."

Finding the king's chamber empty, they ran into the princess's apartment. The princess was sitting pale and trembling, surrounded by a group of ladies, among whom was Dame Agatha. A few gentlemen were gathered round. Just as the lads entered, Sir Robert Hales, the treasurer, ran in.

"Madam," he said, "I beseech you order these gentlemen to sheathe their swords. Resistance is impossible. There are thousands upon thousands of these knaves, and were a sword drawn it would cost your life and that of all within the Tower. They have no ill-will against you, as they showed when you passed through them at Blackheath. I implore you, order all to remain quiet whatever happens, and it were best that all save your personal attendants dispersed to their apartments. Even the semblance of resistance might excite these people to madness, and serve as an excuse for the most atrocious deeds."

"Disperse, I pray you, knights and ladies," the princess said. "I order—nay, I implore you, lose not a moment."

"Come," Dame Agatha said firmly, taking hold of Aline's hand; "and do you follow, my son, with Edgar."

They hurried along the passages, one of which was that by which the lads had entered.

"Go on with them," Edgar said to his friend; "I will follow in a moment. This is the room where we left our disguises."

Running in he gathered the clothes, made them into a rough bundle, and then followed. He overtook his friends as they were mounting a staircase which led to a room in one of the turrets. As they reached the chamber, and the door closed behind them, Dame Agatha burst into tears.

"I have been in such anxiety about you both!" she exclaimed.

"We have fared well, mother," Albert said; "but do you lose no moment of time. We have disguises here. I pray you put on the commonest garment that you have, you and Aline. If you can pass as servants of the palace, we can conduct you safely out of the crowd."

Edgar ran up a narrow flight of stone stairs, at the top of which was a trap-door. He forced back the bolts and lifted it.

"Bring up the clothes, Albert," he called down. "We will put them on while the ladies are changing, and we can watch from this platform what is doing without."

They soon slipped on the countrymen's clothes over their own, and then looked out at the scene below. Every space between the buildings was crowded by the mob shouting and yelling. The garrison still stood immovable on the outer walls.

"You must be right, Albert. Even if there be some traitors among them there must also be some true men, and never would they stand thus impassive had not the strictest orders been laid upon them before the king's departure."

In a minute or two they saw a number of men pour out, hauling along the Archbishop of Canterbury, Sir Robert Hales, the king's confessor, and four other gentlemen. Then with exulting shouts they dragged their prisoners to Tower Hill, and then forced them to kneel.

"They cannot be going to murder them!" Albert exclaimed with horror.

"That is surely their intent," Edgar said sternly. "Would that we were there with but a hundred men-at-arms! Assuredly there would be a stout fight before they had their way."

"I cannot look on!" Albert exclaimed, hurrying to the other side of the platform as a man armed with a heavy sword faced the prisoners.

Edgar did not move, but stood gazing with scowling brow and clenched hand. Presently he turned.

"There is naught more to see, Albert. All are murdered! God assoil their souls!"

At this moment Dame Agatha called out from below that they were ready, and they ran down at once into the chamber. Dame Agatha and her daughter were both dressed in rough garments with hoods pulled over their faces, and might well have passed unnoticed as being the wife and daughter of some small trader, or superior domestics of the palace. Just as they were about to start they heard an uproar on the stairs below. The door had been already fastened.

"Best to open it," Edgar said; "they would but break it in."

Seven rough fellows, whose flushed faces showed that they had already been drinking, rushed into the room.

"Who have we here?" one shouted roughly. "Two wenches and two country lads. But what are all these fine clothes lying about; they must be nobles in disguise. We must take them down to Tyler and hear what he has to say to them. But, first of all, let us have a kiss or two. I will begin with this young woman," and he rudely caught hold of Aline.

Edgar's sword flashed out, and with the hilt he struck the ruffian so terrible a blow on the top of his head that he fell dead. An instant later he ran another through the body, shouting to the ladies: "Quick! to the platform above! Albert, guard the stairs after they pass. I will hold this door. None of these fellows must go out alive."

Taken by surprise for a moment, the men made a rush at him. The nearest was cut down with a sweeping blow that caught him on the neck, and almost severed the head from his body. Albert had drawn his sword as soon as he saw Edgar strike the first blow, and ran one of the men through the body, then engaged another, who made at him fiercely, while Dame Agatha and Aline sped up the steps. There were now but three foes left. While one engaged with Albert and pressed him hotly, the other two attacked Edgar, who was standing with his back to the door; but they were no match for the young swordsman, who parried their blows without difficulty, and brought them one after the other to the ground just as Albert rid himself of his opponent.

"Bring the ladies down, Albert, quickly. We must be out of this before anyone else comes."

Albert ran up. The two ladies were on their knees. "Quick, mother! There is not a moment to be lost. It is all over, and you have to go down as speedily as possible."

Dame Agatha passed through the scene of carnage without a shudder, for she had more than once accompanied Sir Ralph abroad, and had witnessed several battles and sieges, but Aline clung to Albert's arm, shuddering and sobbing. Edgar stood at the door until they had passed out. He closed it behind him, locked it on the outside, and threw the key through a loophole on the stair. They met with no one until they reached the lower part of the Tower, which the rioters were now leaving, satisfied with the vengeance that they had taken upon the archbishop and treasurer, whom they regarded as the authors of the obnoxious poll-tax. The party were unquestioned as they issued out into the yard and mingled with the mob. Here they gathered that the princess, having been roughly kissed by some of those who first entered her apartment, had swooned with terror, and that her attendants had been permitted to carry her down and place her in a boat, and that she had been taken across the river.

The rioters poured out across the drawbridge with almost as much haste as they had pressed over to enter the Tower, anxious to be away before the king's return, when he might turn against them the whole of the garrison. Many had intoxicated themselves by the wine in the royal cellars, and beyond a few rough jests nothing was said to the ladies, who were supposed to be some of the royal servants now being escorted to their country homes by their friends. As soon as possible Edgar and Albert edged their way out of the crowd and soon reached the door of their lodging. As soon as the garden gate closed behind them Aline fainted. Edgar, who was walking beside her, caught her as she fell, and carried her into the house, where he left her for a while in the care of her mother.

The latter said before she closed the door: "Edgar, I charge you to go back to the Tower and speak to my lord as he enters with the king. He will be well-nigh distraught should he find that we are missing, and go up to our chamber to look for us. Albert, do you remain here with us."

A quarter of an hour later she came down to her son.

"Aline has recovered her senses," she said, "but will have to lie quiet for a time. Now tell me what has happened. Have any of the court been killed?"

Albert told her of the murder of the archbishop, the treasurer, and their five companions.

"'Tis terrible!" she said; "and I can well understand that Edgar was so maddened at the sight that when one of those half-drunken wretches insulted Aline he could contain himself no longer. But it was a rash act thus to engage seven men."

"Well, mother, if he had not smitten that man down I should have run him through. My sword was half out when he did so. You would not have had me stand by quietly and see you and Aline insulted by those wretches. But indeed the odds were not so great, seeing that they were but rabble of the town, and already half-drunk. Besides the man that he smote down, Edgar killed four of them, while I had but two to encounter, which was a fair division considering his strength and skill compared with mine. No half-measures would have been of any use after that first blow was struck. It is certain that we should all have been killed had one of them escaped to give the alarm."

"I am far from blaming you, Albert. My own blood boiled at the indignity, and had I carried a dagger I believe that I should have stabbed that fellow myself though I had been slain a moment afterwards."

Looking out from the gate Edgar saw that the mob had

now melted away. Throwing off his disguise, he proceeded
to the Tower. Half an hour later the king rode up at a
furious pace, followed by all who had ridden out with him
save the king's half-brothers, the Earl of Kent and Sir John
Holland, who, knowing their own unpopularity, and alarmed
for their safety, put spurs to their horses and rode away.
The king threw himself from his horse at the entrance at
which Edgar was standing.

"Is the news that has reached me true," he asked him,
"that the princess, my mother, has been grossly insulted
by this foul rabble, and that the archbishop, treasurer, and
others have been murdered?"

"It is quite true, your Majesty; the princess has been
carried across the river in a swoon; the bodies of the gentlemen murdered still lie on the hill."

With an exclamation of grief and indignation the king
ascended the steps.

"What of my dame and daughter, Edgar?" the knight
asked as the king turned away.

"They are both safe, and at their former lodging, Sir
Ralph. Dame Agatha sent me here to acquaint you where
they were to be found; she knew that you would be very
anxious as to their safety."

"I thank her for the thought," the knight said, turning
his horse's head to go there. "Where have you and Albert
been for the last two days?"

"We have slept at the lodgings, Sir Ralph, and during
the day have traversed the city in sober clothes watching
what has been done."

"Then you have seen scenes which must have made you
almost ashamed of being an Englishman," Sir Ralph said
angrily. "This has been a disgraceful business. It was bad
enough to destroy John of Gaunt's palace; for although I
love not Lancaster greatly, it was an ornament to London,

and full of costly treasures. For this, however, there was some sort of excuse, but not so for the burning of the Temple, still less for the destruction of the great house of the Knights of St. John, and also the manor-house of the prior of the order. I hear to-day that great numbers of Flemings have been slain, their houses pillaged, and in some cases burnt. Now comes the crowning disgrace. That the Tower of London, garrisoned by 1200 men, and which ought to have defied for weeks the whole rabbledom of England, should have opened its gates without a blow being struck, and the garrison remained inert on the walls while the king's mother was being grossly insulted, and the two highest dignitaries of the state with others massacred is enough, by my faith, to make one forswear arms, put on a hermit's dress and take to the woods. Here we are!"

The knight's two retainers ran up to take his horse as he entered the gateway; and, vaulting off, he hurried into the house.

"Why, Agatha, you are strangely pale! What has happened? I have not had time yet to question Edgar, and, indeed, have been talking so fast myself that he has had no chance of explaining how you and Aline managed to get here. You came by water, I suppose, and so escaped that crowd of knaves round the Tower?"

"No, Sir Ralph, we escaped under the protection of your son and this brave youth. Had it not been for them we should surely have suffered indignity and perhaps death."

"What! were they in the Tower? How got they there, wife?"

"I have had no time to ask questions yet, husband, having been attending Aline, who fainted after bearing up bravely until we got here. She has but a few minutes since come out of her swoon, and I have stayed with her."

"Tell me what has happened, Albert," the knight said.

"We slept here last night, sir; and upon sallying out found the rioters assembled round the Tower. We were clad in traders' dresses Master Gaiton had given us; and seeing that there was no chance of entering the Tower, while it would not have been safe to have mingled with the mob in such an attire, we knew not what to do until Edgar suggested that we might, if we went down to the wharf, obtain disguises from one of the vessels lying there. We were fortunate, and exchanged our citizen clothes for those of two sailor-men. Then we came back and mingled in the crowd. We saw the drawbridge lowered, and the king ride off with his company, followed by the more orderly portion of the rioters. In a few minutes, headed by Wat the Tyler, those who remained poured across the drawbridge and were masters of the place, not a blow being struck in its defence.

"We made our way, by back passages known to us, to the princess's apartments, where she, with several knights and ladies, among them my mother and sister, were waiting to see what might come. Sir Richard Hales rushed in and prayed that no resistance be offered, as this would inflame the passions of the mob, and cost the lives of all within the Tower. So the princess gave orders for all to leave her save her maids, and to scatter to their own apartments, and remain quiet there. As soon as we reached my mother's room we besought her to put on that sombre dress, and prayed her similarly to attire Aline, so that they might pass with us unnoticed through the crowd. While they were doing this we went up to the platform above, and there witnessed the murder of the archbishop, treasurer, and priest—at least, Edgar did so, for I could not bring myself to witness so horrible a sight.

"In a short time my mother called that she and Aline were ready. We were about to leave the room and hurry away, when suddenly seven rough knaves, inflamed by wine, rushed in. The leader of them said that they saw we were people of quality, and that he would take us down before Wat the Tyler, who would know how to deal with us; but before doing so he and his crew would give the ladies some kisses, and thereupon he seized Aline roughly. I was in the act of drawing my sword, when Edgar dealt him so terrible a blow with the hilt of his that the man fell dead. Then there was a general fight. Edgar shouted to my mother and Aline to run up the steps to the platform above, and to me to hold the stairs, while he placed his back to the door.

"The combat lasted but a short time, for the fellows possessed no kind of skill. In addition to the man that Edgar had first killed he slew four others, while I killed the other two. Then mother and Aline came down from the platform, descended the stairs, and mingled with the mob; they were pouring out exulting in the mischief they had done, but plainly anxious as to the consequences to themselves. We had no difficulty in coming hither. By the remarks we heard, it is clear that they took the ladies for two of the princess's tire-women, and we their friends who were going to escort them to their homes."

"Of a truth 'tis a brave tale, Albert," the knight exclaimed, bringing his hand down on the lad's shoulder with hearty approbation. "By my faith, no knights in the realm could have managed the matter more shrewdly and bravely. Well done, Albert! I am indeed proud of my son. As for you, Edgar, you have added a fresh obligation to those I already owe you. 'Tis a feat, indeed, for one of your age to slay five men single-handed, even though they were inflamed by liquor. Now, wife, what about Aline?"

"She is here to answer for herself," the girl said as she entered the room. "I am better, but still feel strangely weak. I could not lie still when I knew that you were in the house. I take great shame to myself, father. I thought I could be brave, in case of peril, as your daughter should be, but instead of that I swooned like a village maiden."

"You are not to be blamed. So long as there was danger you kept up, and, in truth, it was danger that might well drive the blood from the face of the bravest woman; for the sight of that chamber, after the fight was over, must in itself have filled a maid of your age with horror. Why, the princess herself swooned on vastly less occasion. No, no, girl, I am well pleased with you; as for your mother, she had seen such sights before, but it was a rough beginning for you, and I think that you acted bravely and well."

CHAPTER IX.

DEATH OF THE TYLER.

WHAT befell the king, my lord?" said Edgar.

"As far as he was concerned all went well. A multitude accompanied him to Mile End Fields, and then, on his demanding that they should frankly tell him what were their grievances, they handed to him a parchment containing the four points that have from the first been asked for, and all of which are reasonable enough. The king, after reading them, told them in a loud voice that he was willing to grant their desires, and would forthwith issue a charter bestowing these four points on the people. The rebels set up a great shout, and forthwith marched away in their companies, the men of Herts, Cambridge, and Suffolk, and all those of Essex who were there. Nothing could have been better. We knew not that the Kentish men and some of the Essex bands, together with the rabble of the city, had remained at the Tower, and it was only as we rode back, believing that the trouble was all over, that we heard what had happened."

"Will the king still grant the charter, father?" Albert asked.

"I know not. Everything has been changed by the conduct of these fellows, and the murder of the archbishop, the lord treasurer, and others, to say nothing of the insults to the king's mother, and the insolence of the mob in making themselves masters of the Tower. But, indeed, the king could not himself grant such a charter. It is a matter that must be done both by king and parliament, and when the knights of the shires and the representatives of the great towns meet, they will be equally indisposed to grant concessions to men who have burned palaces, destroyed all deeds and titles wheresoever they could find them, killed every man of law on whom they could lay hands, and throughout all England have risen against the lords of the soil.

"If the rabble could, whenever they had the fancy, rise in arms and enforce any claim that they chose to propose, they would soon be masters of all. It may be that ere long serfdom will cease, and I see not why all men should not have the right of buying and selling in open market. As to fixing the price of land, I think not that that can be done, seeing that some land is vastly more fertile than others, and that the land near towns is of much greater value than elsewhere. But even in my time there have been great changes, and the condition of the serfs is very greatly improved, while the hardships they complain of, and the heavy taxation, are not felt by serfs only, but are common to all.

"However, although for a time I believe that these unlawful and riotous doings will do harm rather than good, and assuredly all those who have taken a leading part in them will be punished, yet in the end it will be seen that it were best that these things that they now ask for should be granted, and that England should be content, and all classes stand together. Undoubtedly these fellows have shown that they can bite as well as growl, and though they would always be put down in the end, it might be only after great effort and much heavy fighting, and after terrible misfortunes befalling, not only towns, but all throughout the country who dwell in houses incapable of making a long defence.

"At present we may be sure that whatever the king may promise these varlets, parliament will grant no such charter. I myself would not that they should do so. It would be fatal to the peace of the land for the Commons, as they call themselves, to think that they have but to rise in arms to frighten the king and government into granting whatsoever they may demand. And now let us eat and drink, for indeed I am both hungry and thirsty, and I doubt not that 'tis the same with you. I told Jenkin, as I came in, to give us something to eat, it mattered not what, so that it were done speedily. 'Tis well that I left the two men here, otherwise we should have found an empty larder."

"That might well have been, father," Albert said, "for our hostess and her servants all went away yesterday, thinking that it would be safer in the city than here; but we told Hob and Jenkin always to keep a store of food, since there was no saying when you would all return, and that, at any rate, even were we out all day Edgar and I might want supper on our return, and a good meal before leaving in the morning."

"What have you both been doing since I saw you last?" the knight asked when the meal was finished.

Albert told how they had seen the Mayor constrained to open the bridge gates; how the Duke of Lancaster's palace at the Savoy had been burned, and the houses in the Temple pillaged and fired; and how the Flemings had been murdered in great numbers, and their houses sacked and in some cases burned.

"In faith, I am glad I was not there," Sir Ralph said, "for I think not that I could have kept my sword in its sheath, even though it had cost me my life."

"You charged us to take no part in broils, Father," Albert said with a smile, "and we felt, therefore, constrained to do nothing save on one occasion."

"Ah! ah!" the knight exclaimed in evident satisfaction; "then you did do something! I hope that you gave a lesson to one or more of these villains. Now that I look at you closely, it seems to me that you use your left arm but stiffly, Albert; and you have your hair cut away in one place, Edgar, and a strip of plaster on it. I thought it was the result of the fray in the Tower."

"No, sir, it was in the other matter. We each got some blows—some of them pretty hard ones—but they were of no great consequence."

"How did it come about, Albert?"

Albert gave a full account of the fray, from the time they came to the assistance of the Flemish girl until they escaped by the secret passage.

"By Saint George, wife," the knight said, "but these young esquires shame us altogether! While the king's knights and courtiers, his garrison of the Tower, and the worshipful citizens of London have not among them struck one blow at this rabbledom, they must have disposed of fully a score between them—seven, you say, in the Tower, and, I doubt not, a good thirteen at the door and on the stair of this Fleming's house—and to think that we considered this boy of ours fit for nothing else than to become a priest! This is the second time since we came up here a fortnight since that they have rescued a fair lady, to say nothing of their fathers, and without counting the saving of yourself and Aline; the sooner they are shipped off to France the better, or they will be causing a dearth of his Majesty's subjects. I am proud of you, lads. Who is this Fleming? Did you learn his name?"

"Yes, sir; it was Van Voorden."

"Say you so? It seems to me that you make choice of useful men upon whom to bestow benefits. Master Robert Gaiton is, as I learn, one of the leading citizens of London, a wealthy man, and one who in a few years is like to be mayor; and now you have befriended Van Voorden, who is the richest and most influential of the Flemish merchants in London. It is to him that the chancellor goes when he desires to raise a loan among the Flemings, and he always manages it without difficulty, he himself, as they say, contributing no small share of it. He is one who may be a good friend to you indeed, and who, should fortune take you to the Low Country, could recommend you to the greatest merchants there."

"He will be out there himself, father. He told us that he had for some little time been thinking of returning to Flanders, and that now he should do so at once. How was it, father, that the men-at-arms did not defend the Tower?"

"It was not altogether their fault. When it was determined that the king should ride out and meet the mob, the most stringent orders were given that on no account should the archers draw a bow upon the rabble. It is true that there were doubts whether many of them were not at heart with the people, which was not altogether unnatural, seeing that they were drawn from the same class and from the same counties. Still, doubtless, most of them would have proved true, and so long as they did their duty the others could hardly have held back; but, in truth, this had naught to do with the order, which was simply given to prevent a broil between the garrison and the mob, for had some of the latter been killed, it might have cost the king his life and the lives of all with him.

"No one, however, thought for a moment that the rabble would have attacked the Tower. We supposed, of course, that the drawbridge would be raised as soon as we had passed over it, but whether the order was not given for it or whether it was misunderstood I know not, but the blunder has cost the lives of the archbishop, the lord treasurer, and others, the insult to the princess, and the disgrace of the Tower having been in the hands of this rascaldom. Well, I must be off there and see what is going to be done."

The knight found that the king had already gone to visit his mother, who had, after landing, been conveyed to a house called the Royal Wardrobe in Bayard's Castle Ward by the Thames, where he remained until the next morning. While there he learned that Wat the Tyler and a portion of the Kentish men had rejected contemptuously the charter with which the men from the counties north of the Thames had been perfectly satisfied, and which was all that they themselves had at first demanded. Another was drawn up craving further concessions. This was also rejected, as was a third.

"The king is going to mass at Westminster," the knight said, "and after that he will ride round the city. I shall go myself to Westminster with him, and you can both ride with me, for it may be that the king on his way may be met by the rabble, which is composed of the worst and most dangerous of all who have been out, for in addition to Tyler's own following, there will be the prisoners released from all of the jails and the scum of the city. We will ride in our armour. They say there are still 20,000 of them, but even if the worst happens we may be able to carry the king safely through them."

In the morning they took horse. The knight was in full armour; Edgar and Albert were in body armour with steel caps. He skirted the walls of the city and rode to Westminster. At the Abbey they found the Lord Mayor and many of the leading citizens also in armour, they having come to form an escort for the king. Richard arrived by water with several knights and gentlemen who had accompanied him on his visit to his mother. Mass was celebrated, and the king then paid his devotions before a statue of the Virgin, which had the reputation of performing many miracles, particularly in favour of English kings. After this he mounted his horse and rode off with the barons, knights, and citizens—in all some sixty persons.

"There they are," Sir Ralph said, as a great crowd were seen gathered in West Smithfield. "I have some curiosity to see this knave Tyler. I hear from one of the knights with the king that he had the insolence to demand, in addition to all the concessions offered, that all forest laws should be abolished, and that all warrens, waters, parks, and woods should be made common land, so that all might fish in all waters, hunt the deer in forests and parks, and the hare wherever they chose."

When they approached the rioters, the king checked his horse, and made a sign that he would speak with them. Wat the Tyler at once rode forward, telling his followers to stand fast until he gave the signal.

"The insolent varlet!" Sir Ralph muttered, grasping the hilt of his sword; "see, he lifts not his cap to the king, but rides up as if he were his equal!"

The Tyler, indeed, rode up until his horse's head touched the flank of the king's horse, and he and Richard were knee to knee. Nothing could exceed the insolence of his demeanour.

M 371

THE LORD MAYOR STABS WAT THE TYLER IN PRESENCE
OF THE BOY-KING.

"King," he said, "do you see all these men here?"

"I see them," Richard replied. "Why dost thou ask?"

"Because," the Tyler said, "they are all at my will, sworn to do whatsoever I shall bid them."

So threatening and insolent was his manner as he spoke, keeping his hand on his sword, that the Lord Mayor, who was riding next to the king, believed that he intended to do Richard harm, and drawing a short sword, stabbed him in the throat. Wat the Tyler reeled on his horse, and Ralph Standish, one of the king's esquires, thrust him through the body, and he fell dead. A great shout arose from his followers, and, fitting their arrows to the strings of their bows, they ran forward with cries of vengeance. The knights and gentlemen drew their swords, but Richard, signing to them not to advance, rode forward.

"What are you doing, my lieges?" he cried. "Wat the Tyler was a traitor. I am your king, and I will be your captain and guide."

The mob stood irresolute. Although they had declared war against his councillors, they had always professed loyalty to the boy king himself. The king then rode back to his party.

"What had we best do now?" he asked the Lord Mayor.

"We had best make for the fields, sire," the latter said; "if they see us attempt to retreat they will gain heart and courage and will rush upon us, while if we advance we may gain a little time. Sir Robert Knowles is gathering a force in the city, and I have issued an order for all loyal citizens to join him; they will soon be with us, then we shall put an end to the matter."

Slowly the party proceeded onwards; the mob, silent and sullen, opened a way for them to pass, and then followed close behind them. Deprived of their leader they knew not what to do, and as no one else came forward to take the command, they did nothing until the king reached the open fields by Islington. As he did so, Sir Robert Knowles, with a following of upwards of a thousand men, rode up from the city and joined him. The mob at once took to flight, some running through the corn-fields, while others threw away their bows and other weapons, dropping upon their knees and crying for mercy.

"Shall I charge them, your Majesty? We will speedily make an end of the affair altogether."

"No," Richard replied, "many of them are but poor varlets who have been led astray. They are no longer dangerous, and we shall have time to deal with their leaders later on."

It was with the greatest difficulty that Sir Robert and the citizens, who were burning with a desire to avenge the dishonour thrown upon the city by the doings of the rioters, were restrained from taking their revenge upon them.

"Nay, nay, gentlemen," the king said, "they are unarmed and defenceless, and it would be an ill deed to slay them unresistingly. Rest content, I will see that due punishment is dealt out."

"The king is right," Sir Ralph said, as he sheathed his sword. "As long as they stood in arms I would gladly have gone at them, but to cut them down without resistance is a deed for which I have no stomach. It was a courageous action of the young king, lads, thus to ride alone to that angry crowd armed with bills and bows. Had one of them loosed an arrow at him all would have shot, and naught could have saved his life, while we ourselves would all have been in a perilous position. Well, there is an end of the matter. The knaves will scarce cease running until they reach their homes."

In the meantime the insurgents throughout the country

had done but little. The nobles shut themselves up in their castles, but the young Bishop of Norwich armed his retainers, collected his friends, and marched against the insurgents in Norfolk, Cambridge, and Huntingdon. He surprised several bodies of peasants and utterly defeated them. The prisoners taken were brought before him, and putting off the complete armour which he wore, he heard the confession of his captives, gave them absolution, and then sent them straight to the gibbet. With the return of the peasants to their homes the gentlemen from the country were able to come with their retainers to town, and Richard found himself at the head of forty thousand men.

He at once annulled the charters that had been wrung from him, while commissioners were sent throughout the country to arrest and try the leaders of the insurrection, and some fifteen hundred men, including all the leaders, were executed. The men of Essex alone took up arms again, but were defeated with great loss, as was to be expected. When parliament met they not only approved the annulment of the charters, but declared that such charters were invalid without their consent, and passed several stringent laws to deter the people from venturing upon any repetition of the late acts. Later on, the Commons presented petitions calling for the redress of abuses in administration, attributing this insurrection to the extortions of the tax-collectors, and the venality and rapacity of judges and officers of the courts of law.

On the day following the death of Wat the Tyler Sir Ralph told the lads that the king desired to see them.

"He was good enough to ask me this morning how you had fared, and I told him how you had rescued my dame and daughter, and also how you had befriended Mynheer Van Voorden, and he at once asked me to bring you again to him."

The king received them in private. "By Saint George, gentlemen," he said, "had all my knights and followers proved themselves as valiant as you, we should have had no difficulty in dealing with these knaves! It seems to me strange, indeed, that, while you are but a year older than myself, you should have fought so valiantly, and killed so many of these rioters."

"Your Majesty should hardly think that strange," Edgar said courteously, "seeing how you yourself performed a far more valiant action, by riding up to twenty thousand angry men with bows drawn and pikes pointed. I trembled, and felt well-nigh sick when I saw you thus expose yourself to what seemed certain death. In our case the risk was but small, for in the fray here we had to deal with men flushed with wine, and knowing naught of the use of their weapons; and it was the same thing in the house of the Fleming, where, moreover, we had the advantage of ground."

The young king was evidently pleased at the compliment. "It seemed to me that it was the only thing to do," he said, "and I had no time to think of the danger. I have told Sir Ralph de Courcy that I would gladly knight you both, in proof of my admiration for your courage; but he has pointed out to me that you are as yet young, and that he would prefer—and believed that you also would do so—to wait until you had an opportunity of winning your spurs in combat with a foreign foe. However, it is but deferred, and I promise you that as soon as you are two years older I will bestow knighthood upon you. I myself would willingly," he added with a smile, "have laid Van Voorden under an obligation. He is a very Crœsus, and I regard him as my banker, for he is ever ready to open his money-bags, and to make me advances upon any tax that may have been ordered. Have you seen him since the fray?"

"No, sire. We are going to him when we leave you, to tell

him that order is restored, and that he may now without danger leave his hiding-place."

"Van Voorden is not the only merchant in London that my son and Master Ormskirk have had the good fortune to aid since their arrival here, your Majesty, for they rescued from an attack by robbers outside Aldersgate, Master Robert Gaiton, who is an alderman and a foreign merchant. He had his daughter with him, and had the lads arrived a minute later the two would have been killed."

"I know him," the king said; "he was one of those who rode with the Lord Mayor from Westminster with me. Please tell me all about it. I love to hear of brave deeds."

Albert told the story of the rescue.

"It was well done indeed," the king said. "I would that I could ramble about and act the knight-errant as you do. 'Tis tiresome to be in the hands of councillors, who are ever impressing upon me that I must not do this or that, as if I were a child. I would gladly have you here about my person, but, as Sir Ralph has told me, you would fain, at any rate for the present, devote yourselves to arms, I did not press the matter; but be assured that at any time you will find in me a friend. You have but to ask a boon, and whatsoever it is, if it be in my power, I will grant it, and I hope that some day I shall find you settled at court, where," and he laughed, "it seems to me that honours, if not honour, are much more easily gained than in the battlefield."

Leaving the king's presence, the lads went into the city. Van Voorden had showed them how the sliding panel might be opened from the outside. Already the city had resumed its usual appearance, and the people were going about their business. They therefore found the door of the house opposite Van Voorden's standing open. Waiting until they saw that no one was near, they entered, opened the sliding panel, and, closing it carefully behind them, descended the stairs. On reaching the iron door Edgar gave three knocks, the signal that they had arranged with the Fleming. It was opened at once.

"Welcome, my friends!" Van Voorden said as they entered. "I have not ventured out, thinking that it would be better to remain quiet for at least a week, rather than run any risk. What news do you bring me?"

"Good news, sir," Edgar replied; "the insurrection is at an end, the men of the northern counties have marched away, the Tyler has been killed and his followers have fled, loyal gentlemen with their retainers are coming in fast, all is quiet here, the shops are open, and save for the ruins of burnt houses there are no signs of the evil days that we have passed through."

"That is good news indeed. My dame is better, but I shall be glad to get her out into the light and air. I will sally out with you at once and look for a lodging, where we may bestow ourselves until I have wound up my affairs and am ready to start for Flanders."

This business was soon settled. The Fleming found a compatriot whose house had escaped sack, but who had been so alarmed that he intended to return home at once, until order was completely restored throughout the country, and he decided to let his house as it stood to Van Voorden. As a vessel was sailing that evening, he arranged to give up possession at once.

"I will, with your permission," said Van Voorden, "fetch my wife and daughter here forthwith. The former has so far recovered from her malady that she will not need to be carried hither, but I want to get her out from the hiding-place where she now is, for, in truth, in spite of the precautions that were taken when it was built, the air is close and heavy."

"By all means do so at once," the Fleming said. "There is plenty of room in the house, for I embarked my wife and family ten days since, and there is no one but myself and the servants here."

On the way Van Voorden had been warmly greeted by many acquaintances, all of whom had believed him to have been killed by the rioters before they fired his house, and on issuing out now he met Robert Gaiton.

"I am glad, indeed, to see you, Mynheer," the latter said. "I feared that you and yours had all perished."

"That we did not do so was owing to the valour of these gentlemen, Master Robert; let me introduce them to you."

"I need no introduction," the merchant said, smiling, "for it is to their valour also that I owe it that you see me here alive. If you can spare time to come and take your meal with me, which should be ready by this time, I will tell you about it, and will hear from you also how they have done you a like service."

"I will do so gladly," Van Voorden said, "for they will not be expecting me back for some time, as they would not deem that I could so soon find a house for them to go to."

"Of course you will come too?" said Gaiton.

"With your permission we will decline your offer," Albert said. "My father is detained at the Tower, and my mother and sister are alone, and will be expecting us."

"Well, I will not press you. I do not suppose that you care about having your good actions talked about."

"Truly, Master Robert, these young gentlemen have rendered us both rare service," Van Voorden said after he and Gaiton had both told their stories. "I see not how I am to discharge any of my obligations to them. If they had taken us both captives in war they would have put us to ransom and we could have paid whatever was demanded, but in this case we do not stand so."

"I feel that myself, Mynheer. A knight considers himself in no ways lowered by taking ransom from a captive, or by receiving a purse of gold from his sovereign. But his notions of honour will scarce admit of his taking money for a service rendered. I have promised to fit them out with arms, armour, and a war-horse when they go on service; but beyond that, which is after all but a trifle to me, I see not what to do."

"I am sorry that you have forestalled me," Van Voorden said, "for I had thought of doing that myself. I may do them a service if they should chance at any time to go to Flanders; but beyond that I see not that I can do aught at present. Later on, when they become knights, and take wives for themselves, I shall step in and buy estates for them to support their rank, and methinks that they will not refuse the gift."

"I shall claim to take part with you in that matter," Robert Gaiton said. "I cannot count guineas with you, but I am a flourishing man, and as I have but one daughter to marry, I have no need for my money beyond what is engaged in trade."

"Well, we won't quarrel over that," the Fleming replied. "However, for the present it were best to say naught of our intentions. They are noble lads. Edgar is the leading spirit, and, indeed, the other told me, when they were waiting till it was safe for them to leave the hiding-place, that he had been a very weakly lad, and had been intended for the Church, but that Edgar had been a great friend of his, had urged him to practise in arms, which so increased his strength that he was, to his father's delight, able to abandon the idea. He said that all he knew of arms he had acquired from Edgar, and that, while he was still but an indifferent swordsman, his friend was wonderfully skilled with his weapon, and fully a match for most men."

"That he has proved for both of our benefits," Robert Gaiton said. "In truth, they are in all ways worthy youths. I have seen much of them during the last few days, and like them greatly, irrespective of my gratitude for what they did for me."

On the following day the king knighted the Lord Mayor, William Walworth, Robert Gaiton, and five other aldermen who had ridden with him, and granted an augmentation to the arms of the city, introducing a short sword or dagger in the right quarter of the shield, in remembrance of the deed by which the Lord Mayor had freed him from the leader of the rioters.

Van Voorden called with Robert Gaiton upon Sir Ralph to thank him for the services his son and Edgar had rendered him, and heard for the first time how they had saved Dame Agatha and Aline from insult, and had slain the seven rioters, of whom five had fallen to Edgar's sword.

"Truly a brave deed, and a prudent one," Sir Robert Gaiton said. "Once begun, it was a matter of life and death that the business should be carried out to the end."

"His Majesty has highly commended them," Sir Ralph said, "and would fain have knighted them had they been a year or two older."

"I see not that age should have stood in the way," Van Voorden broke in. "Of a surety no men could have done better, and as they have behaved as true knights in all respects, methinks they deserve the rank."

"I cannot say you nay there, though I am the father of one of them; nevertheless, they can well wait for a couple of years. They have not yet learned that the first duty of a knight is to obey, and it were well they served under some brave captain, and learned how to receive as well as give orders. To-morrow, gentlemen, I ride to St. Alwyth, for news has come in that the Kentish rebels, as well as those of Essex, are burning and slaying on their way to their homes, and I must go and see to the safety of my castle. A force will march to-morrow morning to deal with the Essex men."

"Then, Sir Ralph, I will ride with you," Sir Robert said. "I have raised a troop of fifty men from my ward to join those the city is gathering for the king's aid. They are stout fellows, and will, I warrant, fight well; and they will do as good service for the king in Kent as they would do in Essex."

"Nay; while thanking you for your offer, I cannot so trouble you, Sir Robert."

"'Tis no trouble. On the contrary, after what your son did for me, it will be a pleasure to lift some small share of the burden of obligation from my shoulders, and if you will not let me ride with you, I shall go down on my own account."

"I thank you heartily, Sir Robert, and assuredly will not refuse so good an offer, for my men in the castle are scarce numerous enough to make defence against a strong attack. I doubt not that all the serfs on the estate have been in the Tyler's following, and my vassals would scarce be enough, even if I could gather them, to make head against a crowd."

"When do you start, Sir Ralph?"

"As soon as the gate at Aldgate is open I shall ride through it."

"Then I will be at the head of the bridge, awaiting you with my men."

"I am afraid that I cannot send a contingent, Sir Knight," Van Voorden said, "for so many of my countrymen have been slaughtered that we could scarce gather a company."

"Nay; I shall have enough with those our good friend will bring me. With him by my side, and my son, and that stout swordsman, young Edgar, and with fifty sturdy Londoners, who have always in their wars proved themselves to be as good fighters as any in our armies, I would ride through a host of the rabble."

"Will you be returning, Sir Ralph?"

"Yes; I leave my wife and daughter here, and as soon as matters are settled, come back to fetch them."

"Then may I beg you to leave them with me?" the Fleming said earnestly. "They will hardly wish to go back to the Tower at present, after their late experience of it. My wife and daughter will do their best to make them comfortable."

"I accept your invitation for them thankfully," the knight replied. "The Tower is already crowded, so many ladies and gentlemen have come in during the last few days; nor do I like to leave them here without protection."

"I thank you most heartily, Sir Knight. It will be a pleasure, indeed, to my wife and daughter to have ladies with them, for indeed both are somewhat shaken from what they have gone through. I will, if it pleases you, be at the gate to-morrow if they will accompany you so far, and will escort them to my house; or, should you prefer it, my wife will come thither with me to take them back after they have had their morning meal."

"Thanks, sir; but I will escort them myself and hand them over to you. Will you kindly bring a servant with you to carry their valises, for I had yesterday all their things removed from that room in the Tower, and at the same time had the dead bodies of the rioters carried down and thrown into the Thames?"

"I wish that there was more that I could do," Van Voorden said to Sir Robert Gaiton as they walked back to the city.

"I will tell you what you can do, Master Van Voorden. I had the intention of doing it myself; but if you wish it I will relinquish it to you. I marked as we rode two days since to Smithfield that our friend's son and Master Edgar Ormskirk had but body armour and wore steel caps, and I intended to buy this afternoon two complete suits for them."

"I thank you greatly for your offer; it would be a relief to me to do something for them. Know you about their size?"

"To within an inch, for I fitted them on two citizen suits. If you like I will go with you to Master Armstrong's. He is accounted the best armourer in the county, and provides no small share of the armour for our knights and nobles."

"I know his name well," the Fleming said. "I shall be glad if you will accompany me to choose them, for indeed I am but a poor judge of such matters."

"I would fain have two suits of the best armour in your store, Master Armstrong," Van Voorden said, as he entered the armourer's shop. "The cost is a matter of no account, but I want the best, and I know that no one can supply better than yourself. My friend, Sir Robert Gaiton, will do the choosing for me."

The armourer bowed to the wealthy Fleming, who was well known to everyone in the city.

"'Tis but a matter of size that I have to decide upon," the alderman said. "See and get the suits somewhat large, for the gentlemen for whom Mynheer Van Voorden intends them have not yet come to their full stature."

The armourer led them to an inner room. "These are

my best suits," he said, pointing to a score of lay-figures in armour ranged along the wall. "They would soon get tarnished were they exposed to the fogs of London. They are all of foreign make save these two, which, as you see, are less ornamented than the rest. The others are all of Spanish or Milanese workmanship. These two suits are my own make. Our craftsmen are not so skilled in inlaying or ornamenting as the foreigners, but I will guarantee the temper of the steel and its strength to keep out a lance thrust, a cross-bow bolt, or a cloth-yard arrow against the best of them."

"Methinks, Mynheer," the alderman said, "that if these suits are of the right size they were better than the Italian or Spanish suits. In the first place, these others would scarce be in keeping with two young men who are not yet knights, seeing that they are such as would be worn by wealthy nobles; in the next place, there is no saying how much the lads may grow; and lastly, I have myself promised their father to present them with a suit of armour when they obtain the rank of knighthood."

"So be it, then," the Fleming said. "If Master Armstrong guarantees the suits equal in strength to the others I care not, and indeed there is reason in what you say as to their fitness for the youths."

"Will you run a yard measure round the shoulders," Sir Robert said. One was forty inches, the other thirty-six.

"That will do well; one is bigger than the other, and the measurement will give them an inch or two to spare. And now as to heights. The one is five feet ten, the other an inch less; but this matters little, seeing that another strip of steel can be added or one taken away from the leg pieces without difficulty. I think that they will do excellently well. And now, what is the price?"

It was a heavy one, for the armour was of exceptional

make and strength by reason of its temper, but was still
light, the excellence of the steel rendering it unnecessary to
get anything like the weight of ordinary armour.

Van Voorden made no attempt to bargain, but merely
said, "Please send them round at once to the Golden Fleece,
in the Poultry, which was till yesterday the abode of Master
Nicholas Leyd, and also furnish me with the bill by your
messenger."

"My son will come," said the armourer, "with two men
to carry the armour, and in a quarter of an hour the suits
shall be at your door."

"Send also, I pray you, swords and daggers of the finest
temper with each suit, and add the charge to the account."

CHAPTER X.

A FIGHT IN THE OPEN.

IT was seven in the evening, and Sir Ralph and his family
had just finished their evening meal, when one of the
retainers announced that two porters had brought a letter
and some goods from Mynheer Van Voorden.

"Let them bring the goods in here," Sir Ralph said, "and
then take them into the kitchen and give them a tankard of
ale and refreshment, and keep them there till we have a
letter ready for their master."

The party were surprised to see the bulky parcels brought
in.   One of the men handed a letter addressed to Sir
Ralph. "Go with my retainers, my good fellows," the latter
said, "and remain until I see what your master says. Here,
Albert, my scholarship is rusty; read what the Fleming
says; it may tell us what are in those crates."

"They are not for you, father," Aline, who had run across to look at them, said: "one is for Albert and the other for Edgar."

The letter was as follows:—

To the good knight, Sir Ralph de Courcy, greeting—It seems to me that, prone as your son and Master Edgar Ormskirk are to rush into danger in order to aid and succour those in peril, it were but right that they should be clad in armour suitable for such adventures, and meet that such armour should be provided for them by one of those who has benefited by their valour, whose life and that of his wife and daughter have been preserved by them. Therefore I send them two suits as the only token I can at present give them of my thankfulness and gratitude. It is feeble testimony indeed, but none the less sincere. I know well that the armour made by Master Armstrong could be borne by none worthier, and trust that the swords will ever be used in the cause of right and in the protection of the oppressed and the unfortunate.

Aline clapped her hands joyfully as Albert finished reading the letter.

"A timely gift indeed," the knight said; and one that does honour both to the giver and those who receive it. Open the crates, lads, and let us see what the worthy Fleming has sent us."

The casques were the first pieces that came to view. Albert carried his to his father, while Aline placed Edgar's on the table in front of Dame Agatha. The knight examined it carefully.

"I know the suit," he said, "for I was in the armourer's shop a week before these troubles began, with the Earl of Suffolk, who had asked me to go with him to choose a suit.

This, and another like it, stood in one corner, and mightily took my fancy, though others were there from the master armourers of Milan and Toledo. These two suits were, however, he thought, not as fine and ornamental as he should like; indeed, they were scarce large enough for him, for he is well-nigh as big as I am myself, and he chose a Milan suit; but Master Armstrong said to me, 'I see you know a good piece of steel, Sir Knight, for methinks those two suits are the best that I have ever forged, and I would not part with them for less than the price of the very finest of those inlaid ones. I have tried their strength in every way and am proud of them, but it may be that I shall keep them here for some time before I sell them. The foreign arms are now all the fashion, and those who can afford the best would take the more showy of the foreign suits, but I would not bate a penny in their price were these two suits to stand in my shop as long as I live. Do you see that tiny mark?—you need to look closely at it to make it out. That was made by a cloth-yard arrow shot by an archer, who is reputed the strongest in the city, and who carries a bow that few others can bend to its full; he shot at a distance of five yards, and I doubt if among all those suits you would find one that would have stood such a test without a deep dint.' 'Tis a noble gift, lads, and the Fleming, whom I should hardly take to be a judge of armour, must either have had a good adviser with him, or he must have trusted himself wholly to Master Armstrong's advice."

"'Tis like enough, father, that Sir Robert Gaiton may have gone with him to choose them when they left us yesterday. I have heard him say that though 'tis in the stuffs of Italy and the East that he chiefly deals, that his agents abroad sometimes send him suits of the finest Milan armour, swords of Damascus, and other such things for which he can always find purchasers among the nobles who deal with him.   He therefore would probably be a good judge."

By this time the crates were completely unpacked, and the armour, with the swords and daggers, laid upon the table, where the two lads surveyed them in silent admiration.

"Put them on," Sir Ralph said.   "I know that you are longing to do so, and it would be strange were you not. Do you buckle them on the lads, dame.   You have done me the service many a time, and it is right that you should be the first to do it for Albert.   Aline, do you wait upon Edgar.   As you are new to such work, your mother will show you how to do it, but seeing that he has struck five mortal blows in your defence, it is right that you should do him this service."

Aline coloured with pleasure.   Her mother first instructed her how to arm Edgar, and then herself buckled on Albert's harness.   Their swords were girt on, and the casques added last of all.

"They look two proper esquires, wife," the knight said; "and as we ride to-morrow I shall make but a sorry show beside them."

"Ah, father!" said Albert, "but your armour has many an honourable mark, and it can be seen that, if it is not as bright as ours, 'tis in battle that its lustre has been lost, while all can see that, bright as our armour may be, it has not had the christening of battle."

"Well put!" his mother said softly.   "There was no more noble figure than your father when I first buckled his armour on for him.   It was a new suit he had taken from a great French lord he had overthrown in battle, and I was as proud of him as I now feel of you, for you have shown yourself worthy of him, and though your arms are unmarked 'tis but because your battles were fought before you had them."

"We had hardly ventured to hope for this, dame," Sir Ralph said, with a strange huskiness in his throat. "No knight could have begun a career more creditably or more honourably. Three times has he fought—once on behalf of you and Aline, twice for men and women in danger. In what better causes could he have first fleshed his sword? Now unbuckle him at once, dame, that he may write in my name a letter of thanks to this noble Fleming. I have not written a letter for years, and our friend would scarce be able to decipher it were I to try." Then he went on as she removed Albert's casque: "There was good taste as well as judgment in the purchase of those arms, Agatha. To me who knows what arms are, they are superb, but to the ordinary eye they would seem no better than those generally worn by knights or by esquires of good family; whereas, had he bought one of these damascened suits it would at once have attracted attention, and the lads would have been taken for great nobles. I doubt not that guided the stout alderman in his choice. He is a man of strong sense and sober taste, and had he not been born a merchant he would have made a rare good fighter."

As soon as Albert's harness was taken off he sat down and wrote, in his fair clerkly hand, a letter of the warmest thanks on the part of Sir Ralph, Edgar, and himself to Van Voorden. After this had been sent off, the swords and daggers were examined and admired, Sir Ralph declaring the former to be of the finest Toledo steel and the latter to come from Damascus. Edgar had said little, but he was even more delighted with his new acquisition than Albert. To have a good suit of armour had been his greatest ambition, but his father was by no means wealthy, and he had thought that his only chance of obtaining such a suit would be to overthrow some French noble in battle.

The next morning they were up betimes, and mounted a few minutes before the hour at which the city gates would be opened. Sir Ralph and his dame rode first, Aline took her place between her brother and Edgar, the latter keeping a watchful eye over her horse, which was fresh after six or seven days' idleness. The two retainers rode behind, having the ladies' valises strapped behind them. The city churches rang out the hour when they were within a hundred yards of the gate, and as this opened, Van Voorden, with his daughter behind him on a pillion, rode out to meet them, followed by two mounted men.

"That is thoughtful and courteous of him, dame," the knight said. "He might well have come alone; but it is kindly of him as well as courteous to bring his daughter."

As the party met, the Fleming bowed deeply to Lady Agatha.

"I have brought my daughter with me," he said, "in that I might introduce her to you, and that she might assure you, in her mother's name, of the pleasure your visit will give her."

"'Tis kind and courteous of you, Mynheer Van Voorden," Dame Agatha said, as, leaning over, she shook his daughter's hand.

"My mother bade me say that she is impatiently waiting your coming, and that your visit will give her the greatest pleasure—and yours also, Mistress Aline," she added as the girl rode up, "and I am sure that it will give me great pleasure too."

Joanna Van Voorden was some two years older than Aline. Both were fair, but of a different type, for while Aline's hair was golden, Joanna's was of a tawny red. Even making allowance for the difference in age, she was of a heavier build than the English girl, and gave signs of growing up into a stately woman.

"And now, Master Van Voorden," the knight said as the latter turned his horse and they proceeded on their way, "I must repeat in person what I said in my letter, how deeply obliged we are to you for the superb suits of armour you sent last night to my son and his friend."

"Speak not of it again, I pray you," the merchant said. "I owe them a debt of gratitude that I never can hope to repay, and the harness was indeed but a slight token of it. I can only hope that some day I may have an opportunity of more worthily testifying my gratitude. We shall scarcely be able to lodge you, lady," he went on, turning to Dame Agatha, "as I could have done in my house at Bread Street, for the one I have hired, although comfortable enough, is much less commodious; still, I doubt not that you will find your rooms more comfortable than those you occupied in the Tower, for indeed, as yet, even English palaces, stately though they be, have not the comforts that we Flemings have come to regard as necessaries."

"So I have understood, sir, but I think that some of our city merchants cannot be far behind you, judging from what my daughter has told me of the abode of Sir Robert Gaiton."

"No; many of the London traders are in this respect far better housed than any of the nobles with whose castles I am acquainted, and Sir Robert has, in Italy and elsewhere, had opportunities of seeing how the merchant princes there live. I have known him for some years. He is one of the foremost men in the city; he has broad and liberal ideas, and none of the jealousy of us Flemings that is so common among the citizens, although my countrymen more directly rival him in his trade than they do many others who grumble at us, though they are in no way injured by our trading."

So they chatted until they reached the spot where the knight required to turn off towards the bridge. There was a moment's pause, the valises were transferred to the saddles of the Van Voorden's followers, while adieux were exchanged. Then the Fleming's party turned to the right, while the knight, Edgar, Albert, and the two retainers trotted down at a smart pace to the bridge. Here Sir Robert Gaiton, in full armour, with fifty stout men-at-arms, were awaiting them.

"Good morrow, Sir Ralph! and you, young sirs!" Sir Robert said as they rode up. "Let me congratulate you on your armour, which becomes you mightily."

"And for which," Sir Ralph put in, "I think we have somewhat to thank you for choosing."

"Yes; I went with Van Voorden to Master Armstrong's, not so much to choose the harness as to give my opinion as to the size required, and these suits greatly took my fancy, the armourer guaranteeing their temper; and they were, as it seemed to me, about the right size, for although just at first they may be somewhat roomy, 'tis a matter that a few months will mend.

"Are they comfortable, Edgar?" he added.

"I suppose as much so as any armour can be, Sir Robert; but 'tis the first time I have worn such things, and they seem to me marvellously to confine me, and with the vizor down I should feel well-nigh stifled in my casque, and as if fighting in the dark."

"You will get accustomed to it in a short time. I know that when I began to be known in the city, and found that I must, like others of the better class of citizens, ride in full armour when occasion offered, I felt just as you do, perhaps more so, for I was some seven or eight years older, and less accustomed to changes; but even now I would far rather fight with my vizor up, save that one must have its protection when arrows or cross-bow bolts are flying; but as against other knights I would always keep it up; the helm itself and the cheek-pieces cover no small part of the face, and nought but a straight thrust could harm one, and I think I could trust my sword to ward that off. However, I have never yet had occasion to try. I have had more than one encounter with Eastern and African pirates during my voyages, but I have never taken my helmet with me on such journeys, and have not suffered by its loss."

By this time they were across the bridge, and proceeding at a sharp trot until beyond the boundaries of Southwark, they broke into a gallop. When, after going at this pace for three or four miles, they reined their horses into a walk, Sir Ralph said, "Albert, if it likes you, you can remove your helmet and carry it on your saddle-bow."

"Thanks, father; indeed I was well-nigh reeling in my saddle with heat. Edgar, will you take yours off?"

"No, thank you, I have got to get accustomed to it, and may as well do so now as at any other time." Under their helmet both wore a small velvet cap. "You are looking quite pale, Albert," Edgar went on, as his friend unhelmed.

"It is not everyone who is made of iron, as you are," Albert laughed. "You must make allowances for me. In another year or two I hope that I too shall be able to bear the weight of all these things without feeling them; but you must remember that it is not two years since I began hard exercise, while you have been at it since your childhood."

"I don't forget it, Albert, and I wonder at you daily."

At Greenwich they heard many tales as to the damage

committed by the peasants on their homeward way. Houses had been sacked and burnt, and many persons of substance killed.

"The king ought to have let us charge the fellows," Sir Ralph said, as they went forward again. "When men find that they get off without punishment for misdeeds, they will recommence them as soon as the danger is past. One lesson would have made itself felt over the whole land. I heard last night that there was news that many manors and the houses of men of law have been destroyed in Essex, and that the rioters have beheaded the Lord Chief Justice of England, Sir John of Cambridge, and the Prior of St. Edmondsbury, and set up their heads on poles in the market-place of Bury, and have destroyed all the charters and documents of the town. We shall have great trouble before order is restored, whereas had we charged the rioters of Kent, who are the worst of all, the others would have been cowed when they heard of the slaughter. By our Lady, we will give these fellows a rough lesson if we find them besieging our castle."

"Is it a strong place, Sir Ralph?"

"No. With a fair garrison it could easily repel any assault by such fellows as these, but it could not stand for a day against an attack by a strong body of men-at-arms, even if they were unprovided with machines."

When within five miles of the castle they obtained sure news that it was attacked by some two thousand of the rioters, but that so far as was known it was still holding out.

"Shall we gallop on, Sir Ralph?" the alderman asked.

"Nay, we will rather go more slowly than before, so that our horses may be in good wind when they arrive. We shall need all their strength, for we may have to charge through them two or three times before they break and run, and then we will pursue and cut them up as long as the horses have breath. These fellows must have a lesson, or we shall never be able to dwell in peace and quiet."

When within half a mile of the castle they saw that the flag was still flying above it, and knew that they had arrived in time. Then Albert put on his helmet again, and the two lads followed the example of Sir Ralph and the aldermen, and lowered their vizors, for, as the knight said, "Though some of the knaves threw away their bows at Smithfield, many of the others took them away." On reaching a field near the castle, they could see that a fierce fight was going on. The rioters had procured ladders, and were striving to climb the walls, while a small party of armed men were defending the battlement.

"By St. Mary, we are but just in time!" the knight said. "We four will ride in front. Sir Robert, will you bid your men form in two lines and follow us, one line twenty yards behind the other. Bid them all keep together in their rank, the second line closing up with the first if the fellows make a stout resistance; but above all things they must keep in their order, and follow close behind us."

The alderman raised his voice, and repeated the orders to the men.

"The reports as to the rascals' numbers were about right," Sir Ralph said. "Now, boys, do you keep between us, and leave a space of some three yards between each horse, so as to give each man room to swing his sword. Now, Sir Robert, let us have at them."

Going slowly at first, they increased their speed to a fierce gallop as they neared the mass of rioters. They had been noticed now. The men on the ladders hastily climbed down again; confused orders were heard, and many were seen separating themselves from the main body and flying. The mass of the rioters, however, held their ground, seeing how small was the number of their opponents. A flight of arrows was shot when they were some sixty yards distant, but as all were bending forward in their saddles, and the arrows were shot in haste, most of them fell harmless; three or four of the horses were struck, and plunged violently from the pain, but still kept on with the others. With a shout the party fell upon the rioters, the weight of the riders and horses throwing great numbers to the ground, while the knights and their followers hewed right and left with their swords.

The bravest spirits had thrown themselves in front, and once the troops had cut their way through these, but little resistance was met with beyond, the peasants seeking only to get out of their way. As soon as they were through the crowd they turned again, and in the same order as before charged the mob, with the same success. As they drew up and again turned, Sir Ralph ordered them to charge this time in single line.

"They are becoming utterly disheartened now," he said, "and we shall sweep a wider path."

This time when they drew up they saw that the crowd had broken up, and the rioters were flying filled with dismay through the fields.

"Chase and slay!" Sir Ralph shouted, raising his vizor that his voice might reach all; "give no quarter; the business must be ended once and for all."

Edgar and Albert both threw up their vizors—there was no fear of arrows now, and both felt half-stifled. There was no longer any order kept, and the horsemen followed the fugitives in all directions. The two lads kept together so as to be able to give each other assistance should any stand be made. None, however, was attempted; the greater portion of the rioters had thrown away their arms, and when overtaken they raised cries for mercy.

"You gave none to the Flemings," the lads shouted in return, infuriated by the scenes that they had witnessed in London; and for an hour they followed the fugitives, sparing none who came within reach of their swords.

"We have done enough now," Albert exclaimed at last; "I am fairly spent, and can scarce lift my sword."

"My horse is spent, but not my strength," Edgar said as he reined up. "Well, we have avenged the Flemings, and have done something towards paying these fellows for their insults to the Princess. Now let us wend our way back; I must say good-bye to Sir Ralph and the sturdy alderman, and will then ride home and see how my father has fared. I have little fear that any harm has befallen him, for his magic would frighten the rioters even more than our swords. Well, our armour has stood us in good stead, Albert. When we charged the first time I was several times struck with bill-hook and pike, and more than one arrow shivered on my breastpiece, but I found that the blows all fell harmless, and after that I wasted no pains in defending myself, but simply struck straightforward blows at my opponents."

"I found the same, Edgar; the weapons glanced off the armour as a stone would fly from a sheet of strong ice."

For a while they rode slowly to give their horses time to recover wind. When they had done so, they rode more rapidly, and, keeping a straight line,—they had before ridden a devious course in pursuit,—they arrived in an hour at the castle. Here they found that most of the horsemen had already returned. Two hundred bodies lay dead on the ground over which they had charged so often; and when notes were compared they calculated that no less than five hundred of the rioters had been slain.

"I think we shall hear no more of rioting in this neighbourhood," Sir Ralph said grimly. "If the king had but taken my advice and ridden out to Blackheath with his knights and half the garrison of the Tower, and with such aid as the loyal citizens would have furnished him, he and the city would have been spared the humiliation that they have suffered. One blow struck in time will save the need of twenty struck afterwards. Had we but killed a thousand on Blackheath it would have spared us the trouble of slaying perhaps ten times that number now; would have saved the lives of many honourable gentlemen throughout the country, to say nothing of the damage that has been wrought in London. So you are riding home, Edgar? You are right, lad; I trust you will find all quiet there."

"Would you like twenty of my men to ride with you?" the alderman asked.

"No, thank you, Sir Robert; my father, who, as I told you, is a man of science, has prepared sundry devices, any one of which would terrify these peasants out of their wits; and if they have troubled him, which is like enough, I will warrant that he has given them as great a scare as we have given these fellows to-day."

"At any rate, Edgar, you had best take a fresh horse. Yours has done a good day's work indeed; and it is just as well that you should bestride an animal that can carry you off gaily should you fall in with another party. There are half a dozen in the stalls. I don't suppose they have been out since we have been away; besides, methinks that after such hot work as we have been doing a cup of wine will do us all good."

Edgar therefore rode into the castle, and while he was taking a cup of wine and a hasty meal in the hall, Sir Ralph's servitors changed his saddle to a fresh horse, and the lad then started for home. Confident as he felt, it was still a great satisfaction to him to see that no signs of violence were visible as he approached the house. The door in the gate was indeed closed, contrary to usual custom.

Dismounting, he rung the bell. A small grille in the door opened, then the servitor's head appeared.

"Now then, Andrew, what are you staring at? Why don't you open the gate?"

"I was not sure that it was yourself, Master Edgar. In that grand helmet I did not at first make you out. Well, I am glad that you have come back safely, young master, for we heard of parlous doings in London."

"Yes, I have come back all right. I hope that everything has gone on well here."

"Ay, ay, sir; we had a bit of trouble, but, bless you, the master sent them running, most scared out of their senses." And the man burst into a fit of laughter.

"Here, take the horse, Andrew; I must go in to see him."

"Hulloa! hulloa!" Mr. Ormskirk exclaimed; "is this really my son?"

"It is, father; and right glad am I to see you safe and well. I told Sir Ralph that I felt sure you would be able to hold your own here; still, I was very pleased when I saw that the gate stood uninjured, and that there were no signs of attack."

"Has Sir Ralph come back?" Mr. Ormskirk asked; "and knows he that the rabble are besieging his castle?"

"Were besieging, father; for with us came a worthy city knight with a troop of fifty stout men; and we have given the rioters such a lesson that methinks there will be no more rioting in this part of Kent, for from four to five hundred of them have been slain, and I believe all the rest are still running!"

"It was a lesson much needed, Edgar, for after their doings in London these fellows would never have been quiet, had they not been roughly taught that they are but like a flock of sheep before the charge of men-at-arms.

"But whence this armour, my son? Truly it is a goodly suit. My coffer is so low that I know not how I shall make shift to pay for it."

"It is a gift, father, and Albert has one like it. 'Tis of the finest steel, and is, as you see, all undinted, though it has had many a shrewd blow from arrow, bill-hook, and pike in to-day's fight. But the story is a long one to tell, and I pray you, before I begin it, to let me know how matters have fared here, for I hear from Andrew that you have not been left entirely alone."

Mr. Ormskirk smiled. "No, I had a goodly company three days ago. Some hundred of men from Dartford, joined, I am sorry to say, by a good share of those at the village, came round here in the evening with the intent, as they were good enough to say, of roasting the witchman in his bed. Andrew had brought me news of their intentions, so I was ready for them. I had gone out and had painted on the door, with that stuff I told you of, the rough figure of a skeleton holding a dart in his hand. It was of the same colour as the door, so that it did not show in the daylight. Then I fixed along on the top of the wall a number of coloured lights that I had seen in use in Italy on fête days, and of which I learned the composition. I had, as I told you before, placed cases of Friar Bacon's powder round the house, and had laid trains to them by which they could be fired from within the wall.

"Had it been dark when they came the skeleton and that skull would have sufficed; but it wanted still an hour before these devices would be of use. I made them out in the distance, and thought that something else would be needed. Therefore I got that eastern gong that I purchased as a curiosity at Genoa, and lighted a fire in the courtyard. As soon as they approached I threw pitch into the fire, making thereby a great column of smoke, and set Andrew to beat the gong furiously, telling him to shout and yell as he pleased. Then I went to an upper window to observe the effect. The crowd had halted some fifty yards away and stood open-mouthed gazing at the place, and indeed it was no wonder that such ignorant men were scared, for truly the yelling of Andrew, and the noise of the gong, were enough to frighten anyone who knew not what it meant.

"For some time it seemed to me that they would depart without venturing farther, but some of the bolder spirits plucked up courage and went about among the others shouting that no true Kentish man would be frightened by a noise that meant nothing, they had but to break down the door and they would soon put an end to it. However, the night began to fall before they got fairly in motion, and I went down and prepared to fire the powder should it be needful, and besides I hoisted the skull above the parapet over the gate. Thinking that the light of the phosphorus might not show up well a short distance away, I placed in addition some red fire in the skull. I then got on the wall, and sat down where I could peep out without being seen. Shouting a great deal to encourage each other, they came on until within a few paces of the gate. Then I heard a sudden cry, and those in front pushed back and stood staring at the door as if bewitched; then all ran away some distance. After much talk they came forward again, timidly pointing to the figure as they advanced.

"This was now, doubtless, plain enough to be well made out fifty yards away. There they came to a halt again. Then I called out to Andrew to light the fire in the skull, and set the jaw wagging, having so balanced it, that having been once set going it would wag for two or three minutes before it stopped. Then he ran one way with a brand from the fire, and I the other, and twelve green fires burst out. There was a yell of horror when the skull was made out. The alarm was doubtless heightened by the green fire, they having never seen such a thing before, and they started to run wildly off. To hasten their flight I ran down and fired four of the powder cases, which exploded with a noise that might have been heard at Dartford.

"After that Andrew and I went quietly to bed, sure that not another soul would venture to attack the house. Andrew went into the village in the morning. He found that some of the men had been well-nigh killed by fright. All sorts of tales were told of great blazing skeletons that dashed out from the gate with dart in hand, and of a skull that breathed out red fire from a blazing mouth, and grinned and gibbered at them. As to the noises and the ghastly green fire, none could account for them, and I do believe that there is not a villager who would approach within a quarter of a mile of the house after dark, on any condition."

CHAPTER XI.

AN INVITATION.

EDGAR laughed heartily at his father's account of the success of his defence of the house. Then he said: "I hope, father, that distorted accounts of the affair may not get you into trouble with the Church."

"I have no fear of that, Edgar. I had shown the Prior my preparations, and he approved of them heartily, being a man of much broader intelligence than is common. Indeed, he begged of me a pot of my shining paste, and with it painted the stone crucifix over the Abbey gateway. And it was well that he did so, for last night some men came out from Dartford with intent to plunder the Priory of its deeds and muniments, but on seeing the glowing crucifix, they went off in fear and trembling, and the villagers were saying this morning that the Priory had been protected by a miracle, while you see in my case they attribute it to the work of the devil. And now, Edgar, tell me all that has befallen you since you went away."

Edgar related the various adventures that had happened.

When he had concluded, his father said: "Truly, Edgar, you have been fortunate indeed, which is another way of saying that you have skilfully grasped the opportunities that presented themselves. The man who bemoans ill fortune is the man too apathetic, too unready, or too cowardly to grasp opportunity. The man who is called fortunate is, on the other hand, he who never lets a chance slip by, who is cool, resolute, and determined. During the time that you have been away you have made friends of two wealthy merchants, and have rendered them both high services; you have also as greatly benefited our neighbour Sir Ralph de Courcy, and have placed your foot so firmly on the ladder, that 'tis your own fault if you do not rise high. And now, what think you of doing?"

"I have the intention of staying at home for a while, father. There will be troubles for a time, but I care not to take part in the hunting down of these poor peasants north of the river, who, unlike these fellows, were well content when the king offered them the charter granting their demands, and retired peacefully to their homes. So I would rather remain here quietly until I have a chance of drawing sword in a foreign war, either against the French or the Scots."

"I think that you are right; and, moreover, although you have proved your manhood against men, you can hardly, when with an army, be regarded as more than a young esquire till another year or two have gone over your head."

Two days later, finding that all was now perfectly quiet, and that there was no probability whatever of a renewal of the troubles, Sir Ralph went up to London with the city knight and his company. They had ridden over on the previous day to call upon Mr. Ormskirk to thank him for the services that Edgar had rendered them, and upon which they entered in much fuller detail than Edgar had allowed himself. In return he gave them a description of the defence of his house, in which Sir Robert was greatly interested, going down into the laboratory and examining the luminous paint and its effect upon the skull.

"It is a goodly device," he said, "and though I myself have, during my visit to Italy, come to believe but little in the superstitions that are held by the mass of the people, I own that my courage would have been grievously shaken if I had encountered suddenly that gibbering head. How long does the effect last?"

"Three or four days. I believe that it is a sort of slow combustion which, although it has no sensible heat, gradually consumes the particles that give rise to it. It may be that further researches will lead to a discovery by which the light might be made permanent, and in that case the invention would be a useful one. I have, however, no time to follow it up, being engaged in more serious matters, and regard this as a mere relaxation from more important work."

"And yet, methinks," the merchant said, "that were men of science, like yourself, to devote themselves to such discoveries, instead of searching for the secrets that always evade them, they might do good service to mankind. Look at this discovery of Friar Bacon's. So far, I grant that it has led to nothing, but I can see that in the future the explosive power of this powder will be turned to diverse uses besides those of machines for battering down walls. Were this light of yours made permanent it would do away with the necessity for burning lamps indoors. What could be more beautiful than a hall with its ceilings, rafters, walls, and pillars all glowing as if in the moonlight? For methinks the light resembles that of the moon rather than any other."

"Were I a young man I would take up such matters, Sir Robert, for I believe with you that the time might be more usefully spent; but 'tis too late now. 'Tis not when one's prime is past that men can embark in a fresh course or lay aside the work for which they have laboured for so many years."

"And which, even if made, might bring more woe than good upon the world," Sir Robert said. "Where would be the value of gold if other metals could at will be transformed into it? When first produced, it might enable monarchs to raise huge armies to wage war against their neighbours; but, after a time, its use would become common. Gold would lose it value, and men would come to think less of it than of iron, for it is not so strong nor so fitted for weapons or for tools; and then some other and rarer metal would take its place, and alchemists would begin their work again in discovering another philosopher's stone that would transmute other metals into the more valuable one."

Mr. Ormskirk was silent. "I think, Sir Robert," he said at last, "that we alchemists do not work solely for the good of mankind, nor give a thought to the consequences that might follow the finding of the philosopher's stone. We dream of immortality, that our name shall pass down through all ages as that of the man who first conquered the secret of nature and made the great discovery that so many thousands of others have sought for in vain."

"It is assuredly an ambition as worthy as many others," Sir Robert said thoughtfully. "A knight would be ready to risk his life a thousand times in order to gain the reputation of being one of the foremost knights of Europe. A king would wring the last penny from his subjects for a rich monument that will, he thinks, carry down his name to all time; and doubtless the discovery of a secret that has baffled research for hundreds of years, is at least as worthy an ambition as these,—far more laudable, indeed, since it can be carried out without inflicting woes upon others. And now farewell, Mr. Ormskirk! I trust that your son will always remember that in me he has a friend ready to do aught in his power for him. I am but a simple citizen of London, but I have correspondents in well-nigh every city in Europe, and can give him introductions that may be valuable wheresoever he goes, and I shall be grieved indeed if he does not avail himself of my good-will and gratitude."

Three days later Sir Ralph returned to St. Alwyth from London with his dame and Aline. For some weeks, time passed quietly and pleasantly to Edgar. The intimacy between the two houses became even closer than before, and Sir Ralph's report of Edgar's doings in London caused him to be frequently invited to the houses of all the well-to-do people in the neighbourhood. In the meantime the insurrection had been finally crushed. The commissioners in various parts of the country were trying and executing all who had taken any lead in the movement, and until a general amnesty was passed two months later, every peasant lived in hourly dread of his life. They had gained nothing by the movement from which they had hoped so much, and for a while, indeed, their position was worse than it had ever been before.

In time, however, as the remembrance of the insurrection died out it bore its fruits, and although there was no specific law passed abolishing serfdom, the result was arrived at insensibly. Privileges were granted, and these privileges became customs with all the effect of the law, and almost without their knowing it the people became possessed of the rights for which their fathers had in vain taken up arms. Three weeks after Edgar's return from London a royal commission came down to Dartford, and the authorities of the town and others were called upon to name the leaders of the insurgents.

Sir Ralph, who was one of those summoned, said that he was altogether unable to give any information. He had been away when the first outbreak took place. On his return he found his castle besieged, but having with him fifty stout men-at-arms he attacked and pursued the insurgents, and nearly five hundred of them were slain. But fighting, as he did, with his vizor down, and having for a time as much as he could do to defend himself, he had recognized no one, and indeed, so far as he knew, he did not see one among the rioters with whose face he was acquainted.

Two days later, as Edgar was riding back from Sir Ralph's castle, he came suddenly upon a man at a cross-road. He was one of the villagers.

"Well, Master Ormskirk," he said, folding his arms, "you can kill me if you will, and it will be best so, for if you do not I shall live but the life of a hunted dog, and sooner or later fall into their hands."

"Why should I kill you, Carter? I have naught against you."

"Then it was not you who denounced me as one of those who fought against you at De Courcy's castle?"

"Not I, assuredly. I have had no communication whatever with the commissioners, nor did I know that you were one of those we encountered there."

"Someone has given my name," the man said moodily. "I suppose it was some of those at Dartford, for it is true enough that I joined the Tyler the day he slew the collector. I thought that he had done rightfully, and it may be that, like a fool, I have exhorted others to join him to win our charter of rights. I thought it was to be got honestly, that no harm was to be done to any man; but when we got to London, and I saw that the Tyler and others intended to slay many persons of high rank and to burn and destroy, I was seized with horror, and made my way back. When the others returned I was fool enough to let myself be persuaded to join in the attack on Sir Ralph's castle: and for that and the speeches, it seems that I am to be tried and hung. You had best run me through, Master Ormskirk, and have done with it; I would rather that than be hung like a dog."

"I shall do nothing of the kind, Carter. I have known you for years as an honest fellow, and a hard-working.

Here are a couple of crowns with which you can make your way to London."

"'Tis no good, sir. I hear that there are parties of men on every road, and that orders have been given in every township to arrest all passers-by and to detain them if they have not proper papers with them. Well, I can die better than some, for I lost my wife last Christmas, and have no children; so if you won't do my business for me I will go straight back to Dartford and give myself up."

"No, no, Carter. Do you go into that wood, and remain there till nightfall; then come to our house and knock at the gate, and you can shelter there as long as you like. As you know, there are few indeed who come there, and if I get you a servitor's suit, assuredly none of our visitors would recognize you, and as for the village folk, you have but to keep out of their way when they come with wood, meat, and other matters. It may not be for long, for 'tis like that I shall be going to the wars soon, and when I do so I will take you with me as my man-at-arms. Moreover, it is probable that when the commissioners have sat for a time, and executed all the prominent leaders of this rioting, there will be an amnesty passed. What do you say to that?"

"I say, God bless you, sir! I know well enough that I deserve everything that has befallen me, for of a surety the murders that were done in London have so disgraced our cause that no one has a right to look for mercy. However, sir, if you are willing to give me such shelter as you say, I will serve you well and faithfully, and will right willingly imperil the last drop of my blood in your service."

"Then it is agreed, Carter. Come soon after nightfall. I am sure that my father will approve of what I am doing, and should the worst come to the worst, and you be discovered, he would be able to say truly that he knew not that you were wanted for your share in the matter, for indeed he takes but small notice of what is passing without. Now you had better be off at once to hiding before anyone else comes along."

"Father," Edgar said when he returned, "I have taken on an additional servitor in the house. He will cost you naught but his food while he is here, and he will ride with me as my man-at-arms if I go abroad. He is a stout fellow, and I beg that you will ask me no questions concerning him, and will take him simply on my recommendation. He will not stir out of the house at present, but you may make him of use in your laboratory if you can."

"I think that I understand, Edgar. After a business like that which is just over, vengeance often strikes blindly, and 'tis enough for me that you declare him to be honest, and that you have known him for some time."

"Andrew," Edgar said to the old servitor after he had left his father, "I know that you are no gossip, and that in the matter of which I am going to speak to you I can rely upon your discretion. I have taken on a stout fellow, who will follow me to the wars as a man-at-arms. It may be that you will know him when you see him; indeed, I doubt not that you will do so. It is good for him at present that he should not stir beyond the walls, and he will, indeed, remain indoors all day. There are a good many others like him, who just at present will be keeping quiet, and you may be sure that I should not befriend the man were it not that I feel certain he has had no hand in the evil deeds performed by others."

"I understand, young master, and you may trust me to keep my lips sealed. I hear that a score have been hung during the last three days, and though I am no upholder of rioters, methinks that now they have had a bitter lesson. The courts might have been content with punishing only those who took a part in the murders and burnings in London. The rest were but poor foolish knaves, who knew no better, and who were led astray by the preachings of some of these Jack Priests and other troublers of the peace."

"Think you that it would be best to speak to old Anna?"

"Not a bit, Master Ormskirk. Save to go to mass, she never stirs beyond the house, and she is so deaf that you have to shout into her ear to make her hear the smallest thing. I will simply say to her that you have got a man-at-arms to go with you to the wars, and that until you leave he is to remain here in the house. You did not tell me whether I was to take your horse round to the stable."

"No; I am going to ride into Dartford now, to get the man some apparel suited to his station here."

Edgar returned in an hour, bringing with him a servitor's suit. As soon as Hal Carter arrived, Edgar himself opened the gate to him.

"Strip off those clothes, and put on this suit; it were best that you be not seen in your ordinary attire. However, you can trust old Andrew, and as to Anna, there is little chance of her recognizing you, and I don't suppose she as much as knows that there has been trouble in the land."

A month later a mounted messenger brought Edgar a letter—it was the first that he had ever received. Telling the man to alight, and calling Carter to take his horse, he led the man into the kitchen and told Anna to give him some food. He then opened the letter. It ran as follows:—

To Master Edgar Ormskirk, with hearty greeting,

Be it known to you, good friend, that having wound up my business affairs, I am about to start for Flanders, and shall in the first place go to Ghent, having a mission from those in authority at Court here to carry out in that city. It would greatly please me if you would accompany me. The times are troubled in Flanders, as you doubtless know, and you would see much to interest you; and, moreover, as at present there is nought doing in England, save the trying and executing of malefactors, you could spend your time better in seeing somewhat of a foreign country than in resting quietly at St. Alwyth. I need not say that the trip will put you to no cost, and that by accepting, you will give pleasure to my wife and daughter as well as to myself.

Yours in friendship,

NICHOLAS VAN VOORDEN.

P.S.—I am writing at the same time to Master De Courcy, who, I hope, will also accompany me.

Edgar went down at once to his father's laboratory and handed him the letter. Mr. Ormskirk read it.

"It is a hearty invitation, Edgar," he said, "and after the kindness of the Fleming in presenting you with that splendid suit of armour, you can scarce refuse it; but, indeed, in any case I should be glad for you to accompany him to Flanders. The Flemings are mostly our allies against France, and it would be well for you to pass some time among them, to learn as much as you can of their language, and to acquaint yourself with their customs. Their towns are virtually independent republics, like those of Athens, Sparta, and Thebes. The power lies wholly in the hands of the democracy, and rough fellows are they. The nobles have little or no influence, save in the country districts. The Flemings are at present on ill terms with France, seeing that they, like us, support Pope Urban, while the French, Spaniards, and others hold to Pope Clement.

"Possibly neither may care very much which pope gets the mastery, but it makes a convenient bone of contention, and so is useful to neighbours on bad terms with each other. Go, by all means. You had best write a reply at once, and hand it to the messenger. Have you heard yet whether he has been to the De Courcys' castle?"

"I did not ask him, father, for I did not read the letter until I had handed him over to Anna to get some food in the kitchen. I will go and ask him now, and if he has not yet gone there I will ride with him. 'Tis a cross-road, and he might have difficulty in finding it; besides, perhaps if I tell Sir Ralph that I am going, it may influence him to let Albert go also."

He went down to the kitchen and found that the messenger had not yet been to the castle. Telling him that he would go with him and act as his guide, and would be ready to start in a quarter of an hour, Edgar sat down to write to the Fleming. It was the first time that he had ever indited a letter, and it took him longer than he expected. When he went down, the messenger was already standing by his horse, while Carter was walking Edgar's up and down.

Albert and Aline were at the castle gate as they rode up.

"We were in the pleasaunce when we saw you coming, Edgar. We did not expect you until to-morrow."

"I have come over with a messenger, who is the bearer of a letter to you."

"You mean to my father, I suppose?"

"No, indeed; it is for yourself, and I have had a similar one. I have written an answer, and I hope you will write one in the same strain."

"Who can it be from?" Aline said, as Albert took out his dagger and cut the silk that held the roll.

"It is from our good friend Mynheer Van Voorden,"

Edgar said. "He is just leaving for Flanders, and has written to ask Albert and myself to accompany him thither."

"And I suppose that you have accepted," Aline said pettishly.

"Yes, indeed; my father thinks that it will be very good for me to see something of foreign countries, and especially Flanders. As there is nothing doing here now, I am wasting my time, and doubtless in the great Flemish cities I shall be able to find masters who can teach me many things with the sword."

"And how are we going to get on without you, I should like to know," she asked indignantly, "especially if you are going to take Albert away too?"

"Albert will decide for himself—at least Sir Ralph will decide for him, Mistress Aline."

"It is all very well to say that, but you know perfectly well that Albert will be wanting to go if you are going, and that Sir Ralph will not say no, if you and he both want it."

"Well, you would wish us to become accomplished knights some day, and assuredly, as all say, that is a thing better learned abroad than in England."

"I am quite satisfied with you as you are," she replied, "and I call it a downright shame. I thought, anyhow, I was going to have you both here until some great war broke out, and here you are, running away for your amusement. It is all very well for you to contend that you think it may do you good, but it is just for change and excitement that you want to go."

By this time Albert had finished reading the letter.

"That will be splendid," he said. "I have always thought that I should like to see the great Flemish cities. "Why, what is the matter, Aline?" he broke off, seeing tears in his sister's eyes.

"Is it not natural that I should feel sorry at the thought of your going away? We have to stay all our lives at home, while you wander about, either fighting or looking for danger wherever it pleases you."

"I don't think that it is quite fair myself, Aline, but I did not have anything to do with regulating our manners and customs; besides, it is not certain yet that my father will let me go."

They had by this time reached the spot where Sir Ralph was watching a party of masons engaged in heightening the parapet of the wall, as the experience of the last fight showed that it did not afford sufficient protection to its defenders.

"Well, Albert, what is your news?" he said, as he saw by their faces that something unusual had happened.

"A letter from Mynheer Van Voorden to ask me to accompany him to Flanders, whither he is about to sail. He has asked Edgar too, and his father has consented."

"Read me the letter, Albert. 'Tis a fair offer," he said, when Albert came to the end, "and pleases me much. I had spoken but yesterday with your mother, saying that it was high time you were out in the world, the only difficulty being with whom to place you. There are many knights of my acquaintance who would gladly enough take you as esquire, but it is so difficult to choose. It might be that, from some cause or other, your lord might not go to the wars, unless, of course, it were a levy of all the royal forces, and then it would be both grief to you and me that I had not put you with another lord under whom you might have had a better opportunity.

"But this settles the difficulty. By the time you come back there may be some chance of your seeing service under our own flag. Lancaster has just made a three years' truce with the Scots, and it may be that he will now make preparations in earnest to sail with an array to conquer his kingdom in Spain. That would be an enterprise in which an aspirant for knighthood might well desire to take part. The Spaniards are courtly knights and brave fellows, and there is like to be hard fighting. This invitation is a timely one. Foreign travel is a part of the education of a knight, and in Flanders there are always factions, intrigues, and troubles. Then there is a French side and an English side, and the French side is further split up by the Flemings inclining rather to Burgundy than to the Valois. Why, this is better than that gift of armour, and it was a lucky day indeed for you when you went to his daughter's aid. Faith, such a piece of luck never fell in my way."

"Shall I go and write the letter at once, father?"

"There is no hurry, Albert. The messenger must have ridden from town to-day, and as he went first to Master Ormskirk's, that would lengthen his journey by three or four miles, therefore man and horse need rest, and it were best, I should think, that he sleep here to-night, and be off betimes in the morning. It would be dark before he reached the city, and the roads are not safe riding after nightfall; besides, it can make no difference to Van Voorden whether he gets the answer to-night or by ten o'clock to-morrow morning."

Dame Agatha did not, as Aline had somewhat hoped, say a word to persuade Sir Ralph to keep Albert longer at home. She looked wistfully at the lad as the knight told her of the invitation that had come, and at his hearty pleasure thereat, but she only said: "I am sorely unwilling to part with you, Albert, but I know that it is best for you to be entering the world, and that I could not expect to have you many months longer. Your father and I were agreeing on that

yesterday. A knight cannot remain by a fireside, and it is
a comfort to me that this first absence of yours should be
with the good Flemish merchant, and I like much also his
wife and daughter, who were most kind to us when we
tarried with them in London when your father was away.
I would far rather you were with him, than in the train of
some lord bound for the wars. I am glad, too, that your
good friend Edgar is going with you. Altogether, it is
better than anything I had thought of, and though I cannot
part with you without a sigh, I can feel that the parting
might well have been much more painful. What say you,
Aline?"

"I knew, as you say, mother, that it was certain that
Albert would have to leave us, but I did not think that it
would be so soon. It is very hateful, and I shall miss him
dreadfully."

"Yes, my dear; but you must remember it was so I felt
the many times that your father went to the war. It is so
with the wife of every knight and noble in the land. And
not only these, but also the wives of the men-at-arms and
archers, and it will be yours when you too have a lord.
Men risk their lives in battle; women stay at home and
mind their castles. We each have our tasks. You know the
lines that the priest John Ball used, they say, as a text for
his harangues to the crowds, *When Adam delved and Eve span.*
You see, one did the rough part of the toil, the other sat at
home and did what was needful there; and so it has been
ever since. You know how you shared our feelings of delight that your brother had grown stronger, and would be
able to take his own part as his fathers had done before
him, to become a brave and valiant knight, and assuredly
it is not for you to repine now that a fair opportunity
offers for him to prepare for his career."

"I was wrong, mother," Aline said penitently. "I was very cross and ill-behaved, but it came suddenly upon me, and it seemed to me hard that Albert and Edgar should both seem delighted at what pained me so much. Forgive me, Albert."

"There is nothing to forgive, dear. Of course I understand your feeling that it will be hard for us to part when we have been so much together. I shall be very sorry to leave you, but I am sure you will agree with me that it is less hard to do so now than it would have been if I had been going to be shut up in a convent to prepare for entering the Church, as we once thought would be the case."

"I should think so," the girl said. "This will be nothing to it. Then you would have been going out of our lives; now we shall have an interest in all you do, and you will often be coming back to us; there will be that to look forward to. Well, you won't hear me say another word of grumbling until you have gone. And when are you to go?"

"To-morrow or next day," her father said. "Mynheer Van Voorden says, 'I am about to start', which may mean three days or six. It will need a whole day for your mother and the maids to see to Albert's clothes, and that all is decent and in order. To-day is Monday, and I think that if we say that Albert will arrive there on Thursday by noon it will do very well. Will you be ready by that time, Edgar?"

"Easily enough, Sir Ralph; for indeed, as we have no maid, my clothes need but little preparation. I wear them until they are worn out, and then get new ones; and I doubt not that I shall be able to replenish my wardrobe to-morrow at Dartford."

Well pleased to find that Albert was to accompany him Edgar rode home. As he passed in at the gates Hal Carter ran up to him. "Master tells me that you are going away, Master Edgar. Are you going to take me with you?"

"Not this time, Hal. I am going to Flanders as a guest of a Flemish gentleman, and I could not therefore take a man-at-arms with me; besides, as you know naught of the language, you would be altogether useless there. But do not think that I shall not fulfil my promise. This is but a short absence, and when I return I shall enter the train of some warlike knight or other, and then you shall go with me, never fear."

"Thank you, sir! 'Tis strange to me to be pent up here; not that I have aught in the world to complain of; your father is most kind to me, and I do hope that I am of some use to him."

"Yes, my father has told me several times how useful you were to him in washing out his apparatus and cleaning his crucibles and getting his fires going in readiness. He wonders now how he got on so long without a helper, and will be sorry when the time comes for you to go with me. Indeed he said, but two days ago, that when you went he should certainly look for someone to fill your place."

"So long as he feels that, Master Edgar, I shall be willing enough to stay; but it seemed to me that I was doing but small service in return for meat and drink and shelter. I should feel that I was getting fat and lazy were it not that I swing a battle-axe every day for an hour as you bade me."

"Look through your apparel, Edgar," his father said that evening, "and see what you lack. To-morrow morning I will give you moneys wherewith you can repair deficiencies. The suits you got in London will suffice you for the present, but as winter approaches you must get yourself cloth garments, and these can be purchased more cheaply in Flanders than here. Of course I know not how long your stay there may

be; that must depend upon your host. It would be well if
at the end of a month you should speak about returning,
then you will see by his manner whether he really wishes
you to make a longer stay or not. Methinks, however, that
it is likely he will like you to stay with him until the spring
if there is no matter of importance for which you would
wish to return. I am sure that he feels very earnestly how
much he owes to you, and is desirous of doing you real service; and to my thinking he can do it in no better manner
than by giving you six months in Flanders."

Accordingly, three days later the two friends again rode to
London. Each was followed by a man on horseback leading
a sumpter-horse carrying the baggage; and Hal Carter was
much pleased when he was told that he was to perform this
service. Both, for the convenience of carriage, wore their
body-armour and arm-pieces, the helmets and greaves being
carried with their baggage. On their arrival they were
most cordially received by Van Voorden and his family,
and found that they were to start on Saturday. On the
following morning the lads went to the Tower to pay their
respects to the king.

"Be sure you do not neglect that," Sir Ralph had said;
"the king is mightily well disposed to you, as I told you.
I had related to him in full the affairs in which you took part
in London, and on my return after the fight here, I, of course,
told him the incidents of the battle, and he said, 'If all
my knights had borne themselves as well as your son and his
friend I should not have been in so sore a strait. I should
be glad to have them about my person now; but I can well
understand that you wish your son to make a name for himself as a valiant knight, and that for a time I must curb my
desire.'"

The king received them very graciously. "Sir Ralph and

you did good work in dispersing that Kentish rabble, and doing with one blow what it has taken six weeks to accomplish in Essex and Hertford. So you are going to Flanders? You will see there what has come of allowing the rabble to get the mastery. But of a truth the knaves of Ghent and Bruges are of very different mettle to those here, and fight as stoutly as many men-at-arms."

" 'Tis true, your Majesty," Edgar said, "but not because they are stouter men, for those we defeated so easily down in Kent are of the same mettle as our archers and men-at-arms who fought so stoutly at Cressy and Poictiers, but they have no leading and no discipline. They know, too, that against mail-clad men they are powerless; but if they were freemen, and called out on your Majesty's service, they would fight as well as did their forefathers."

"You are in favour, then, of granting them freedom?"

"It seems to me that it would strengthen your Majesty's power, and would add considerably to the force that you could put in the field, and would make the people happier and more contented. Living down among them as we do, one cannot but see that 'tis hard on men that they may not go to open market, but must work for such wages as their lords may choose to give them, and be viewed as men of no account, whereas they are as strong and able to work as others."

"You may be right," the young king said, "but you see, my councillors think otherwise, and I am not yet rightly my own master. In one matter, however, I can have my way, and that is in dispensing honours. You know what I said to you before you went hence, that, young as you were, I would fain knight you for the valiant work that you had done. Since then you have done me good service, as well as the realm, by having, with Sir Ralph de Courcy and Sir

н 371

EDGAR AND ALBERT ARE KNIGHTED BY KING RICHARD.

Robert Gaiton, defeated a great body of the Kentish rebels, who were the worst and most violent of all, though there were with you but fifty men-at-arms. This is truly knightly service, and their defeat drove all rioters in that part to their homes, whereas, had they not been so beaten, there might have been much more trouble, and many worthy men might have been slain by them.

"Moreover, as you are going to Flanders with our good friend Mynheer Van Voorden, who is in a way charged with a mission from us, it is well that you should travel as knights. It will give you more influence, and may aid him to further my object. Therefore, I am sure that all here who know how stoutly you have wielded your swords, and how you gave aid and rescue to the worshipful Mynheer Van Voorden and his family, to stout Sir Robert Gaiton, Dame De Courcy and her daughter, and how you bore yourselves in the fight down in Kent, will agree with me that you have right well won the honour."

Then, drawing his sword, he touched each slightly on the shoulder:

"Rise, Sir Albert de Courcy, and Sir Edgar Ormskirk."

As the lads rose they were warmly congratulated by several of the nobles and knights standing round.

"I will not detain you," the king said a short time later. "Doubtless you have many preparations to make for your voyage. I hope that things will fare well with you in Flanders. Bear in mind that if you draw sword for Mynheer Van Voorden you are doing it for England."

CHAPTER XII.

THE TROUBLES IN FLANDERS.

ON re-entering the city gates they first went to an armourer's, where they purchased and buckled on some gilded spurs.

"Truly, Albert, I can scarce believe our good fortune," Edgar said as they left the shop. "It seems marvellous that though we have not served as esquires, we should yet at seventeen be dubbed knights by the king."

"You have well deserved it, Edgar; as for me, I have but done my best to second you."

"And a very good best it was, Albert," Edgar laughed. "'Tis true that in the skirmish outside Aldersgate I might have managed by myself, but in the Fleming's affair and in the Tower I should have fared hardly indeed had it not been for your help. I fancy that we have the Fleming to thank for this good fortune. You see he had already told the king that we were to accompany him, and perhaps he may have pointed out to him that it might be to the advantage of his mission that we should be made knights. He has great influence with the court, seeing that he has frequently supplied the royal needs with money. First let us visit our good friend Sir Robert Gaiton."

The knight received them most warmly. "I heard from Van Voorden that you were going to Flanders with him. You are like to see stirring events, for Ghent has long been in insurrection against the Count of Flanders, and things are likely to come to a head ere long. Ah, and what do I see—gold spurs! Then the king has knighted you! That is well, indeed, and I congratulate you most heartily. I tell you that I felt some shame that I, who had not even drawn a sword, should have been knighted, while you two, who had fought like paladins, had not yet your spurs, and I was glad that I had an opportunity, down in Kent, of showing that I was not a mere carpet knight."

"'Tis for that affair that the king said he knighted us, Sir Robert," Edgar said. "The other matters were private ventures, though against the king's enemies; but that was a battle in the field, and the success put an end to rioting down there."

"I shall not forget my promise about the knightly armour," the merchant said, "but methinks that it were best to wait for a while. The armour the Fleming bought you is as good as could be made, but doubtless you will outgrow it, so it would be best for me to delay for two or three years. It is not likely that you will have much to do with courtly ceremonies before then, and when you get to twenty, by which time you will have your full height if not your full width, I will furnish you with suits with which you could ride with Richard when surrounded by his proudest nobles and best knights."

"We thank you, indeed, Sir Robert, and it would be much better so. The first shine is not off our armour at present, and it would be cumbrous to carry a second suit with us, therefore we would much rather that you postponed your gift."

He now went with them into the ladies' room. "Dame and daughter," he said, "I have to present to you Sir Edgar Ormskirk and Sir Albert de Courcy, whom his Majesty has been pleased this morning to raise to the honour of knighthood, which has been well won by their own merits and bravery."

The dame gave an exclamation of pleasure and her daughter clapped her hands.

"'Tis well deserved, indeed," the former exclaimed, "and I wish them all good fortune with their new dignity. How much we owe them, Robert!"

"That do we," the merchant said heartily.

"I am pleased," the girl said, coming forward and frankly shaking hands with both.

"I can scarce credit our good fortune, Mistress Ursula," Albert said. "'Tis but a few months since I deemed that I was unfit for martial exercise, and that there was nought for me but to enter the Church, and now, thanks entirely to Edgar and to good luck, I am already a knight; 'tis well-nigh past belief. That meeting with you and your father was the beginning of our great fortune."

"That was a terrible night," the girl said with a little shudder at the recollection. "Heaven surely sent you to our aid."

While they were talking, Sir Robert said a word apart to his wife, and left the room. He presently returned with a small coffer, which he handed to her.

"It seems to me, young knights," she said, "that your equipment is incomplete without a knightly chain. My husband, I know, is going to give you armour for war; it is for us to give you an ornament for court. These are the work of Genoese goldsmiths, and I now, in the name of my daughter and myself, and as a small token of the gratitude that we owe you, bestow these upon you."

So saying she placed round their necks two heavy gold chains of the finest workmanship. Both expressed their thanks in suitable terms.

"When do you sail?" the merchant asked Edgar.

"To-morrow morning," he replied, "and the ship will unmoor at noon. We will come to say farewell to you in the morning."

Mynheer Van Voorden and his family were no less

delighted than Sir Robert Gaiton at the honour that had befallen them.

"Methinks, Mynheer," Edgar said, "that 'tis to you that we in part owe the honour the king has bestowed on us, for he said that as you had a mission from him it would be well that we should have the rank of knighthood."

"I may have said as much to the king," Van Voorden admitted, "but it was not until Richard had himself said that he intended at the first opportunity to knight you both. On that I spoke, and pointed out that the presence of two English knights with me would add weight to my words. On which he gladly assented, saying that it had before been his intention to do so ere you left London, had not Sir Ralph said it would be better for you to earn it in the field; but as, since that time, you had fought in a stiff battle, and done good service to the realm by putting down the insurgents in Kent, who had been the foremost in the troubles here, he would do so at once.

"I think now that it were well you should each take a man-at-arms with you—a knight should not ride unattended. When we get across there I will hire two Flemings, who speak English, to ride with your men. You will need them to interpret for you, and they can aid your men to look after your horses and armour. If the two fellows here start at once for your homes, the others can be back in the morning."

"One of them is the man I should take with me," Edgar said. "I promised him that he should ride behind me as soon as occasion offered. He has no horse, but I doubt not that I shall be able to purchase one out there."

"I will see to that," Van Voorden said, "and to his armour. Do not trouble yourself about it in any way. And now about your man, Sir Albert?"

"I will ask my father to choose a good fellow for me, and one who has armour and a horse."

"Then it were best to lose no time. There is pen and parchment on that table. Doubtless you will both wish to write to tell your fathers of the honour that the king has bestowed upon you."

Both at once sat down and wrote a short letter. Edgar, after telling his father that he had been knighted, said:

Mynheer Van Voorden says it will be as well if we each take a man-at-arms with us, so I shall, with your permission, take Hal Carter as I had arranged with you to do so when I went to the wars. He is a stout fellow, and will, I am sure, be a faithful one. I hope that you will find no difficulty in replacing him.

Sir Ralph himself arrived at the house the next morning. "I could not let you go without coming to congratulate you both on the honour that has befallen you. It might have been well that it should have come a little later, but doubtless it will be of advantage to you in Flanders, and should there be fighting between Ghent and the Earl you will be more free to choose your own place in battle, and to perform such journeys and adventures as may seem good to you as knights, than you would be as private gentlemen, or esquires, following no leader, and having no rank or standing save that of gentlemen who have come over as friends of Mynheer Van Voorden.

"Your mother is greatly pleased, and as for Aline she would fain have ridden hither with me, but as I intend to return this afternoon, and as she saw you both but two days since, I thought it best that she should stay at home. I have brought up with me John Lance. I thought that he was the one who would suit you best. In some respects the other is the more experienced and might be of more value were you going on a campaign, but he is somewhat given to the ale jug, so I thought it best to bring Lance, who is a stout fellow and can wield his sword well. He is civil and well-spoken, and as I have told him he is to obey your orders just the same as if they were mine, I believe that you will have little trouble with him. His arms and armour are in good condition, and he has been furnished with a fresh suit out of the chest.

"I saw your father, Edgar, late yesterday evening. I myself took over your letter to him. He said that whatever a man's calling may be, it is well that he should go into it with all his heart, and that since you have taken to arms it is well indeed that you should so soon have distinguished yourself as to be deemed worthy of knighthood. He said that he would get another to take the place of the man you keep with you, and he wishes you God-speed in Flanders."

At eleven o'clock Van Voorden, his wife, and daughter, mounted, together with Edgar, Albert, and their two men-at-arms; both the latter were in body armour, with steel caps; the Fleming had secured a strong and serviceable horse for Hal. His own servants had gone on an hour before with three carts carrying the baggage; Sir Ralph accompanied them across London Bridge to Rotherhithe, where the barque was lying alongside a wharf. The horses were first taken on board, and placed in stalls on deck. These Van Voorden had had erected so that the horses should suffer no injury in case they encountered rough weather. As soon as the animals were secured in their places Sir Ralph said good-bye to them all, the hawsers were thrown off and the vessel dropped out into the tide, the baggage having been lowered into the hold before they came down.

There were no other passengers, the Fleming having secured all the accommodation for his party. There were two small cabins in the stern, one of which was set apart for the merchant's wife and daughter, the other for their two maids. The cabin where they sat and took their meals was used by the merchant and the two young knights as a sleeping place. The Fleming's four men-servants and the two men-at-arms slept in a portion of the hold under the stern cabins. The wind was favourable, and although speed was not the strong point of the ship, she made a quick passage, and forty-eight hours after starting they entered the port of Sluys.

" Will you tell us, Mynheer," Edgar said as they sailed quietly down the Thames, " how it comes about that Ghent is at war with the Earl of Flanders, for it is well that we should have some knowledge of the matter before we get into the midst of it?"

" 'Tis well, indeed, that it should be so, Edgar. The matter began in a quarrel between two men, John Lyon and Gilbert Mahew. Lyon was a crafty and politic man, and was held in great favour by the Earl. There was a citizen who had seriously displeased Louis, and at his request John Lyon made a quarrel with him and killed him. The matter caused great anger among the burgesses, and Lyon had to leave the city, and went and dwelt at Douay, living in great state there for three years, at the Earl's expense. At the end of that time the Earl used all the influence he possessed at Ghent, and obtained a pardon for Lyon, and the restoration of his property that had been forfeited for his crime, and, moreover, made him chief ruler of all the ships and mariners.

" This caused great displeasure to many not only in Ghent but in all Flanders. Mahew and his seven brothers were the leading men among the mariners, and between their family and that of Lyon there was a long-standing feud, went presently to the Earl and told him that if things were properly managed and certain taxes put on the shipping, the Earl would derive a large annual sum from it, and the Earl directed Lyon to carry this out. But owing to the general opposition among the mariners, which was craftily managed by Mahew's brothers, Lyon was unable to carry the Earl's orders into effect. Gilbert Mahew then went to the Earl and said that if he were appointed in Lyon's place he would carry the thing out. This was done, and Mahew, from his influence with the mariners, and by giving many presents to persons at the Earl's court, gained high favour, and used his power to injure Lyon.

"The latter, however, kept quiet and bided his time. This came when the people of Bruges, who had long desired to make a canal,—which would take away most of the water of the river Lys for their benefit,—but who had never been able to do so owing to the opposition offered by Ghent, now set a great number of men upon this work. This caused a great agitation in Ghent, especially among mariners, who feared that if the river Lys were lowered their shipping-trade would be much injured. Then people began to say that if Lyon had remained their governor in Ghent the people of Bruges would never have ventured on such action. Many of them went secretly to Lyon to sound him on the matter. He advised them that they had best revive the old custom of wearing white hoods, and that they should then choose a governor whom they would obey.

"In a few days a great number of white hoods appeared in the streets, and a popular meeting was held. John Lyon was elected leader, and with two hundred companies marched from Ghent to attack the pioneers digging the channel. These, on hearing that a great force from Ghent was marching against them, hastily retired. John Lyon and his force returned home, and the former again resumed his position as a quiet trader. The White Hoods, however, dominated the town. In a short time some of them demanded that a mariner, who was a burgess of Ghent, and who was confined in the Earl's prison at Eccloo, should be liberated, as, according to the franchise of the city, no burgess could be tried save by its courts.

"'This trouble Lyon carefully fostered, and as the new and heavy dues injured the trade of Ghent, his party increased rapidly. In public, however, he always spoke moderately, remaining quietly in his house, and never going out except with an escort of two or three hundred of the White Hoods. An embassy was sent to the Earl to ask that the rights of the city should be respected. The Earl answered them mildly, ordered the prisoner to be given up to them, and promised to respect the franchise of the city, but at the same time asked that the wearing of white hoods should be discontinued. Lyon, however, persuaded the White Hoods not to accede to this request, saying that it was the White Hoods that had wrung those concessions from the Earl, and that if they disappeared from the streets, the franchise would be speedily abolished.

"In this Lyon was right, and he at once set to work to organize the White Hoods, dividing them into companies, and appointing a captain to each hundred men; a lieutenant to fifty; and a sub-officer to ten. In a short time the Bailie of Ghent, with two hundred horse, rode into the city, the Earl having agreed with Gilbert Mahew that John Lyon and several other leaders should be carried off and beheaded. As soon as the Bailie arrived at the market-place he was joined by the Mahews and their adherents. The White Hoods at once gathered at John Lyon's house, and he set out for the market-house with four hundred men.

These were joined by many others as they went. As soon as they appeared, the Mahews, with their party, fled. Then the White Hoods rushed upon the Bailie, unhorsed and slew him, and tore the Earl's banner to pieces. His men-at-arms, seeing how strong and furious were the townsmen, at once turned their horses and rode away.

"A search was then made for the Mahews, but they had fled from the town and ridden away to join the Earl. Their houses were all sacked and destroyed. The White Hoods were now undisturbed masters of the place; most of the rich burgesses, however, were much grieved at what had taken place. A great council was held, and twelve of their number went to the Earl to beg for pardon for the town. The Earl received them sternly, but at their humble prayer promised to spare the city and to punish only the chief offenders. While they were away, however, Lyon called an assembly of the citizens in a field outside the town. Ten thousand armed men gathered there, and they at once sacked and burnt the palace of Andrehon, which was the Earl's favourite residence and a very stately pile.

"The Earl, on hearing the news, called the burgesses, who were still with him, and sent them back to Ghent with a message to the town that they should have neither peace nor treaty until he had struck off the heads of all those whom he chose. John Lyon began the war by marching to Bruges, which, being wholly unprepared, was forced to admit him and his men, and to agree to an alliance with Ghent. He then marched to Damme, where he was taken ill, and died, not without strong suspicion of having been poisoned. The people of Ghent sent a strong force to Ypres. The knights and men-at-arms of the garrison refused to admit them, but the craftsmen of the town rose in favour of Ghent, slew five of the knights, and opened the gates.

The men of the allied cities then tried to attack Tormonde, where the Earl was, but were unable to take it; they afterwards besieged Oudenarde. The Duke of Burgundy, however, interposed, and peace was agreed upon, on condition that the Earl should pardon all and come to live in Ghent. The Earl kept his promise so far as to go there, but he only stayed four days and then left the town.

"The peace was of very short continuance, for some relations of the bailie and some other knights took forty ships on the river, put out the eyes of the sailors, and sent them into Ghent, in return for which a strong body marched out from Ghent, surprised Oudenarde, and stayed there a month, during which time they hewed down the gates and made a breach in the walls by destroying two towers. After the men of Ghent had left Oudenarde the Earl went there and repaired the damage they had done, and then marched to Ypres and beheaded many of those who had risen against him, and had slain his knights. In the meantime Ghent prepared for the war by sacking and destroying all the houses of the gentry in the country round the city.

"Several battles were fought, and in these the White Hoods had the worst of it, for although they fought stoutly they were greatly outnumbered. Bruges and Damme opened their gates to the Earl, and Ghent was left without an ally. Then Peter de Bois, who was now the chief of the White Hoods, seeing that many of the townsmen were sorely discouraged by their want of success, went to Philip van Artevelde (the son of Jacob van Artevelde, who was murdered by the townsfolk for making an alliance with England) and persuaded him to come forward as the leader of the people. On his doing so Philip was at once accepted by the White Hoods. Two of the leaders of the party of peace were at once murdered. As his father had been a great man and an excellent ruler, Philip was joyfully accepted by the whole population, and was given almost arbitrary power.

"Since that time," went on Van Voorden, "Ghent has been straitly besieged, and had it not been that they sent out a strong force, who bought large supplies at Brussels and at Liege, and managed to convey them back to the city, most of the inhabitants would have died from hunger.

"So matters stand at present. The mission with which I am charged at present is to see Von Artevelde, and to find out whether he, like his father Jacob, is well disposed towards the English, and if so, to promise that some aid shall be sent to him."

"And what are your own thoughts on the matter, Mynheer?"

"As to Ghent, I say nothing," the merchant replied. "The population have ever been rough and turbulent, swayed by agitators, and tyrannized over by the craftsmen; but I can well see that it is for the interest of England that Ghent should be upheld, for these troubles in Flanders greatly disturb both the Duke of Burgundy and the King of France, whose interests never run together. Again, I see that the independence of Ghent, Bruges, and other large towns is for the good of Flanders, since, were it not for that, the country would be but an appanage of Burgundy or France. Heavy imposts would be laid upon the people, their franchises abolished, and the trade greatly injured; and it would therefore be a sore misfortune for the country were the Earl of Flanders to crush Ghent, for did he do so he could work his will in all the other towns.

"These, you see, are something like your city of London; they exist and flourish owing to the rights they have gained. They curbed the power of the nobles, and have built up great wealth and power for themselves. Their merchants have the revenues of princes, and carry on a great trade with all countries. You see how readily the Earl fell in with Mahew's suggestion, and laid heavy taxes on the shipping of Ghent. In the same way, were he supreme master, he and his lords could similarly tax the trade of other towns of Flanders, to the great benefit of the merchants of foreign countries. Thus, you see, as a Fleming I should wish to see Ghent—although I love not the turbulent town—preserved from the destruction that would surely fall upon it were the Earl to capture it. Why, at Ypres, not only did he kill many thousands of the citizens in an ambush, but when he entered the town he beheaded well-nigh six hundred of the citizens. If he did that at Ypres, which had offended comparatively little, what would he do to Ghent, which has killed his bailie, sacked and burned his palace, defied his authority, and holds out against all his force?"

"Thank you very much, Mynheer; I knew but little of the matter before, and I am glad to be so thoroughly informed in it. I see it is the same there as it was in London when the rioters came thither; the better class were overborne by the baser. Had it not been for the death of Wat the Tyler, and the dispersal of his rabble, it is likely that every trader's house in London would have been pillaged, and all the better class murdered, as were the Flemings."

As soon as the vessel drew alongside the wharf at Sluys, a Flemish trader came on board. He was a correspondent of Van Voorden's, and to him the merchant had written asking him to secure lodgings for him and his party for a day or two. Van Voorden was well known to him, for the merchant had occasion to cross to Flanders three or four times every year, and his correspondent often came over to

London. After greeting the merchant, his wife and daughter, he said:

"I was in much fear for you, Van Voorden, when I heard the reports of the wild doings of the rabble in London, and how they specially directed their fury against our people, and killed very many worthy merchants. You have said in your letters to me that you had been in some danger, but that, as you would see me shortly, you would not write at length."

"I will tell you of it anon, Rochter. First, how about the lodging?"

"As to that, there is no difficulty. It would be strange indeed were you to go elsewhere than to my house, which you have always used hitherto when you passed through."

"Yes; when I was alone. Now I have my wife and daughter, and these two young English knights, to say nothing of the maids and the men-at-arms."

"We can take them all without difficulty. As you know, the house is a large one, and there are but my wife and myself and my daughter Marie. There is the room you always occupy for yourself and madam, a bed has been put up in Marie's room for your daughter, the large room over it will be allotted to these gentlemen, your maids can sleep with ours, and there is a large room in the attic for your servants and the knights' men."

"So be it," Van Voorden said, "and it will be far more pleasant to be with you and your good wife than in a strange place. How about the horses, of which we have six?"

"The accommodation I have for them is small, but I have arranged with a friend for the disposal of the horses in his stables, which are commodious, and of which he makes but little use."

The house of Mynheer Rochter surprised the young knights by its size. It was massively and strongly built, and apparently there was no pressure for room, as was the case in the busy streets of London. The hall was of great size, panelled with a dark wood, and with a flooring so smooth and polished that both knights narrowly escaped falling, on stepping on it for the first time. A great staircase led to the family apartments upstairs. The main room would have held four of either those of Van Voorden or Sir Robert Gaiton in London, and the rest of the house was on the same scale. All was dark, massive, and rich, with an air of great comfort. The furniture and floors were polished until they reflected the light from the casements, and heavy rugs and carpets were stretched in front of the fireplaces and windows, and at other points where the family were accustomed to sit.

There were heavy curtains to the windows, and others before the doors, so that all draught should be cut off. Although not so handsome as the rooms of the two merchants in London, everything was so substantial, well kept, and comfortable, that the two friends were greatly struck by it. It was now October, and great wood fires blazed in the hall below and in all the upstairs rooms, and these quite dispelled any air of gloom that might otherwise have been caused by the darkness of the furniture.

"Truly, Edgar," Albert said in a low tone, while the ladies were talking together, "I think that I shall change my vocation once again, abandon the cutting of throats, and establish myself as a Flemish merchant."

"It would be years before you could acquire the necessary knowledge," Edgar laughed, "to say nothing of the capital required for the business; but truly the comfort of this house is wonderful, and it is clear to me that, although we Englishmen have learned to fight, we are mightily behind others in the art of making our lives comfortable."

Before the meal was served the friends went upstairs
to their room, took off the rough clothes in which they
had travelled, and apparelled themselves in the plainest of
their two suits. When dinner was announced they went
into a room leading from that in which they had before
been. As the numbers were equal, the four gentlemen each
offered his hand to a lady, and led her to the table. It was
almost dark now, and the room was lighted with many wax
candles, which were novelties to the young knights. Tallow
candles had indeed come into partial use at the beginning
of the century, but they had never seen wax used, save on
occasions of great ceremony in the churches. It was now
for the first time that Frau Rochter obtained a fair view
of the faces of her guests.

"You are young indeed, gentlemen, are you not, to have
attained the rank of knighthood?" she said; "but I believe
that in England 'tis a title that goes with the land."

"It is so," Van Voorden said, before either of the young
knights could reply; "but in this case it has been won
by distinguished bravery, for which King Richard himself
bestowed knighthood upon them. No one can testify to
their bravery more strongly than ourselves, for it was
thanks alone to them that my life certainly, and probably
those of my wife and daughter, were preserved on that
evil day in London," and as the meal proceeded he gave a
full narrative of the manner in which they had defended
his house while his wife was removed from her sick-bed
and carried down to the hiding-place below. "It was not
only for this single act of bravery that they received
knighthood. Young though they are, they saved the life
of a worshipful London citizen—who has since himself become a knight—when he had fallen into the hands of a party
of robbers. When the Tower was in the hands of the

rioters, they, without assistance, killed seven men who had entered the ladies' chamber; and, lastly, they rode, with two knights and fifty men-at-arms, at a mob consisting of some two thousand of the worst of the rebels, and entirely defeated them with the loss of five hundred, and it was for this last act that they were knighted."

"Mynheer Van Voorden omits to say," Edgar added, "that it was largely to his own good offices that we owe the honour."

"I said nothing to the king but what was true and just," the merchant replied; "and he told me that he had already determined to promote you on the first opportunity; indeed, even had I not spoken I believe that he would have done so before we left London."

"I am sure that they deserved it if it had only been for what they did for us," his daughter said warmly. "Several times, while you were getting mother down the stairs, I ran out to the landing and looked down at the fight. It was terrible to see all the fierce faces, and the blows that were struck with pole-axe and halbert, and a marvel that two young men should so firmly hold their ground against such odds."

"We all owe them our lives assuredly," Madame Van Voorden said. "Had it not been for them, undoubtedly I should have died that day. I was very near to death as it was, and had I seen my husband slaughtered before my eyes, it would have needed no blow of knife to have finished me."

CHAPTER XIII.

A STARVING TOWN.

MANY of the leading citizens, hearing of Van Voorden's arrival, called in the course of the evening. The conversation, of course, turned upon the state of public affairs in Flanders; and Van Voorden inquired particularly as to the feeling in Bruges, and the sides taken by leading citizens there.

"That is difficult to say," one of the merchants replied. "Bruges has always been a rival to Ghent, and there has been little good-will between the cities. The lower class are undoubtedly in favour of Ghent; but among the traders and principal families the feeling is the other way. Were Ghent in a position to head a national movement with a fair chance of success, no doubt Bruges would go with her for she would fear that, should it be successful, she would suffer from the domination of Ghent. At present, however, the latter is in a strait, the rivers are blockaded by the Earl's ships, and the town is sorely pressed by famine. After the vengeance taken by the Earl on the places that, at the commencement of the trouble, threw in their lot with Ghent, she can expect no aid until she shows herself capable of again defeating the prince's army."

"Of course, at present I know but little how matters stand," Van Voorden said. "I have been so long settled in England that I have hardly kept myself informed of affairs here. I am thinking now of making Flanders my home again, but I would not do so if the land is like to be torn by civil war; I shall, therefore, make it my business to sojourn for a time in many of the large towns, and so to learn the general

feeling throughout the country towards the Earl, and to
find out what prospect there is of the present trouble coming to a speedy end.   France, Burgundy, or even England
may interfere in the matter if they see a prospect of gain
by it, and in that case the fighting might become general."

"Is the feeling of England in favour of Ghent?" one of
the burghers asked anxiously.

"So far I have heard but little on the matter. The English have had troubles of their own, and have had but little
time to cast their eyes abroad. Nevertheless, if the struggle
continues they may remember that a Van Artevelde was
their stout ally, and that Ghent, after his murder, again
submitted itself to them. There is, too, the bond of sympathy that Flanders accepts the same pope as England, and
that in aiding her they aid the pope's cause, and strike a
blow at France, with whom they are always at daggers
drawn. Therefore, methinks more unlikely things have
happened than that, if France gives aid to the Earl, the
English may strike in for Ghent."

"I trust not," one of the burghers said earnestly, "for
Sluys might well be the landing point for an English expedition, and then the first brunt of the war would fall upon
us."

"I say not that there is much chance of such a thing,"
Van Voorden said; "I was but mentioning the complication
that might arise if Ghent is able to prolong the struggle."

On the following morning the party started from Sluys.
They made a good show, for Van Voorden had the evening
before engaged two mounted men, well armed, to ride with
the young knights as men-at-arms. Behind the merchant
and his party came the two maids and the four retainers
who had accompanied them from England. These carried
swords and daggers, but no defensive armour. Behind were

the two English men-at-arms and the two freshly taken on,
all wearing breast- and back-pieces and steel caps. They
tarried but a day or two at Bruges, Van Voorden finding
that among the burgesses the trade animosity against Ghent
overpowered any feeling of patriotism, and moreover it was
felt that the success of that town would give such encouragement to the democracy elsewhere that every city
would become the scene of riot and civil strife.

They learnt that, unless they fell in with one of the
parties that was stationed to prevent strong forces of
foragers issuing from Ghent to drive in cattle, they would
find no difficulty in entering the town, for the citizens had
shown themselves such stout fighters, that the Earl, believing
that the city must fall by famine, had drawn off the greater
portion of his army. Travelling by easy stages, the party
approached the town on the second evening. Soon after they
started that morning they came upon a body of the troops
of the Earl of Flanders. The officer in command rode up
to the merchant and asked him for his name and his object
in going to Ghent, and also who were the two knights with
him. As soon as Van Voorden mentioned his name, and
said that he had for many years been established in London,
the officer at once recognized it.

"I am well acquainted with your name as one of the
foremost among our countrymen at King Richard's court,
and that you have several times acted as our representative
when complaints have been made of injury to Flemish
traders by English adventurers, but I must still ask, what
do you propose doing at Ghent?"

"I am over here for a time with my wife and daughter,
and am paying visits to friends and business correspondents
in the various towns, and it may be that if these troubles
come to an end I may retire from business altogether and

settle down here. These knights have done me a signal
service, having saved the lives of myself and daughter
during the riots in London, therefore I have asked of them
the courtesy to ride with me through Flanders. Having a
desire to visit foreign countries, they accepted my invitation."

"Adieu, then, Master Van Voorden! I know that you
are a man of influence among the merchants, and trust that
you will do your best to persuade the stiff-necked burghers
of Ghent to submit themselves to their lord."

"Methinks, from what I hear," the merchant replied,
"that if it depended upon the burgesses and traders there
would be a speedy end to these troubles, but they are overborne by the demagogues of the craftsmen."

"That is true enough," the officer replied. "Numbers of
the richer burgesses have long since left Ghent, and many
have established themselves in trade in other cities where
there was better chance of doing their business in peace and
quiet."

The party now rode on, and without further interruption
arrived at Ghent. They put up for the night at a hostelry,
but in the morning the merchant had no difficulty in hiring
the use of a house for a month, for many of the better-class
houses were standing empty. Then he called on several of
the leading burgesses, some of whom were known to him
personally, and had long and earnest talk with them upon
the situation.

Late in the afternoon he sent a letter to Philip Van
Artevelde saying that he had just arrived from England,
and would be glad to have a private parley with him. An
answer was received from Van Artevelde saying that he
would call that evening upon him, as it would be more
easy to have quiet speech together there than if he visited
him at his official residence. At eight o'clock Van Artevelde

arrived. He was wrapped in a cloak, and gave no name, simply saying to the retainer who opened the door that he was there by appointment with his master. Van Voorden received him alone. They had met on two or three occasions previously, and saluted each other cordially.

"I think it best that we should meet quietly," the merchant said, as they shook hands. "I know the Ghentois, how greedily they swallow every rumour, how they magnify the smallest things, and how they rage if their desires are not gratified, and give themselves wholly up to the demagogues. 'Tis for that reason that I think it well that you have come to see me privately.

"I have no official mission to you, but I am charged by King Richard, or rather by his council—when they heard that I was coming over here on my private affairs—to find out in the first place how things really stand here; and secondly, to learn your own opinion and thoughts on the matters in hand."

By this time they had seated themselves by the fire.

"The position is grievous enough in that we are straitened for food," was the reply; "indeed although we have of late been fortunate in obtaining supplies, the pressure cannot be borne. Of one thing you may be sure, Ghent will not tamely be starved out. If we cannot obtain fair terms, every man will arm himself and sally out, and, if need be, we will sweep the whole country clear of its flocks and herds, and bring in such stores as we want from all quarters, carrying our arms to the gates of Brussels and Malines in one direction, to Lisle in another, and to Ypres and Dixmuide south of the Lys. Earl though he be, Louis cannot bar every road to us, nor for ever keep up a force sufficient to withstand us. Already the feudal lords have kept their levies under arms far beyond the time they have a right to require them, but this cannot go on. War costs us no more than peace, and whenever we will we can march with 20,000 men in any direction that may please us. As to defending ourselves against assault, I have no fear whatever. Thus, then, so long as Ghent chooses she can maintain the war." He put an emphasis on the last words.

"That means, I take it," the merchant said, "as long as the people are willing to go on fasting."

"That is so. There is a sore pinch, food is distributed gratuitously; for as all trade is stopped there is little work to be had. So long as they could live in idleness, obtain enough food, and a small sum paid daily, there were no signs of discontent; and there is still plenty of money in the coffers, for the goods and estates of many who have fled, and who are known to be favourable to the Earl, have been confiscated; but money cannot provide food. Thus, it seems to me that, save for the lack of food, matters could go on as at present. But if fair terms cannot be obtained, the people will demand to be led against their enemy. We shall lead them, but what will come after that I cannot say.

"As you doubtless know, I am here by no choice of my own. I had nought to do with the rising of Ghent, or what has been done hitherto, but when Lyon died and the leaders who succeeded him were killed, they sent to me to be their governor. For a time I refused, but I was overborne. I was living quietly and peaceably on my estates, with no love for strife; but it was pointed out that I alone could unite the factions, that many of the better classes of citizens, who held aloof from the demagogues of the streets, would feel confidence in me, that my name would carry weight, and that other cities might make alliance with me when they would have nought to say to butchers and skinners and such like, and that possibly the Earl would be more likely to grant

terms to me than to those whom he considers as the rabble.
I took up the position reluctantly, but, having taken it up,
I shall not lay it down. Like enough it will cost me my
life, as it cost the life of Jacob Van Artevelde before me, but
it may be that aid will come from some unexpected quarter."

"That is the next point. Do you look for aid from
France?"

"France is never to be relied upon," Artevelde replied
gloomily. "The Valois has, of course, made us vague
promises, but all he cares for is that the war should go on,
so that if he and Burgundy come to blows, Flanders can
give no aid to the Duke. I have no hope in that quarter.
Of late, however, Burgundy and Berry have prevailed in his
councils, and we hear that he has decided to join the Duke
against us. We have sent, as doubtless you know, to the
King of England, to ask him to ally himself with us."

"'Tis concerning that matter he has charged me. It was
known when I left England that Burgundy had promised
his aid to the Earl, but nought was known of France joining
in. The king is well disposed towards you, but his Council
hold that, so long as Ghent stands alone, England can make
no alliance with her, for she would have to fight, not only
Burgundy and France, but the rest of Flanders. But if
Ghent makes herself master of Flanders England will gladly
ally herself with you, and will send troops and money."

"'Tis reasonable," Artevelde said, "and we will bestir
ourselves. I myself have done all that is possible to obtain
peace, and in three days I am going, with twelve of the
principal citizens, to Bruges, where the Earl arrived yesterday. We shall offer to submit ourselves to his mercy if
he will have pity on the city. If he demands the entire
mastership we shall fight in earnest. If he will content
himself with taking our lives, we are ready to give them

for the sake of the city. We know that we have a strong body of friends in every town, and should it come to blows, methinks it is not improbable that all Flanders will join, and if we are supported by England, we may well hope to withstand both France and Burgundy."

"I have two young English knights with me, Van Arte-velde; they are young, but have already shown themselves capable of deeds of the greatest bravery. During the late riots in London they defended my house against a mob many hundreds strong, and so gave time for myself, my wife, and daughter to gain a place of hiding; they did many other brave feats, and so distinguished themselves that, though very young, the king has knighted them. I invited them to accompany me hither, in order that they might see service, and I would fain commend them greatly to you. The fact that they are English knights would be of advantage to you, seeing that it will in the eyes of the people be taken as a proof that the sympathy of England is with us, and should there be fighting, or any occasion for the use of brave men, you can rely upon them to do their utmost."

"I will gladly accept their services, Van Voorden, and, as you say, the people will certainly draw a good augury from their presence."

The merchant left the room, and returned in a minute with the two young knights.

"These are the gentlemen of whom I have spoken to you, Van Artevelde," he said, "Sir Edgar Ormskirk and Sir Albert de Courcy, both very valiant gentlemen, and high in the esteem of King Richard."

"I greet you gladly, sir knights," Van Artevelde said, "both for your own sakes and for that of Mynheer Van Voorden, my worthy friend, who has presented you, and right glad shall I be if you will aid us in this sore strait into which we have fallen."

"I fear that our aid will not be of much avail to you, sir," Edgar said, "but such service as we can render we will right willingly give. I shall be glad to see service for the first time under one bearing the name of the great man who lost his life because he was so firm an ally of England."

"At present, gentlemen, things have not come to a crisis here, and for a few days I must ask your patience; by that time we shall know how matters are to go. If it be war, gladly, indeed, will I have you ride with me in the field."

Two days later Philip Van Artevelde rode away with the twelve citizens, who, like himself, went to offer their lives for the sake of the city. The scene was an affecting one, and crowds of haggard men and half-starved women filled the streets. Most of them were in tears, and all prayed aloud that Heaven would soften the Earl's heart and suffer them to come back unharmed to the city. Three days later they returned. As they rode through the streets all could see that their news was bad, and that they had returned because the Earl had refused to accept them as sacrifices for the rest. An enormous crowd gathered in front of the town-hall, and in a few minutes Van Artevelde and his companions appeared on the balcony.

There was a dead hush among the multitude. They felt that life or death hung on his words. He told them that the Count had refused altogether to accept twelve lives as ransom for the city, and that he would give no terms save that he would become its master and would execute all such as were found to have taken part in the rebellion against him.

A despairing moan rose from the square below.

"Fellow citizens," Van Artevelde went on, "there is now

but one of two things for us to do. The one is to shut our gates, retire to our houses, and there die either by famine or by such other means as each may choose. The other way is, that every man capable of bearing arms shall muster, that we shall march to Bruges, and there either perish under the lances of his knights, or conquer and drive him headlong from the land. Which choose ye, my friends?"

A mighty shout arose: "We will fight!"

"You have chosen well," Van Artevelde said. "Have we not before now defeated forces of men-at-arms superior in numbers to ourselves? Are we less brave than our fathers? Shall we not fight as stoutly when we know that we leave famishing wives and children behind who look to us to bring them back food? Return to your homes! A double ration of bread shall be served out from the magazines to all. Two hours before daybreak we will muster in our companies, and an hour later start for Bruges."

Among those who shouted loudest, "We will fight!" were the two young knights. They had, as soon as it was known that Van Artevelde and his party had entered the town, gone with Van Voorden to the house of a friend of his in the great square. They heard with indignation the refusal of the Earl of Flanders to accept the noble sacrifice offered by the twelve burgesses, who had followed the example of the governor of Calais and its leading citizens in offering their lives as a sacrifice for the rest. They had met, however, with a less generous foe, whose terms would, if accepted, have placed the life and property of every citizen of Ghent at his mercy. What that was likely to be had been shown at Ypres. Now the young knights felt indeed that the cause was a righteous one, and that they could draw their swords for Ghent with the conviction that by so doing they were fighting to save its people from massacre.

"By heavens!" Van Voorden exclaimed, "were I but younger I too would go out with the Ghentois to battle. I care but little myself as to the rights of the quarrel, though methinks that Ghent is right in resisting the oppressive taxes which, contrary to their franchise, the Earl has laid on the city. But that is nothing. One has but to look upon the faces of the crowd to feel one's blood boil at the strait to which their lord, instead of fighting them boldly, has, like a coward, reduced them by famine. But now when I hear that he has refused the prayer for mercy, refused to stay his vengeance, or to content himself with the heads of the noblest of the citizens offered to him, but instead would deluge the streets with blood, I would march with them as to a crusade. I will presently see Van Artevelde if but for a moment, tell him that you will ride with him, and ask where you shall take your station."

Late that evening Van Voorden returned. "I have been present at the council," he said. "The gates will not be open to-morrow, but on Thursday five thousand men will set out early."

"But five thousand is a small number," Edgar said, "to march against Bruges, a city as large as this, and having there the Earl, and no doubt a strong body of his own troops."

"That is true; but most of the men are so weakened that it is thought that it will be best to take but a small number of the strongest and most capable. They will carry with them the three hundred hand-guns. What little provision there is must be divided; half will go with those who march, the other half will be kept for those here to sustain life until news comes how matters have fared in the field."

"But with only five thousand men, without machines for the siege, they can never hope to storm the walls of Bruges.

It would be a feat that as many veteran soldiers might well hesitate to undertake."

"They have no thought of doing so. It has been agreed that this would be impossible, but the force will camp near the city, and, seeing the smallness of their number, the people of Bruges will surely sally out and attack them. Then they will do their best for victory, and if they beat the enemy our men will follow on their rear hotly and enter the city."

"'Tis a bold plan," Edgar said; "but at least there seems some hope of success which no other plan, methinks, could give. At any rate we two will do our best, and being well fed and well armed may hope to be able to cut our way out of the mêlée if all should be lost. We fight for honour and from good-will. But this is not a case in which we would die rather than turn bridle, as it would be were we fighting under the banner of England and the command of the king."

"Quite so, Edgar; I agree with you entirely," the merchant said. "You have not come to this country to die in the defence of Ghent. You came hither to do, if occasion offers, some knightly deeds, and feeling pity for the starving people here you offer them knightly aid, and will fight for them as long as there is a chance that fighting may avail them, but beyond that it would be folly indeed to go; and when you see the day hopelessly lost, you and your men-at-arms may well try to make your way out of the crowd of combatants, and to ride whither you will. I say not to return here, for that would indeed be an act of folly, since Ghent will have to surrender at once and without conditions, as soon as the news comes that the battle is lost. Therefore your best plan would be to ride for Sluys, and there take ship again. As for me, I shall wait until news comes and then ride for Liege, and remain there with friends

quietly until we see what the upshot of the affair is likely
to be."

During the day preparations were made for the expedition.
Five thousand of those best able to carry arms were chosen,
but the store of provisions was so small that there were but
five cartloads of biscuit and two tuns of wine for those
who went, and a like quantity for the sustenance of those
who stayed. The young knights were to ride in the train
of Van Artevelde himself. In the morning the merchant
had asked them what colours they would wear, for, so far,
they had not provided themselves with scarves.

"You should have scarves, and knightly plumes also," he
said, "and, if you carry lances, pennons; but as you say
that you shall fight with sword, that matter can stand over.
Tell me what colours you choose, and I will see that you
have them."

Albert answered that he should carry his father's
colours, namely, a red sash, and red and blue plumes.
Edgar replied that he had never thought about it, but
that he would choose white and red plumes, and a scarf of
the same colour. These the merchant purchased in the
afternoon, and his wife and daughter fastened the plumes
in their helmets. At the appointed hour in the morning
they clad themselves in full armour, and when they went
down they found the merchant's wife and daughter were
already afoot, and these fastened the scarves over their
shoulders. On going down to the courtyard they found,
to their surprise, that their two horses both carried armour
on the chest, body, and head.

"It is right that you should go to battle in knightly
fashion," the merchant said, "and I have provided you
with what is necessary. Indeed, that is no more than is
due. I brought you out here, and involved you in this

business, and 'tis but right that I should see that you are
protected as far as may be from harm."

The reins were supplemented by steel chains, so that the
riders should not be left powerless were the leather cut by
a sweeping blow.   When they mounted, the merchant himself went with them to the spot where Van Artevelde's
following were to assemble.   The two men-at-arms, in high
spirits at the thought of a fight, rode behind them, together
with the two Van Voorden had engaged at Sluys, both of
whom were able to speak a certain amount of English.

"If you are unhorsed, comrade," one of them said to Hal
Carter, "and in an extremity, remember that the cry for
mercy is '*Misericorde*'."

"By my faith," Hal replied, "'tis little likely that they
will get that cry from me; as long as I can fight I will fight,
when I can fight no longer they can slay me.   Still, it is as
well that I should know the word, as I should not like to
kill any poor wretch who asks for quarter."

They found Van Artevelde already at the place of assembly.   He greeted the young knights most cordially.

"Your presence here," he said, "will be invaluable to
me.   The word will soon go round to our host that you are
English knights, and it will be held as a token that England is with us."

They waited half an hour, and then Van Voorden bade
them adieu, as the cavalcade moved forward.   Already the
greater part of the armed men had moved out from the
city, each band having assembled in its own quarter, and
moved through the gates as soon as its number was complete.   The instructions had been that each company, as it
issued from the gates, was to follow the road to Bruges, and
as soon as the sun rose it was to halt, when they were all
to form up and move in order.   Van Artevelde introduced

the young knights to many of those who rode with him, as having lately arrived from England, and as being willing to take part in a battle for so good a cause.

The road was broad and wide, but the cavalcade rode in single file, so as to pass without difficulty the masses of marching men. Just as the sun rose they reached the head of the column. A halt was called; the country was flat, and the companies were now formed on a front half a mile wide, so that they could march at once faster and in an orderly body, as it was possible that some spy might have sent the news of their coming to Bruges, and they might be attacked on their way. There were no horses, save those of Van Artevelde and his immediate followers, the seven carts being dragged by men. As the march proceeded, Edgar and Albert requested Van Artevelde to give them leave to ride with their four men across the country, and to take with them a score of the most active foot-men.

"It will be hard," they said, "if we cannot come across a few cattle, sheep, or horses, or some sacks of flour, which would mightily help us. If we keep ahead of the main body we may, too, come by surprise on some of the farm-houses, and shall be able to send back news to you should there be any armed force approaching."

"By all means do so, and thanks for the offer."

Artevelde gave orders at once that twenty men of the company next to him should proceed as rapidly as they could ahead with the English knights, and should hold themselves under their command.

"We will go on, good fellows," Edgar said to them; "if we meet with a force too strong for us we shall ride back, but if we can capture aught in the way of food we will wait until you come up and leave it in your charge to hold until the others arrive."

Riding on fast the friends were soon two miles ahead of the main body. The villages on the road were found to be completely deserted, the people having removed weeks before; for, lying as they did between the rival cities, they were likely to suffer at the hands of both. The party soon turned off and made across the country. Here and there a few animals could be seen over the flat expanse. Presently they came upon a mill; the water of the canal that turned its wheel was running to waste, and the place was evidently deserted.

"Hew down the door, Hal," Edgar said to his follower.

"That will I right willingly, my lord, for, in truth, I begin to feel well-nigh as hungry as those of Ghent. We have had good lodgings, and the beasts have fared well on hay, but had it not been for the food we brought from the last halting-place, verily I believe that we should not have had a bite from the time we entered the place five days ago to now."

"We have been in almost as bad a plight, Hal. It was well indeed that we filled up our panniers, in the knowledge that there was little to be obtained in Ghent; though in truth we knew not that the pressure of want was so great."

A few strokes with the heavy axe Hal carried at his saddle-bow stove in the door, and they entered.

The interior of the mill was in great confusion, and by the manner in which things were thrown about it was evident that it had been deserted in great haste, and probably some months before, when the fighting was going on hotly. "Look round, lads," Edgar exclaimed. "They may well have left something behind when they fled so suddenly."

A shout was raised when the men-at-arms entered the next chamber. In one corner stood ten sacks of flour, and the bin into which the flour ran from the stones was half full, and contained enough to fill five or six others. One of the Flemish men-at-arms was at once ordered to ride back at full speed to the road to intercept the twenty footmen. These were to be directed to come at once to take charge of the mill, and the messenger was then to ride on till he met Van Artevelde, and to beg him to send forward as many bakers as there might be among his following, and to inform him that there was flour enough to furnish a loaf for every man in the force. As soon as the foot-men arrived, Edgar and Albert set them to work. The three men had already collected a quantity of wood and lighted the fire in a great oven that they had found, and from which it was evident that the miller was also a baker, and supplied the villagers round them. The two knights, with their followers, again started on horseback, and after four hours' riding, returned with twelve cattle, four horses, and a score of sheep they had found grazing masterless over the country. By this time fifty bakers were at work, and five hundred men were sitting down round the mill waiting to carry the loaves, when baked, to the army. The animals were given over to the charge of ten of these men, who were ordered to drive them after the army until this halted. The young knights and their men-at-arms then rode away.

CHAPTER XIV.

CIVIL WAR.

EDGAR and Albert came up with the force after an hour-and-a-half's riding, and found it halted some four miles from Bruges. The news that the English knights had discovered a store of flour had passed quickly through the ranks, and they were loudly cheered as they rode in.

"Truly you have rendered us a vast service," Van Arte-velde said as they joined him, "for it will not be needful to break in this evening upon our scanty store, and this is of vital importance, since we must perforce wait until the Earl and the men of Bruges come out to attack us. Your men said that it was some fifteen sacks of flour that you had found?"

"About that, sir. There were ten full, and under the millstones was a great bin holding, I should say, half as much more. Moreover, we have ridden far over the country, and have gathered up twelve head of cattle, four horses, and a score of sheep. These are following us, and will give meat enough for a good meal to-day all round, and maybe something to spare, and to-morrow I trust that we may bring in some more."

A murmur of satisfaction broke from the four or five burghers with Van Artevelde.

"This is a good beginning indeed of our adventure," the latter said, "and greatly are we beholden to these knights. They have dispelled the apprehension I had that if the people of Bruges deferred their attack for a couple of days they might find us so weakened with hunger as to be unable to show any front against them."

Two hours later the animals arrived, and were handed over to the company of the butchers' guild, who proceeded at once to cut them up. They were then distributed among the various companies, with orders that but half was to be eaten that night and the rest kept for the morrow. In the meantime men had been sent on to some of the deserted villages, and had returned with doors, shutters, broken furniture, and beams, and fires were speedily lighted. Before the meat was ready half of those who had remained at the mill arrived laden with bread, and said that the rest would be up in two hours. For the first time for weeks the Ghentois enjoyed a hearty meal, and as Van Artevelde, with the young knights and burghers with him, went round on foot among the men, they were greeted with loud cheers and shouts of satisfaction.

The next day the force remained where it had halted. The two knights and the men-at-arms scoured the country again for some miles round, and drove in before them twenty-two head of cattle, and these sufficed, with what had remained over, to furnish food for the day and to leave enough for the troops to break their fast in the morning.

So deserted was the country that it was not until the next morning early that the news reached the Earl that the men of Ghent had come out against him. Rejoicing that they should thus have placed themselves in his power, he sent out three knights to reconnoitre their position and bring an account of their numbers. After breakfast Philip van Artevelde had moved his followers a short distance away from their halting-ground and taken up a position near to a small hill, where he addressed them.

Some friars and clergy who were with the force celebrated mass at various points, and then confessed the troops, and exhorted them to keep up their courage, telling them that small forces had, with the help of God, frequently defeated large ones, and as all had been done that was possible to obtain peace but without avail, He would surely help them against these enemies who sought to destroy them utterly. Then they prepared for battle. Each man carried with him a long and sharp stake, as was their custom, in the same fashion as did the English archers, and they gathered in a square and set a hedge of these stakes round them. The

enemy's knights had ridden near them without being interfered with, for the Ghentois wished nothing better than
that the smallness of their numbers should be clearly seen.

After they had ridden off, Van Artevelde, confident that
their report would suffice to bring out the Earl with his
people, now ordered that the wine and bread brought out with
them, which had hitherto been untouched, should be served
out. The men then sat down and quietly awaited the attack.
As Van Artevelde had hoped, the message taken back by
the knights as to his strength and position was sufficient to
induce the Earl to give battle at once, as he feared that
they might change their mind and retreat. The alarm-bells
called all the citizens to arms. They fell in with their companies, and marched out forty thousand strong, including the
knights and men-at-arms of the Earl. The citizens of Bruges,
delighted at the thought that the opportunity for levelling
their haughty rival to the dust had now arrived, marched
on, until they reached the edge of a pond in front of the
position of the Ghentois.

Van Artevelde had placed the whole of the men with
guns in the front rank, with the strictest orders that no
shot was to be fired until the order was given. Waiting
until the enemy had gathered in great masses, Van Artevelde gave the word, and the three hundred guns, many of
these being wall-pieces, were fired at once, doing great destruction. The sun was behind the Ghentois, and its direct
rays, and those reflected from the pond, rendered it difficult
for the men of Bruges to see what their foes were doing,
and observing the great confusion from the effect of the
volley, the men of Ghent, with a mighty cheer, pulled up
their stakes, and rushing round the ends of the pond, fell
upon their enemies with fury

The men of Bruges, who had anticipated no resistance, and

M 371

THE TWO YOUNG KNIGHTS CHARGE DOWN UPON THE
PANIC-STRICKEN CROWD.

had marched out in the full belief that the Ghentois would lay down their arms and crave for mercy as soon as they appeared, were seized with a panic. The two young knights, with their four men-at-arms, had placed themselves at the head of the foot-men, and, dashing among the citizens, hewed their way through them, followed closely by the shouting Ghentois. Numbers of the men of Bruges were slain with sword, axe, and pike. The others threw away their arms and fled, hotly pursued by their foes. Louis of Flanders, who, by a charge with his knights and men-at-arms, might well have remedied the matter, now showed that he was as cowardly as he was cruel, drew off with them, and, without striking a single blow, he himself and some forty men galloped to Bruges. The rest of his knights and followers scattered in all directions.

Great numbers of the flying citizens were killed in the pursuit. It was now dark; the Earl on arriving had ordered the gate by which he entered to be closed, and had set twenty men there. Thus the retreat of the citizens into the town was prevented, and many were slaughtered. In consequence, the rest fled to other gates, where they were admitted, but with them rushed in their pursuers. Philip van Artevelde begged the two English knights to each take a strong party, and to proceed round the walls in different directions, seizing all the gates, and setting a strong guard on them, that none should enter or leave; and then, with the main body of his following he marched without opposition to the market-place.

The Earl, when he found that the town was lost and the gates closed, disguised himself, and found shelter for the night in a loft in the house of a poor woman. Van Artevelde had issued the strictest orders that he was on no account to be injured, but was, when found, to be brought at once to him, so that he might be taken to Ghent, and there obliged to make a peace that would assure to the city all its privileges, and give rest and tranquillity to the country. In spite, however, of the most rigid search, the Earl was not found; but the forty knights and men-at-arms who had entered with him were all captured and killed. No harm whatever was done to any of the inhabitants of Bruges, or to any foreign merchants or others residing there.

On the following night the Earl of Flanders managed to effect his escape in disguise. That day being Sunday the men of Ghent repaired to the cathedral, where they had solemn mass celebrated, and a thanksgiving for their victory and for their relief from their sore strait. The young knights were not present, for as soon as the city was captured Van Artevelde said to them:

"Brave knights, to you it is chiefly due that we are masters here to-day, instead of being men exhausted, without hope, and at the mercy of our enemies. It was you who found and brought us food, and so enabled us to hold out for two days, and to meet the enemy strong and in good heart. Then, too, I marked how you clove a way for our men to follow you through the ranks of the foe, spreading death and dismay among them. Sirs, to you, then, I give the honour of bearing the news to Ghent. I have ordered that fresh horses shall be brought you from the prince's stable. Councillor Moens will ride with you to act as spokesman; but before starting, take, I pray you, a goblet of wine and some bread. It were well that you took your men-at-arms with you, for you might be beset on the road by some of the people who did not succeed in entering the gates, or by some of the cowardly knights who stood by and saw the citizens being defeated without laying lance in rest to aid them. Fresh horses shall be prepared for your men also, and they shall sup before they start. There is no lack of food here."

Much gratified at the mission intrusted to them, the young knights at once ordered their men-at-arms to prepare for the ride.

"When you have supped," Albert said, "see that you stuff your saddle-bags and ours with food for Van Voorden's household first, and then for those who most need it."

The meals were soon eaten. As they were about to mount Van Artevelde said to them:

"There will be no lack of provisions to-morrow, for in two hours a great train of waggons, loaded with provisions, will start under a strong guard, and to-morrow at daybreak herds of cattle will be brought in and driven there; you may be sure also that the rivers will be open as soon as the news is known, for none will now venture to interfere with those bringing food into Ghent."

The councillor was ready, and in a few minutes they had passed out of the city, and were galloping along the road to Ghent, just as the bell of the cathedral tolled the hour of ten. Two hours later, without having once checked the speed of their horses, they heard the bells ringing midnight in Ghent. In ten minutes they approached the gate, and were challenged from the walls.

"I am the Councillor Moens," the knights' companion shouted. "I come from Philip van Artevelde with good news. We have defeated the enemy, and captured Bruges."

There was a shout of delight from the walls, and in a minute the drawbridge was lowered and the great gate opened. The councillor rode straight to the town-hall. The doors were open, and numbers of the citizens were still gathered there. Moens did not wait to speak to them, but, running into the belfry, ordered the men there to ring their most joyous peal. The poor fellows had been lying about, trying to deaden their hunger by sleep, but at the order they leapt to their feet, seized the ropes, and Ghent was electrified by hearing the triumphant peal bursting out in the stillness of the night.

In the meantime those in the hall had crowded round the young knights and their followers, but these, beyond saying that the news was good, waited until Moens' return. It was but a minute, and he at once shouted:

"The enemy have been beaten! We have taken Bruges! By the morning food will be here!"

Now from every belfry in the city the notes from the town-hall had been taken up, the clanging of the bells roused every sleeper, and the whole town poured into the street shouting wildly, for though they knew not yet what had happened, it was clear that some great news had arrived. All the councillors and the principal citizens had made for the town-hall, which was speedily thronged. Moens took his place with the two young knights upon the raised platform at the end, and lifted his hand for silence. The excited multitude were instantly still, and those near the doors closed them, to keep out the sound of the bells. Then Moens, speaking at the top of his voice that all might hear him, said: "I am now but the mouthpiece of these English knights, to whom Van Artevelde has given the honour of bearing the news to you, but since they are ignorant of our language I have come with them as inter-preter. First, then, we have met the army of Bruges and the Earl, forty thousand strong; we have defeated them with great slaughter, and with but small loss to ourselves."

A mighty shout rose from the crowd, and it was some minutes before the speaker could continue.

"Following on the heels of our flying foes, we entered the city, and Bruges is ours."

Another shout, as enthusiastic as the first, again interrupted him.

"A great train of waggons filled with wine and provisions was to start at midnight, and will be here to-morrow morning at daybreak. Herds will be driven in, and despatched at once. By to-morrow night, therefore, the famine will be at an end, and every man, woman, and child in Ghent will be able to eat their fill."

Those at the door shouted the glad news to the multitude in the square, and a roar like that of the sea answered, and echoed the shouts in the hall.

"Tell us more, tell us more!" the men cried, when the uproar ceased. "We have seven or eight hours to wait for food; tell us all about it."

"I will tell you first, citizens, why I am speaking to you in the name of these English knights, and why they have been chosen to have the honour of bringing these good tidings hither."

He then told them how, the force being without horsemen and bound to keep straight along by the road, the two knights had volunteered to ride out to see if any hostile force was approaching, and also to endeavour to find provisions.

"The latter seemed hopeless," the councillor went on. "Every village had long since been deserted, and no living soul met the eye on the plain. They had been gone but three hours when one of their men-at-arms rode in, asking that all the bakers should be sent forward at once, for that, in a mill less than two miles from the road, they had discovered fifteen sacks of flour left behind. The bakers started at once with five hundred men to bring on the bread as fast as it was baked to the spot where we were to halt.

"This was not all, for, later on, the knights with some of the men joined us at the camp with sufficient cattle, sheep, and horses, that the knights had found straying, to give every man a meal that night, and one the following morning. The next day they drove in a few more, and so it was not until to-day that we touched the store we took with us. It was the food that saved us. Had we been forced to eat our scanty supply that first night, we should have been fasting for well-nigh forty-eight hours, and when the Earl, with his knights and men-at-arms and the townsmen of Bruges, in all forty thousand men, marched out to meet us, what chance would five thousand famished men have had against them? As it was, the food we got did wonders for us; and every man seemed to have regained his full strength and courage. When they came nigh to us we poured in one volley with all our guns, which put them into confusion. The sun was in their eyes, and almost before they knew that we had moved, we were upon them.

"These two knights and their four men-at-arms flung themselves into the crowd and opened the way for our footmen, and in five minutes the fight was over. It may be that many of the craftsmen of Bruges were there unwillingly, and that these were among the first to throw down their arms and fly. However it was, in five minutes the whole force was in full flight. The Earl's knights and their men-at-arms struck not a single blow, but, seeming panic-struck, scattered and fled in all directions, the Earl and forty men alone gaining Bruges. There they closed the gate against the fugitives, but these fled to other gates, and so hotly did we pursue them that we entered mixed up with them.

"Van Artevelde committed to the two English knights the task of seizing all the gates, and of setting a guard to prevent any man from leaving, while the rest of us under him pushed forward to the market-place. There was no resistance. Thousands of the men had fallen in the battle and flight. Thousands had failed to enter the gates. All who did so were utterly panic-stricken and terrified. Thus the five thousand men you sent out have defeated forty thousand, and have captured Bruges, and I verily believe that not more than a score have fallen. Methinks, my friends, you will all agree with me that your governor has done well to give these knights the honour of carrying the good news to Ghent."

A mighty shout answered the question. The crowd rushed upon the two young knights, each anxious to speak to them and praise them. With difficulty the councillor, aided by some of his colleagues, surrounded them, and made a way to a small door at the end of the platform. Once beyond the building, they hurried along by-streets to Van Voorden's house, to where, on entering the hall, they had charged the men-at-arms at once to take the horses, to hand over as much of the provisions as were needed for the immediate wants of the household, and then to carry the rest to the nuns of a convent hard by,—for these were, they knew, reduced to the direst straits before the expedition started.

"Welcome back, welcome back!" the Fleming exclaimed as they entered, and the words were repeated by wife and daughter. "Your men-at-arms told my wife what had happened, and I myself heard it from the lower end of the town-hall, where I arrived just as Moens began to speak. I saw you escape from the platform, and hurried off, but have only this instant arrived. The crush was so great in the square that it was difficult to make my way through it, but forgive us if we say nothing further until we have eaten that food upon the table, for indeed we have had but one regular meal since you left the town. Tell me first

though, for all were too excited to ask Moens the question
—has the Earl been captured?"

"He had not, up to the moment when we left. The
strictest search is being made for him. It is known that
he must be somewhere in the town, for he and a party, not
knowing that Van Artevelde was in the market-place, well-
nigh fell into his hands, and he certainly could not have got
through any of the gates before we had closed them and
had placed a strong guard over them. Van Artevelde has
given strict orders that he is to be taken uninjured, and
he purposes to bring him here, and to make him sign a
peace with us."

"I trust that he will be caught," Van Voorden said; "but
as for the peace, I should have no faith in it, for be sure
that as soon as he is once free again he would repudiate
it, and would at once set to work to gather, with the aid of
Burgundy, a force with which he could renew the war, wipe
out the disgrace that has befallen him, and take revenge
upon the city that inflicted it. Now let us to supper."

"We will but look on," Albert said with a smile. "We
supped at Bruges at half-past nine, but it will be a pleasure
indeed to see you eat it."

"We must not eat much," the merchant said to his wife
and daughter. "Let us take a little now, and to-morrow we
can do better. It might injure us to give rein to our
appetite after well-nigh starving for the last two days."

As soon as the meal was eaten all sallied out into the
streets, the young knights first laying aside their armour, as
they did not wish to attract attention. The bells were still
ringing out with joyous clamour; at every house flags, carpets,
and curtains had been hung out; torches were fixed to every
balcony, and great bonfires had been lighted in the middle
of the streets, and in the open spaces and markets. The

people were well-nigh delirious with joy; strangers shook hands and embraced in the streets; men and women forgot their weakness and hunger, though many were so feeble but an hour before that they could scarcely drag themselves along. The cathedral and churches were all lighted up and crowded with worshippers, thanking God for having preserved them in their hour of greatest need.

"Then, in truth, Sir Edgar," the Fleming said as they went along, "the people of Bruges showed themselves to be but a cowardly rabble, and the fighting was poor indeed."

"It could scarce be called fighting at all," Edgar said. "A few blows from halbert and bill, and a few thrusts of the pike struck my armour as I charged among them, but after that it was but a matter of cutting down fugitives. The rabble down in Kent fought with far greater courage, for we had to charge through and through them several times before they broke. I doubt not that very many were outside Bruges against their wills, they had not dared disobey the summons to arms. It was a panic, and a strange one. They had doubtless made up their minds that when we saw their multitude we should surrender without a blow being struck. The sudden discharge of the guns shook them, and at our first charge they bolted away panic-struck. The strangest part of the affair was that the Earl, who had a strong following of knights and men-at-arms, made no effort to retrieve the battle. Had they but charged down upon our flank when we had become disordered in the pursuit they could have overthrown us without difficulty.

"How it came about that they did not do so is more than I can say. It is clear that the Earl showed himself to be a great coward, and his disgrace this day is far greater than that of the burghers of Bruges, since he and his party fled

(M 371)   R without the loss of a single drop of blood, while thousands of the citizens have lost their lives."

"'Tis good that he so behaved," Van Voorden said. "The story that he so deserted the men of Bruges, who went to fight in his quarrel, will speedily be known throughout Flanders, and that, with the news of our great victory, will bring many cities to our side. I trust that Van Artevelde will treat Bruges with leniency."

"He has already issued a proclamation that none of the small craftsmen of Bruges shall be injured, but exception is made in the case of the four guilds that have always been foremost against Ghent; members of which are to be killed when found."

"'Tis a pity, but one can scarce blame him. And now, my friends, that we have seen Ghent on this wonderful night it will be well that we get home to bed. My wife and daughter are still weak from fasting, and I myself feel the strain. As to you, you have done a heavy day's work indeed, especially having to carry the weight of your armour."

The young knights were indeed glad to throw themselves upon their pallets. They slept soundly until awakened by a fresh outburst of the bells. They sat up; daylight was beginning to break.

"'Tis the train of provisions," Edgar said. "We may as well go out and see the sight, and give such aid as we can to the council, for the famishing people may well be too eager to await the proper division of the food."

In a few days there was an abundance of everything in Ghent, for Damme and Sluys opened their gates at once. In the former there were vast cellars of wine, of which 6000 tuns were sent by ships and carts to Ghent, while at Sluys there was a vast quantity of corn and meal in the ships and storehouses of foreign merchants. All this was bought and paid for at fair prices and sent to the city. Besides food and wine, Ghent received much valuable spoil. All the gold and silver vessels of the Earl were captured at Bruges, with much treasure, and a great store of gold and jewels was taken at his palace at Male, near Bruges.

Philip Van Artevelde at once sent messages to all the towns of Flanders summoning them to send the keys of their gates to Ghent, and to acknowledge her supremacy. The news of the victory had caused great exultation in most of these cities, and with the exception of Oudenarde all sent deputations at once to Ghent to congratulate her, and to promise to support her in all things. In the meantime the gates and a portion of the wall of Bruges had been beaten down, and five hundred of the burgesses were taken to Ghent as hostages. The young knights remained quietly there until Philip Van Artevelde returned. He was received with frantic enthusiasm. He had assumed the title of Regent of Flanders, and now assumed a state and pomp far greater than that which the Earl himself had held. He had an immense income, for not only were his private estates large, but a sort of tribute was paid by all the towns of Flanders, and Ghent for a time presented a scene of gaiety and splendour equal to that of any capital in Europe.

Siege was presently laid to Oudenarde, where the garrison had been strongly reinforced by a large party of men-at-arms and cross-bowmen sent by the Earl. Every city in Flanders sent a contingent of fighting men to join those of Ghent, and no less than a hundred thousand men were assembled outside Oudenarde. Thither went the two young friends as soon as the siege began. They had come out to see fighting and not feasting, and they had lost the society of

Van Voorden, he having been requested by Van Artevelde
to return to England, to conclude a treaty between her
and Ghent. Flanders was indeed master of itself, for the
Earl was a fugitive at the court of his son-in-law the Duke
of Burgundy, who was endeavouring to induce France to
join him against Flanders.

For a time he failed, for the king was much better disposed to the Flemings than he was to the Earl; but when,
some time later, Charles died, and Burgundy became all-
powerful with the young king, his successor, France also
prepared to take the field against Flanders. Thus a close
alliance between the latter and England became of great
importance to both, and had it not been for the extreme
unpopularity of the Duke of Lancaster and his brother
Gloucester, the course of events might have been changed.
For war with France was always popular in England, and
the necessary supplies would at once have been voted by
parliament had it not been thought that when an army
was raised Lancaster would, instead of warring with France,
use it for furthering his own claims in Spain. Many English knights, however, came over on their own account to
aid the Flemings, and no less than two hundred archers at
Calais quietly left the town, with the acquiescence, if not
with the encouragement, of the authorities, to take service
with Van Artevelde.

One day the two friends returned to camp after being
away for some time watching what was going on. On entering their tent Albert, who was the first to enter, gave a shout
of surprise and pleasure. Edgar pushed in to see what could
have thus excited his friend, and so moved him from his
usual quiet manner. He, too, was equally surprised, and
almost equally pleased, when he saw Albert standing with
his hand clasped in that of his father.

"I thought that I should surprise you," Sir Ralph said, "by coming over both to see this great gathering, and also to have a look at you. We heard of your doings from Van Voorden. He was good enough, after his first interview with the king and council, to ride down to tell us how it fared with you, and it gave us no small pleasure, as you may well suppose, to hear that you had already gained so much credit, and that you both were well in health. I went back to town with him, and stayed three weeks there. There was much talk in the council. All were well content that there should be an alliance with the Flemings, but it seems to me there is not much chance of an English army taking the field to help them at present.

"The king is altogether taken up with his marriage, and is thinking much more of fêtes and pageants than of war. Then 'tis doubtful whether the Commons would grant the large sum required. The present is a bad time; the rebellion has cost much money, and what with the destruction of property, with the fields standing untilled, and the expenses of the court, which are very heavy, in truth the people have reasonable cause for grumbling thereat. Then, again, if an army were sent to Flanders Lancaster would most surely have the command, and you know how much he is hated, and, I may say, feared. Naught will persuade men that he has not designs upon the crown. For this I can see no warrant, but assuredly he loves power, and he and Gloucester overshadow the king.

"Then, again, his wishes are, certainly, to lead a great army into Spain, and he would oppose money being spent on operations in Flanders. Thus, I fear, our alliance is like to be but of little use to Ghent or Flanders. Were but the Black Prince or his father upon the throne things would be different indeed, and we should have a stout army here before many weeks are over. We of the old time feel it hard indeed to see England playing so poor a part. There is another reason, moreover, why our barons do not press matters on. In the first place, they are jealous of the influence that the king's favourites have with him, and that those who, by rank and age, should be his councillors meet with but a poor reception when they come to court.

"But methinks that even these things hinder much less than the conduct of the people of Ghent. Since Bruges was captured there have been, as you know, parties going through the land as far as the frontiers of France plundering and destroying all the houses and castles of the knights and nobles, under the complaint that they were favourable to the Earl, but in truth chiefly because these knaves hate those of gentle blood and are greedy of plunder. Our nobles deem it—and methinks that they have some reason for doing so—to be a business something like that which we have had in England, save that with us it was the country people, while here it is those of the towns who would fain pull down and destroy all those above them in station. Certainly their acts are not like to win the friendship and assistance of our English nobles and knights."

"Indeed I see that, Sir Ralph," Edgar said. "At first we were greatly in favour of Ghent, seeing that they were in a desperate strait and that all reasonable terms were refused them, but of late we have not been so warm in their cause. Van Artevelde himself is assuredly honest and desirous of doing what is right, but methinks he does wrong in keeping up the state of a king and bearing himself towards all those of the other cities of Flanders as if Ghent were their conqueror, and laying heavy taxes upon them, while he himself is swayed by the councils of the most violent of the demagogues of Ghent."

"But now tell me,—how goes on the siege?"

"It goes not on at all. Oudenarde is a strong place; it is defended by many broad ditches, and has a garrison of knights and men-at-arms of the Earl, who, as we know, take upon themselves all the defence, knowing that there are men in the town who would fain surrender, and fearing that these would throw open the gates to us, or give us such aid as they could were there a chance. Still more, the siege goes on but slowly, or rather we may say goes on not at all, for want of a leader. Van Artevelde himself knows nothing whatever of the business of war, nor do any of those about him.

"The men of the towns will all fight bravely in a pitched field, as they have often shown, but as to laying a siege they know naught of it, and it seems to us that the matter might go on for a year and yet be no nearer its end. They are far more occupied in making ordinances and collecting contributions, and in doing all they can for the honour and glory of Ghent, than in thinking of taking Oudenarde, which indeed, when captured, would be of no great consequence to them."

Sir Ralph nodded. "Methinks you are right, Edgar. I arrived here just as you went out this morning, and hearing from your men that you were not like to return till midday, I have ridden round to see what was being done, and to my surprise saw that, in the three months since this great host sat down before Oudenarde, naught of any use whatever has been accomplished. With such an army, if Flanders wishes to maintain her freedom, she should have summoned Burgundy to abstain from giving aid to the Earl, and on his refusal should have marched with her whole force against him, captured some of his great towns, and met his host in a fair field. Methinks you two are doing no good to yourselves here, and that it will be just as well for you both to go back to England for a time, until you see how matters shape themselves."

CHAPTER XV.

A CRUSHING DEFEAT.

THE two young knights were both pleased to hear Sir Ralph's counsel, for they themselves had several times talked the matter over together, and agreed that there was little prospect of aught being done for many months. They felt that they were but wasting their time remaining before Oudenarde, where they were frequently offended by the overbearing manner of the Ghentois, who, on the strength of their defeat of the people of Bruges, considered themselves to be invincible. They had, during the four months that they had been in Flanders, learned enough of the language to make themselves easily understood. They had paid visits to Brussels and other places of importance, and were likely to learn nothing from the events of the siege, which, they could already see, was not going to be attended with success.

It was their first absence from home, and in the lack of all adventure and excitement they would be glad to be back again. Therefore, after remaining three days, which only confirmed Sir Ralph in his view, they took leave of Van Artevelde, saying that they hoped to rejoin him as soon as there was any prospect of active service, and, riding to Sluys, took ship with their followers. At Sir Ralph's suggestion they retained in their train the two Flemings, whom they had found stout and useful fellows.

"Are you glad to go home again, Hal?" Sir Edgar said.

"Well, master, I should not be glad were there aught doing here, though now that they have granted a pardon to all concerned in Wat the Tyler's business I can show my face without fear. But it has been a dull time. Except just for a score of blows in that business with the Bruges people there has been nought to do since we came over, except to groom the horses and polish the armour. One might as well have been driving a cart at St. Alwyth as moping about this camp."

"Perhaps there will be more stirring times when we come back again, Hal. Burgundy is arming, and it is like enough that France may join him, and in that case there will be fighting enough even to satisfy you; but we may have a few months at home before that is likely to take place."

The knights were landed at Gravesend, and their road lay together as far as St. Alwyth. It was late in the afternoon, and Sir Ralph and Albert rode straight home, telling Edgar that they should expect to see him in the morning. Edgar found his father going on just as usual. He received his son with pleasure, but without surprise, as Sir Ralph had called before he left, and had said that if he found that naught was doing at Oudenarde he would recommend his own son and Edgar to return home for a while.

"Well, Sir Knight," Mr. Ormskirk said smiling, "I have not yet congratulated you on your honour, but, believe me, I was right glad when I heard the news. You have had but little fighting, I hear."

"None at all, father, for the affair near Bruges could scarcely be called fighting. It was as naught to the fight we had down here before we went away; save for that, I have not drawn sword. I have returned home somewhat richer, for Van Artevelde gave Albert and myself rich presents as our share of the spoil taken there."

"You have grown nigh two inches," Mr. Ormskirk said, as Edgar laid aside his armour.

"I have done little else but eat and sleep, ride for an hour or two every day, and practise arms other two hours with Albert, for indeed there were few among the Flemings who knew aught of the matter save to strike a downright blow. They are sturdy fellows and strong, and can doubtless fight well side by side in a pitched battle, but they can scarce be called men-at-arms, seeing that they but take down their weapons when these are required, and hang them up again until there is fresh occasion for their use. So that I have doubtless grown a bit, having nothing else to do."

"And for how long are you home, Edgar?"

"That I know not, father. Sir Ralph will go up with us to London next week. He says that it will be well we should present ourselves at court, but after that we shall do nothing until affairs change in Flanders, or till a force goes from here to their aid."

Edgar rode over to the De Courcys' place the next morning, and received a warm welcome.

Four days later they rode to town with Sir Ralph. The king received them with much favour.

"Philip Van Artevelde sent me by Master Van Voorden a most favourable report of you," he said, "and told me that he was mightily beholden to you for his victory over the men of Bruges, for that had it not been for your collecting supplies for his men they would have been too famished to have given battle, and that you led the charge into the midst of their ranks. I was pleased to find that my knights had borne themselves so well. And how goes on the siege of Oudenarde?"

"It can scarcely be called a siege, your Majesty," Edgar said; "there are a few skirmishes, but beyond that naught is done. If your Majesty would but send them out a good knight with skill in such matters they might take Oudenarde in ten days. As it is, 'tis like to extend to the length of the siege of Troy, unless the Burgundians come to its relief."

"I could send them a good knight, for I have plenty of them, but would they obey him?"

"Methinks not, sire," Edgar replied frankly. "Just at present they are so content with themselves that they would assuredly accept no foreign leader, and have indeed but small respect for their own."

The king laughed. "What thought you of them, Sir Ralph?"

"'Tis what might be looked for, your Majesty. It is an army of bourgeois and craftsmen, stout fellows who could doubtless defend their walls against an attack, or might fight stoutly shoulder to shoulder, but they have an overweening conceit in themselves, and deem that all that is necessary in war is to carry a pike or a pole-axe and use it stoutly. A party of children would do as well, or better, were they set to besiege a town. Leadership there is none. Parties go out to skirmish with the garrison; a few lives are lost, and then they return, well content with themselves. 'Tis a mockery of war!"

The king asked them many questions about the state of things in Flanders, to which they replied frankly that Flanders was united at present, and that they thought that,—with five thousand English archers and as many men-at-arms under a commander of such station as would give him authority not only over his own troops but over the Flemings,—they might be able to resist the attacks of Burgundy, or even of Burgundy allied with France; but that by themselves, without military leaders, they feared that matters would go ill with the Flemings.

The king bade the two friends come to the court that evening; and when they did so he presented them to the young queen, speaking of them in very high terms.

"They were," he said, "the only men who did their duty on that day when the rioters invaded the Tower during our absence, killing with their own hands seven men who invaded the apartment of Lady De Courcy, and carrying her and her daughter safely through the crowd. Had all done their duty but a tenth part as well, the disgrace this rabble brought upon us would never have occurred, and the lives of my trusty councillors would have been saved."

"The king has already told me of your exploit here, and of other deeds as notable done by you; and Mynheer Van Voorden also spoke to me of the service you rendered him," the queen said graciously, "but I had scarcely looked to see the heroes of these stories such young knights."

She spoke to them for some time, while the king's favourites looked on, somewhat ill pleased at such graciousness being shown to the new-comers. The haughty De Vere, who had just been created Duke of Dublin, and who was about to start to undertake the governorship of Ireland, spoke in a sneering tone to a young noble standing next to him. Sir Ralph happened to overhear him, and touched him on the shoulder.

"My lord duke," he said, "methinks you need not grudge the honour that has fallen to those two young knights; you yourself have achieved far greater honour, and that without, so far as I know, ever having drawn your sword. But it were best that, if you have aught to say against them, you should say it in their hearing, when, I warrant me, either of them would gladly give you an opportunity of proving your valour. Your skill, indeed, would be needed, since I would wager either of them to spit you like a fly within five minutes; or should you consider them too young for so great a noble to cross swords with, I myself would gladly take up their quarrel."

The favourite flushed hotly, and for a moment hesitated. "I have no quarrel with them, Sir Ralph de Courcy," he said, after a short hesitation. "My words were addressed to a friend here."

"You spoke loud enough for me to hear, my lord duke, and should know that such words so spoken are an insult."

"They were not meant as such, Sir Ralph."

"Then, sir, I will give you my advice to hold your tongue more under government. Those young knights have earned royal favour not by soft words or mincing ways, but by their swords; and it were best in future that any remarks you may wish to make concerning them should be either in strict privacy or openly and in their hearing."

So saying, he turned his back on the disconcerted young courtier, who shortly afterwards left the royal presence overcome by chagrin and confusion, for the knight's words had been heard by several standing round, and more than one malicious smile had been exchanged among his rivals for court favour.

De Vere had a fair share of bravery, but the reports of the singular feats of swordsmanship by the young knights convinced him that he would have but small chance with either of them in a duel. Even if he came well out of it there would be but small credit indeed to him in overcoming a young knight who had not yet reached manhood, while, if worsted, it would be a fatal blow to his reputation. That evening he had a private interview with the king, and requested leave to start the next day to take up his new governorship. Sir Ralph related the incident to the lads as they returned to the hostelry where they had taken up their lodging.

"It was a heavy blow for his pride," he said. "I think not that he is a coward—the De Veres come of a good stock; but he saw that such a duel would do him great harm. The king himself, if he learned its cause, as he must have done, would have been greatly displeased, and the queen equally so, and there would have been no credit to him had he wounded you; while if he had been wounded, it would have been deemed a disgrace that he, the Duke of Dublin and Governor of Ireland, should have been worsted by so young a knight; therefore I blame him not for refusing to accept the challenge I offered him, and it will make him soberer and more careful of his speech in future. It was a lesson he needed greatly, for I have often heard him among his companions using insolent remarks concerning men who were in every respect his superiors, save that they stood not so high in the favour of the king."

They remained a week in London, attending the court regularly and improving their acquaintance with many whom they had met there in the troubled times. There was scarce a day that they did not spend some time at the house of Sir Robert Gaiton, Albert especially being always ready with some pretext for a visit there. Van Voorden had left London, sailing thence on the very day before they had arrived at Gravesend.

The summer passed quietly. Oudenarde still held out, and indeed no serious attack had been made upon it. Van Artevelde had sent a messenger to the King of France, begging him to mediate between the Flemings and the Duke of Burgundy, but the king had thrown the messenger into prison without returning answer, and in the autumn

had summoned his levies to aid the duke in the invasion of
Flanders. Seeing that fighting in earnest was likely to
commence shortly, the knights took ship with their followers
early in October, and after a fair voyage landed at Sluys
and rode to Oudenarde. A formal alliance had by this
time been made between the two countries, but no steps
had been taken towards gathering an army in England.
The two knights were, however, very cordially received by
Van Artevelde.

"You have arrived just in time to ride with me to-morrow,"
he said. "I am going to see that all has been done to prevent the French from crossing the river. All the bridges
have been broken save those at Comines and Warneton,
and Peter de Bois is appointed to hold the one, and Peter
de Winter the other."

The following morning some twenty horsemen started
with Van Artevelde and rode to Ghent, and thence followed
the bank of the Lys. Most of the bridges had been completely destroyed, and those at Comines and Warneton had
both been so broken up that a handful of men at either
could keep it against an army.

"We may feel safe, I think, sir knights," Van Artevelde
said to his friends when they brought their tour of inspection
to an end on the second day after starting.

"Assuredly we are safe against the French crossing by
the bridges," Edgar said, "but should they find boats they
may cross where they please."

"I have ordered every boat to be brought over to this
side of the river, Sir Edgar, and a number of men have, by
my orders, been engaged in doing so."

"Doubtless, sir. I have kept a look-out the whole distance
and have not seen one boat on the other side of the stream;
but there are numerous channels and canals by which the

country folk bring down their produce, and however sharp
the search may be some boats may have escaped notice.
Even a sunken one, that might seem wholly useless, could
be raised and roughly repaired, and in a few trips could
bring a number of men across under shadow of night. So
far as I have read, it is rarely that an army has failed to
find means of some kind for crossing a river."

But Philip van Artevelde was not now, as he had been a
year before, ready to take hints from others, and he simply
replied carelessly, "I have no doubt that my orders have
been strictly carried out, sir knight;" and rode forward again.

"I don't think things will go well with us, Albert," Edgar
said. "With a general who knows nothing whatever of
warfare, an army without officers, and tradesmen against
men-at-arms, the look-out is not good. Van Artevelde
ought to have had horsemen scattered over on the other
side of the river, who would have brought us exact news as
to the point against which the main body of the French
is marching. They ought to have a man posted every
two hundred yards along the river bank for fifteen miles
above and below that point, then I should have four bodies
of five thousand men each posted at equal distances three
miles behind the river, so that one of these could march
with all haste to the spot where they learned that the
French were attempting to cross, and could arrive there
long before enough of the enemy had made a passage, to
withstand their onslaught.

"I will wager that the Lys will not arrest the passage of
the French for twenty-four hours. Were Peter de Bois a
reasonable man, I would ask leave of Van Artevelde to ride
and take up our post with him; but he is an arrogant and
ignorant fellow with whom I should quarrel before I had
been in his camp an hour."

Two days passed quietly at Oudenarde, then the news came that the enemy had passed the Lys at Comines. Seeing that the bridge could not be crossed, the French army had halted. Some of the knights went down to the river, and after a search discovered some boats, in which they passed over with four hundred men-at-arms before nightfall, unperceived by the Flemings. They then marched towards Comines, hoping that the Flemings would leave their strong position near the head of the bridge to give battle, in which case they doubted not that the Constable would find means so far to repair the bridge that the passage could begin.

Peter de Bois, however, was not to be tempted to leave his position, and the French had to remain all night on the marshy ground without food for themselves or their horses. In the morning, however, the Fleming, fearing that others might cross and reinforce the party, marched out against them. The knights and men-at-arms met them so stoutly that in a very short time the Flemings took to flight. The French at once set to work to repair the bridge, and by nightfall a great portion of the army had crossed. The weather was very wet and stormy, and the French army had suffered much.

There were, besides Edgar and Albert, some other English knights in the camp, and these gathered together as soon as the news came, and talked over what in their opinion had best be done.

"I think," said Sir James Pinder, a knight who had seen much service on many stricken fields, "it would be best to remain where we are, and to throw up fortifications behind which we can fight to better advantage, while the French cavalry would be able to do but little against us. The French troops must be worn out with marching, and with the terrible weather; they will find it difficult to procure food, and might even abstain altogether from coming against us, while, from what I see of this rabble, they may fight bravely, but they will never be able to withstand the shock of the French knights and men-at-arms. 'Tis like the French will be three or four days before they come hither, and by that time, with fifty thousand men to work at them, we should have works so strong and high that we could fearlessly meet them. Moreover, the threescore English archers who still remain would be able to gall them as they pressed forward, whereas in a pitched battle they would not be numerous enough to avail anything."

The other six knights all agreed with Sir James, who then said, "I hear that Van Artevelde has summoned his leaders to consult them as to the best course. I will go across and tell them what in our opinion had better be done."

He returned in half an hour. "'Tis hopeless," he said, shrugging his shoulders. "These Flemings are as obstinate as they are ignorant; not one of those present agreed with my proposal, many indeed broke into rude laughter; and so I left them."

After crossing the Lys the French came to Ypres, and on the same day the Flemings broke up their camp before Oudenarde and marched, fifty thousand strong, to Courtray. On the following day they moved forward to ground which Van Artevelde and his counsellors deemed good for fighting. Behind them was a hill, a dyke was on one wing, and a grove of wood was on the other. The French were camped at Rosbecque, some four miles away. That evening Van Artevelde invited all the principal men and officers to sup with him, and gave them instructions for the morrow. He said that he was not sorry that no large force of Englishmen had come to their aid, for had they done so they

would assuredly have had the credit of the victory. He
also gave orders that no prisoners should be taken save
the king himself, whom they would bring to Ghent and
instruct in the Flemish language.

A false alarm roused the camp at midnight, and although
it proved to be ill-founded, the Flemings were so uneasy
at the thought that they might be attacked unawares, that
great fires were lighted and meat cooked and wine drunk
until an hour before daylight, when they arranged themselves in order of battle and also occupied a heath beyond
the wood. A large dyke ran across in front of them, and
behind them the ground was covered by small bushes.
Philip Van Artevelde was in the centre with 9000 picked
men of Ghent, whom he always kept near his person, as he
had but little faith in the good-will of those from other towns.

Beyond these were the contingents of Alost and Gram-
mont, of Courtray and Bruges, Damme and Sluys. All were
armed with maces, steel caps, breast-pieces, and gauntlets
of steel. Each carried a staff tipped with iron; each company and craft had its own livery, and colours and standards
with the arms of their town. The morning was misty, and
no sign could be seen of the French. After a time the
Flemings became impatient, and determined to sally out to
meet the enemy.

"It is just madness," Sir James said to the English
knights, who, with their followers, had gathered round him.
"I had great hopes that, with the dyke in their front
to check the onrush of the French, they might withstand
all attacks and come out victors; now they are throwing
away their advantage, and going like sheep to the shearers.
By my faith, friends, 'tis well that our horses have rested of
late, for we shall need all their speed if we are to make our
escape from this business."

As they moved forward in the mist they caught sight of some French knights, who moved backwards and forwards along their front and then rode away, doubtless to inform their countrymen that the Flemings were advancing against them. In the French army were all the best knights and leaders of France, and as soon as they heard that the Flemings were advancing they divided into three bodies, the one carrying the royal banner, which was to attack the Flemings in front; the two others were to move on either side and fall upon their flanks. This arranged, they moved forward with full confidence of victory.

The central division fell first upon the Flemings, but it was received so roughly that it recoiled a little, and several good knights fell. In a few minutes, however, the other two divisions attacked the Flemings' flanks. The English knights, who were stationed on the right, seeing what was coming, had in vain tried to get the companies on this side to face round so as to oppose a front to the attack. The consequence was that the weight of the attack fell entirely upon the extreme end of the line, doubling it up and driving it in upon the centre, while the same took place on the right. Thus in a very few minutes the Flemings were driven into a helpless mass, inclosed on three sides, and so pressed in that those in front could scarce use their arms, many falling stifled without having struck a blow.

The centre fought well, but their rough armour could not resist the better-tempered swords of the French knights, which cleft through the iron caps as if they had been but leather, while the steel points of the lances pierced breast- and back-piece. But chiefly the knights fought with axes and heavy maces, beating the Flemings to the ground, while their own armour protected them effectually from any blows in return. The noise was tremendous. The shouts of the leaders were unheard in the din of the blows of sword and mace on helm and steel cap. Specially fierce was the French assault against the point where Van Arte-velde's banner flew. He himself had dismounted and was fighting in the front rank, and in the terrible mêlée was ere long struck down and trampled to death; and indeed to every man that fell by the French weapons many were suffocated by the press, and on the French side many valiant knights, after fighting their way into the thick of the battle, met with a similar fate.

When the French division bore down on the right flank the seven English knights with their men-at-arms had fallen back. Single-handed it would have been madness had they attempted to charge against the solid line of the French.

"Keep well back!" Sir James Pinder cried. "If we get mixed up with the foot-men we shall be powerless. Let us bide our time, and deliver a stroke where we see an opportunity.'

They continued, therefore, to rein back, as the Flemings were doubled up, powerless to give any aid or to press forward towards the front line.

"Didst ever see so fearful a sight!" Sir James said. "Sure never before was so dense a mass. 'Tis like a sea raging round the edge of a black rock, and eating it away piece-meal. Were there but five thousand Flemings they might do better, for now their very numbers prevent them from using their arms. Ah! here is a party with whom we may deal;" and he pointed to a small body of French knights who were about to fall on the rear of the Flemings. "Now, gentlemen, *St. George, St. George!*"

Putting spurs to their horses, the seven knights and their followers dashed at the French. The latter were also mounted, unlike the majority of their companions, who before attacking had dismounted and handed their horses to their pages. The party were fully double the strength of the English, but the impetus of the charge broke their line, and in a moment a fierce mêlée began. Edgar and Albert fought side by side. The former, as no missiles were flying, had thrown up his vizor, the better to be able to see what was passing round him. He was fighting with a battle-axe, for a sword was a comparatively poor weapon against knightly armour. His three first opponents fell headlong, their helmets crushed in under the tremendous blows he dealt them. Then, warding off a blow dealt at him, he turned swiftly and drove his horse at a French knight who was on the point of striking at Albert with a mace while the latter was engaged with another opponent.

The sudden shock rolled rider and horse over. He heard Hal Carter shout, "Look out, Sir Edgar!" and, forcing his horse to leap aside, he struck off the head of a lance that would have caught him in the gorget, and an instant later swept a French knight from his saddle. He looked round. Three of his companions were already down, and although many more of the French had fallen, the position was well-nigh desperate.

"We must cut our way through," he shouted, "or we shall be lost. Let all keep close together—forward!" and he and Albert, spurring their horses, fell furiously upon the French opposed to them.

Their splendid armour now proved invaluable, sword blows fell harmless on it, and lances glanced from its polished face. As he put spurs to his horse Edgar had dropped his vizor down again, for he wanted to strike now, and not to have to defend himself. With crushing blows he hewed his way through his opponents. The other two

English knights kept close, and the men-at-arms fought as
stoutly as their masters, until the party emerged from among
their assailants. As they did so the knight next to Edgar
reeled in his saddle. Edgar threw his arm round him, and
supported him until they had ridden a short distance. Then,
as they halted, he sprung from his horse and lowered him
to the ground.

"Thanks!" the knight murmured as he opened his vizor.
"But I am hurt to death. Leave me here to die quietly,
and look to yourselves. All is lost."

Edgar saw that indeed his case was hopeless. A lance
had pierced his body, and had broken short off; a minute
later he had breathed his last. Edgar sprung upon his horse
again and looked round. Of the whole of their retainers
but four remained, and all of these were wounded.

"Art hurt, Albert?" he asked.

"Naught to speak of, but I am sorely bruised, and my
head rings with the blows I have had on my helmet."

"And you, Sir Eustace? I fear that you have fared less
well."

"Wounded sorely," the English knight said. "But I
can sit my horse, and methinks that it were best to ride off
at once, seeing the Flemings are flying. We can assuredly
do no good by remaining."

Edgar agreed. "Methinks that we had best ride for
Sluys, and get there before the news of the defeat."

As they rode off they looked back. Behind them were a
host of flying men, and many of them were throwing away
their steel caps and armour to run the more quickly. The
battle had lasted only half an hour, but by that time nine
thousand Flemings had fallen, of whom more than half had
been suffocated by the press. The flight, however, was far
more fatal than the battle, for the French, as soon as the

fight was won, mounted their horses, and chased the Flemings so hotly that twenty-five thousand were killed. The body of Van Artevelde was found after the battle. It was without a wound, but was so trampled on as to be almost unrecognizable. His body was taken and hung on a tree.

As they galloped off, Edgar reined back to Hal Carter, who was one of the survivors.

"I see that you are badly hurt, Hal. As soon as we get fairly away we will halt, and I will bandage your wounds."

"They are of no great account, Sir Edgar. It was worth coming over from England to take part in such a fray; the worst part of it was that it did not last long enough."

"It lasted too long for many of us, Hal. You saved my life by that warning shout you gave, for, most assuredly, I must have been borne from my saddle had the blow struck me unawares."

"It was a cowardly trick to charge a man when he was otherwise engaged," Hal said. "But you paid him well for it, master; you fairly crushed his helmet in."

Three miles on they halted in a wood to give the horses breathing time, when those unhurt bandaged the wounds of the others. It was found that Sir Eustace was so severely wounded that he could not go much farther, and that two of the men-at-arms were in as bad a case; the third was a Fleming.

"It were best to leave us here," Sir Eustace said. "We cannot ride much farther."

"That we will not do," Edgar said. "Torhut is but four miles away. We can ride at an easy pace, for the Flemings will make for Courtray and Ghent, and the French will pursue in that direction. 'Tis not likely that any will ride so far south as this."

"I have friends in Torhut," the Fleming said. "I come

from that neighbourhood, and I can bestow Sir Eustace, my master, in a place of safety, and will look after him and these two who can go no farther."

"That will be well, indeed. Is it in the town itself?" Edgar asked.

"I have friends there, but an uncle of mine resides in a farm-house three-quarters of a mile from the town. We can get help and shelter there."

"That would be safer, good fellow," Sir Eustace said. "I should not care to enter a town now, for some who saw us come in might be willing to gain favour with the French by saying where we were hidden. Moreover, we should be detained and questioned as to the battle. I have money wherewith to pay your uncle well for the pains to which he will be put. Well, let us forward; the sooner we are in shelter the better."

They rode slowly now until they saw the steeple of Torhut, and then turned off the road, and in half an hour came to a farm-house. The Fleming had ridden on a short distance ahead.

"My uncle will take them in," he said. "He has a loft in the top of his house, and can bestow them there safely, for none would be likely to suspect its existence, even if they searched the house. My uncle is a true Fleming, and would have taken them in without payment, but I say not that he will refuse what my master may be willing to pay."

Ten minutes later, Edgar and Albert continued their way, followed now by Hal Carter alone. The latter had washed the blood from his face and armour, and had thrown a short cloak over his shoulders, so that they could pass without its being suspected that they had taken part in a desperate fray. After riding for some hours they stopped at a wayside inn, and, avoiding Bruges, rode the next day into Sluys, where they found a vessel sailing that evening for England. No rumour of the disastrous battle of Rosebeque had as yet reached Sluys; but the two young knights, calling upon the merchant who had entertained them at their first landing, informed him of what had happened.

"'Tis well that it is so," he said, "for, in truth, the domination of the craftsmen of Ghent and the other great cities would have been far harder to bear than that of the Earl, or of France, or of Burgundy. Already the taxes and imposts are four times as heavy as those laid upon us by the Earl, and had they gained a victory these people would soon have come to exercise a tyranny altogether beyond bearing. 'Tis ever thus when the lower class gain dominion over the upper."

CHAPTER XVI.

A WAR OF THE CHURCH.

YOU have been but a short time absent this voyage," Sir Ralph said as his son and Edgar rode up to the castle.

"Truly we have been but a short time, father," Albert said, "but we have seen much. Of course the news has not yet reached you, but the army of Flanders has been utterly broken by the French. Whether Van Artevelde was killed we know not, but of the fifty thousand men who marched to battle we doubt whether half ever returned to their homes."

"That was indeed a terrible defeat. And how bore you yourselves in the battle?"

"It was rough work, though short, father. Five other English knights were with us; four of these were killed,

and one we left behind at a farm, grievously wounded.
Each of us had two men-at-arms, and of the fourteen two
were left behind wounded sorely, one remained in charge
of his master and them, and Edgar's man here is the only
one who rode to Sluys with us; the rest are dead. So, too,
might we have been but for the strength and temper of our
armour."

"Did not the Flemings fight sturdily then?"

"They fought sturdily for a time, but altogether without
leader or order. They took up a strong position, but, impatient of an hour's delay, marched from it to give battle,
and being attacked on both flanks as well as in front, were
driven into a close mass, so that few could use their arms,
and, were it only to find breathing space, they had to fly."

"'Tis bad news indeed. Had they prevailed, their alliance with us would have brought about great things, for
Artevelde would have put Flanders under English protection, and between us we could have withstood all the
attacks of France and Burgundy."

"Think you that Ghent will be taken, Edgar?"

"That I cannot say, Sir Ralph. However great their loss
may be, the Ghentois are like to make an obstinate defence,
judging from the way in which they withstood their Earl
with all Flanders at his back. They will know that they
have no mercy to expect if they yield, and I believe that so
long as there is a man left to wield arms the city will hold
out. As to the other towns of Flanders, they are as fickle as
the wind, and will all open their gates to the King of France,
who, seeing that it is by his power alone that Flanders
has been taken, will assuredly hold it as his own in the
future."

"Now that you have returned, it would be well, Edgar,
that you and my son should practise with the lance. 'Tis

a knightly weapon, and a knight should at least know how
to use it well. There is a piece of ground but a quarter of
a mile away that I have been looking at, and find that it
will make a good tilting-ground, and I will teach you all
that I know in the matter."

Edgar thankfully embraced the offer, and after going into
the castle to pay his respects to the dame and her daughter,
went home with Hal Carter, whose wounds were still sore.

The news that came from Flanders to England from time
to time was bad. It was first heard how terrible had been
the slaughter of the Flemings after the victory, and that
in all thirty-four thousand had been killed. Then the news
came that Courtray, although it opened its gates without
resistance, had been first pillaged and then burnt, and that
Bruges had surrendered, but had been only spared from
pillage by the payment of a great sum of money. None
of the other towns had offered any resistance, but Ghent
had shut her gates, and the French, deeming that the
operations of the siege would be too severe to be under-
taken in winter, had marched away, their return being
hastened by the news of an insurrection in France.

The king, however, had declared Flanders to be a portion
of France, and the Earl of Flanders had done homage to
him as his liege lord. The news of the merciless slaughter
of the Flemings, and of the cruel treatment of Courtray,
aroused great indignation in England, which was increased
when it was heard that all the rich English merchants in
Bruges had been obliged to fly for their lives, and that all
other Englishmen found in the towns had been seized by
the Earl of Flanders, and thrown into prison and their
goods confiscated.

The young knights practised at tilting daily under the
eye of Sir Ralph, and at the end of three months could

carry off rings skilfully, and could couch their lances truly, whether at breast-piece or helm. It was nigh two years since they had first ridden to London, and both had grown tall and greatly widened. Edgar was still by far the taller and stronger, and was now an exceptionally powerful young man. Albert was of a fair strength and stature, and from his constant practice with Edgar had attained almost as great a skill with his weapons. When they jousted they always used lighter spears than when they practised at the ring, for in a charge Edgar's weight and strength would have carried Albert out of his saddle, and that with such force as might have caused him serious injury; the lances therefore were made so slight as to shiver at the shock.

"You are like to be employing your weapons to better advantage soon," Sir Ralph said one day on his return from London. "You know of the rivalry between the two popes, and that we hold for Urban while France champions Clement."

"Yes, sir," Edgar said; "but how is that likely to give occasion for us to betake ourselves to arms again?"

"Urban is going to use us as his instrument against France and Spain. A bull was received yesterday, of which copies have also been sent to all the bishops, calling upon Richard to engage in a sort of Holy War to this end. He has ordered that all church property throughout England shall be taxed, and that the bishops shall exhort all persons to give as much as they can afford for the same purpose. To all those who take part in the war he gives absolution from all sins, and the same to those who, staying at home, contribute to the Church's need.

"The sum of money thus raised, which I doubt not will be great, is to be devoted partly to an expedition against France, and partly to one under Lancaster against Spain. As it is a Church war, the expedition to France is to be led by a Churchman, and Urban has chosen Sir Henry Spencer, Bishop of Norwich, who, if you will remember, bore himself so stoutly against the insurgents in his diocese as the nominal leader. The king has taken the matter up heartily, and many of the knights whom I met at court are also well content, seeing that the war is to be conducted at the expense of the Church and not of themselves; and I doubt not that a large number of knights and gentlemen will take part in the expedition, which is of the nature of a crusade.

"More than that, I met an old friend, Sir Hugh Calverley, with whom I have fought side by side a score of times, and whose name is, of course, well known to you. He is minded also to go, partly because he hates the French, and partly because of the pope's blessing and absolution. Seeing that, I said to him, 'As you are going, Sir Hugh, I pray you to do me a favour.'

"'There is no one I would more willingly oblige, old friend,' he said.

"'My son,' I went on, 'and a friend of his whom I regard almost as a son, were knighted more than a year since, as you may have heard, for their valiant conduct in the time of the troubles here.'

"'I have heard the story,' he said. 'It is well-known to all at court.'

"'Since then, Sir Hugh, they have been over in Flanders, where they gained the approbation of Van Artevelde by their conduct, and fought stoutly at the grievous battle of Rosbecque. But hitherto they have had no knightly leader. They have gained such experience as they could by themselves, but I would that they should campaign in the train of a valiant and well-known knight like yourself, under whose eyes they could gain distinction as well as a knowledge of military affairs.'

"'I will take them with me gladly,' he said. 'They must be young knights of rare mettle, and even apart from my regard for you I should be right glad to have them ride with me.'

Both the young knights gave exclamations of pleasure. It was hard for a knight unattached to the train of some well-known leader to rise to distinction, and there was no English knight living who bore a higher reputation than Sir Hugh Calverley, so that to ride under him would be an honour indeed. But some months passed before the preparations were complete. Throughout England the bishops and priests preached and incited the people to what they considered a Holy War. The promises of absolution of past and future sins were in proportion to the money given. In the diocese of London alone a tun full of gold and silver was gathered, and by Lent the total amounted to what at that time was the fabulous sum of 2,500,000 francs. Thomas, Bishop of London and brother to the Earl of Devonshire, was appointed by Urban to go with the Duke of Lancaster to Spain as chief captain, with two thousand spears and four thousand archers, and half the money gathered was to be spent on this expedition, and the other half on that of the Bishop of Norwich.

The expeditions were to set out together, but one progressed far more rapidly than the other. The Bishop of Norwich was very popular. He was of ancient lineage, had personally shown great bravery, and was highly esteemed. Upon the other hand, the Duke of Lancaster was hated. Thus great numbers of knights and others enlisted eagerly under the Bishop, while very few were willing to take service under the Duke. Five hundred spearmen and fifteen hundred men at-arms and archers were soon enrolled under the Bishop's banner. A great number of

priests, too, followed the example of the Bishop, threw aside
the cassock, and clad themselves in armour to go to the war
in the spirit of crusaders.

Great numbers passed over from Dover and Sandwich in
parties to wait at Calais for the arrival of their leaders.
At Easter, the Bishop, Sir Hugh Calverley, and two of the
principal knights attended the king and his council, and
swore to do their best to bring to an end the matter on
which they were engaged, and to war only against the sup-
porters of Clement. The king begged them to wait for a
month at Calais, promising that he would send them over
many men-at-arms and archers, and Sir William Beauchamp
as marshal to the army. The Bishop promised the king
to do this, and he and his party sailed from Dover and
arrived at Calais on April 23, 1383.

The young knights had gone up to town a month before
by invitation of Sir Robert Gaiton, and had stayed with him
for a week. At the end of that time he presented each of
them with a superb suit of Milan steel, richly inlaid with
gold, and two fine war-horses.

"It is a gift that I have long promised you," he said.
"I gave orders to my agents in Italy a year since to spare
neither time nor trouble to obtain the best that the armourers of Milan could turn out. The horses are of Yorkshire breed, and are warranted sound at every point."

"It is a princely present, Sir Robert," Edgar said, "and,
indeed, a most timely one, for truly we have well-nigh grown
out of the other suits, although when we got them it seemed
to us that we should never be able to fill them properly;
but of late we have been forced to ease the straps, and to
leave spaces between the pieces, by which lance or arrow
might well find entrance."

Sir Ralph had gone up with them and introduced them to

Sir Hugh, who promised to give them two days' warning when they were to join him at Sandwich or Dover. During this week Edgar for the most part went about alone, Albert, at first to his surprise, and then to his amusement, always making some pretext or other for not accompanying him, but passing, as he found on his return, the greater portion of the time in the house, in discourse, as he said, with Dame Gaiton, but, as Edgar shrewdly guessed, chiefly with Ursula, who, he found, obligingly kept his friend company while the dame was engaged in her household duties. It seemed to him, too, that on the ride back to St. Alwyth Albert was unusually silent and depressed in spirits.

Edgar himself, however, experienced something of the same feeling when he took his last farewell from the De Courcys before starting for Dover. On this occasion each took with him four men-at-arms, stout fellows, Albert's being picked men from among the De Courcy retainers, while Hal Carter had selected his three mates from among the villagers, and had, during the last three months, trained them assiduously in the use of their arms.

"How long do you think that you are likely to be away, Edgar?" his father asked, the evening before the party started.

"I cannot tell you, father, but I do not think that it will be long. If the expedition had started six months ago it would have arrived in Flanders in time to have helped the Flemings, and with their aid the French might have been driven flying over the frontier; but I cannot see what two or three thousand men can do. We cannot fight the whole strength of France by ourselves."

"It seems to me a hair-brained affair altogether," Mr. Ormskirk said; "almost as mad, only in a different way, as the crusade of Peter the Hermit. The Church has surely

(M 371)   T trouble enough in these days, what with men like Wickliffe, who denounce her errors, and point out how far she has fallen back from the simple ways of old times, what with the impatience or indifference of no small part of the people, the pomp and wasteful confusion of the prelates, and the laziness of the monks—she has plenty of matters to look after without meddling in military affairs.

"What would she say if a score of nobles were to take upon themselves to tell her to set her house in order, to adopt reforms, and to throw aside sloth and luxury; and yet the Church is stirring up a war, and raising and paying an army of fighting men—and for what? To settle which of two men shall be pope. The simple thing would be to hold a high tournament, and to let Urban and Clement don armour and decide between themselves in fair fight who should be pope. They might as well do that as set other men to fight for them. I see not what good can come of it, Edgar."

"Albert and myself are of the same opinion, father. Certainly with two or three thousand men we can hardly expect to march to Paris and force the King of France to declare for our pope. Still we shall march in good company, and shall both be proud to do so under the banner of so distinguished a knight as Sir Hugh Calverley."

"I say naught against that, Edgar; but I would rather see you start with him as knights-errant, willing at all times to couch a lance for damsels in distress. The day has passed for crusades. Surely we have had experience enough to see that solid advantages are not to be won by religious enthusiasm. Men may be so inspired to deeds of wondrous valour, but there is no instance of permanent good arising out of such expeditions. As for this in which you are going to embark, it seems to me to be the height of folly."

The next day the two young knights rode to Canterbury, and thence to Dover. The following evening the Bishop of Norwich with his train, Sir Hugh Calverley, and other knights arrived, and the next morning embarked with their following and horses on board three ships, and sailed to Calais. Those who had preceded them were already impatient to take the field. The news that there was to be a further delay of a month until Sir William Beauchamp with reinforcements should arrive, caused much disappointment and vexation.

" 'Tis unfortunate," Sir Hugh said one evening a few days later to the knights of his party, "that there are not more men here accustomed to war, and who have learned that patience and obedience are as needful as strong arms, if a campaign is to be carried out successfully. The Bishop of Norwich is young and fiery, and he hath many like himself round him, so that he frets openly at this delay. Moreover, Sir Thomas Trivet and Sir William Helmon are too full of ardour to act with discretion, and are ready enough to back up the Bishop in his hot desire to be doing something. I regret that this army is not, like the army which fought at Crecy and Poictiers, composed of men well inured to war, with a great number of good archers, and led by experienced warriors, instead of a hasty gathering of men who have been fired by the exhortations of the priests and the promises of the pope.

"We are but a small gathering. We may take some castles, and defeat the forces that the nobles here gather against us, but more than that we cannot do unless England arms in earnest. I foresaw this, and spoke to the Council when they prayed me to go with the Bishop; but when they pointed out that what I said made it all the more needful that one of grave experience and years should go with him, and prayed me to accept the office, I consented."

On the 4th of May the Bishop of Norwich took advantage of Sir Hugh's absence—he having gone for two days to see a cousin who was commander of Guines—to call the other leaders together, and said that it was time they did some deed of arms, and rightly employed the money with which the Church had furnished them. All agreed with him, and the Bishop then proposed that instead of entering France they should march to Flanders, which was now a portion of France. To this Sir Thomas Trivet and Sir William Helmon cordially agreed.

When Sir Hugh returned another council was called, and the matter was laid before him. Sir Hugh opposed it altogether. In the first place, they had given their word to the king to wait for a month for the promised reinforcements; in the second place, they had not come over as Englishmen to fight the French, but as followers of Pope Urban to fight those of Clement, and the men of Flanders were, like themselves, followers of Urban. The Bishop answered him very hotly, and as the other knights and all present agreed with the Bishop, Sir Hugh reluctantly gave way, and said that if they were determined upon going to Flanders he would ride with them. Accordingly notice was given through the town that the force would march the next morning. All assembled at the order, to the number of three thousand, and marched from Calais to Gravelines.

No preparations for defence had been made there, for there was no war between England and Flanders. However, the burghers defended the place for a short time, and then withdrew, with their wives and families, to the cathedral, which was a place of strength. Here they defended themselves for two days. The church was then stormed, and all its defenders put to the sword. The news excited the greatest surprise and indignation in Flanders, and the Earl at once sent two English knights who were with him to Gravelines to protest, and with orders to obtain from the Bishop a safe-conduct to go to England to lay the matter before the English king and his council.

When they arrived at Gravelines the Bishop refused their request for a safe-conduct, but told them to tell the Earl that he was not warring against Flanders, nor was his army an army of England but of Pope Urban, and that although the greater portion of Flanders was Urbanist, the Lord of Bar—in whose dominion Gravelines stood—was for Clement, and so were his people. If he and they would acknowledge Pope Urban, he would march away without doing damage, and paying for all he took, but unless they did so he would force them to submit. The people of Artois, however, who were French rather than Flemings, took the matter in their own hands, and twelve thousand men, under some knights from Nieuport and other towns, marched to Dunkirk and then to Mardyck, a large village not far from Gravelines.

Edgar and Albert had taken no part in the attack upon the cathedral, but remained with Sir Hugh Calverley in the house that he occupied as soon as resistance of the entry to the town had ended.

"On the field I will fight with the rest," he said, "but I will have no hand in this matter. There has been no defiance sent to the Earl of Flanders nor received from him, and 'tis not my habit to fight burghers against whom we have no complaint, and who are but defending their homes against us."

The two young knights were well pleased with this decision. It was an age when quarter was but seldom given, and wholesale slaughters followed battles, so that they had, naturally, the ideas common to the time. Still, they both felt that this attack was wholly unprovoked and altogether beyond the scope of the expedition, and were well pleased that their leader would have naught to do with it. It was, however, a different matter when they heard that an army twelve thousand strong was coming out against them, and they were quite ready to take their share in the fight.

While waiting at Gravelines several other knights had joined the army, among them Sir Nicholas Clifton and Sir Hugh's cousin, the commander of Guines, Sir Hugh Spenser, nephew of the bishop, and others.

The force consisted of six hundred mounted men, sixteen hundred archers, and the rest foot-men. They found that the Flemings had fallen back to Dunkirk, and had taken up a position in front of that town. The Bishop, on approaching them, sent forward a herald to ask them whether they were for Pope Urban or Clement, and that if they were for Urban he had no quarrel with them. As soon, however, as the herald approached, the Flemings fell upon him and killed him. This excited the most lively indignation among the English, for among all civilized people the person of a herald was held to be sacred.

The bishop and knights at once drew up the force in order of battle. The men on foot were formed into a wedge. The archers were placed on the two flanks of the unmounted men-at-arms, while the cavalry prepared to charge as soon as opportunity offered. The army was preceded by the standard of the Church. The trumpets on both sides sounded, and as they came within range the English archers poured flights of arrows among the Flemings. These advanced boldly to the attack of the foot-men. Again and again the horsemen charged down upon them, but were unable to break their solid lines, and for a time the battle was doubtful, but the English archers decided the fate of the day. The Flemings, although they resisted firmly the charge of the men-at-arms, were unable to sustain the terrible and continuous rain of arrows, and their front line fell back.

As soon as they did so the second line wavered and broke. Then the Bishop with his knights and men-at-arms charged furiously down upon them, and the battle was over. The Flemings broke and fled in wild disorder, but the English pursued them so hotly that they entered Dunkirk with them. Here again and again they attempted to make a stand, but speedily gave way before the onslaught of the English. No one distinguished themselves in the battle more than did the priests and monks who were fighting on the side of the Bishop, and it was said among the others that these must have mistaken their vocation, and that had they entered the army instead of the Church they would have made right valiant knights.

The English loss was four hundred, that of the Flemings was very much heavier. There died, however, among them no knights or persons of quality, for the rising was one of the people themselves, and as yet the Earl of Flanders was waiting for the King of England's reply to the message he had sent by the two knights from Sluys. The English, however, considered that the absence of any horsemen or knights was due to the fact that these remembered what terrible havoc had been made among the chivalry of France at Crecy and Poictiers, and cared not to expose themselves to that risk.

CHAPTER XVII.

PRISONERS.

AFTER the capture of Dunkirk all the seaports as far as Sluys were taken by the English, who then marched to Ypres, to which town they at once laid siege, and were joined by twenty thousand men from Ghent. Their own number had swollen considerably by the arrival from England of many knights and men-at-arms besides numbers of foot-men, attracted as much by the news of the great spoil that had been captured in the Flemish towns as by the exhortations and promises of the clergy.

Ypres had a numerous garrison commanded by several knights of experience. The works were very strong, and every assault was repulsed with heavy loss. One of these was led by Sir Hugh Calverley. The force crossed the ditches by throwing in great bundles of wood with which each of the foot-men had been provided, and having reached the wall, in spite of a hail of cross-bow bolts and arrows, ladders were planted, and the leaders endeavoured to gain the ramparts. Sir Hugh Calverley succeeded in obtaining a footing, but for a time he stood almost alone. Two or three other knights, however, sprang up. Just as they did so one of the ladders broke with the weight upon it, throwing all heavily to the ground.

Edgar and Albert were with a party of archers who were keeping up a rain of arrows. Seeing that the situation was bad they now ran forward, followed by four of their men-at-arms, the others having charge of the horses in the camp. A few more men-at-arms had gained the ramparts by the time they arrived at the foot of the ladders, where numbers waited to take their turns to ascend.

"There is not much broken off this one, Sir Edgar," Hal Carter said, "not above three feet, I should say. We might make a shift to get up with that."

"Pick it up, Hal, and bring it along a short distance. Possibly we may be able to mount unobserved, for the fight is hot above, and the attention of the enemy will be fixed there."

Followed by their own men-at-arms, and by a few others who saw what their intentions were, they kept along at the foot of the wall until they reached an angle some thirty yards away. Searching about they found several stones that had been dislodged from the battlements during the siege. With these they built up a platform, and, raising the ladder on this, they found that it reached to within a foot of the top.

"Now," Edgar said, "follow us as quickly as you can, but do not try the ladder too heavily; it has broken once, so the wood cannot be over strong."

Then, followed closely by Albert and the men-at-arms, he ascended the walls. So intent were the defenders upon the strife going on round Sir Hugh Calverley that Edgar was not noticed until, putting his hands upon the wall, he vaulted over it. He held his sword between his teeth, and betaking himself to this fell so fiercely and suddenly upon the enemy that several were cut down and the rest recoiled so far that Albert and the four men-at-arms were able to join him before the enemy rallied. Every moment added to the strength of the party, and as soon as some twenty had gathered behind him, Edgar flung himself upon the enemy with a shout of "*St. George! St. George!*" and, in spite of the opposition of the defenders, fought his way along the wall until he joined Sir Hugh and the little group who were defending themselves against tremendous odds.

Sir Hugh himself was seriously wounded. Two or three of his knights lay dead beside him, and had it not been for the arrival of the reinforcement the fight would speedily have terminated, for the English were so penned up against the wall that there was no footing for more to join them. The suddenness of the attack drove the enemy back some little distance, and this enabled a score of those upon the ladders to make their way on to the rampart.

"Bravely done!" Sir Hugh Calverley said, as he leant against the wall utterly exhausted by his efforts and loss of blood. A moment later he would have fallen had not Albert sprung to his side.

"We must save Sir Hugh at all risks," he said to two of the knight's companions, who were also wounded. "Will you, sir knights, aid in lowering him down the ladder, and see that he is carried off? You have done your share. It is our turn now, and we can at least hold the rampart until he is in safety."

Leaning over, he shouted to the men on one of the ladders to descend and leave the ladder clear, as Sir Hugh was to be lowered down.

"Methinks I can carry him, Sir Albert," Hal Carter said. "I have carried two sacks of wheat on my shoulder before now, and methinks that I can carry one knight and his armour."

He took his place on the ladder, and Sir Hugh was lowered to him, and laying him on his shoulder Hal carried him safely down. The two wounded knights followed, and then Hal sprang up the ladder again. While this was being done Edgar and his party had been holding the enemy at bay. Hal was followed by some of the men-at-arms, and others poured up by the other ladders. Edgar saw that they were now strong enough to take the offensive, and as the English numbered nearly a hundred, he fell upon the enemy to the right, while Albert led another party to the left.

For some time the fury with which the English fought drove the enemy before them on either hand. Every moment they were joined by fresh men, who were now able to pour in a steady stream up the ladders. The enemy, too, were harassed by the English archers, who, advancing to the edge of the ditch, sent their shafts thick and fast among them. The town bells were clanging fiercely, drums beating, and horns sounding as the alarm spread that the besiegers had gained a footing on the walls, and great numbers of the garrison could be seen pouring along the streets leading to the threatened point.

Had there been more ladders so that reinforcements could have arrived more rapidly, the place might have been won. As it was, it was evident that success was impossible. Edgar's party still gained ground slowly, but he saw that Albert was being pressed backwards.

"Fall back, men!" he shouted, "slowly, and keeping your face to the enemy. The odds are too heavy for us."

Foot by foot, fighting silently and obstinately, the English fell back until their party joined that of Albert, at the spot where the wall had been won. Their exulting foes pressed hotly upon them, but Edgar's sword and the heavy long-handled mace wielded by Hal Carter did such terrible execution that the rest were able to retreat in good order.

"Jump down, my men!" Edgar shouted. "You will break the ladders if you try to go by them. The ground is but soft, and the wall of no great height. Do not hurry. We will cover you and then follow."

Gradually the number of the party on the walls was lessened as by threes and fours they leapt down; while many, getting on to the ladders, slipped rapidly to the ground.

When there were but half a dozen left, Hal suddenly exclaimed: "Sir Albert has fallen—wounded!"

Edgar freed himself from his opponent of the moment by a sweeping blow, and then with a spring placed himself astride of his friend. Hal Carter joined him. The rest of their followers remaining on the wall either jumped over or were cut down. Fortunately Albert had fallen close to the parapet, and his two defenders could not be attacked from behind. For some minutes the fight continued, and then for a moment the enemy drew back astonished at the manner in which two men kept them at bay; then one of the assailants lowered his sword.

"Sir knight," he said, "you have done enough for honour. Never have I seen a stouter fighter. I pray you, then, to surrender, on promise of good treatment and fair terms of ransom to you, to the knight at your feet, and to this stout man-at-arms. I am Sir Robert de Beaulieu."

"Then I yield to you," Edgar said. "I am Sir Edgar Ormskirk, and this knight is my brother-in-arms, Sir Albert de Courcy. I yield in his name and my own, and am glad that, as fortune has declared against us, it should be to so good a knight as Sir Robert de Beaulieu that I surrender my sword."

"Keep it, Sir Edgar, for never have I seen one better wielded. No small damage, indeed, has it done us."

"The stout man-at-arms is my own retainer, and I prythee, sir knight, suffer him to remain with us."

"Assuredly he shall do so."

As soon as the parley began Hal Carter laid down his weapon, and, kneeling beside Albert, unlaced his helmet.

"He lives, Sir Edgar!" he said; "he is but stunned, methinks, with the blow of a mace, which has deeply dinted his casque, though, indeed, he has other wounds."

M 371

SIR EDGAR AT LAST SURRENDERS TO SIR ROBERT DE BEAULIEU.

By Sir Robert de Beaulieu's orders four men now formed a litter with their spears. Albert was laid on it, and Sir Robert, Edgar, and Hal Carter walking in front, and half a score of men-at-arms accompanying them, they made their way to a large house where the knight lodged. Sir Robert had sent on for a leech to be in attendance, and he was there when they arrived. Hal at once took off Albert's armour.

" 'Tis well for him that this armour was good," Sir Robert said. Had it not been, it would have gone hard with him. It must be steel of proof indeed, for I saw the blow struck, and there are but few helmets that would not have been crushed by it."

" He has a deep gash near the neck," the leech said. " The lacings and straps of the helmet and gorget must have been cut by a sharp sword, and another blow has fallen on the same spot. Methinks he has dropped as much from loss of blood as from the blow on the head."

Edgar had by this time taken off his own helmet. As soon as he did so, Sir Robert de Beaulieu, who was somewhat grizzled with age, said:

" In truth, sir knight, you and your companion are young indeed to have fought so doughtily as you have done to-day; you are young to be knights, and yet you have shown a courage and a skill such as no knight could have surpassed. We had thought the affair finished when that stout knight Sir Hugh Calverley was down with two others, and but three or four remained on their feet. Then suddenly your party burst upon us, coming from we knew not where, and had you but been reinforced more rapidly the town would have been lost."

Edgar made no reply, for at the moment Hal Carter leant heavily against him.

"I can do no more, Sir Edgar," he murmured, "I am spent."

Edgar caught the brave fellow in his arms and supported him, while two men-at-arms who had assisted to carry Albert in, unstrapped Hal's armour and gently laid him down on a couch. He was bleeding from half a dozen wounds, and his face was pale and bloodless. Edgar knelt by his side and raised his head.

"I will see to him, sir knight," the surgeon said. "I have bandaged your comrade's injuries, and methinks that he will soon come round."

Then he examined Hal's wounds.

"He will do," he said. "Assuredly there are none of them that are mortal; 'tis but loss of blood that ails him. I will but bandage them hastily now, for there are many other cases waiting for me; and methinks, sir, that you yourself need looking to."

"I am unhurt," Edgar said in surprise.

"Your doublet is stained with blood from the shoulder to the wrist," Sir Robert said. "A spear-head has penetrated at the shoulder-joint and torn a gash well-nigh to the neck. 'Tis well that it is not worse."

Two of his men-at-arms had by this time taken off Sir Robert's armour also.

"You have ruined my helmet, Sir Edgar, and cut so deep a notch in it that I know not how my head escaped. You have gashed a hole in my gorget and dinted the armour in half a dozen places, and I failed to make a single mark on yours. Never was I engaged with so good a swordsman. I could scarcely believe my eyes when you lifted your vizor, for it seemed to me that you must be in the prime of your manhood, and possessed of strength altogether out of the common."

"I have practised a good deal," Edgar said quietly, "having indeed little else to do, so it is not surprising that my muscles are hard."

At the knight's order a servant now brought in two goblets of wine. Sir Robert and Edgar then drank to each other, both draining the cups to the bottom.

Albert was not long before he opened his eyes. He looked round in wonder, and smiled faintly when he saw Edgar, who hastened to his side.

"We are out of luck this time, Albert; we are both prisoners. Still, things might have been worse. You were struck down with a mace, but the leech says that the wound on your head is of no great consequence, and that you fainted rather from loss of blood from other gashes than from the blow on the head. I have got off with a scratch on the shoulder. Hal Carter, who fought like a tiger over your body, has come off worst, having fully half a dozen wounds, but it was not before he had killed at least twice as many of his assailants with that terrible mace of his."

So far Edgar had spoken in English. He went on in French:

"This is the good knight Sir Robert de Beaulieu, who is our captor, and will hold us on ransom."

"You may congratulate yourself, Sir Albert," the knight said courteously, "that you had such stout defenders as your comrade here and his man-at-arms, because for fully five minutes they held the whole of us at bay, and so stoutly did they fight that we were all glad when Sir Edgar yielded himself to me. Truly, between you, you have done us ill service, for not only have you and your party killed a large number of our men, but you have enabled Sir Hugh Calverley to be carried off, and for so famous a captain we should have claimed a goodly ransom, and it would have been an honour and glory to have taken so fearless a knight. As it is, with the exception of yourselves, no single prisoner has fallen into our hands, and methinks that in all there were not more than ten or twelve in the storming party killed, while we must have lost nigh a hundred. 'Tis the first time I have fought against the English, and in truth you are doughty foemen. It was well that you came into the land but some four or five thousand strong, for had you brought an army you might have marched to Paris. Now, Sir Edgar, I will show you your room."

He led the way along a broad corridor to a large room, the men-at-arms carrying the couch on which Albert was lying.

"I should like to have my man-at-arms brought here also, Sir Robert," Edgar said. "He is a faithful fellow, and I have known him for years. He speaks but little of any language but English, and will, methinks, do better with my nursing than with any other."

In a fortnight Albert was quite convalescent, and Hal was rapidly gaining strength. Three days after they had been taken prisoner Sir Robert had said to Edgar:

"It will be best, Sir Edgar, that you should not go abroad in the streets. The townsmen here, as in other towns in Flanders, are rough fellows. They are, of course, suffering somewhat from the siege, and they murmur that any prisoners should have been taken. They say that your people showed no mercy at Gravelines and Dunkirk, which, methinks, is true enough, and that none should be given here. Yesterday some of their leaders came to the house where I was sitting in council with other knights, and represented that all English prisoners should be put to the sword at once. I pointed out to them that, for their own sakes, as many prisoners should be taken as possible. We hope to defend the town until succour comes, but were the English to capture it, and to find that prisoners who had surrendered had been killed, no mercy would be shown, but every man within the walls would be slain and the city laid in ashes.

"To this they had no answer ready, and retired grumbling. But, in any case, it were better that you did not show yourself in the street, for a tumult might arise, and your life might be sacrificed before any of us could come to your assistance."

"I thank you, Sir Robert, and will gladly take your advice. I have seen somewhat of the townsmen of Ghent and Bruges, and know that, when the fit seizes them, they are not to be restrained."

After that time Sir Robert de Beaulieu seldom left the house, and Edgar found that the doors were kept closed, and that the knight's followers and men-at-arms were also kept in the house. Several times he heard shouts in the street of, "Death to the English!"

He took his meals with the knight, while Albert and Hal were served in their room. At the end of the week, however, Albert was able to join the two knights, and a fortnight later Hal was again up and about.

"I fear, Sir Robert, that our presence here is a source of trouble to you," Edgar said one day. "If it could be managed, we would gladly give you our knightly word to send you our ransom at the first opportunity, and not to serve in arms again until it is paid, if you would let us go free."

"I would do so gladly, Sir Edgar, but I fear that it would be difficult to manage. Both before and behind the house there are evidently men on the watch to see that no one passes out. My own men-at-arms have been stopped and questioned, and were you to issue out methinks that there would on the instant be an uproar, for so great a crowd would gather in a few minutes that even had you a strong guard you might be torn from them. You see, though some eight of us knights and three hundred men-at-arms were placed here to aid in the defence, we could do naught without the assistance of the townsmen, who have on all occasions fought stoutly. Were there to be a fray now, the safety of the town would be compromised, for the crafts-men of all these towns are as fickle as the wind. The men of Ypres fought by the side of those at Ghent at one time, and when the Count of Flanders came here, great numbers of the townspeople were executed. At present, why I know not, they are fighting stoutly for the Count, while the men of Ghent are with the besiegers; but were there to be troubles between them and us, they might to-morrow open their gates to the English."

"That I can quite believe, Sir Robert. I can only say that we are in your hands, and are ready to pursue any course that you may think best, either to stay here quietly and take the risk of what may come of it, or endeavour to escape in disguise if so it could be managed."

"I would that it could be managed, for the matter is causing us grave anxiety. My comrades are, of course, all with me, and hold that even if it comes to a struggle with the mob, the lives of prisoners who have surrendered on ransom must be defended. I suggested that we should hold counsel here, that two should remain, and that you should sally out with the others, but our faces are all so well known in the town that there would be little chance indeed of your passing undetected."

"Think you, Sir Robert, that we could pass along the roofs, enter a casement a few houses along, and then make our way out in disguise?"

" It would be well-nigh impossible. The roofs are all so sloping that no one could maintain a footing upon them."

" When it gets dusk I will, with your permission, Sir Robert, go up to one of the attics and take a look out."

" By all means do so. Escape in that manner would certainly be the best way out of the dilemma, though I much fear that it cannot be done."

When it became so dark that while he could take a view round, his figure could not be recognized at a short distance, Edgar, with Albert and Hal, went up to the top of the house, and the former got out of the highest of the dormer-windows, and, standing on the sill, looked out. The roof was indeed so steep that it would be impossible to obtain a footing upon it. Its ridge was some twenty feet above the window. The houses were of varying heights, some being as much as thirty feet lower than others. Still it seemed to Edgar that it would not be very difficult to make their way along if they were provided with ropes. Descending, he told Sir Robert the result of their investigations.

" It would," he said, " be very desirable, if possible, to come down into some house which was either uninhabited, or where the people were friendly. Still that would not be absolutely necessary, as we might hope to make our way down to the door unperceived."

" There is one house which is empty," Sir Robert said, " for the owner left the town with his family before the siege began, he having another place of business at Liege. He was an old man, and was therefore permitted to leave; for he could have been no good for the defence, and there would, with his family and servants, have been ten mouths more to feed had he remained. It is the sixth house along, I think, but I will see when I go out. Once in the street and away from here, there would be no difficulty. I would meet you a short distance away, and go with you to the walls, from which you could lower yourself down. One or two of my comrades would give their aid, for, naturally, all would be pleased that you should escape, and so put an end to this cause of feud between us and the townsmen. You would, of course, require some rope; that I can easily procure for you."

"We shall want several lengths, Sir Robert, and two or three stout grapnels. We shall also want a strong chisel for forcing open a casement."

"All these you shall have; one of my men shall fetch them to-morrow."

On the following day the ropes and grapnels were brought in, and Sir Robert, who had been out, ascertained that he had been correct, and that the empty house was indeed the sixth from that he occupied. "I have been speaking with two of my comrades," he said, "and they will be with me at ten o'clock to-night at the end of the street that faces the house through which you will descend. I shall accompany you to the foot of the walls. The citizens are on guard there at night, and if they ask questions, as they may well do, my comrades will say that you are bearers of a message to the King of France to pray him to hasten to our aid. I shall not myself go up on to the walls, for were I to do so suspicion might fall upon me. Should you be interrupted as you go along the street to meet us, give a call and we will run to your assistance."

"And now as to our ransom, Sir Robert?" Edgar went on.

"Trouble not yourselves about it," he replied; "you are but young knights, and 'tis a pleasure to me to have been of service to two such valiant young gentlemen. Moreover, I consider that I have no right to a ransom, since, instead of letting you go free to obtain it, or holding you in honourable captivity until it is sent to you, you are obliged to risk your lives, as you assuredly will do, by climbing along those roofs to obtain your liberty; therefore, we will say nothing about it. It may be that some day you will be able to treat leniently some young Flemish or French knight whom you may make captive. As to your armour, I see not how you can carry it away with you, for you will have to swim the ditches; but the first time that there is a flag of truce exchanged I will send it out to you, or should there be no such opportunity, I will, when the siege is over, forward it by the hands of some merchant trading with England, to any address that you may give me there."

The two young knights thanked Sir Robert de Beaulieu most cordially for his kindness to them, and at his request gave him their word not to serve again during the campaign. This, indeed, they were by no means sorry to do, for they had keenly felt the slight paid to Sir Hugh Calverley by the haughty bishop in acting altogether contrary to his advice. They also had been thoroughly disgusted by the massacre at Gravelines, and the sack of so many towns against which England had no cause for complaint.

In the afternoon Sir Robert brought three doublets and caps for them to put over their own clothes, so that they could pass as citizens. They employed some time in wrapping strips of cloth round the grapnels, so that these would fall noiselessly on to the tiles.

At nine o'clock Sir Robert said good-bye to them and went out; and half an hour later they ascended to the upper story. They were well provided with ropes, and had made all their arrangements. Edgar was the first to fasten a rope round his body, and while this was held by his companions he was to get out on the window-sill and throw a grapnel over the ridge and pull himself up by the rope attached to it.

The others were to fasten the rope round their bodies at

distances of twenty feet apart, so that if one slipped down
the others could check him. Edgar took off his shoes and
tied them round his neck, and then stood out on the window-sill, and threw the grapnel over the ridge of the roof;
then he drew the rope in until he found that the hook
caught on the ridge.

"That is all right," he said to his comrades. "Now keep
a firm hold on the rope, but let it gradually out as I climb;
if you hear me slipping draw it in rapidly so as to stop me
as I come past the window. But there is no fear of that
unless the hook gives way."

Then he swung himself up to the roof of the dormer-
window and proceeded to haul himself by the rope up the
steep incline, helping himself as much as possible with his
feet and knees. He was heartily glad when he gained the
ridge, and had thus accomplished the most dangerous part
of the work. He was able now to fix the grapnel firmly,
and, sitting astride of the roof, he called down that he was
ready. It was easier work for Albert to follow him. Not
only was the latter certain that the grapnel was safely
fixed, but Edgar, pulling upon the rope, was enabled to give
him a good deal of assistance. In two or three minutes
Hal Carter joined them.

"In faith, master," he said panting, "I had not deemed
that so much of my strength had gone from me. If it had
not been for the help you gave me I doubt if I could have
climbed up that rope."

They now made their way along to the end of the roof.
The grapnel was fixed, and Edgar slid down the rope to
the next roof, which was some fifteen feet below them.
They did not attempt to free the grapnel, fearing that in
its fall it might make a clatter; they therefore used another
to mount to the next house, which was as high as that

м 371

THE PRISONERS MAKE THEIR ESCAPE OVER THE ROOFS OF YPRES.

which they had left. There was but a difference of four
feet in the height of the next, and they had not to use the
grapnel again until they reached the sixth house, which was
ten feet below that next to it.

There was light enough to enable them to make out the
position of the dormer-window below them, and, fixing the
grapnel, Edgar, aided by his companions lowering him,
made his way down beside it, and knelt upon the sill, his
companions keeping a steady strain upon the rope. With
his chisel he had but little difficulty in prising open the casement. His companions were not long in joining him. Once
inside the house they made their way with great caution.
They had no means of striking a light, and were forced to
grope about with their swords in front of them to prevent
their touching any piece of furniture, till at last they discovered the door. It was not fastened, and passing through,
and, as before, feeling the floor carefully as they went, they
presently found the head of the stairs.

After this it was comparatively easy work, though a
stoppage was necessary at each landing. At last, to their
satisfaction, they found themselves in a flagged passage,
and knew that they were on the ground-floor. They made
their way along the passage, and soon reached the door.
It was locked with so massive a fastening that it would
have been difficult to unfasten it from the outside; but with
the aid of the chisel they had but little difficulty in forcing
back the lock. They paused for a minute to listen, as a
passer-by might have been startled by the sound of the
bolts being shot in an empty house. All was quiet, however, and, opening the door cautiously, Edgar stepped out.

"The street is all clear," he said; "except half a dozen
fellows watching in front of the house we have left there is
not a soul in sight. The others joined him, closing the door

silently behind them. They had not put on their shoes again, so with noiseless steps they crossed the street and turned up the one that had been indicated by Sir Robert. After going a few paces they stopped, put on their shoes, and then walked boldly along. When they reached the end of the street three figures came out from a deep doorway to meet them.

"Is all well?" one asked.

This was the signal that had been agreed upon.

"All is well, Sir Robert. We have escaped without any difficulty or aught going wrong."

"The saints be praised!" the knight ejaculated. "These with me are Sir Oliver Drafurn and Sir François Regnault."

"Right glad we are, knights," one of them said, "that we can assist in giving you your freedom. A foul shame indeed would it have been had two such gallant fighters been massacred by this rascally mob, after yielding themselves to a knight."

"Truly, sirs, we are greatly beholden to you," Edgar replied, "and trust that an occasion may occur in which we may repay to some of your countrymen the great service you are now rendering us."

They had gone but a short distance further when the door of a tavern opened and twelve or fifteen half-drunken soldiers poured out.

"Whom have we here?" one of them shouted. "Faith, if they are burghers they must pay for being thus late in the streets."

"Silence, knaves!" Sir François Regnault said sternly. "What mean ye by this roystering? Disperse to your quarters at once, or by St. James some of you shall hang in the morning, as a lesson to others that the burgesses of Ypres are not to be insulted by drunken revellers."

As by this time the speaker had moved on into the light that streamed through the open door, the soldiers saw at once that it was a knight, and, muttering excuses, went hastily down the street. No one else was encountered until they reached the foot of the wall. Here Sir Robert took a hearty farewell of them. The two knights first mounted the steps to the wall.

As they reached the top a sentry close by challenged.

"France!" Sir Oliver replied; "and, hark ye, make no noise. I am Sir Oliver Drafurn, and I am here with Sir François Regnault to pass three messengers over the wall, bearers of important despatches. We do not wish the news to get abroad, so take your halbert and march up and down."

Hal Carter had brought one of the ropes, twisted round him for the purpose.

"You are on the side facing the English camp," Sir Oliver said. "Those are the lights that you see ahead. You will have three ditches to swim, and will find it cold work, but there is no other way for it."

After giving hearty thanks to the knights, the three were lowered one at a time, and the rope was then dropped down. It was a good deal longer than was necessary for descending the wall, but Edgar, rather to the surprise of the others, had chosen it for the purpose. The first ditch was but ten yards away; it was some thirty feet across."

"Now," Edgar said, "I will cross first. I am much the strongest, for neither of you has fully recovered his strength. The water will be icy cold, therefore I will swim across first, and do you, when I am over, each hold to the rope and I will pull you across.

Short as was the distance the work was trying, for the night was bitterly cold, and the ditches would have been frozen hard were it not that twice a day the besieged went out and broke the ice, which had now began to bind again. At last, however, Edgar got across.

"Do you take the rope, Albert, and let Hal hold on by you, for the passage I have made is but narrow."

A few strong pulls on Edgar's part brought them across.

"It is well," he said as they climbed out, "that the knights promised to go one each way, to tell the watchers on the walls to take no heed of any sounds that they might hear of breaking ice, for that those leaving the town were doing so by their authority."

The two other ditches were crossed in the same way, but the work was more difficult, as the besieged only broke the ice of these once a day.

"We should never have got across without your aid, Edgar," Albert said. "I could scare hold on to the rope. My hands are dead, and I feel as if I were frozen to the bone."

"Let us run for a bit, Albert, to warm our blood. Another quarter of a mile and we shall be challenged by our sentries."

CHAPTER XVIII

A NOBLE GIFT.

THE pace at which the party started soon slackened, for neither Albert nor Hal Carter could maintain it. However, it was not long before they heard the sentry challenge:

"Who go there?"

"Sir Albert de Courcy and Sir Edgar Ormskirk, escaped from Ypres," Edgar answered.

"Stand where you are till I call the sergeant," the man said, and shouted "Sergeant!" at the top of his voice. In five minutes a sergeant and two men-at-arms came up.

"Hurry, sergeant, I pray you!" Edgar said. "We have swum three ditches, and my companions, being weakened by their wounds, are well-nigh perished."

"Come on," the sergeant said, "it is clear at any rate that you are Englishmen." He had brought a torch with him, and as they came up looked at them narrowly, then he saluted. "I know you, Sir Edgar, disguised as you are. I was fighting behind you on the wall five weeks since, and had it not been for the strength of your arm I should have returned no more to England."

"How is Sir Hugh Calverley?" Edgar asked as they hurried towards the camp.

"His wounds are mending fast," the sergeant said, "and he went out of his tent to-day for the first time. I saw him myself."

A quarter of an hour's walking brought them to the tent occupied by Sir Hugh and his followers. A light was still burning there, and they heard voices within.

"May we enter?" Edgar said as he slightly opened the flap of the tent.

"Surely that must be the voice of Sir Edgar Ormskirk!" Sir Hugh exclaimed.

"It is I, sure enough, and with me is Sir Albert de Courcy and my brave man-at-arms."

As he spoke he stepped into the tent. Two knights were there, and they and Sir Hugh advanced with outstretched hands to meet the new-comers.

"Welcome back, welcome back!" Sir Hugh exclaimed in

a tone of emotion. "My brave knights, I and my two comrades here have to thank you for our lives, for although in truth I know naught about it, I have heard from Sir Thomas Vokes and Sir Tristram Montford how you brought the band to our assistance, and how you kept the enemy at bay, while this good fellow of yours bore me down the ladder on his shoulder; while from those who escaped afterwards we heard how you both, with but two or three others, kept the foe back, and gave time for the rest to jump from the walls or slide down the ladders. But your faces are blue, and your teeth chattering?"

"We have had to swim three ditches, and the ice having formed pretty thickly it was no child's work."

"First, do you each drain a goblet of wine," Sir Hugh said, "and then to your tent. All your things are untouched. Knights, will you go with them and rub them down till their skin glows, and then wrap them up in blankets." He called, and two servants came in. "Heat three bottles of wine in a bowl with plenty of spices," he said, "and carry it to these knights' tent, and take a portion to the tent of their men-at-arms for the use of this good fellow. See that your comrades rub you down," he said to Hal. "They will be glad indeed to see you back; for although we heard from a prisoner that the two knights were alive we knew not whether any others had been taken with them. Tell Hawkins to light two torches at once and fix them in the knights' tent, and put two others in that of the men-at-arms. Mind, Sir Edgar, once between the blankets you stay there till morning. Your story will keep until then."

After throwing off their wet clothes, and being rubbed down until they glowed, Edgar and Albert were soon covered up in blankets, and after drinking the hot spiced wine, soon

fell asleep. In the morning they related their story to Sir
Hugh Calverley and the other two knights.

"'Tis Sir Edgar who should tell the tale," Albert said,
"for indeed I know but little about it from the time I saw
you lowered over the wall. Things went well with us for
a time; we were joined by more men, and were strong
enough to divide into two parties, Edgar going to the
right while I went to the left. We cleared the wall for
some distance, and methinks had there been ladders, so
that we could have been helped more quickly, the town
would have been won; but the enemy were reinforced more
quickly than we were, and we began to lose ground. Then
came a body of knights who beat us back till we were close
to the point where the ladders were set. Then a knight
made at me with a mace. I saw his arms raised, and after
that I knew nothing more."

"The last man who jumped from the wall, Sir Albert,
told us that he saw that you were down and that Sir Edgar
and one of his men-at-arms were fighting like demons over
you. Now, Sir Edgar, tell us how the matter ended."

"We made a shift to keep them back, Sir Hugh, for some
five minutes, when one of the French knights offered to
give us terms of surrender on ransom, and seeing no use in
fighting longer when the matter could only have terminated
one way, I surrendered."

Then he related the good treatment they had met with
at the hands of Sir Robert de Beaulieu, and the manner in
which he had enabled them to escape the fury of the rabble
of Ypres, and had sent them away free from ransom.

"It was well done, indeed, of him," Sir Hugh said
warmly. "Truly a courteous and knightly action. And so
you have both given your pledge to fight no more in this
campaign. By St. George, I should not be ill-pleased if

someone would put me under a similar pledge, for I tell you
that I am heartily sick of it! Never did so disordered an
army start from England. An army led by bishops and
priests is something strange. Bishops have before now
ridden often in battle, but never before did they assume
command. Methinks when I go home that I will ask the
king to give me the direction of Westminster Monastery
and Abbey; at any rate I could not make a worse hand of
it than the Bishop of Norwich is doing of this. And you
say that De Beaulieu promised to send your armour on the
first opportunity! That is, indeed, a generous action, for
the armour of a prisoner is always the property of his
captor, and your armour is of great value. I would that
we could do something to show the good knight that we
appreciate his generosity."

"We have our chains," Edgar said. "Of course we did
not carry them about us when we should have to fight, and
they are very heavy and of the finest workmanship. These
would we gladly send to him, would we not, Albert, in
token of our gratitude? Though costly as they are, they
are of much less value than the armour."

"I would gladly add something of my own account," Sir
Hugh said, "seeing that you are in my train, and one
does not like to be surpassed by a foreign knight. As to
the matter of the ransom, that does not trouble me, and
indeed, seeing that you surrendered to him, and that he
felt that he could not give protection, and you had to risk
your lives in getting away, it was but reasonable that he
should remit it, but in the matter of the armour the case is
different. I will add to your chains a reliquary which was
presented to me by Pedro of Castile when I saved his life
in the fight at Najarra. He told me that it contained a
nail of the true cross, and that it was brought to Spain by

a Spaniard of royal blood who was a knight commander of
the Temple.

"I do not know how far this is true, for as one gets older
one loses faith in these monkish stories of reliquaries.
However, the casket is set with gems of value, and there is
with it a parchment setting forth its history; at any rate it
is a gift that is worthy of even a prince's acceptance. I
will send it to him as a token that Sir Hugh Calverley
recognizes his chivalrous behaviour to the knights who were
captured while covering his carriage from the ramparts of
Ypres, and, therefore, sends this gift to him in all honour
and courtesy, together with the gold chains of the knights
themselves. We shall not have long to wait. There are
fights well-nigh every day, and when these are over there
is a truce of an hour to carry off the wounded and dead."

The young knights thanked Sir Hugh for thus gener-
ously supplementing their own offering in return for their
armour, but he waved it aside.

"You saved my life," he said; "or at any rate you saved
me from capture, and had I fallen into their hands methinks
that I should have had to pay a far heavier ransom before
they let me out again."

Two days later there was heavy fighting again and much
loss on both sides. It ceased as usual without any advantage being won by the besiegers. The fighting ended soon
after mid-day, and at one o'clock the trumpet sounded a
truce. Sir Hugh mounted, with his two knights, saying to
Edgar: "It were perhaps best that you should not ride
with me. 'Tis likely that the townsmen still think that you
are in Beaulieu's house, and were it known that you had
escaped it might bring trouble upon him and the two
knights who aided your escape from the wall."

He took with him a pursuivant and trumpeter, and, riding

through the English and Flemish men-at-arms, who were already engaged in carrying away the dead and wounded, he rode up to within a short distance of the wall, then the pursuivant and trumpeter advanced to the edge of the moat, and the latter blew a loud blast.

In a short time a knight appeared on the wall, and the pursuivant cried in a loud voice:

"Sir Hugh Calverley, a valiant and puissant knight of England, desires speech with Sir Robert de Beaulieu, a brave and gentle knight of Flanders."

"I am Sir Robert de Beaulieu. Pray tell Sir Hugh Calverley to do me the courtesy to wait for me a quarter of an hour, and I will then issue forth and speak to him."

At the end of that time Sir Robert rode out, and crossed the bridge which had been lowered across the ditch for the passage of the soldiers engaged in collecting the dead. He was followed by two esquires and four men-at-arms, the latter bearing something behind them on their horses. The two knights saluted each other courteously, and Sir Hugh introduced his two companions to Sir Robert.

"I am glad indeed," the latter said to Calverley, "thus to have the opportunity of meeting one of the most famous knights in Europe. My men-at-arms are bearers of the armour of Sir Edgar Ormskirk and Sir Albert de Courcy, who are, I believe, knights riding in your train. I promised them that I would send the armour on the first opportunity, and am glad indeed that the occasion has come so speedily."

He and Sir Hugh had both dismounted after saluting each other, and the latter held out his mailed hand to the Fleming.

"Sir Robert de Beaulieu," he said, "I have heard of you as a brave and honourable knight, and you have in this matter proved yourself to be a chivalrous and generous one in thus rendering up the spoil fairly won by you, without ransom; but it is not our custom to be outdone in generosity. The armour is of no ordinary value, and as these knights of mine were made prisoners while covering my removal when insensible and helpless, I feel that the debt is mine as well as theirs. They have begged me to give you these two chains, both, as you see, of value, and of the best Italian work. To these I add, as a token of my esteem for you, this casket, which was given to me by Don Pedro of Spain when I rode with the Black Prince to aid him in his struggle with Don Henry. As you will see by the parchment attached to the casket, it contains a nail of the true cross, brought from Palestine by a Spanish grandee who was knight commander of the Spanish branch of the Knights Templar. I pray you to accept it, not as part of the ransom for my knights' armour, but as a proof of my esteem for one who has shown himself a flower of knightly courtesy."

"It would be churlish, Sir Hugh Calverley, for me to refuse so noble a gift thus courteously tendered. I shall prize it beyond any in my possession, not only for its own value and holiness, but as the gift of so noble and famous a knight. As to the chains, I pray you to return them to your brave young knights. Never did I see men who bore themselves more gallantly, and Sir Edgar especially withstood with honour a score of us for some time, and at last he yielded, not because he was conquered, but to save further bloodshed. They are young, and may, like enough, some day be again made prisoners. In that case they may find the chains, which are of singular beauty, of value to them; therefore, I pray you, hand them back to them again as a token of how warmly I appreciate their bravery and conduct."

"Right gladly will I do so. As you put it in that way, Sir Robert, they will appreciate the gift as much as I do, and, as you say, maybe the chains will be useful to them some day, for they are not of those who battle for spoil, and, like myself, have refused all share in that which the army has taken in Flanders, holding that we had no cause of dispute with your people, and that our assault upon them was unfairly and unjustly made."

After some more compliments had been exchanged, the two knights grasped each other's hands courteously, remounted, and then saluting again, rode off. While the conversation had been going on, Sir Robert's men-at-arms had handed over the armour to the three retainers who had ridden behind Sir Hugh and his two knights.

Edgar and Albert were delighted at regaining their armour. It would have been impossible for them to have replaced the harness by similar suits, and, moreover, they felt that they would have been humiliated had they, on their return to England, been obliged to confess to Sir Robert Gaiton that they had lost the splendid presents that he had given them. They were less pleased at the return of their chains, but Sir Hugh assured them that it would be an act of discourtesy were they to send them back to De Beaulieu.

There was now nothing to detain them longer in the camp, and taking leave of Sir Hugh, they started the next morning with Hal Carter and the other surviving retainers, and rode by easy stages to Gravelines, where they took ship for Dover. Instead of riding directly home, they journeyed to London, as they were bearers of a letter from Sir Hugh Calverley to the council, and one also to the king. The latter received them with marked pleasure.

"What! back from the wars, sir knights?" he said as

they handed him Sir Hugh's letter. "Surely Calverley might have chosen as his messengers some whose swords could have been better spared."

"We were chosen, your Majesty, because we had the misfortune to be taken prisoners at Ypres, and it was a condition of our release that we should take no further part in the campaign, and as we were returning in consequence, Sir Hugh committed to us this letter to yourself, and one to the council."

"Prisoners!" the king said with a laugh; "that you had got yourselves killed would not have surprised me, but that you should surrender never entered my mind."

The two young knights coloured.

"It cannot be said that Sir Albert surrendered," Edgar said, "seeing that he was insensible from his wounds. As for myself, your Majesty, as I and one of my men-at-arms stood alone on the walls of Ypres surrounded by foes, I trust that your Majesty will see that it was wiser for me to yield, and so to have the opportunity of fighting again some day under your royal banner, than to give away my life uselessly."

"Assuredly, assuredly!" the young king said hastily. "I did but jest, Sir Edgar, for I know that so long as a chance of victory remained you would not lower your sword. However, let me see what the stout knight says. I know already that he does not approve of the way in which the war is being carried on; and indeed had we thought that the headstrong bishop would have disregarded Sir Hugh's counsel and embroiled us with the Flemings, whom we regard as our allies, we should not have placed him at the head of the army, for though it is but, as the Bishop maintains, a church army and not an English army, Europe will assuredly hold us responsible for its doings."

He cut with his dagger the silk that bound the roll of parchment together.

The king read the letter carefully, and when he concluded said:

"Truly, young sirs, you have borne yourselves right gallantly and well; Sir Hugh Calverley speaks strongly indeed in your favour, and says that he owes his freedom if not his life to you. And now tell me, think you that Ypres will be taken?"

"I fear not, your Majesty," Edgar said. "I thought that the siege of Oudenarde was worse conducted than anything I had ever read of, but the siege of Ypres is to the full as faulty. The place is strong, and stoutly defended, and it can only be taken by regular works erected against it and machines placed to batter a breach. Nothing of this sort has been attempted. The troops march valiantly against the walls, but they throw away their lives in vain; and if, as is said, the French king is marching to its assistance with a strong army, there will be naught for us but to retreat to the ports unless strong aid arrives from England."

"But the Bishop has some eight thousand Englishmen and twenty thousand Ghentois," the king said. "Surely we might fight and win, as our grandfathers did at Crecy."

"Yes, sire; but the English army at Crecy was commanded by a king, and was composed of good fighting men, with a great number of knights and nobles to lead them. The army in Flanders is commanded by a bishop, and there are many of the men who have gone over for the sake of plunder, and they will make but a poor stand in battle."

"My uncle of Lancaster has gathered a large force, and is ready to cross over to their aid," the king said.

"So we have heard by the way, sire. and if he joins the Bishop all may be well, for his authority would be paramount, but at present he has not crossed, and unless he arrives before the King of France, things will assuredly go badly with the Bishop."

"I have no doubt that Sir Hugh has set forth these matters in his letter to the council," the king said, "but assuredly Lancaster should be there in time. And now, tell me how you made your escape from Ypres?"

Edgar related the circumstances.

"Your captor was an honourable gentleman," the king said, "and it is well that you escaped, for these Flemish burghers are masterful men and might well have murdered you. I must now to the council, I have summoned it to assemble. Have you been home yet?"

"No, sire. Our first duty was to bring you the letters, but, with your permission, we shall ride down into Kent to-morrow."

"Do you know that your friend Van Voorden has again returned to London? He found that he could do naught in Flanders, which at present is wholly at the orders of the King of France."

They rode first to Sir Robert Gaiton's house, where, as always, they were welcomed most warmly, and Albert narrated their adventures in Flanders, and how they still owned the armour he had given them.

After staying there for some time they went to the house where Van Voorden was lodging, having obtained his address from Sir Robert Gaiton. They had not seen him since they had parted from him in Ghent, a year before.

"I thought you intended to settle in Flanders, Mynheer?" Edgar said after the first greetings were over.

"I hoped to do so, and after I left Antwerp I went to Louvain and took a house there; but when the King of France defeated and killed Van Artevelde, and all Flanders save Ghent came under his power, the country was no longer safe for me.   It was known, of course, that I was for many years here, and that I had done all in my power to effect a league between Ghent and England, so three months ago I crossed hither, leaving my wife and daughter at Louvain. I stopped for a short time at Ghent, and had much to do with bringing it about that Ghent should send an army to assist the English; but I fear that the doings of the Bishop's troops — the sacking of towns by them — has so set the Flemings against England that there is no hope of a general alliance being made with Flanders.

"There were other things for which I wished to come over.   I had hoped to return before this, but matters seem to be going on but badly, and if the King of France and his army defeat or drive out the Bishop, his power will be greater than ever in Flanders, and in that case I shall send for my wife and daughter to come over again, and establish myself here finally."

On taking leave of them he handed a wooden box to each, saying:

"I pray you not to open these until you reach home."

The next day Edgar and Albert rode down into Kent. Great was the surprise that their presence excited when they arrived at De Courcy's castle.   Aline ran down into the courtyard and embraced her brother warmly, and then, as was the custom, held up her cheek to be kissed by Edgar.

"What, tired of the wars already?" she said laughing. "Or have you killed all your enemies? or how is it that you are here?"

"We have been prisoners, Aline," her brother said, "and have been bound to take no farther part in the war."

"Prisoners!" she repeated; "you are joking with me,

Albert. Surely you and Edgar would never have surrendered unharmed?"

"Nor did we, Aline. I was cut down and stunned by the blow of a mace, and was lying insensible."

"And what was Edgar doing?" she asked, looking reproachfully at him.

"Edgar was not near me when I was struck down, Aline, but no sooner did I fall than he with his man-at-arms, Hal Carter, stood over me and kept at bay a host of knights and soldiers, and slew so many that they were glad at last to give him terms of surrender."

The girl's face flushed, and she would have spoken had not Sir Ralph and her mother at that moment issued from the door.

"Why! what brings you home, lads?" Sir Ralph asked heartily.

"They have been taken prisoners, father," Aline interposed, "and Albert has been wounded, and they have both been obliged to give their parole not to serve again through the war."

"That is bad news indeed," the knight said. "It means another farm gone, and perhaps two, to pay for Albert's ransom. However, it is the fortune of war. Now come in and tell us all about it; but doubtless you are both hungry, and the matter will keep till you have dined. The meal is already on the table. You are not looking much the worse for your wounds, Albert," his father went on as they seated themselves at table.

"I have been healed of them for the last month, father. I was brought down by the blow of a mace, which would have finished me had it not been for the good work put into my helmet by the Milanese armourer. Also I had a wound on the neck, but fortunately it was not very deep."

"And did you come out of it scatheless, Edgar?"

"Nearly scatheless, for I knew not that I had been wounded until the fight was over, and it was but a pike thrust that entered at the shoulder-joint and cut the flesh thence to the neck. It was but an affair of a bandage and a bit of plaster. The only one seriously hurt was Hal Carter,—it was some three weeks before he began to mend. He had half a dozen wounds. Another of my men was killed and two of Albert's."

"Now let us hear all about it," Sir Ralph said, when the meal was over; "that you bore yourselves well I have no doubt, but I would fain hear the details of the matter."

Albert told the whole story of the assault and the escape, interrupted by Edgar, who protested that Albert was always belittling his own doings, and giving him credit when everything had been done equally by them both.

"You blame Albert unjustly, Edgar," Sir Ralph said when the story was concluded. "Albert has behaved well, but he has neither your strength, your skill, nor your quickness. It was you who thought of carrying the broken ladder to another spot, and so taking the besieged on the wall by surprise, and you were the first to mount it. It was you who, when you saw that the case had become altogether hopeless, ordered the soldiers to save themselves, while you held the enemy at bay. Albert would like enough have been killed, had you not so stoutly defended him that they gave terms of surrender to you both. You, again, had the idea of making your escape along the roofs, and took the lead in it. There is all credit due to Albert that he well seconded you, but it was you who led. Again it is probable that neither he nor your man-at-arms would have been able to cross those half-frozen ditches, had you not first broken the ice for them and then dragged them over. You have done wonders for Albert, but you could not accomplish miracles. You have transformed him from a weakling into a brave young knight, of whom I am proud, but you cannot give him your strength or your quickness. If you go on as you have begun, Edgar, you will become a famous captain. He will remain, and will be content to remain, your companion and lieutenant. What have you in those boxes that were strapped behind your saddles?"

"I know not, Sir Ralph," Albert said. "They were given to us by Mynheer Van Voorden, and he charged us not to open them until we arrived here."

"It is a mystery then!" Aline exclaimed. "Let us send for them and open them at once. I am glad one of the boxes was not given to me to take care of, for I am afraid I should never have had the patience to wait until I arrived here before opening it."

Sir Ralph ordered the boxes to be brought in. "They are light enough," he said, "and I should judge from their weight that they contain papers of some sort. Open yours first, Albert."

They were fastened by three skeins of silk, the Fleming's seal being affixed to the knots.

"Cut them, Albert!" Aline exclaimed, as her brother proceeded to break the seals and untie the knots.

"No, no," he said; "silk is not to be picked up on the wayside, and it will be little trouble to undo them."

Indeed, in a minute he had unfastened the knots and raised the lid. At the top lay a piece of paper, on which was written, *A slight testimony of gratitude for inestimable services rendered to yours gratefully, John Van Voorden.* Underneath was a roll of parchment.

"What have we here?" Sir Ralph said. Albert ran his

eye over the crabbed black-letter writing, and gave an exclamation of surprise.

"Now then, Albert," Aline exclaimed impatiently; "don't keep it all to yourself. We are burning to know what it is all about!"

Albert made no reply, but continued to read. "It is an assignment to me," he said at last, in a low and agitated voice, "of the lands, castle, messuages, tenements, &c., of Cliffe."

Sir Ralph leapt to his feet. "A princely gift, Albert! The lands are four times as large as mine, and, as I have heard, a fair castle has been rising there for months past. Art sure that there is no mistake?"

"There can be no mistake in the deed, father; but can I accept such a gift at the hands of the Fleming?"

"That you can, my son, and without any hesitation. Van Voorden is known to be the richest Fleming in England. He has on various occasions lent vast sums to the king and council, and noble as the gift is, it is one that he can doubtless well afford. You have saved the lives of himself, his wife, and daughter, and he may well feel grateful. He told me when he gave you that suit of armour that it was no recognition of what he felt he owed you, and that he hoped in the future to discharge the debt more worthily. Now, Edgar, let us see what is in your box."

Edgar had been quietly untying the knots of the silk, and the box was already open. The words on the top were similar to those in Albert's box.

"Please read it, Albert," he said, handing over the parchment. "You can decipher the characters better than I can." Albert read it through to himself.

"'Tis similar to mine," he said, "and assigns you the land, manors, the castle, and all rights and privileges thereto appertaining of the hundred of Hoo."

"Bravo, bravo!" Sir Ralph exclaimed. "Another noble gift, and fully equal to that of Albert. This Fleming is a very prince. I congratulate you, Edgar, with all my heart. I had heard that Sir John Evesham had sold his estates, which comprise the whole hundred of Hoo, a year since, in order to live at court, but none seemed to know who was the purchaser. I heard, too, that a large number of men had been employed in building a castle on the heights looking down the Medway past Upnor to Chatham. Why, lads, if you ever win to the rank of knight banneret, you will have land enough to support the dignity, and to take the field with two or three knights and a fair following of men-at-arms in your train. I have gained good sums for the ransom of prisoners, but I never had the luck to save the life of a Flemish merchant and his family."

"It seems well-nigh impossible," Edgar said.

"You must remember, Edgar, that these rich Flemings are the bankers of half the princes in Europe. You, who have been in their houses, know that they live in comfort and luxury such as none of our nobles possess. They could find the money for a king's ransom, or pay beforehand the taxes of a country. If a king can grant estates like these to his favourites,—and not only the king, but many of our nobles can do so,—it is not strange that one of the richest of these Flemings should make such gifts to those who have saved his life, without feeling that he has in any way over-paid the service."

"I must be riding on now," Edgar said, "to carry this wonderful news to my father."

While they had been dining, Hal Carter had been getting a hearty meal in the kitchen, where he and Albert's two retainers were surrounded by all the men-at-arms, who were anxious to hear the details of the expedition. When Edgar sent down for his horse, Sir Ralph went down with him to the courtyard, and as Hal brought the horses round, the old knight put his hand upon his shoulder.

"My brave fellow," he said, "I have heard how you stood with your master across my son's body, and how doughtily you fought. Do not forget that I am your debtor, but for the present I can only say that I thank you for the part you played."

"It would have been strange indeed, Sir Ralph, had I not hit my hardest, for my own life depended upon it, and it was not like that I should draw back a foot when Sir Albert, whom I love only next to my master, was lying there; but, indeed, it was a right merry fight, the only one that came up to my expectations of what a stiffly fought mêlée would be. I would not have missed it for anything."

CHAPTER XIX.

WELL SETTLED.

WELL, well, well!" Mr. Ormskirk exclaimed when Edgar brought the story of all that had happened since he had been away to an end, "indeed you surprise me. I know that many knights fit out parties and go to the wars, not so much for honour and glory as for the spoils and ransoms they may gain, and that after Crecy and Poictiers there was not a single soldier but came back laden with booty and with rich jewels, gold chains, and costly armour gathered from the host of French nobles who fell on those fields; while knights who were fortunate enough to capture counts, earls, or princes, gained ransoms that enabled them to purchase estates, and live without occasion to go

further to the wars during their lives. But I never thought
that you would benefit by such a chance. As it is to my
mind more honourable to save life than to take it, I rejoice
that you have come to your fortune, not by the slaying of
enemies, but by the saving the lives of a man, his wife, and
daughter, who are rich enough to reward you.

"Assuredly, if a man like Mynheer Van Voorden had fallen
into the hands of the Count of Flanders, the latter would
have extracted from him, as the price of his freedom, a sum
many times larger than that which he has expended on
the purchase of these two estates, and the building of the
castles. Well, Edgar, I congratulate you heartily. You
can now ride to the wars when the king's banner is spread
to the winds, and do your duty to your country, but there
will be no occasion for you to become a mere knight adven-
turer—a class I detest, ever ready to sell their swords to
the highest bidder, and to kill men, against whom they
have no cause of complaint, as indifferently as a butcher
would strike down a bullock with a pole-axe.

"Between these men and those who fight simply in the
wars of their own country the gulf is a wide one, as wide
as that betwixt a faithful house-dog and a roving wolf.
When are you going to receive your new acquisition, or
are you intending to ride first to London to thank the
Fleming for his noble gift?"

"Assuredly, we should have first ridden to London, father,
but we each found in the bottom of our boxes a short letter
which we had at first overlooked. The letters were the
same, save for our names. Mine ran:—

"*Dear Sir Edgar,*

"*It has given me very great pleasure to prepare
this little surprise for you. I pray you, do not mar it in any*

*way by returning me thanks. The gift is as naught in compari-
son with the service rendered. I am proceeding to the North to-
morrow on business with Earl Percy, and shall not return for
some weeks. When we meet next, I pray you let there be no
word of thanks concerning this affair, for I consider myself still
greatly your debtor. You will find an agent of mine at your
castle. He has been there some time, has made the acquaintance
of all the vassals and others, and will introduce you to them as
their lord. He has my instructions either to remain there to
manage your affairs for six months, or for any less time you may
choose. But methinks you will do well to keep him for that time,
as he is a good man of business, and you will need such an one
until you have mastered all the details, and can take matters
entirely in your own hands."*

"So you see, father, we shall be free to start to-morrow.
Sir Ralph, Lady De Courcy, and Mistress Aline will ride
with us, and I trust that you will come also. We shall
first go to Cliffe, which will be on our road, and, indeed,
I believe that for some distance Albert's lands join mine.
Then we shall go on to my castle—it sounds absurd, doesn't
it, father?—and doubtless we shall be able to stay in Hoo,
or if not, 'tis but two or three miles to Stroud, where we
are sure to find good lodging."

"I should like to ride with you, Edgar, but it is years
since I have bestridden a horse."

"We shall ride but slowly, father, for Dame De Courcy
loves not for her palfrey to go beyond a walk. If you like
you could bestride Hal Carter's horse, which is a strong
and steady animal, and he can walk alongside, so as to be
ready to catch the rein if it be needed. He will be very

glad to go, for the honest fellow is in the highest delight at the news of my good fortune."

"I think that I could do that, Edgar, yet I will not go by Cliffe, but straight to Hoo. I can then travel as I like, and shall not have to join in talk with Dame De Courcy nor the others, nor feel that my bad horsemanship makes me a jest."

"Very well, father, perhaps that would be the pleasantest way for you."

"If I get there before you, Edgar, I shall stop at a tavern in the main street of Hoo,—there is sure to be one there, —and will rest until you come along. If Hal Carter learns that you have passed through before my arrival, I will come straight on to the castle."

Accordingly, early the next morning Mr. Ormskirk started with Hal, and Edgar, after seeing them fairly on their way, rode over to the De Courcys. All were in readiness for the start.

"Is not Mr. Ormskirk coming with us?" Dame De Courcy asked. "Recluse though he is, I thought he would surely tear himself from his books on such an occasion."

"He has done so, dame, and is already on the road to Hoo, under the charge of Hal Carter. 'Tis so many years since he has bestridden a horse that he said that he should be ill at ease riding with such a party, and that he would therefore go on quietly with Hal walking beside him, and would join us when we came to Hoo."

They mounted at once. Dame De Courcy rode on a pillion behind Sir Ralph. Aline bestrode—for side-saddles had not yet come into use—her own pony. Two retainers followed, one leading a sumpter horse, with two panniers well filled with provisions and wine, together with some women's gear, in case the weather should turn bad, and a change be required at the halting-place for the night. They started briskly, and Edgar was glad that his father had gone on alone, the pace would have sorely discomposed him. Alternately walking and going at a canter they arrived in three hours at Cliffe.

"There is your castle, Albert," Aline exclaimed. "It seems well-nigh if not quite finished, and is strongly posted on that hill, overlooking the whole country from Dartford to Sheerness. You will need a chatelaine before long, brother mine."

Albert laughed, but coloured a little.

"Time enough to think of that, Aline."

"Nay, I am in earnest. Many are betrothed, if not married, long before they attain your age."

"I may say the same to you, Aline. 'Tis the fashion now for girls to be betrothed between twelve and fourteen. I have been wandering about and fighting and have had no time to think of love-making."

Aline shrugged her shoulders. "You had better ask Sir Ralph and my mother for their views about me, Albert. It is not for a maid to make her own marriage, but a valiant knight like yourself can manage your own affairs. Methought perhaps that you would have to tell us that the Fleming's fair daughter was to assist you in the management of the castle that her father has given you."

"Joanna Van Voorden!" Albert exclaimed indignantly, while Edgar burst into laughter; "why, she is well-nigh as big as her mother already, and promises to be far bigger. Thank you, Aline! If the castle and estate had been offered me on the condition that I married her, I would have had none of them."

"Well, sir, shall I make another guess?" Aline asked mischievously.

"No, no, Aline," Albert said hastily. "No more guessing, if you please."

They had by this time approached the castle. "Look, father!" Aline exclaimed, clapping her hands; "they must have been on the watch for us. See! they are raising a flag on that staff on the turret; and see, there are your arms blazoned on it."

"'Tis a goodly castle for its size," the knight said, as he drew rein and turned his horse so that his dame might get a better view of it. "There is a dry moat, which is lined with stonework. The walls are not very high, but they are well defended by those flanking towers, and the place could stand any sudden assault. I should say that it was about the same strength as our own. So far as I can see, the other arrangements are quite different. There is no keep, and it seems to me that the house is built rather for comfort than for defence; the windows are large, and it looks more like a Flemish house built within a castle wall than an English place of strength. Now let us ride on;" and they pressed their horses forward.

The gates were thrown open when they approached within a hundred yards, the drawbridge over the moat had been already lowered.

"Ride you first, Albert," Sir Ralph said; "you are lord of the place."

As they came to the head of the drawbridge a middle-aged man of grave aspect, dressed in the garb of a citizen, appeared at the gate, and six men-at-arms in steel caps and body armour, armed with pike and sword, drew up behind him.

The man bowed deeply to Albert. "Welcome to Cliffe Castle, sir knight!" he said. "I am Nicholas Hocht, and have, by the orders of my master, Mynheer Van Voorden, been here for the last year to superintend the building of this castle, and in carrying out his other commands respecting it, with further orders to remain here, should you desire it, for the further space of six months as your steward. I received a message from him yesterday, saying that possibly you would be here to-day, and I must, therefore, have everything in readiness for you. The warning was somewhat short, but I have done my best, and I trust that you will pardon any shortcomings."

"I am much beholden to you, Master Hocht," Albert said. "You have done well indeed, for a fairer castle and one better placed no one could desire."

The men-at-arms saluted as he rode on. Entering the gate, they were able to see the house itself. It was, as Sir Ralph had said, rather a Flemish house than a knightly castle; the lower range of windows were small and heavily barred, but above there were large casements, pointed roofs, and projecting gables. It had an air of comfort and brightness. On the top of the broad steps leading to the great door were four retainers all similarly attired in doublets of russet cloth and orange hose. As soon as the party alighted they ascended the steps, led by the steward. When they entered the great hall a general exclamation of surprise broke from them.

They had expected to see bare walls and every sign of the place having only just left the builder's hands; instead of this everything was complete, the massive oak beams and panels of the ceilings were varnished, the walls were wainscotted, the oak floor highly polished; Eastern rugs lay here and there upon it, carved benches ran along the sides, and a large banqueting table stood in the centre; rich curtains hung by the window, and a huge fire was piled on the hearth."

"Why, this is a work of enchantment, Master Hocht!"
Dame Agatha said.

"I have had but little to do with it, lady," the steward
replied. "The woodwork was all made in London, to my
master's orders, and I had but to superintend its being
placed in position."

He led them from room to room, their surprise and
delight continually increasing; all were furnished richly in
the Flemish style with cabinets, tables, settees, and armoires.
There were hangings to the windows and rugs on the floors;
everything was ready for habitation, the linen presses were
full of table-cloths and napkins and sheets. The beds were
ready for sleeping in, with their great bags of soft feathers,
their thick blankets, and silken coverlets. These more than
anything else excited the dame's admiration. Never had
she seen beds approaching these in softness and daintiness.

"With the exception of the furniture in the hall," Master
Hocht explained, "everything has come direct from Flanders,
having been selected by Mynheer Van Voorden himself, and
sent by sea to Gravesend."

After having inspected the whole of the house they returned to the hall. Here the table had been spread. A
silver skewer, to act as a fork, an article then unknown in
England, was placed before each, and an admirable repast
was served; the steward himself officiating as carver, while
the four servitors carried the platters, which were of fine
Flemish ware, to the guests. Albert had begged his father
to take the head of the table, but the latter refused positively.
He sat on one side of his son and his dame on the other.
Fish of several kinds, meats, and poultry were served. All
cut up their meat with their daggers, and carried it to their
mouths on the point of the skewer.

Albert and Edgar had learned the use of them in Flanders.

Lady Agatha and Aline said that they were charming, but Sir Ralph declared that he greatly preferred using his fingers. After the meal was concluded, water was brought round in a silver bowl, with a damask napkin for them to wipe their fingers on.

"The wine is excellent," Sir Ralph said. "You can scarcely have purchased this at Cliffe or Gravesend."

"It is from the cellar, Sir Ralph, which is well stocked with the wines of France and Spain."

"Truly, Albert," Dame Agatha said, "this is not a castle; it is a veritable enchanted palace. Mynheer Van Voorden is like one of the good genii the Saracens believe in, who can, at will, summon up from the ground a vast palace, ready built and furnished. I trust that it will not at once vanish as soon as we leave it. Were it to do so I should scarcely be more surprised than I have been at its splendour and comfort."

"Do you tarry here to-night, Sir Albert?" the steward asked as they rose from the table.

"No, we are going to take horse at once and ride to Hoo."

"Will you take the men-at-arms with you? They have horses in the stables."

"Not to-day," Albert said. "We are a family party, and travelling quietly."

As they rode into the street of Hoo Mr. Ormskirk came out of a tavern, where he had been resting. After greeting the ladies and Sir Ralph, he said, "I had begun to think that you must have changed your minds, and that you were not coming hither to-day. I expected you three hours ago."

"We have been viewing the marvels of an enchanted castle, Mr. Ormskirk," Dame Agatha said. "We will not tell you about them, for doubtless you will see others like them here, and it would be a pity for me to prepare you for what you are to see."

The castle was indeed in all respects an almost exact duplicate to that of Cliffe. They were received as before by the Flemish steward. There were the same number of men-at-arms and servitors, and the fittings and furnishings were as perfect as those of Cliffe. After going over it, Edgar drew Sir Ralph aside.

"Sir Ralph," he said, "the castle, perfect as it is, still lacks one thing—a mistress. I have long hoped that the time would some day come that I should ask you for the hand of Mistress Aline, but though I have been fortunate, and have won rank and some distinction, I was but a landless knight, and in no position to ask for your daughter's hand. That obstacle has now been removed, and I pray you to give her to me. I love her very truly. My thoughts have never wandered for a moment from her, and I trust that I shall be able to make her happy. Unless the banner of England is hoisted I shall go no more to the wars."

"I am in no way surprised at your request, Edgar," the knight said; "and indeed for the past two years my dame and I have talked this over, and hoped that it might be. I have during the past year had more than one request for her hand, but have refused them, for her mother told me she believed that Aline's fancy has long inclined towards you."

He called Dame Agatha to join him, and on hearing Edgar's request she heartily concurred with the knight.

"Nothing could please us better," she said. "We have long regarded you almost as our son, and we need have no fear that Aline will thwart our wishes and yours. Have you spoken to your father?"

"I spoke to him last night, lady, and told him what my hopes have long been, and that Van Voorden's noble gift now rendered it possible for me to speak; that it might be some time before it could be more than a betrothal, since, although I had rank and land, I was still without money to enable me to make the castle comfortable for her abode. Now that, owing to the Fleming's generosity, this difficulty is also removed, I hope that you will not think it necessary that our marriage should be delayed."

"I see no reason at all," Sir Ralph said.   "Here is everything ready for her, and no noble in England could offer so comfortable a home to his bride. The castle lacks a mistress, and the sooner it has one the better. Therefore you can take her as soon as her mother can get her ready."

They now joined Albert, Aline, and Mr. Ormskirk, who had mounted to the top of one of the turrets and were admiring the view.

"'Tis a fair home," Sir Ralph said.

"It is indeed, father."

"What say you to becoming its mistress, daughter? Sir Edgar has asked for your hand, and has gained mine and your mother's hearty consent. What say you?"

The girl coloured up to her forehead as her father spoke. "I am ready to obey your orders father," she said in a low tone, "the more so as my heart goes wholly with them."

"Take her, Edgar. 'Tis not often that a young knight gains castle, and land, and bride in twenty-four hours. May your good luck continue all your life!"

"You have robbed me of my chatelaine, Edgar," Albert said after the first congratulations were over.   "Aline had half promised to come and keep house for me for the present."

"You must follow Edgar's example," Sir Ralph said. "Who is it to be, lad?"

"I had intended to speak to you shortly, father, but as you ask me I will do so at once. I have seen no one whom I could love so well as Mistress Ursula, daughter of Sir Robert Gaiton, and methinks that I am not indifferent to her."

"She is a fair maid," Sir Ralph said, "and her father is a right good fellow, though but a city knight. Still, others of higher rank than yourself have married in the city, and as Sir Robert has no other children, and is said to be one of the wealthiest of the London citizens, she will doubtless come to you better dowered than will Aline, for, as Edgar knows, my estates bring me in scarcely enough to keep up my castle and to lay by sufficient to place my retainers in the field should the king call on me for service. So be it then, my son. As we have settled to sleep here to-night, it will be to-morrow afternoon before we get home. The next day I will ride with you to London, and will ask Sir Robert for his daughter's hand for you."

Not the least happy of the party at the castle was Hal Carter. He passed the afternoon in walking sometimes round the walls, sometimes going out and making a circuit of the moat, or walking away short distances to obtain views of the castle from various points. The news that his master and Aline de Courcy would shortly be married raised his delight to the highest pitch, for it pointed to an early occupation of the castle. The thought that he, Hal Carter, was to be the captain of the men-at-arms in a castle like this seemed to him a huge joke. It was but two years before that he had been hunted as a rioter, and would have been executed if caught. That so famous a leader as Sir Hugh Calverley should have praised him greatly, and that he was now to have men under his command, seemed to him as wonderful a thing as that his master, whom he had known as a young boy, should stand high in the king's favour, and should be lord of a castle and a wide estate.

"Of course, father," Edgar said, as early the next morning he took a turn upon the battlements with him, "you will leave St. Alwyth and come here?"

"I don't think that I could do that, Edgar," Mr. Ormskirk said doubtfully.

"You will find it very lonely there, father; and of course we can fit you up a laboratory here, and you can go on just the same way as you did at home."

"I do not see that I shall be more lonely than I have been for the last two years, Edgar, and, indeed, as you know, even when you were at home I lived very much my own life, and only saw you at meals and for an hour or so of an evening; therefore, your being established here will make but little difference in my life, and, indeed, whenever I feel lonely I can ride over here for a day or two. I thank you all the same, Edgar, but at any rate for the present I will continue to live at St. Alwyth. I have the good prior, who often comes in for a talk with me in the evening, and makes me heartily welcome should I, as I do sometimes, go to the monastery for an hour after sunset. Sir Ralph never passes my door on his way down to Dartford without dismounting and coming in. I am happy in my own life, and as long as I have health and strength shall hope to continue it. Should my interest in my work flag, or when I feel that I am getting too old for useful work, which will, I trust, be not for many years yet, I will then gladly come and end my days here."

So the matter was left for the time, and although Edgar more than once tried to shake his father's determination, and Aline added her persuasions to his, he failed to alter Mr. Ormskirk's resolution. Sir Ralph and Albert returned

from London after staying there for a few days. Sir Robert
Gaiton had consented willingly to his daughter's marriage
with Albert, and had announced his intention of giving her
a dowry greater than that which most nobles could have
bestowed on a daughter. The king had expressed very
great satisfaction at hearing of the gift Master Van Voorden had bestowed on the young knights, and took great
interest in their approaching marriages.

"They will then have enough land for a knight banneret's
feu," he said; "that pleases me much. I should, on the
report of Sir Hugh Calverley, have appointed them to that
rank, but at present there are no estates in my gift, and I
waited till some might fall in before I appointed them.
Now, however, there is no further need for delay, and I
will order the patent appointing them to be made out at
once, for they can now, if called upon for service, take the
field with the proper following of their rank. Has Sir
Edgar adopted any cognizance? Of course your son will
take yours."

"I don't think that he has ever so much as thought of
it, sire."

"I will talk it over with my heralds," the king said, "and
see if we can fix upon something appropriate, and that is
not carried by any noble or knight. When will the weddings be?"

"In two months' time, sire. Sir Robert Gaiton and his
dame asked for that time. My son will, of course, be
married in London, and will be wed in St. Paul's. I have
not yet thought about my daughter's marriage, but it will
doubtless be at the chapel in the castle."

"'Tis a pity that they could not be married together here,
Sir Ralph."

"I believe that my daughter's tastes and those of Sir

Edgar would incline to a quiet wedding, with just our
neighbours and friends, and doubtless Albert's would also
lie that way; but in this matter Sir Robert must, of course,
carry out the arrangements as he wishes; and as an alderman and like to be lord-mayor in two years he would wish
to make a brave show on the occasion."

Before the time for the weddings approached came the
news that things had gone badly in Flanders.   At the
approach of the French army a council was held among the
leaders, and it was agreed that the allied army could not
fight with any hope of success against it. Accordingly, the
men of Ghent retired to their own city, and the English
marched with great haste to the coast and shut themselves
up in Bruckburg, while the Bishop himself galloped as far
as Bergues.   Bruckburg surrendered on the arrival of the
French army; all the English being permitted to embark
with the great spoil that had been taken. Sir Hugh Calverley, whose advice throughout had been always disregarded,
had ridden to Gravelines with his small body of men-at-
arms and thence took ship to England.   The Bishop, on his
arrival home was, with the knights who had been his councillors, very badly received; for it was held that by their
conduct and ignorance of affairs, and by the manner in
which they had behaved in Flanders, they had brought
great discredit upon England.

Sir Hugh Calverley, on the other hand, was received
with honour, it being well known that all that had been
done had been contrary to his advice, and that had this
been followed the event would have turned out very
differently.   The people at large, however, considered that
the blame for the ill ending of the expedition was due
entirely to the delay on the part of the Duke of Lancaster
in crossing over with the army under him.   It was known

that he had been altogether opposed to the expedition, which had prevented the one he desired from sailing to Spain, and that he was minded to bring ruin upon it by delaying, under many false pretences, from crossing to France. He had been extremely unpopular before, but this added very greatly to the ill-feeling with which he was regarded.

But, in truth, the Bishop's expedition failed from its own weakness. In no case could an army so collected and led have effected any great thing; but the headstrong folly and arrogance of the Bishop, and his unprovoked attack upon the Flemings, precipitated matters, and the scornful neglect of all the counsel tendered by the veteran knight who accompanied the expedition rendered it a shameful disaster.

The marriage of Sir Edgar with Aline was celebrated a fortnight before that of the bride's brother. The ceremony took place at the castle of the De Courcys, and was attended only by neighbours and friends, and by Sir Robert Gaiton, who rode down from town and presented the bride with a superb casket of jewels.

On the following day Sir Edgar with his wife rode to his castle at Hoo, where for the first time his banner with the cognizance chosen by the king, a very simple one, being a sword with the words "*For King and Honour*", was hoisted at their approach, while the banneret denoting Edgar's new rank flew from another tower. The number of the men-at-arms had been increased to ten, and great was Hal Carter's pride as he took his place in front of them and saluted as Sir Edgar rode in. Ten days later they started for London to attend Albert's wedding, which was celebrated with much pomp in St. Paul's; the king himself and most of the nobles of the court being present.

Neither of the two young knights ever rode to the wars

again, for in King Richard's time the royal banner was never again raised in France; and yet they were not without a share of fighting. Many depredations were committed along the coasts and at the mouths of rivers by French freebooters and lawless people, and the castles of Hoo and Cliffe were well placed for preventing such incursions by men landing anywhere in the Hundred, either from the Medway or the Thames. There was no fear of such marauders sailing up the Medway past Hoo, for Upnor Castle barred the way, and indeed Rochester was too large a place, defended as it was by its castle, to be attacked by such pirates; but below Hoo a landing could be effected anywhere, and boats with a few hands on board could row up the creeks in the marshes, pounce upon a quiet hamlet, carry off anything of value, and set the place on fire.

Such incursions had been carried far up the Thames and great damage done, but as the ships of Fowey and other places were equally busy damaging French commerce and ravaging their sea-coast, no complaints could be made to France even during the very brief period when there was a truce between the two countries. Not only from across the Channel did these marauders come, but from the islands of Friesland and Zeeland, where the inhabitants—hardy sailors to a man—were lawless and uncontrolled. After having suffered several times from these pirates, and been moved by the constant complaints of their tenants, Edgar and Albert went up to town and laid the matter before the king and council, pointing out that these attacks were becoming more frequent and general all along the coast, and praying that measures might be adopted for putting a stop to them.

"But what do you propose should be done, sir knights?" the king asked.

"I would suggest, your Majesty, that either a few fast ships should be placed at various points, such as the mouth of the Medway, Harwich, Dover, Hastings, and South-ampton, that might keep a watch for these pirates, or else that some of your vassals round the coast should be appointed to keep forces of some strength always under arms, just as the Percys are at all times in readiness to repel the incur-sions of the Scots; but should you and the council think this too weighty a plan, we would pray you to order better protection for the Thames. It was but the other day some pirates burnt six ships in Dartford Creek, and if they carry on these ravages unpunished, they may grow bolder and will be sailing higher still, and may cause an enormous loss to your merchants by setting fire to the vessels at the wharves or to those anchored out in the stream."

"The matter would be serious, assuredly," the king said, "and would cause so great a trouble to the citizens of London that it would be well that some means should be taken to prevent it. I will talk the matter over with the council, sir knights, and will let you know in an hour's time whether we can do aught in the matter."

When the young knights returned, the king said:

"There is a royal manor at Bromley at present vacant; 'tis of the value of fifty-six pounds a year. This we will hand over to you jointly, upon your undertaking to keep thirty men-at-arms fully equipped and ready for service, each of you; and also that each of you shall maintain, at the spots which may seem to you the most advisable, a galley with oars, in the which you can put out and attack these pirates."

Edgar begged permission to consult with his friend.

"You see, Albert, we have already each of us ten men-at-arms, and the revenue of the manor should well-nigh, if not quite, pay the expenses of the others. As to the galleys, we could keep them in the little creek beween Cliffe and Gravesend. It would give us employment, and should we ever be called upon to take the field, the sixty men-at-arms will make a good beginning for the force we should gather."

Albert assented, and, returning, they informed the council that they were ready to undertake the charge of keeping thirty men-at-arms each always in readiness for service, and for fighting the pirates by land or water. Returning home, preparations were speedily made, and the men enrolled and drilled. A watch-tower was raised on an eminence that was visible from both castles, and a look-out place also erected at the mouth of the Medway. This was some sixty feet high. A great cresset was placed at the summit ready for firing, and an arrangement made with the tenants, on whose land it stood, that a man should be on watch night and day. His duty would be to keep a vigilant eye on the river, and to light the beacon if any suspicious vessels were seen coming up. The smoke by day or the fire at night could be seen at both castles, and by a pre-arranged system signals could then be exchanged between Edgar and Albert by means of the watch-tower on the hill.

Albert had two large and fast galleys constructed, for his wife's dowry enabled him to spend money more freely than Edgar. They had a good many encounters with the freebooters. Two or three times strong parties that had landed from ships were attacked by the garrisons of both castles, joined by the tenantry near, and were driven to the boats with heavy loss.

Once the beacon from the mouth of the Medway signalled that three ships had entered the mouth of that river. Edgar signalled to Cliffe, and when at ten o'clock the French landed just below Hoo, thinking to make an easy capture of the village, and perhaps even to carry the castle by surprise, they were allowed to ascend the hill undisturbed, and were then attacked by the sixty men-at-arms, led by the two knights, together with a number of villagers and countrymen armed with bows and bills. Although superior in numbers the French were driven down the hill with great slaughter. Only a few succeeded in regaining their ships, but the tide had not yet turned, and there was little wind. Boats were obtained at Upnor, the vessels boarded, and all on board put to the sword.

Three or four sharp engagements also took place between the galleys and the pirates ascending the Thames, and at various times rich prizes that the pirates had taken higher up the river were recovered from them; so that in time the depredations greatly abated, and the city of London presented the two knights with costly swords and a vote of thanks for the great services they had rendered to the city, and to those trading with it.

They were both too happy in their homes to care to go often to court, but they viewed with pain the increasing unpopularity of the king, brought about by his reckless extravagance, his life of pleasure, and the manner in which he allowed himself to be dominated by unworthy favourites. Van Voorden, who had permanently settled in England, often came down with his wife and daughter to stay for a few days with them, and declared that he had never laid out money so well as that which had established two such happy households. The last few years of Mr. Ormskirk's life were spent at Hoo, where he still dabbled a little in his former occupation, but never succeeded in finding the elixir he had laboured so long to discover. On the departure of the Flemish steward, Hal Carter was appointed to the post, with the understanding that if his lord should ever ride to battle that he was to revert to the command of the men-at-arms.   Hal was ignorant of figures, but he had a young assistant given him to manage this part of the work, and his honesty, his acquaintance with farming, and his devotion to his master made up for any deficiency on that score. Both knights sent contingents under their sons to fight at Agincourt, and were only prevented from taking the field themselves by the entreaties of their wives and daughters, and by the thought that it would be as well to give their sons the opportunity of distinguishing themselves, as they themselves had done, in their early youth.

THE END.

PRINTED BY BLACKIE AND SON, LIMITED, GLASGOW.

BLACKIE & SON'S
BOOKS FOR YOUNG PEOPLE.

BY G. A. HENTY.

In crown 8vo, cloth elegant, olivine edges.

At Agincourt: A Tale of the White Hoods of Paris. With 12 page Illustrations by WAL PAGET. 6s.

"Mr. Henty's admirers, and they are many, will accord a hearty welcome to the sturdy volume entitled *At Agincourt.*"—*Athenæum.*

With Cochrane the Dauntless: A Tale of the Exploits of Lord Cochrane in South American Waters. With 12 page Illustrations by W. H. MARGETSON. 6s.

"This tale we specially recommend; for the career of Lord Cochrane and his many valiant fights in the cause of liberty deserves to be better known than they are."—*St. James's Gazette.*

The Tiger of Mysore: A Story of the War with Tippoo Saib. By G. A. HENTY. With 12 Illustrations by W. H. MARGETSON, and a Map. 6s.

"Mr. Henty not only concocts a thrilling tale, he weaves fact and fiction together with so skilful a hand that the reader cannot help acquiring a just and clear view of that fierce and terrible struggle which gave to us our Indian Empire."—*Athenæum.*

A Knight of the White Cross: A Tale of the Siege of Rhodes. By G. A. HENTY. With 12 full-page Illustrations by RALPH PEACOCK. 6s.

"Mr. Henty is a giant among boys' writers, and his books are sufficiently popular to be sure of a welcome anywhere. . . . In stirring interest, this is quite up to the level of Mr. Henty's former historical tales."—*Saturday Review.*

When London Burned: A Story of Restoration Times and the Great Fire. By G. A. HENTY. With 12 page Illustrations by J. FINNEMORE. 6s.

"No boy needs to have any story of Henty's recommended to him, and parents who do not know and buy him for their boys should be ashamed of themselves. Those to whom he is yet unknown could not make a better beginning than with *When London Burned.*"—*British Weekly.*

A

BY G. A. HENTY.

"Among writers of stories of adventure for boys Mr. Henty stands in the very first rank."—*Academy*.

In crown 8vo, cloth elegant, olivine edges.

The Lion of St. Mark: A Tale of Venice in the Fourteenth Century. By G. A. HENTY. With 10 page Illustrations by GORDON BROWNE. 6s.

"Every boy should read *The Lion of St. Mark*. Mr. Henty has never produced any story more delightful, more wholesome, or more vivacious. From first to last it will be read with keen enjoyment."—*The Saturday Review*.

By England's Aid: The Freeing of the Netherlands (1585–1604). By G. A. HENTY. With 10 page Illustrations by ALFRED PEARSE, and 4 Maps. 6s.

"The story is told with great animation, and the historical material is most effectively combined with a most excellent plot."—*Saturday Review*.

With Wolfe in Canada: or, The Winning of a Continent. By G. A. HENTY. Illustrated with 12 page Pictures by GORDON BROWNE. 6s.

"A model of what a boys' story-book should be. Mr. Henty has a great power of infusing into the dead facts of history new life, and as no pains are spared by him to ensure accuracy in historic details, his books supply useful aids to study as well as amusement."—*School Guardian*.

Bonnie Prince Charlie: A Tale of Fontenoy and Culloden. By G. A. HENTY. Illustrated with 12 page Pictures by GORDON BROWNE. 6s.

"Ronald, the hero, is very like the hero of *Quentin Durward*. The lad's journey across France with his faithful attendant Malcolm, and his hairbreadth escapes from the machinations of his father's enemies make up as good a narrative of the kind as we have ever read. For freshness of treatment and variety of incident, Mr. Henty has here surpassed himself."—*Spectator*.

For the Temple: A Tale of the Fall of Jerusalem. By G. A. HENTY. With 10 page Illustrations by S. J. SOLOMON, and a Coloured Map. 6s.

"Mr. Henty's graphic prose pictures of the hopeless Jewish resistance to Roman sway adds another leaf to his record of the famous wars of the world. The book is one of Mr. Henty's cleverest efforts."—*Graphic*.

True to the Old Flag: A Tale of the American War of Independence. By G. A. HENTY. With 12 page Illustrations by GORDON BROWNE. 6s.

"Does justice to the pluck and determination of the British soldiers. The son of an American loyalist, who remains true to our flag, falls among the hostile redskins in that very Huron country which has been endeared to us by the exploits of Hawkeye and Chingachgook."—*The Times*.

"Mr. Henty undoubtedly possesses the secret of writing eminently successful historical tales; and those older than the lads whom the author addresses in his preface may read the story with pleasure."—*Academy*.

STEPHEN BEATS OFF THE GREAT WAR-CANOE SINGLE-HANDED.

BY G. A. HENTY.

"Mr. Henty is one of our most successful writers of historical tales."—*Scotsman.*

In crown 8vo, cloth elegant, olivine edges.

The Lion of the North: A Tale of Gustavus Adolphus and the Wars of Religion. By G. A. Henty. With 12 page Pictures by J. Schönberg. 6s.

"A praiseworthy attempt to interest British youth in the great deeds of the Scotch Brigade in the wars of Gustavus Adolphus. Mackay, Hepburn, and Munro live again in Mr. Henty's pages, as those deserve to live whose disciplined bands formed really the germ of the modern British army."—*Athenæum.*

The Young Carthaginian: A Story of the Times of Hannibal. By G. A. Henty. With 12 page Illustrations by C. J. Staniland, R.I. 6s.

"The effect of an interesting story, well constructed and vividly told, is enhanced by the picturesque quality of the scenic background. From first to last nothing stays the interest of the narrative. It bears us along as on a stream whose current varies in direction, but never loses its force."—*Saturday Review.*

Redskin and Cow-boy: A Tale of the Western Plains. By G. A. Henty. Illustrated by Alfred Pearse. 6s.

"It has a good plot; it abounds in action; the scenes are equally spirited and realistic, and we can only say we have read it with much pleasure from first to last. The pictures of life on a cattle ranche are most graphically painted, as are the manners of the reckless but jovial cow-boys."—*Times.*

With Clive in India: or, The Beginnings of an Empire. By G. A. Henty. Illustrated by Gordon Browne. 6s.

"Among writers of stories of adventure for boys Mr. Henty stands in the very first rank. Those who know something about India will be the most ready to thank Mr. Henty for giving them this instructive volume to place in the hands of their children."—*Academy.*

In Greek Waters: A Story of the Grecian War of Independence (1821–1827). By G. A. Henty. With 12 page Illustrations by W. S. Stacey, and a Map. 6s.

"There are adventures of all kinds for the hero and his friends, whose pluck and ingenuity in extricating themselves from awkward fixes are always equal to the occasion. It is an excellent story, and if the proportion of history is smaller than usual, the whole result leaves nothing to be desired."—*Journal of Education.*

The Dash for Khartoum: A Tale of the Nile Expedition. By G. A. Henty. With 10 page Illustrations by J. Schönberg and J. Nash, and 4 Plans. 6s.

"It is literally true that the narrative never flags a moment; for the incidents which fall to be recorded after the dash for Khartoum has been made and failed are quite as interesting as those which precede it."—*Academy.*

BY G. A. HENTY.

"Mr. Henty is the king of story-tellers for boys."—*Sword and Trowel.*

In crown 8vo, cloth elegant, olivine edges.

Through the Fray: A Story of the Luddite Riots. By

G. A. HENTY. With 12 page Illustrations by H. M. PAGET. 6s.

"Mr. Henty inspires a love and admiration for straight-forwardness, truth, and courage. This is one of the best of the many good books Mr. Henty has produced, and deserves to be classed with his *Facing Death*."—*Standard.*

Captain Bayley's Heir: A Tale of the Gold Fields of California. By G. A. HENTY. Illustrated by H. M. PAGET. 6s.

"A Westminster boy who makes his way in the world by hard work, good temper, and unfailing courage. The descriptions given of life are just what a healthy intelligent lad should delight in."—*St. James's Gazette.*

St. Bartholomew's Eve: A Tale of the Huguenot Wars. By G. A. HENTY. Illustrated by H. J. DRAPER. 6s.

Reduced Illustration from "A Knight of the White Cross".

"What would boys do without Mr. Henty? Ever fresh and vigorous, his books have at once the solidity of history and the charm of romance. *St. Bartholomew's Eve* is in his best style, and the interest never flags. The book is all that could possibly be wished from a boy's point of view."—*Journal of Education.*

In Freedom's Cause: A Story of Wallace and Bruce. By

G. A. HENTY. Illustrated by GORDON BROWNE. 6s.

"His tale of the days of Wallace and Bruce is full of stirring action, and will commend itself to boys."—*Athenæum.*

By Right of Conquest: or, With Cortez in Mexico. By

G. A. HENTY. With 10 page Illustrations by W. S. STACEY. 6s.

"*By Right of Conquest* is the nearest approach to a perfectly successful historical tale that Mr. Henty has yet published."—*Academy.*

BY G. A. HENTY.

"Mr. Henty is one of the best of story-tellers for young people."—Spectator.

In crown 8vo, cloth elegant, olivine edges.

Beric the Briton: A Story of the Roman Invasion. By

G. A. HENTY. Illustrated by W. PARKINSON. 6s.

"We are not aware that anyone has given us quite so vigorous a picture of Britain in the days of the Roman conquest. Mr. Henty has done his utmost to make an impressive picture of the haughty Roman character, with its indomitable courage, sternness, and discipline. *Beric* is good all through."—*Spectator.*

By Pike and Dyke:

A Tale of the Rise of the Dutch Republic. By G. A. HENTY. With 10 page Illustrations by MAYNARD BROWN, and 4 Maps. 6s.

"The mission of Ned to deliver letters from William the Silent to his adherents at Brussels, the fight of the *Good Venture* with the Spanish man-of-war, the battle on the ice at Amsterdam, the siege of Haarlem, are all told with a vividness and skill which are worthy of Mr. Henty at his best."—*Academy.*

Reduced Illustration from "At Agincourt".

Wulf the Saxon: A Story of the Norman Conquest. By

G. A. HENTY. Illustrated by RALPH PEACOCK. 6s.

"*Wulf the Saxon* is second to none of Mr. Henty's historical tales, and we may safely say that a boy may learn from it more genuine history than he will from many a tedious tome. The points of the Saxon character are hit off very happily, and the life of the period is ably reconstructed."—*The Spectator.*

Through the Sikh War: A Tale of the Conquest of the

Punjaub. By G. A. HENTY. With 12 page Illustrations by HAL HURST, and a Map. 6s.

"The picture of the Punjaub during its last few years of independence, the description of the battles on the Sutlej, and the portraiture generally of native character, seem admirably true. . . . On the whole, we have never read a more vivid and faithful narrative of military adventure in India."—*The Academy.*

BY G. A. HENTY.

"No more interesting boys' books are written than Mr. Henty's stories."—
Daily Chronicle.

In crown 8vo, cloth elegant, olivine edges.

With Lee in Virginia: A Story of the American Civil War. By G. A. HENTY. With 10 page Illustrations by GORDON BROWNE, and 6 Maps. 6s.

"The story is a capital one and full of variety, and presents us with many picturesque scenes of Southern life. Young Wingfield, who is conscientious, spirited, and 'hard as nails', would have been a man after the very heart of Stonewall Jackson."—*Times.*

Under Drake's Flag: A Tale of the Spanish Main. By G. A. HENTY. Illustrated by GORDON BROWNE. 6s.

"There is not a dull chapter, nor, indeed, a dull page in the book; but the author has so carefully worked up his subject that the exciting deeds of his heroes are never incongruous or absurd."—*Observer.*

On the Irrawaddy: A Story of the first Burmese War. With 8 Illustrations by W. H. OVEREND. Crown 8vo, cloth elegant, olivine edges, 5s.

"Stanley Brook's pluck is even greater than his luck, and he is precisely the boy to hearten with emulation the boys who read his stirring story."—*Saturday Review.*

Through Russian Snows: A Story of Napoleon's Retreat from Moscow. By G. A. HENTY. With 8 Illustrations by W. H. OVEREND, and a Map. 5s.

"Julian, the hero of the story, early excites our admiration, and is altogether a fine character such as boys will delight in, whilst the story of the campaign is very graphically told. . . . Will, we think, prove one of the most popular boys' books this season."—*St. James's Gazette.*

In the Heart of the Rockies: A Story of Adventure in Colorado. By G. A. HENTY. Illustrated by G. C. HINDLEY. 5s.

"Few Christmas books will be more to the taste of the ingenuous boy than *In the Heart of the Rockies.*"—*Athenæum.*

"Mr. Henty is seen here at his best as an artist in lightning fiction."—*Academy.*

One of the 28th: A Tale of Waterloo. By G. A. HENTY. With 8 page Illustrations by W. H. OVEREND, and 2 Maps. 5s.

"Written with Homeric vigour and heroic inspiration. It is graphic, picturesque, and dramatically effective . . . shows us Mr. Henty at his best and brightest. The adventures will hold a boy of a winter's night enthralled as he rushes through them with breathless interest 'from cover to cover'."—*Observer.*

Facing Death: or, The Hero of the Vaughan Pit. A Tale of the Coal Mines. By G. A. HENTY. With 8 page Pictures by GORDON BROWNE. 5s.

"If any father, godfather, clergyman, or schoolmaster is on the look-out for a good book to give as a present to a boy who is worth his salt, this is the book we would recommend."—*Standard.*

BY G. A. HENTY.

"Ask for Henty, and see that you get him."—*Punch.*

In crown 8vo, cloth elegant, olivine edges.

The Cat of Bubastes: A Story of Ancient Egypt. By
G. A. HENTY. Illustrated by J. R. WEGUELIN. 5s.

"The story, from the critical moment of the killing of the sacred cat to the perilous exodus into Asia with which it closes, is very skilfully constructed and full of exciting adventures. It is admirably illustrated."—*Saturday Review.*

Maori and Settler: A Story of the New Zealand War. By
G. A. HENTY. With 8 page Illustrations by ALFRED PEARSE. 5s.

"It is a book which all young people, but especially boys, will read with avidity."—*Athenæum.*

"A first-rate book for boys, brimful of adventure, of humorous and interesting conversation, and of vivid pictures of colonial life."—*Schoolmaster.*

St. George for England: A Tale of Cressy and Poitiers.
By G. A. HENTY. Illustrated by GORDON BROWNE. 5s.

"A story of very great interest for boys. In his own forcible style the author has endeavoured to show that determination and enthusiasm can accomplish marvellous results; and that courage is generally accompanied by magnanimity and gentleness."—*Pall Mall Gazette.*

The Bravest of the Brave: With Peterborough in Spain.
By G. A. HENTY. With 8 full-page Pictures by H. M. PAGET. 5s.

"Mr. Henty never loses sight of the moral purpose of his work—to enforce the doctrine of courage and truth, mercy and lovingkindness, as indispensable to the making of an English gentleman. British lads will read *The Bravest of the Brave* with pleasure and profit; of that we are quite sure."—*Daily Telegraph.*

For Name and Fame: or, Through Afghan Passes. By
G. A. HENTY. Illustrated by GORDON BROWNE. 5s.

"Not only a rousing story, replete with all the varied forms of excitement of a campaign, but, what is still more useful, an account of a territory and its inhabitants which must for a long time possess a supreme interest for Englishmen, as being the key to our Indian Empire."—*Glasgow Herald.*

A Jacobite Exile: Being the Adventures of a Young Englishman in the Service of Charles XII. of Sweden. By G. A. HENTY.
With 8 page Illustrations by PAUL HARDY, and a Map. 5s.

"Incident succeeds incident, and adventure is piled upon adventure, and at the end the reader, be he boy or man, will have experienced breathless enjoyment in a romantic story that must have taught him much at its close."—*Army and Navy Gazette.*

Held Fast for England: A Tale of the Siege of Gibraltar.
By G. A. HENTY. Illustrated by GORDON BROWNE. 5s.

"Among them we would place first in interest and wholesome educational value the story of the siege of Gibraltar. . . . There is no cessation of exciting incident throughout the story."—*Athenæum.*

BY G. A. HENTY.

"Mr. Henty's books are always alive with moving incident."—*Review of Reviews.*

In crown 8vo, cloth elegant.

Condemned as a Nihilist: A Story of Escape from Siberia.

By G. A. HENTY. Illustrated by WALTER PAGET. 5s.

"The best of this year's Henty. His narrative is more interesting than many of the tales with which the public is familiar, of escape from Siberia. Despite their superior claim to authenticity these tales are without doubt no less fictitious than Mr. Henty's, and he beats them hollow in the matter of sensations."—*National Observer.*

Orange and Green: A Tale of the Boyne and Limerick.

By G. A. HENTY. Illustrated by GORDON BROWNE. 5s.

"The narrative is free from the vice of prejudice, and ripples with life as vivacious as if what is being described were really passing before the eye. . . . Should be in the hands of every young student of Irish history."—*Belfast News.*

In the Reign of Terror: The Adventures of a Westminster

Boy. By G. A. HENTY. Illustrated by J. SCHÖNBERG. 5s.

"Harry Sandwith, the Westminster boy, may fairly be said to beat Mr. Henty's record. His adventures will delight boys by the audacity and peril they depict. The story is one of Mr. Henty's best."—*Saturday Review.*

By Sheer Pluck: A Tale of the Ashanti War. By G. A.

HENTY. With 8 full-page Pictures by GORDON BROWNE. 5s.

"Morally, the book is everything that could be desired, setting before the boys a bright and bracing ideal of the English gentleman."—*Christian Leader.*

The Dragon and the Raven: or, The Days of King

Alfred. By G. A. HENTY. With 8 page Illustrations by C. J. STANILAND, R.I. 5s.

"A story that may justly be styled remarkable. Boys, in reading it, will be surprised to find how Alfred persevered, through years of bloodshed and times of peace, to rescue his people from the thraldom of the Danes. We hope the book will soon be widely known in all our schools."—*Schoolmaster*

A Final Reckoning: A Tale of Bush Life in Australia.

By G. A. HENTY. Illustrated by W. B. WOLLEN. 5s.

"All boys will read this story with eager and unflagging interest. The episodes are in Mr. Henty's very best vein—graphic, exciting, realistic; and, as in all Mr. Henty's books, the tendency is to the formation of an honourable, manly, and even heroic character."—*Birmingham Post.*

The Young Colonists: A Tale of the Zulu and Boer Wars.

By G. A. HENTY. With 6 Illustrations by SIMON H. VEDDER. 3s. 6d.

"Fiction and history are so happily blended that the record of facts quicken the imagination. No boy can read this book without learning a great deal of South African history at its most critical period."—*Standard.*

A Chapter of Adventures: or, Through the Bombard-

ment of Alexandria. By G. A. HENTY. With 6 page Illustrations by W. H. OVEREND. 3s. 6d.

"Jack Robson and his two companions have their fill of excitement, and their chapter of adventures is so brisk and entertaining we could have wished it longer than it is."—*Saturday Review.*

BY KIRK MUNROE.

In crown 8vo, cloth elegant, olivine edges.

Through Swamp and Glade: A Tale of the Seminole War. By KIRK MUNROE. Illustrated by VICTOR PERARD. 5s.

"The hero of *Through Swamp and Glade* will find many ardent champions, and the name of Coachoochie become as familiar in the schoolboy's ear as that of the headmaster."—*St. James's Gazette.*

At War with Pontiac: or, The Totem of the Bear. By KIRK MUNROE. Illustrated by J. FINNEMORE. 5s.

"Is in the best manner of Cooper. There is a character who is the parallel of Hawkeye, as the Chingachgooks and Uncas have likewise their counterparts."—*The Times.*

The White Conquerors of Mexico: A Tale of Toltec and Aztec. By KIRK MUNROE. Illustrated by W. S. STACEY. 5s.

"Mr. Munroe gives most vivid pictures of the religious and civil polity of the Aztecs, and of everyday life, as he imagines it, in the streets and market-places of the magnificent capital of Montezuma."—*The Times.*

Crown 8vo, cloth elegant.

Two Thousand Years Ago: or, The Adventures of a Roman Boy. By Professor A. J. CHURCH. With 12 page Illustrations by ADRIEN MARIE. 6s.

"Adventures well worth the telling. The book is extremely entertaining as well as useful, and there is a wonderful freshness in the Roman scenes and characters."—*The Times.*

The Clever Miss Follett. By J. K. H. DENNY. With 12 page Illustrations by GERTRUDE D. HAMMOND. 6s.

"Just the book to give to girls, who will delight both in the letterpress and the illustrations. Miss Hammond has never done better work."—*Review of Reviews.*

The Heiress of Courtleroy. By ANNE BEALE. With 8 page Illustrations by T. C. H. CASTLE. 5s.

"We can speak highly of the grace with which Miss Beale relates how the young 'Heiress of Courtleroy' had such good influence over her uncle as to win him from his intensely selfish ways."—*Guardian.*

Under False Colours: A Story from Two Girls' Lives. By SARAH DOUDNEY. Illustrated by G. G. KILBURNE. 4s.

"Sarah Doudney has no superior as a writer of high-toned stories—pure in style and original in conception; but we have seen nothing from her pen equal in dramatic energy to this book."—*Christian Leader.*

BY GEORGE MANVILLE FENN.

"Mr. Fenn stands in the foremost rank of writers in this department."—*Daily News.*

In crown 8vo, cloth elegant.

Dick o' the Fens: A Romance of the Great East Swamp. By
G. MANVILLE FENN. Illustrated by FRANK DADD. 6s.

"We conscientiously believe that boys will find it capital reading. It is full
of incident and mystery, and the mystery is kept up to the last moment. It is
rich in effective local colouring; and it has a historical interest."—*Times.*

Devon Boys: A Tale of the North Shore. By G. MANVILLE
FENN. With 12 page Illustrations by GORDON BROWNE. 6s.

"An admirable story, as remarkable for the individuality of its young heroes
as for the excellent descriptions of coast scenery and life in North Devon. It is
one of the best books we have seen this season."—*Athenæum.*

The Golden Magnet: A Tale of the Land of the Incas. By
G. MANVILLE FENN. Illustrated by GORDON BROWNE. 6s.

"There could be no more welcome present for a boy. There is not a dull page
in the book, and many will be read with breathless interest. 'The Golden Magnet' is, of course, the same one that attracted Raleigh and the heroes of *Westward Ho!*"—*Journal of Education.*

In the King's Name: or, The Cruise of the *Kestrel*. By
G. MANVILLE FENN. Illustrated by GORDON BROWNE. 6s.

"The best of all Mr. Fenn's productions in this field. It has the great quality
of always 'moving on', adventure following adventure in constant succession."—
Daily News.

Nat the Naturalist: A Boy's Adventures in the Eastern
Seas. By G. MANVILLE FENN. With 8 page Pictures. 5s.

"This sort of book encourages independence of character, develops resource,
and teaches a boy to keep his eyes open."—*Saturday Review.*

Bunyip Land: The Story of a Wild Journey in New Guinea.
By G. MANVILLE FENN. Illustrated by GORDON BROWNE. 4s.

"Mr. Fenn deserves the thanks of everybody for *Bunyip Land*, and we may venture to promise that a quiet week may be reckoned on whilst the youngsters have
such fascinating literature provided for their evenings' amusement."—*Spectator.*

Quicksilver: or, A Boy with no Skid to his Wheel. By
GEORGE MANVILLE FENN. With 6 page Illustrations by FRANK
DADD. New edition, 3s. 6d.

"*Quicksilver* is little short of an inspiration. In it that prince of story-writers
for boys—George Manville Fenn—has surpassed himself. It is an ideal book for
a boy's library."—*Practical Teacher.*

Brownsmith's Boy: A Romance in a Garden. By G.
MANVILLE FENN. With 6 page Illustrations. 3s. 6d.

"Mr. Fenn's books are among the best, if not altogether the best, of the stories
for boys. Mr. Fenn is at his best in *Brownsmith's Boy*."—*Pictorial World.*

*** For other Books by G. MANVILLE FENN, see page 22.

BY GEORGE MACDONALD.

In crown 8vo, cloth elegant.

A Rough Shaking. By GEORGE MACDONALD. With
12 page Illustrations by W. PARKINSON. 6s.

"One of the very best books for boys that has been written. It is full of material peculiarly well adapted for the young, containing in a marked degree the elements of all that is necessary to make up a perfect boys' book."— *Teachers' Aid.*

At the Back of the North Wind. By GEORGE MAC-
DONALD. With 75 Illustrations by ARTHUR HUGHES. 5s.

"The story is thoroughly original, full of fancy and pathos. . . . We stand with one foot in fairyland and one on common earth."—*The Times.*

Ranald Bannerman's Boyhood. By GEO. MACDONALD.
With 36 Illustrations by ARTHUR HUGHES. 5s.

"The sympathy with boy-nature in *Ranald Bannerman's Boyhood* is perfect. It is a beautiful picture of childhood, teaching by its impressions and suggestions all noble things."—*British Quarterly Review.*

The Princess and the Goblin. By GEORGE MACDONALD.
With 32 Illustrations. 3s. 6d.

"Little of what is written for children has the lightness of touch and play of fancy which are characteristic of George MacDonald's fairy tales. Mr. Arthur Hughes's illustrations are all that illustrations should be."—*Manchester Guardian.*

The Princess and Curdie. By GEORGE MACDONALD.
With 8 page Illustrations. 3s. 6d.

"There is the finest and rarest genius in this brilliant story. Upgrown people would do wisely occasionally to lay aside their newspapers and magazines to spend an hour with Curdie and the Princess."—*Sheffield Independent.*

BY ASCOTT R. HOPE.

Young Travellers' Tales. By ASCOTT R. HOPE. With
6 Illustrations by H. J. DRAPER. 3s. 6d.

"Possess a high value for instruction as well as for entertainment. His quiet, level humour bubbles up on every page."—*Daily Chronicle.*

The Seven Wise Scholars. By ASCOTT R. HOPE. With
nearly 100 Illustrations by GORDON BROWNE. 5s.

"As full of fun as a volume of *Punch*; with illustrations more laughter-provoking than most we have seen since Leech died."—*Sheffield Independent.*

Stories of Old Renown: Tales of Knights and Heroes.
By ASCOTT R. HOPE. With 100 Illustrations by GORDON BROWNE. 3s. 6d.

"A really fascinating book worthy of its telling title. There is, we venture to say, not a dull page in the book, not a story which will not bear a second reading."—*Guardian.*

BY HARRY COLLINGWOOD.

In crown 8vo, cloth elegant.

The Log of a Privateersman. By HARRY COLLING-
WOOD. With 12 page Illustrations by W. RAINEY, R.I. 6s.

"The narrative is breezy, vivid, and full of incidents, faithful in nautical colouring, and altogether delightful."—*Pall Mall Gazette.*

The Pirate Island:
A Story of the South Pacific. By HARRY COLLINGWOOD. With 8 page Pictures by C. J. STANILAND and J. R. WELLS. 5s.

"A capital story of the sea; indeed in our opinion the author is superior in some respects as a marine novelist to the better-known Mr. Clark Russell."—*The Times.*

The Log of the "Flying Fish":
A Story of Aerial and Submarine Adventure. By HARRY COLLINGWOOD. With 6 page Illustrations by GORDON BROWNE. 3s. 6d.

Reduced Illustration from "The Log of a Privateersman".

"The *Flying Fish* actually surpasses all Jules Verne's creations; with incredible speed she flies through the air, skims over the surface of the water, and darts along the ocean bed. We strongly recommend our schoolboy friends to possess themselves of her log."—*Athenæum.*

** For other Books by Harry Collingwood, see pages 22 and 23.

Banshee Castle. By ROSA MULHOLLAND. With 12 page Illustrations by JOHN H. BACON. 6s.

"One of the most fascinating of Miss Rosa Mulholland's many fascinating stories."—*Athenæum.*

Giannetta: A Girl's Story of Herself. By ROSA MULHOLLAND.
With 8 page Illustrations by LOCKHART BOGLE. 5s.

"One of the most attractive gift-books of the season."—*The Academy.*

BY ROBERT LEIGHTON.

In crown 8vo, cloth elegant, olivine edges.

Olaf the Glorious. By ROBERT LEIGHTON. With 8 page
Illustrations by RALPH PEACOCK, and a Map. 5s.

"Is as good as anything of the kind we have met with. Mr. Leighton more
than holds his own with Rider Haggard and Baring-Gould."—*The Times.*

"Among the books best liked by boys of the sturdy English type few will take
a higher place than *Olaf the Glorious.* . . . "—*National Observer.*

The Wreck of "The Golden Fleece": The Story of a
North Sea Fisher-boy. By ROBERT LEIGHTON. With 8 page
Illustrations by F. BRANGWYN. 5s.

"This story should add considerably to Mr. Leighton's high reputation. Excellent in every respect, it contains every variety of incident. The plot is very
cleverly devised, and the types of the North Sea sailors are capital."—*The Times.*

The Pilots of Pomona: A Story of the Orkney Islands.
By ROBERT LEIGHTON. Illustrated by JOHN LEIGHTON. 5s.

"A story which is quite as good in its way as *Treasure Island,* and is full of
adventure of a stirring yet most natural kind. Although it is primarily a boys'
book, it is a real godsend to the elderly reader."—*Glasgow Evening Times.*

The Thirsty Sword: A Story of the Norse Invasion of
Scotland (1262-63). By ROBERT LEIGHTON. With 8 page Illustrations by A. PEARSE. 5s.

"This is one of the most fascinating stories for boys that it has ever been our
pleasure to read. From first to last the interest never flags."—*Schoolmaster.*

BY SHEILA E. BRAINE.

To Tell the King the Sky is Falling. By SHEILA E.
BRAINE. With over 80 quaint and clever Illustrations by ALICE
B. WOODWARD. 8vo, cloth, decorated board, gilt edges, 5s.

"It is witty and ingenious, and it has certain qualities which children are
quick to perceive and appreciate—a genuine love of fun, affectionateness, and
sympathy, from their points of view."—*Bookman.*

A Girl's Loyalty. By FRANCES ARMSTRONG. With 8 page
Illustrations by JOHN H. BACON. 5s.

"There is no doubt as to the good quality of *A Girl's Loyalty.* The book is
one which would enrich any girls' book-shelf."—*St. James's Gazette.*

A Fair Claimant: Being a Story for Girls. By FRANCES
ARMSTRONG. Illustrated by GERTRUDE D. HAMMOND. 5s.

"As a gift-book for big girls it is among the best new books of the kind. The
story is interesting and natural, from first to last."—*Westminster Gazette.*

THE GNOMES BRING THE GONDOLA TO TOYLAND.

The Universe: or, The Infinitely Great and the Infinitely Little. A Sketch of Contrasts in Creation, and Marvels revealed and explained by Natural Science. By F. A. POUCHET, M.D. With 272 Engravings on wood, of which 55 are full-page size, and 4 Coloured Illustrations. Twelfth Edition, medium 8vo, cloth elegant, **gilt edges**, 7s. 6d.; also morocco antique, 16s.

"Dr. Pouchet's wonderful work on *The Universe*, than which there is no book better calculated to encourage the study of nature."—*Pall Mall Gazette.*

"We know no better book of the kind for a schoolroom library."—*Bookman.*

BY G. NORWAY.

In crown 8vo, cloth elegant.

A Prisoner of War: A Story of the Time of Napoleon Bonaparte. By G. NORWAY. With 6 page Illustrations by ROBT. BARNES, A.R.W.S. 3s. 6d.

"More **hairbreadth escapes** from death by starvation, by ice, by fighting, &c., were never **before surmounted**. . . . It is a fine yarn."—*The Guardian.*

A True Cornish Maid. By G. NORWAY. With 6 page Illustrations by J. FINNEMORE. 3s. 6d.

"There is some excellent reading. . . . Mrs. Norway brings before the eyes of her readers the good Cornish folk, their speech, their manners, and their ways. *A True Cornish Maid* deserves to be popular."—*Athenæum.*

*** For other Books by G. NORWAY see p. 23.

Dr. Jolliffe's Boys: A Tale of Weston School. By LEWIS HOUGH. With 6 page Pictures. 3s. 6d.

"Young people **who** appreciate *Tom Brown's School-days* will find this story a worthy companion to that fascinating book."—*Newcastle Journal.*

The Bubbling Teapot. A Wonder Story. By Mrs. L. W. CHAMPNEY. With 12 page Pictures by WALTER SATTERLEE. 3s. 6d.

"Very literally a 'wonder story.' Nevertheless it is made realistic enough, and **there** is a good deal of information to be gained from it."—*The Times.*

Thorndyke Manor: A Tale of Jacobite Times. By MARY C. ROWSELL. Illustrated by L. LESLIE BROOKE. 3s. 6d.

"Miss Rowsell has never written a **more** attractive **book than** *Thorndyke Manor*."—*Belfast News-Letter.*

Traitor or Patriot? A Tale of the Rye-House Plot. By MARY C. ROWSELL. Illustrated. 3s. 6d.

"**Here** the Rye-House Plot serves as the groundwork for a **romantic love** episode, whose true characters are lifelike beings."—*Graphic.*

BY DR. GORDON STABLES.

In crown 8vo, cloth elegant.

For Life and Liberty: A Story of Battle by Land and Sea. By Dr. GORDON STABLES, R.N. With 8 Illustrations by SYDNEY PAGET, and a Map. 5s.

"The story is lively and spirited, with abundance of blockade-running, hard fighting, narrow escapes, and introductions to some of the most distinguished generals on both sides."—*The Times.*

To Greenland and the Pole. By GORDON STABLES, M.D. With 8 page Illustrations by G. C. HINDLEY, and a Map. 5s.

"His Arctic explorers have the verisimilitude of life. It is one of the books of the season, and one of the best Mr. Stables has ever written."—*Truth.*

Westward with Columbus. By GORDON STABLES, M.D. With 8 page Illustrations by A. PEARSE. 5s.

"We must place *Westward with Columbus* among those books that all boys ought to read."—*The Spectator.*

'Twixt School and College: A Tale of Self-reliance. By GORDON STABLES, C.M., M.D., R.N. Illustrated by W. PARKINSON. 5s.

"One of the best of a prolific writer's books for boys, being full of practical instructions as to keeping pets, and inculcates in a way which a little recalls Miss Edgeworth's 'Frank' the virtue of self-reliance."—*Athenæum.*

With the Sea Kings: A Story of the Days of Lord Nelson. By F. H. WINDER. Illustrated by W. S. STACEY. 4s.

"Just the book to put into a boy's hands. Every chapter contains boardings, cuttings out, fighting pirates, escapes of thrilling audacity, and captures by corsairs, sufficient to turn the quietest boy's head. The story culminates in a vigorous account of the battle of Trafalgar. Happy boys!"—*The Academy.*

Storied Holidays: A Cycle of Red-letter Days. By E. S. BROOKS. With 12 page Illustrations by HOWARD PYLE. 3s. 6d.

"It is a downright good book for a senior boy, and is eminently readable from first to last."—*Schoolmaster.*

Chivalric Days: Stories of Courtesy and Courage in the Olden Times. By E. S. BROOKS. With 20 Illustrations. 3s. 6d.

"We have seldom come across a prettier collection of tales. These charming stories of boys and girls of olden days are no mere fictitious or imaginary sketches, but are real and actual records of their sayings and doings."—*Literary World.*

Historic Boys: Their Endeavours, their Achievements, and their Times. By E. S. BROOKS. With 12 page Illustrations. 3s. 6d.

"A wholesome book, manly in tone; altogether one that should incite boys to further acquaintance with those rulers of men whose careers are narrated. We advise teachers to put it on their list of prizes."—*Knowledge.*

[11] B

BY HUGH ST. LEGER.

In crown 8vo, cloth elegant.

An Ocean Outlaw: A Story of Adventure in the good ship
Margaret. With Illustrations by WILLIAM RAINEY, R.I. **4s.**

"We know no modern boys' book in which there is more sound, hearty, good-humoured fun, or of which the tone is more wholesome and bracing than Mr. St. Leger's."—*National Observer.*

Hallowe'en Ahoy! or, Lost on the Crozet Islands. By
HUGH ST. LEGER. With 6 Illustrations by H. J. DRAPER. **4s.**

"One of the best stories of seafaring life and adventure which have appeared this season. It contains a capital 'fo'c's'le' ghost and a thrilling shipwreck. No boy who begins it but will wish to join the *Britannia* long before he finishes these delightful pages."—*Academy.*

Sou'wester and Sword. By HUGH ST. LEGER. With 6
page Illustrations by HAL HURST. **4s.**

"As racy a tale of life at sea and war adventure as we have met with for some time. . . . Altogether the sort of book that boys will revel in."—*Athenæum.*

Meg's Friend. By ALICE CORKRAN. With 6 page Illustra-
tions by ROBERT FOWLER. **3s. 6d.**

"One of Miss Corkran's charming books for girls, narrated in that simple and picturesque style which marks the authoress as one of the first amongst writers for young people."—*The Spectator.*

Margery Merton's Girlhood. By ALICE CORKRAN. With
6 page Pictures by GORDON BROWNE. **3s. 6d.**

"Another book for girls we can warmly commend. There is a delightful piquancy in the experiences and trials of a young English girl who studies painting in Paris."—*Saturday Review.*

Down the Snow Stairs: or, From Good-night to Good-morn-
ing. By ALICE CORKRAN. Illustrated by GORDON BROWNE. **3s. 6d.**

"A gem of the first water, bearing upon every page the mark of genius. It is indeed a Little Pilgrim's Progress."—*Christian Leader.*

Grettir the Outlaw: A Story of Iceland. By S. BARING-
GOULD. With 6 page Illustrations by M. ZENO DIEMER. **4s.**

"Is the boys' book of its year That is, of course, as much as to say that it will do for men grown as well as juniors. It is told in simple, straightforward English, as all stories should be, and it has a freshness, a freedom, a sense of sun and wind and the open air, which make it irresistible."—*National Observer.*

Gold, Gold, in Cariboo: A Story of Adventure in British
Columbia. By CLIVE PHILLIPPS-WOLLEY. With 6 page Illustrations by G. C. HINDLEY. **3s. 6d.**

"We have seldom read a more exciting tale of wild mining adventure in a singularly inaccessible country. There is a capital plot, and the interest is sustained to the last page."—*The Times.*

BY CHARLES W. WHISTLER.

In crown 8vo, cloth elegant.

Wulfric the Weapon-Thane: The Story of the Danish

Conquest of East
Anglia. With 6
Illustrations by W.
H. MARGETSON.
4s.

"A picturesque and energetic story. A worthy companion to his capital story, *A Thane of Wessex*. One that will delight all active-minded boys."—*Saturday Review.*

A Thane of Wessex: Being the

Story of the Great
Viking Raid of 845.
By CHARLES W.
WHISTLER. With
6 Illustrations by
W. H. MARGETSON.
3s. 6d.

"This is one of the best books of the season. . . . The story is told with spirit and force, and affords an excellent picture of the life of the period."—*Standard.*

*Reduced Illustration
from "Wulfric the Weapon-Thane".*

His First Kanga-

roo: An Austra-
lian Story for Boys. By ARTHUR FERRES. Illustrated by PERCY
F. S. SPENCE. 3s. 6d.

"A lively story of life on an Australian stock-station, where the monotony of things is agreeably diversified by not only the bounding kangaroo, but also the up-sticking bushranger."—*Scotsman.*

A Champion of the Faith: A Tale of Prince Hal and the

Lollards. By J. M. CALLWELL. With 6 page Illustrations by
HERBERT J. DRAPER. 4s.

"Will not be less enjoyed than Mr. Henty's books. Sir John Oldcastle's pathetic story, and the history of his brave young squire, will make every boy enjoy this lively story."—*London Quarterly.*

BY ANNIE E. ARMSTRONG.

In crown 8vo, cloth elegant.

Violet Vereker's Vanity. With 6 page Illustrations by GERTRUDE DEMAIN HAMMOND. 3s. 6d.

"A book for girls that we can heartily recommend, for it is bright, sensible, and with a right tone of thought and feeling."—*Sheffield Independent.*

Three Bright Girls: A Story of Chance and Mischance. By ANNIE E. ARMSTRONG. Illustrated by W. PARKINSON. 3s. 6d.

"Among many good stories for girls this is undoubtedly one of the very best."—*Teachers' Aid.*

A Very Odd Girl: or, Life at the Gabled Farm. By ANNIE E. ARMSTRONG. Illustrated. 3s. 6d.

"The book is one we can heartily recommend, for it is not only bright and interesting, but also pure and healthy in tone and teaching."—*The Lady.*

The Captured Cruiser: By C. J. HYNE. Illustrated by FRANK BRANGWYN. 3s. 6d.

"The two lads and the two skippers are admirably drawn. Mr. Hyne has now secured a position in the first rank of writers of fiction for boys."—*Spectator*

Afloat at Last: A Sailor Boy's Log of his Life at Sea. By JOHN C. HUTCHESON. 3s. 6d.

"As healthy and breezy a book as one could wish to put into the hands of a boy."—*Academy.*

Picked up at Sea: or, The Gold Miners of Minturne Creek. By J. C. HUTCHESON. With 6 page Pictures. 3s. 6d.

Brother and Sister: or, The Trials of the Moore Family. By ELIZABETH J. LYSAGHT. 3s. 6d.

Life's Daily Ministry: A Story of Everyday Service for Others. By Mrs. E. R. PITMAN. With 4 page Illustrations. Cloth extra, 3s. 6d.

"Full of stirring interest, genuine pictures of real life, and pervaded by a broad and active sympathy for the true and good."—*Christian Commonwealth.*

Dora: or, A Girl without a Home. By Mrs. R. H. READ. With 6 page Illustrations. 3s. 6d.

"It is no slight thing, in an age of rubbish, to get a story so pure and healthy as this."—*The Academy.*

BY EDGAR PICKERING.

In crown 8vo, cloth elegant.

Two Gallant Rebels: A Story of the Great Struggle in La Vendée. By EDGAR PICKERING. With 6 Illustrations by W. H. OVEREND. 3s. 6d.

"There is something very attractive about Mr. Pickering's style. . . . Boys will relish the relation of those dreadful and moving events, which, indeed, will never lose their fascination for readers of all ages."—*The Spectator.*

In Press-Gang Days. By EDGAR PICKERING. With 6 Illustrations by W. S. STACEY. 3s. 6d.

"It is of Marryat we think as we read this delightful story; for it is not only a story of adventure with incidents well conceived and arranged, but the characters are interesting and well-distinguished."—*Academy.*

An Old-Time Yarn: Wherein is set forth divers desperate mischances which befell Anthony Ingram and his shipmates in the West Indies and Mexico with Hawkins and Drake. By EDGAR PICKERING. Illustrated by ALFRED PEARSE. 3s. 6d.

"And a very good yarn it is, with not a dull page from first to last. There is a flavour of *Westward Ho!* in this attractive book."—*Educational Review.*

Silas Verney: A Tale of the Time of Charles II. By EDGAR PICKERING. With 6 page Illustrations by ALFRED PEARSE. 3s. 6d.

"Altogether this is an excellent story for boys."—*Saturday Review.*

BLACKIE'S NEW THREE-SHILLING SERIES.

Beautifully illustrated and handsomely bound.

Highways and High Seas: Cyril Harley's Adventures on both. By F. FRANKFORT MOORE. With 6 page Illustrations by ALFRED PEARSE. 3s.

"This is one of the best stories Mr. Moore has written, perhaps the **very best**. The exciting adventures are sure to attract boys."—*Spectator.*

Under Hatches: or, Ned Woodthorpe's Adventures. By F. FRANKFORT MOORE. Illustrated by A. FORESTIER. 3s.

"The story as a story is one that will just suit boys all the world over. The characters are well drawn and consistent."—*Schoolmaster.*

Perseverance Island: or, The Robinson Crusoe of the 19th Century. By DOUGLAS FRAZAR. With 6 page Illustrations. 3s.

"This is an interesting story, written with studied simplicity of style, much in Defoe's vein of apparent sincerity and scrupulous veracity; while for practical instruction it is even better than *Robinson Crusoe*."—*Illustrated London News.*

Girl Neighbours: or, The Old Fashion and the New. By SARAH TYTLER. Illustrated by C. T. GARLAND. 3s.

"One of the most effective and quietly humorous of Miss Sarah Tytler's stories. It is very healthy, very agreeable, and very well written."—*The Spectator.*

THREE-SHILLING SERIES—Continued.

Beautifully illustrated and handsomely bound.

The Missing Merchantman. By HARRY COLLINGWOOD.
With 6 page Illustrations by W. H. OVEREND. **3s.**

"One of the author's best sea stories. The hero is as heroic as any boy could desire, and the ending is extremely happy."—*British Weekly.*

Menhardoc: A Story of Cornish Nets and Mines. By G.
MANVILLE FENN. Illustrated by C. J. STANILAND, R.I. **3s.**

"The Cornish fishermen are drawn from life, and stand out from the pages in their jerseys and sea-boots all sprinkled with silvery pilchard scales."—*Spectator.*

Yussuf the Guide: or, The Mountain Bandits. By G. MAN-
VILLE FENN. With 6 page Illustrations by J. SCHÖNBERG. **3s.**

"Told with such real freshness and vigour that the reader feels he is actually one of the party, sharing in the fun and facing the dangers."—*Pall Mall Gazette.*

Patience Wins: or, War in the Works. By GEORGE MAN-
VILLE FENN. With 6 page Illustrations. **3s.**

"Mr. Fenn has never hit upon a happier plan than in writing this story of Yorkshire factory life. The whole book is all aglow with life."—*Pall Mall Gazette.*

Mother Carey's Chicken: Her Voyage to the Unknown
Isle. By G. MANVILLE FENN. With 6 page Illustrations by A. FORESTIER. **3s.**

"Undoubtedly one of the best Mr. Fenn has written. The incidents are of thrilling interest, while the characters are drawn with a care and completeness rarely found in a boy's book."—*Literary World.*

Robinson Crusoe. With 100 Illustrations by GORDON
BROWNE. **3s.**

"One of the best issues, if not absolutely the best, of Defoe's work which has ever appeared."—*The Standard.*

Gulliver's Travels. With 100 Illustrations by GORDON
BROWNE. **3s.**

"Mr. Gordon Browne is, to my thinking, incomparably the most artistic, spirited, and brilliant of our illustrators of books for boys, and one of the most humorous also, as his illustrations of 'Gulliver' amply testify."—*Truth.*

The Wigwam and the War-path: Stories of the Red
Indians. By ASCOTT R. HOPE. With 6 page Illustrations. **3s.**

"Is notably good. It gives a very vivid picture of life among the Indians, which will delight the heart of many a schoolboy."—*Spectator.*

THREE-SHILLING SERIES—Continued.

Beautifully illustrated and handsomely bound.

The Loss of John Humble: What Led to It, and What

Came of It. By G. NORWAY. With 6 page Illustrations by JOHN SCHÖNBERG. *New Edition.* 3s.

"This story will place the author at once in the front rank. It is full of life and adventure. The interest of the story is sustained without a break from first to last."—*Standard.*

Hussein the Hostage: or, A Boy's

Adventures in Persia. By G. NORWAY. With 6 page Illustrations by JOHN SCHÖNBERG. 3s.

"*Hussein the Hostage* is full of originality and vigour. The characters are lifelike, there is plenty of stirring incident, the interest is sustained throughout, and every boy will enjoy following the fortunes of the hero."—*Journal of Education.*

Cousin Geoffrey and

I. By CAROLINE AUSTIN. With 6 page Illustrations by W. PARKINSON. 3s.

Reduced Illustration from "Cousin Geoffrey".

"Miss Austin's story is bright, clever, and well developed."—*Saturday Review.*

The Rover's Secret: A Tale of the Pirate Cays and Lagoons

of Cuba. By HARRY COLLINGWOOD. With 6 page Illustrations by W. C. SYMONS. 3s.

"*The Rover's Secret* is by far the best sea story we have read for years, and is certain to give unalloyed pleasure to boys."—*Saturday Review.*

The Congo Rovers: A Story of the Slave Squadron. By

HARRY COLLINGWOOD. With 6 page Illustrations. 3s.

"No better sea story has lately been written than the *Congo Rovers*. It is as original as any boy could desire."—*Morning Post.*

BLACKIE'S HALF-CROWN SERIES.

Illustrated by eminent Artists. In crown 8vo, cloth elegant.

Marooned on Australia, being the Narration of Diedrich Buys of his Discoveries in Terra Australis Incognito about the year 1630. By ERNEST FAVENC.

"A remarkably interesting and well-written story of travel and adventure in the Great Southern Land."—*School Guardian.*

My Friend Kathleen. By JENNIE CHAPPELL.

"A pleasantly-written story for elder girls, who will admire Kathleen's courage, and learn much from her nobility of character."—*Board Teacher.*

A Girl's Kingdom. By M. CORBET-SEYMOUR.

"The story is bright, well told, and thoroughly healthy and good."—*Ch. Bells.*

Laugh and Learn: The Easiest Book of Nursery Lessons and Nursery Games. By JENNETT HUMPHREYS.

"One of the best books of the kind imaginable, full of practical teaching in word and picture, and helping the little ones pleasantly along a right royal road to learning."—*Graphic.*

Reefer and Rifleman: A Tale of the Two Services. By Lieut.-Col. PERCY-GROVES.

"A good, old-fashioned, amphibious story of our fighting with the Frenchmen in the beginning of our century, with a fair sprinkling of fun and frolic."—*Times.*

A Musical Genius. By the Author of the "Two Dorothys".

"It is brightly written, well illustrated, and daintily bound, and can be strongly recommended as a really good prize-book."—*Teachers' Aid.*

For the Sake of a Friend: A Story of School Life. By MARGARET PARKER.

"An excellent school-girl story. . . . Susie Snow and her friend, Trix Beresford, are charming girls."—*Athenæum.*

Under the Black Eagle. By ANDREW HILLIARD.

"The rapid movement of the story, and the strange scenes through which it passes, give it a full interest of surprise and adventure."—*Scotsman.*

The Secret of the Australian Desert. By ERNEST FAVENC.

"We recommend the book most heartily; it is certain to please boys and girls, and even some grown-ups."—*Guardian.*

A Golden Age: A Story of Four Merry Children. By ISMAY THORN. Illustrated by GORDON BROWNE.

"Ought to have a place of honour on the nursery shelf."—*The Athenæum.*

HALF-CROWN SERIES—Continued.

Illustrated by eminent Artists. In crown 8vo, cloth elegant.

BY BEATRICE HARRADEN.

Things Will Take a Turn. By BEATRICE HARRADEN.

With 44 Illustrations by JOHN H. BACON.

" Perhaps the most brilliant is *Things Will Take a Turn.* . . . A tale of humble child life in East London. It is a delightful blending of comedy and tragedy, with an excellent plot."—*The Times.*

From "Things will Take a Turn". (*Reduced.*)

The Whispering Winds, and the Tales that they Told.

By MARY H. DEBENHAM. With 25 Illustrations by PAUL HARDY.

" We wish the winds would tell *us* stories like these. It would be worth while to climb Primrose Hill, or even to the giddy heights of Hampstead Heath in a bitter east wind, if we could only be sure of hearing such a sweet, sad, tender, and stirring story as that of Hilda Brave Heart, or even one that was half so good."—*Academy.*

Hal Hungerford. By J. R. HUTCHINSON, B.A.

" Altogether, Hal Hungerford is a distinct literary success."—*Spectator*

The Secret of the Old House. By E. EVERETT-GREEN.

" Tim, the little Jacobite, is a charming creation."—*Academy.*

White Lilac: or, The Queen of the May. By AMY WALTON.

" Every rural parish ought to add *White Lilac* to its library."—*Academy.*

Miriam's Ambition. By EVELYN EVERETT-GREEN.

" Miss Green's children are real British boys and girls."—*Liverpool Mercury.*

The Brig "Audacious". By ALAN COLE.

" Fresh and wholesome as a breath of sea air."—*Court Journal.*

HALF-CROWN SERIES—Continued.

Illustrated by eminent Artists.　In crown 8vo, cloth elegant.

Jasper's Conquest.　By ELIZABETH J. LYSAGHT.
"One of the best boys' books of the season."—*Schoolmaster.*

Little Lady Clare.　By EVELYN EVERETT-GREEN.
"Reminds us in its quaintness of Mrs. Ewing's delightful tales."—*Liter. World.*

The Eversley Secrets.　By EVELYN EVERETT-GREEN.
"Roy Eversley is a very touching picture of high principle."—*Guardian.*

The Hermit Hunter of the Wilds.　By G. STABLES, R.N.
"Will gladden the heart of many a bright boy."—*Methodist Recorder.*

Sturdy and Strong.　By G. A. HENTY.
"A hero who stands as a good instance of chivalry in domestic life."—*The Empire.*

Gutta-Percha Willie.　By GEORGE MACDONALD.
"Get it for your boys and girls to read for themselves."—*Practical Teacher.*

The War of the Axe: or, Adventures in South Africa.　By J. PERCY-GROVES.
"The story is well and brilliantly told."—*Literary World.*

The Lads of Little Clayton.　By R. STEAD.
"A capital book for boys."—*Schoolmaster.*

Ten Boys who lived on the Road from Long Ago to Now.　By JANE ANDREWS.　With 20 Illustrations.
"The idea is a very happy one, and admirably carried out."—*Practical Teacher.*

A Waif of the Sea: or, The Lost Found.　By KATE WOOD.
"Written with tenderness and grace."—*Morning Advertiser.*

Winnie's Secret.　By KATE WOOD.
"One of the best story-books we have read."—*Schoolmaster.*

Miss Willowburn's Offer.　By SARAH DOUDNEY.
"Patience Willowburn is one of Miss Doudney's best creations."—*Spectator.*

A Garland for Girls.　By LOUISA M. ALCOTT.
"These little tales are the beau ideal of girls' stories."—*Christian World.*

Hetty Gray: or, Nobody's Bairn.　By ROSA MULHOLLAND.
"Hetty is a delightful creature—piquant, tender, and true."—*World.*

Brothers in Arms: A Story of the Crusades.　By F. BAYFORD HARRISON.
"Sure to prove interesting to young people of both sexes."—*Guardian.*

Miss Fenwick's Failures.　By ESMÉ STUART.
"A girl true to real life, who will put no nonsense into young heads."—*Graphic.*

Gytha's Message.　By EMMA LESLIE.
"This is the sort of book that all girls like."—*Journal of Education.*

A Little Handful.　By HARRIET J. SCRIPPS.
"He is a real type of a boy."—*The Schoolmaster.*

HALF-CROWN SERIES—Continued.

Illustrated by eminent Artists.   In crown 8vo, cloth elegant.

Hammond's Hard Lines. By Skelton Kupford.

"It is just what a boy would choose if the selection of a story-book is left in his own hand."—*School Guardian.*

Dulcie King: A Story for Girls. By M. Corbet-Seymour.

"An extremely graceful, well-told tale of domestic life. . . . The heroine, Dulcie, is a charming person, and worthy of the good fortune which she causes and shares."—*Guardian.*

Hugh Herbert's Inheritance. By Caroline Austin.

"Will please by its simplicity, its tenderness, and its healthy interesting motive. It is admirably written."—*Scotsman.*

Nicola: The Career of a Girl Musician. By M. Corbet-Seymour.

Jack o' Lanthorn: A Tale of Adventure. By Henry Frith.

Reduced Illustration from "A Girl in Spring-time".

My Mistress the Queen. By M. A. Paull.
The Stories of Wasa and Menzikoff.
Stories of the Sea in Former Days.
Tales of Captivity and Exile.
Famous Discoveries by Sea and Land.
Stirring Events of History.
Adventures in Field, Flood, and Forest.

"It would be difficult to place in the hands of young people books which combine interest and instruction in a higher degree."—*Manchester Courier.*

A Rough Road: or, How the Boy Made a Man of Himself. By Mrs. G. Linnæus Banks.

'Mrs. Banks has not written a better book than *A Rough Road.*"—*Spectator.*

HALF-CROWN SERIES—Continued.

The Two Dorothys. By Mrs. HERBERT MARTIN.
"A book that will interest and please all girls."—*The Lady.*

A Cruise in Cloudland. By HENRY FRITH.
"A thoroughly interesting story."—*St. James's Gazette.*

Marian and Dorothy. By ANNIE E. ARMSTRONG.
"This is distinctively a book for girls. A bright wholesome story."—*Academy.*

Stimson's Reef: A Tale of Adventure. By C. J. HYNE.
"It may almost vie with Mr. R. L. Stevenson's *Treasure Island*."—*Guardian.*

Gladys Anstruther. By LOUISA THOMPSON.
"It is a clever book: novel and striking in the highest degree."—*Schoolmistress.*

BLACKIE'S TWO-SHILLING SERIES.

Illustrated by eminent Artists. In crown 8vo, cloth elegant.

Sydney's Chums: A Story of East and West London. By H. F. GETHEN.

Daddy Samuel's Darling. By the Author of "The Two Dorothys".

May, Guy, and Jim. By ELLINOR DAVENPORT ADAMS.

A Girl in Spring-time. By Mrs. MANSERGH.

In the Days of Drake. Being the Adventures of Humphrey Salkeld. By J. S. FLETCHER.

Wilful Joyce. By W. L. ROOPER.

Proud Miss Sydney. By GERALDINE MOCKLER.

Queen of the Daffodils. By LESLIE LAING.

The Girleen. By EDITH JOHNSTONE.

The Organist's Baby. By KATHLEEN KNOX.

School-Days in France. By AN OLD GIRL.

The Ravensworth Scholarship. By Mrs. HENRY CLARKE.

Sir Walter's Ward: A Tale of the Crusades. By WILLIAM EVERARD.

Raff's Ranche: A Story of Adventure among Cow-boys and Indians. By F. M. HOLMES.

The Joyous Story of Toto. By LAURA E. RICHARDS.

Our Dolly: Her Words and Ways. By Mrs. R. H. READ.

Fairy Fancy: What she Heard and Saw. By Mrs. READ.

New Light through Old Windows. By GREGSON GOW.

Little Tottie, and Two Other Stories. By THOMAS ARCHER.

TWO-SHILLING SERIES—Continued.

Illustrated by eminent Artists.   In crown 8vo, cloth elegant.

An Unexpected Hero. By Eliz. J. Lysaght.

The Bushranger's Secret. By Mrs. Henry Clarke, M.A.

The White Squall. By John C. Hutcheson.

The Wreck of the "Nancy Bell". By J. C. Hutcheson.

The Lonely Pyramid. By J. H. Yoxall.

Bab: or, The Triumph of Unselfishness. By Ismay Thorn.

Brave and True, and other Stories. By Gregson Gow.

The Light Princess. By George Mac Donald.

Nutbrown Roger and I. By J. H. Yoxall.

Sam Silvan's Sacrifice. By Jesse Colman.

Insect Ways on Summer Days in Garden, Forest, Field, and Stream. By Jennett Humphreys. With 70 Illustrations.

Susan. By Amy Walton.

A Pair of Clogs. By Amy Walton.

The Hawthorns. By Amy Walton.

Dorothy's Dilemma. By Caroline Austin.

Marie's Home. By Caroline Austin.

A Warrior King. By J. Evelyn.

Aboard the "Atalanta". By Henry Frith.

The Penang Pirate. By John C. Hutcheson.

Teddy: The Story of a "Little Pickle". By John C. Hutcheson.

A Rash Promise. By Cecilia Selby Lowndes.

Linda and the Boys. By Cecilia Selby Lowndes.

Swiss Stories for Children. From the German of Madam Johanna Spyri. By Lucy Wheelock.

The Squire's Grandson. By J. M. Callwell.

Magna Charta Stories. Edited by Arthur Gilman, A.M.

The Wings of Courage; and The Cloud - Spinner. Translated from the French of George Sand, by Mrs. Corkran.

Chirp and Chatter: Or, Lessons from Field and Tree. By Alice Banks. With 54 Illustrations by Gordon Browne.

Four Little Mischiefs. By Rosa Mulholland.

TWO-SHILLING SERIES—Continued.

Illustrated by eminent Artists.   In crown 8vo, cloth elegant.

Naughty Miss Bunny.   By CLARA MULHOLLAND.
Adventures of Mrs. Wishing-to-be.   By ALICE CORKRAN.

LIBRARY OF FAMOUS BOOKS FOR BOYS AND GIRLS.

In Crown 8vo.   Illustrated.   Cloth extra, 1s. 6d. each.

Autobiographies of Boyhood.
Holiday House.   By CATHERINE SINCLAIR.
Log-book of a Midshipman.
Parry's Third Voyage.
Passages in the Life of a Galley-Slave.
The Downfall of Napoleon.   By SIR WALTER SCOTT.
What Katy Did.   By SUSAN COOLIDGE.
What Katy Did at School.
Wreck of the "Wager".
Miss Austen's Northanger Abbey.
Miss Edgeworth's The Good Governess.
Martineau's Feats on the Fiord.
Marryat's Poor Jack.
The Snowstorm.   By MRS. GORE.
Life of Dampier.
The Cruise of the Midge. M. SCOTT.
Lives and Voyages of Drake and Cavendish.
Edgeworth's Moral Tales.

Marryat's The Settlers in Canada.
Michael Scott's Tom Cringle's Log.
Natural History of Selborne.
Waterton's Wanderings in S. America.
Anson's Voyage Round the World.
Autobiography of Franklin.
Lamb's Tales from Shakspeare.
Southey's Life of Nelson.
Miss Mitford's Our Village.
Two Years Before the Mast.
Children of the New Forest.
Scott's The Talisman.
The Basket of Flowers.
Marryat's Masterman Ready.
Alcott's Little Women.
Cooper's Deerslayer.
The Lamplighter. By MISS CUMMINS.
Cooper's Pathfinder.
The Vicar of Wakefield.
Plutarch's Lives of Greek Heroes.
Poe's Tales of Romance and Fantasy.

BLACKIE'S EIGHTEENPENNY SERIES.

With Illustrations.   In crown 8vo, cloth elegant.

A Chum Worth Having.   By FLORENCE COOMBE.
Penelope and the Others.   By AMY WALTON.
The "Saucy May".   By HENRY FRITH.
The Little Girl from Next Door.   By GERALDINE MOCKLER.
Uncle Jem's Stella.   By Author of "The Two Dorothys".
The Ball of Fortune.   By C. PEARSE.
The Family Failing.   By DARLEY DALE.
Warner's Chase: or, The Gentle Heart.   By ANNIE S. SWAN.

Climbing the Hill.   By ANNIE S. SWAN.
Into the Haven.   By ANNIE S. SWAN.
Down and Up Again.   By GREGSON GOW.
Madge's Mistake.   By ANNIE E. ARMSTRONG.
The Troubles and Triumphs of Little Tim.   By GREGSON GOW.
The Happy Lad: A Story of Peasant Life in Norway.   By B. BJÖRNSON.
A Box of Stories.   Packed for Young Folk by HORACE HAPPYMAN.
The Patriot Martyr, and other Narratives of Female Heroism.

THE EIGHTEENPENNY SERIES.—Continued.

With Illustrations. In crown 8vo, cloth elegant.

Olive and Robin: or, A Journey to Nowhere. By the author of "The Two Dorothys".

Mona's Trust: A Story for Girls. By PENELOPE LESLIE.

Reduced Illustration
From "A Chum Worth Having".

Little Jimmy: A Story of Adventure. By Rev. D. RICE-JONES, M.A.

Pleasures and Pranks. By ISABELLA PEARSON.

In a Stranger's Garden: A Story for Boys and Girls. By CONSTANCE CUMING.

A Soldier's Son: The Story of a Boy who Succeeded. By ANNETTE LYSTER.

Mischief and Merry-making. By ISABELLA PEARSON.

Littlebourne Lock. By F. BAYFORD HARRISON.

Wild Meg and Wee Dickie. By MARY E. ROPES.

Grannie. By ELIZABETH J. LYSAGHT.

The Seed She Sowed. By EMMA LESLIE.

Unlucky: A Fragment of a Girl's Life. By CAROLINE AUSTIN.

Everybody's Business: or, A Friend in Need. By ISMAY THORN.

Tales of Daring and Danger. By G. A. HENTY.

The Seven Golden Keys. By JAMES E. ARNOLD.

The Story of a Queen. By MARY C. ROWSELL.

Edwy: or, Was he a Coward? By ANNETTE LYSTER.

The Battlefield Treasure. By F. BAYFORD HARRISON.

Joan's Adventures at the North Pole. By ALICE CORKRAN.

Filled with Gold. By J. PERRETT.

Our General: A Story for Girls. By ELIZABETH J. LYSAGHT.

Aunt Hesba's Charge. By ELIZABETH J. LYSAGHT.

By Order of Queen Maude: A Story of Home Life. By LOUISA CROW.

The Late Miss Hollingford. By ROSA MULHOLLAND.

Our Frank. By AMY WALTON.

A Terrible Coward. By G. MANVILLE FENN.

Yarns on the Beach. By G. A. HENTY.

Tom Finch's Monkey. By J. C. HUTCHESON.

Miss Grantley's Girls, and the Stories she Told Them. By THOS. ARCHER.

The Pedlar and his Dog. By MARY C. ROWSELL.

Town Mice in the Country. By M. E. FRANCIS.

Phil and his Father. By ISMAY THORN.

Prim's Story. By L. E. TIDDEMAN.

₊ *Also a large selection of Rewards at 1s., 9d., 6d., 3d., 2d., and 1d. A complete list will be sent post free on application to the Publishers.*

BLACKIE'S
SCHOOL AND HOME LIBRARY.

Under the above title the publishers have arranged to issue, for School Libraries and the Home Circle, a selection of the best and most interesting books in the English language. The Library includes lives of heroes, ancient and modern, records of travel and adventure by sea and land, fiction of the highest class, historical romances, books of natural history, and tales of domestic life.

The greatest care has been devoted to the get-up of the Library. The volumes are clearly printed on good paper, and the binding made specially durable, to withstand the wear and tear to which well-circulated books are necessarily subjected.

In crown 8vo volumes.   Strongly bound in imperial cloth.   Price 1s. 4d. each.

Dana's Two Years before the Mast.
Southey's Life of Nelson.
Waterton's Wanderings in S. America.
Anson's Voyage Round the World.
Lamb's Tales from Shakspeare.
Autobiography of Benjamin Franklin.
Marryat's Children of the New Forest.
Miss Mitford's Our Village.
Scott's Talisman.
The Basket of Flowers.
Marryat's Masterman Ready.
Alcott's Little Women.
Cooper's Deerslayer.
Parry's Third Voyage.
Dickens' Old Curiosity Shop. 2 vols.
Plutarch's Lives of Greek Heroes.
The Lamplighter.
Cooper's Pathfinder.
The Vicar of Wakefield.
White's Natural History of Selborne.
Scott's Ivanhoe. 2 vols.
Michael Scott's Tom Cringle's Log.
Irving's Conquest of Granada. 2 vols.

Lives of Drake and Cavendish.
Michael Scott's Cruise of the Midge.
Edgeworth's Moral Tales.
Passages in the Life of a Galley-Slave.
The Snowstorm. By Mrs. Gore.
Life of Dampier.
Marryat's The Settlers in Canada.
Martineau's Feats on the Fiord.
Marryat's Poor Jack.
The Good Governess. By Maria Edgeworth.
Northanger Abbey. By Jane Austen.
The Log Book of a Midshipman.
Autobiographies of Boyhood.
Holiday House. By Catherine Sinclair.
Wreck of the "Wager".
What Katy Did. By Miss Coolidge.
What Katy Did at School. By Do.
Scott's Life of Napoleon.
Essays on English History By Lord Macaulay.
The Rifle Rangers. By Captain Mayne Reid.

"The Library is one of the most intelligent enterprises in connection with juvenile literature of recent years. . . . A glance at the list proves that the editing is in the hands of some one who understands the likings of healthy boys and girls. . . . One of the healthiest juvenile libraries in existence."—Bookman.

Detailed Prospectus and Press Opinions will be sent post free on Application.

LONDON:
BLACKIE & SON, Limited, 50 OLD BAILEY, E.C.